THE LOVE OF

Harriet Evans works in publishing
writing books. *The Love of Her Life*
Home and *A Hopeless Romantic*, both
likes old films, liquorice allsorts a
recently invented, called 'The Harrie' (one part sloe gin to three
parts sparkling wine).

Visit www.AuthorTracker.co.uk for exclusive updates on Harriet
Evans.

Praise for Harriet Evans:

'Fabulous . . . I loved it.' Sophie Kinsella

'Touching and engrossing . . . a rollicking ride of joy, disappointment, and self-discovery.' *Daily Telegraph*

'Delicious.' *Marie Claire*

'Harriet Evans has scored another winner . . . witty, entertaining
and full of characters you'll grow to love.' *Heat*

'A joy from start to finish – sharp, funny and modern as well
as warm, cosy and nostalgic.' Fiona Walker

'Hard to resist.' *Elle*

'A lovely, funny heartwarmer . . . Evans' comic style and love-
able characters make it effortlessly readable.' *Marie Claire*

'Harriet Evans' debut novel is a great romcom, packed with
intrigue and suspense.' *New Woman*

'An endearing tale of broken and rescued hearts . . .' *In Style*

'A contemporary romance that is as sparkly as its cover suggests.'
Daily Mail

'An entertaining page-turner.' *Closer*

'A superior romcom with heart and soul.' *Bella*

'Few debuts are set to make such an impact as this.'
Daily Mirror

By the same author

Going Home
A Hopeless Romantic

HARRIET EVANS

The Love of Her Life

HARPER

Harper
An imprint of HarperCollins*Publishers*
77–85 Fulham Palace Road,
Hammersmith, London W6 8JB

www.harpercollins.co.uk

A Paperback Original 2008
4

Excerpt from 'Moving On' in *I Feel Bad About My Neck*
reprinted by permission of International Creative Management, Inc.
Copyright © 2006 by Nora Ephron

A catalogue record for this book is
available from the British Library

ISBN: 978 0 00 724382 2

Set in Meridien Roman by Palimpsest Book Production Limited,
Grangemouth, Stirlingshire

Printed and bound in Great Britain by
Clays Ltd, St Ives plc

Find out more about HarperCollins and the environment at
www.harpercollins.co.uk/green

It's not love. It's just where I live.
Nora Ephron, *Moving On*

Set me a seal upon thine heart, as a seal upon thine arm; for love is stronger than death.
Song of Solomon, ch VIII, v6

Darling Kate,

I'm sorry.

Perhaps one day, when you're grown-up, you'll understand why I've done it. Relationships are complicated, that's the truth. Darling, I love you, and your father loves you. You mustn't blame yourself. You are our little girl, and we're both very proud of you.

You must come and see me soon.

Lots and lots of love,

Mummy

xxx

PS Happy belated fourteenth birthday, darling. I do hope you like the telescope, is it the one you wanted?
Zoe helped me choose it, so I do hope so. Lots of love xxxxx

PART ONE

CHAPTER ONE

New York, 2007

Her father wasn't well. They kept saying she shouldn't worry too much, but she should still come back to London. He had had an operation – emergency kidney transplant, he'd been bumped right up the list. He was lucky to get one, considering his lifestyle, his age, everything. They kept saying that, too. Earlier, before it was an emergency, Kate had even been tested, to see if she could be a donor. She couldn't, which made her feel like a bad daughter.

It all happened so suddenly. It was Monday afternoon when she got the call telling her it had happened, the previous day, after a kidney miraculously became available. He'd been unwell for a few years now, the diabetes and the drinking; and the stress of his new life, he was busier than ever – but how had it got to this, got so far? Apparently he had collapsed; the next day he'd been put at the top of the transplant list; and that afternoon, Daniel was given a new kidney. Kate's stepmother Lisa had rung the following day to let her know.

'I think he'd very much like to see you.' Lisa's rather nasal voice was not improved by the tinny phone line.

'Of – of course,' Kate said. She cast around for something to say. 'Oh god. How . . . how is he now?'

'He's alive, Kate. It was very sudden. But he's got much much worse these last few months. So he's not that well. And he'd like to see you. Like I say. He misses you.'

'Yes,' said Kate. Her throat was dry, her heart was pounding. 'Yes. Yes, of course.'

'He's going to be in intensive care for a few days, you know. Can you come next week? You can get the time off at the office, I presume.' Lisa made no other comment, but a variety of the comments she could make hung in the air, and rushing in next to them came millions of other guilty thoughts, all jostling for attention in front of Kate till she couldn't see anything. She rubbed her eyes with one hand as she cradled the phone on her shoulder. Her darling dad, and she hadn't seen him for eighteen months, hadn't been back to London in nearly three years. How the hell . . . was this emergency, his rapid decline, was it her fault? No, of course it wasn't, but still, Kate couldn't escape the thought that she had made him ill herself, as certainly as if she had stuck a knife into him.

Out of the window, Manhattan looked calm and still, the grey monolithic buildings giving no clue to the arctic weather, the noise, the hustle, the sweet crazy smell of toasted sugar and tar that hit you every time you went outside, the city she had grown used to, fallen in love with, the city that had long ago replaced London in her affections. Kate looked round the office of the literary agency where she worked. It was a small place, only four full-time members of staff. Bruce Perry, the boss, was in his office, talking on the phone. Kate could see his head bobbing up and down as he violently agreed with someone and what they were saying. Doris, the malevolent old bookkeeper from Queens, who openly hated Kate, was pretending to type but in reality listening to Kate's conversation, trying to work out what was going on. Megan, the junior agent, was in the far corner, tapping a pencil against her keyboard.

'Kate?' said Lisa, breaking into Kate's thoughts. 'Look, I can't force you to come back, but . . .' She cleared her throat, and Kate could hear the sound echo in the cavernous basement kitchen of her father and Lisa's flashy new home in Notting Hill.

'Of course I'll come,' Kate heard herself say, and she crouched into herself, flushed with shame, hoping Doris hadn't heard her.

'You will?' Lisa said, and Kate could hear incredulity and something else, yes – pleading in her voice, and she was horrified at herself, at how cold she was capable of being to Lisa. Her father was ill, for god's sake. Dad.

It was time to get a grip and go back home. And so Kate put the phone down, booked a flight for Saturday evening, getting into London on Sunday morning. Then she went into Bruce Perry's office to ask for two weeks off. No more. She wasn't staying there any longer than she had to.

Bruce had grimaced a bit, but he'd been fine about giving her the time off. Perry and Co was not exactly the fast-paced business unit it might have been, which is why Kate had got her job as assistant there in the first place. In fact, to the outside eye, but for one author it would seem to be a mystery that they managed to stay in business, employing as they did five people, and with no books sold to any major publisher, no scripts sold to any studio, for years and years, so it would seem.

But one day, seventeen years ago, a middle-aged lady called Anne Graves had arrived in Bruce's office with the idea for a crime series set in her hometown in Ohio. And that day Bruce had got lucky, very lucky. It was Anne Graves who kept them afloat, Anne Graves who paid their salaries, for the lunches, for the midtown offices a block or two from the Rockefeller Plaza. Anne Graves, and her creation Jimmy Potomac and his dog, Thomas. Jimmy and Thomas lived in Ravenna, Ohio, and solved crimes together. A flagpole goes missing. The local sheriff loses his golden wedding anniversary present. Some kids make a little disturbance. That kind of thing. The books had sold one hundred million copies, and the NBC series, *Jimmy Potomac*, now in its third season, pulled in sixteen million viewers a week. When the dog playing Thomas had died, the studio had received five thousand letters of sympathy.

Kate had been the office assistant at Perry and Co now for over two years. She had yet to meet a single person who'd read a Jimmy Potomac book.

'Where will you stay?' Bruce asked. 'Will you go to your dad?'

'No,' said Kate firmly. 'I've – I've actually got a place there.' Bruce raised his eyebrows, and Kate could see Doris put down her ledger and look up, intrigued.

'Your own place?'

'It's . . . kind of,' Kate told him. She cleared her throat. 'I part own it. I was renting it out, but they've just left. Last month.'

'Good timing,' said Bruce, pleased. 'That's great!'

'Yes,' said Kate. She wasn't sure it was that good timing, the ending of Gemma's rental lease coinciding with her father's emergency kidney transplant, but still, look for the silver lining, as her mother was always telling her. She shook her head, still trying to come to terms with it. 'Wow,' she said out loud. 'I'm going back to London. Wow.' She bit her thumb. 'I'd better see if I can get hold of Dad, Lisa said he'd be awake in a little while . . .'

'Well, what will we do without you,' Bruce said, more for effect than sounding like he meant it. He stood up languidly. 'Hurry back now!'

'I will,' said Kate, although she was kind of sure she could simply not ever appear again and all they'd need to do after a few weeks would be to hire a temp to filter through the fan letters to Anne Graves. 'I'm sorry to leave you in the lurch like this –'

'Oh honey,' Doris said, standing up and coming over. She patted Kate's arm. Kate reared back in horror, since usually Doris wore an expression of murderous hate every time she came near Kate. 'Don't you worry about that. My niece, Lorraine, she can cover for you. She'll do a real good job too, you know it, Bruce.'

'Great idea!' Bruce said happily.

Kate nodded. It made sense. Lorraine had temped for her before, when Kate and her friend Betty had driven across the States the previous summer. She had put all the files back in extraordinary places, none of Kate's messages had been checked, nor her emails, but she had, during the handover session they'd had, managed to walk behind Bruce, murmuring, 'Oh, excuse me, Mr Perry,' brushing her enormous breasts against his back and that, not her shorthand skills, was the reason she'd be welcomed back at Perry and Co anytime. That, plus she was the kind of girl who made herself genial, asking questions about folks, smiling brightly at people, even when on the phone.

'That OK with you?' said Bruce, as if it were up to Kate, and he'd ring up a temping agency right away if she vetoed Lorraine. He rubbed his hands together.

'Oh sure, sure,' said Kate. 'That's cool, and you know, I'll be –'

'I'll call her now,' said Doris, waddling back to her desk, and smiling gleefully down at her own monstrous nails. 'Say,

Bruce! Lorraine did say to tell you hi last week anyway. She'll be thrilled, you know!'

'I'm thrilled too, Doris,' Bruce said, solemnly. 'Real thrilled.' He went back into his office, whistling, as Kate swung back around to face her computer. She bit her lip, not sure whether she wanted to laugh or cry.

Kate walked home that night, the twenty-odd blocks that took her back to her mother and Oscar's apartment, a feeling of slight unease hanging over her about the task that lay ahead, and the conversation she would have to have with her mother and stepfather. It was a milder March night than it had been thus far that year, and though it was dark, and the clocks wouldn't go forward till Sunday, there was still a sense that spring was in the air. She walked up Broadway, following its slicing path through her beloved Manhattan. She didn't try to think about anything, just walked her usual walk, drinking it all in. This was her home. Here she could walk the streets and be part of the glorious, jostling mass of humanity, anonymous even if she wore a pink wig and rode a giraffe. No one here cared, no one here recognized her, knew her. Here she bumped into no old school friends, ex-work colleagues, here she saw no ghosts getting in her way. Just the wide stretch of the road, leaving mid-town behind, heading up past the Lincoln Center, the lights getting dimmer, a little cosier, people out running, walking their dogs, living their lives in the thick of the metropolis – that was what she loved best about New York.

She knew she was nearly home when she got to Zabar's. The huge, cheery, famous deli was as busy as ever. Families doing late-night shopping, solitary coffee drinkers hunched over a paper in the café. Warmth, light, colour, bursting out of every window and door. Kate stared in. They were advertising gefilte fish for Passover, only a few weeks away in mid-April. I'll be back by then, she thought. Only a couple of weeks. Really, that's all it is.

He's going to be fine, she told herself, as the traffic purred beside her and she looked around wildly, wondering where she was for a moment. She thought about him for the moment, wondering with terrified fascination what it would be like to see him again. Her father, so tall, so commanding, so handsome and charismatic, always the centre of the room – what would he be like now, what would his life be like after this operation? What if the kidney didn't work? How had it come to this, that she could push down the love she had for him, push it down so far inside her she had been able to pretend, for a while, that it was all OK?

But she knew the answer. She'd become an expert at the answer since she'd left London.

Deep inside her came a stabbing pain at the top of her breast bone. Kate gently rubbed her collarbone; her eyes filled with painful tears. But she could not cry, not here, not now. If she started, she might never stop. Come on, she told herself. She carried on walking, turned the corner.

I'll go back, see Dad, make sure he's OK, check on the flat, try and find a new tenant.

And I'll see Zoe.

At the thought of seeing her best friend after all this time, the hairs on Kate's neck stood up, and though the memory of what had happened still sliced at her she smiled, a small smile, until she realized she was grinning through the window at a rather bewildered old man with thick white hair, who was trying to read his paper in peace. Kate blushed, and hurried on.

It was Oscar's sixtieth birthday in a few weeks' time, and Venetia had given him his present – a brand-new baby grand piano – early, back in January. As Kate arrived at

11

the apartment building, on the corner of Riverside Drive, the window of Venetia and Oscar's apartment was open, and the sound of the piano came floating down to her on the sidewalk.

'Hello there, Kate!' Maurice the doorman called happily, opening the door for her into the small marbled foyer. He pushed the button for the elevator. Kate smiled at him, a little wearily.

'How are you, Maurice?' she said.

'I'm just fine,' said Maurice. 'I'm pretty good. That spray you told me to get, for my back – well, I bought it yesterday, I meant to say. And it's done a lot of good.'

'Really?' said Kate, pleased. 'That's great, Maurice. I'm so glad.'

'I owe you Kate, that's for sure. It just went away after I used that spray.'

Kate got into the lift. 'Good-o. That's brilliant.'

'Hold the elevator!' came a querulous voice, and Mrs Cohen, still elegant, tall, refined in a powder-blue suit, shuffled into the lobby. 'Kate, dear, hold the elevator! Hello Maurice. Would you be a dear, and –'

'I'll get the bags from the cab,' said Maurice, nodding. 'You wait here.'

There were times when the geriatric street theatre of the apartment block made Kate's day; there were other times when she would have given fifty dollars to see someone her own age in the lift. Just once. When they were installed in the lift, bags and all, and when Kate had helped Mrs Cohen to her door, and put her bags in her hallway, she climbed the last flight up to her mother's apartment, hearing the sound of the piano again, as she reached the sixth floor.

Venetia was born to be a New Yorker; it was hard to believe she'd ever lived anywhere else. Of course, Kate could remember her in London, but it seemed rather unreal, now. The mother she'd had until the age of fourteen when, the day after Kate's birthday, Venetia had left, was like a character Kate remembered watching in a film, not her actual, own mother. She had to remind herself that it was Venetia who'd picked her up from school every day, Venetia who'd smoothed her hair back when she'd been sick after some scrambled eggs when she was eight, Venetia who'd collected her from the Brownie camp in the New Forest a day early after Kate had cried all night for her. The idea that she and Kate's father had lived together no longer had any substance. That Venetia had taken Kate to the Proms to watch Daniel play, had entertained myriad friends of Daniel's in their cluttered basement in the tall house in Kentish Town, had wiped down tables, collected up wine bottles, fielded calls from agents and journalists and critics and young, lithe music students: that Venetia had long disappeared. She was a New Yorker now, and more importantly, Kate thought, she was the star of her *own* show.

Venetia and Oscar's apartment was straight out of Annie Hall, from the framed Saul Steinberg prints and posters of the *Guys and Dolls* revival that Oscar had done a couple of years ago, to the copies of *The New Yorker* on the coffee table, and the view over Riverside Drive from the long, low room that served as sitting room, dining room, den and Oscar's office (he worked at home mostly; he was an arranger, a composer, and a conductor).

There were also pictures of Kate in silver frames that she always found hugely embarrassing: her as a baby, sucking her toes, sitting on a lawn somewhere (Kate never knew where; there was no lawn in the Kentish Town house); smiling rather rigidly outside her college after getting her degree; with her mother, the first time she came to New York to visit, when Kate was fifteen, just after Venetia had married Oscar. And there was one she always wanted to take down, just because: Kate, beaming, holding the first issue of *Venus*, the magazine she'd worked on in London. There had been other photos, other remnants of Kate's life. They had been taken down – no one wanted to see them, now.

As Kate opened the door to the apartment, a smell of onions, something warming, hit her. Her mother was in the tiny galley kitchen singing; 'Some Enchanted Evening' was being played in the long room.

'Hi!' she called, injecting a note of jollity into her voice. 'Something smells nice.'

'Hello darling!' Venetia appeared in the corridor, wiping her hands on her apron. 'I'm making risotto, it's going to be lovely.' She kissed her daughter. 'Thanks for calling. It'll be ready in about fifteen minutes. How was your day? Did you get hold of Betty? She rang earlier. She was wondering if you wanted to meet for a drink on Friday.'

Kate disentangled herself from her scarf, and from her mother, backing away towards the door to hang her things up. She pulled her long dark blonde hair out from her coat, and turned to her mother, chewing a lock of hair as she did.

'I'm starving,' she said indistinctly. 'I'll give her a call in a minute. Mum –'

Oscar called from the long room. 'Hello, Katy! Come and say hi!'

Kate poked her head around the door. 'Hi, Oscar,' she said. 'How was your day?'

'Honey, I'm home!' Oscar said joyously, launching into a ragtime version of 'Luck Be A Lady'. 'I've been home all day!'

Oscar made this joke roughly three times a week. Kate smiled affectionately at him.

'What a lovely evening,' she said, staring out over the Hudson, at the purple, grey sunset. 'I had such a nice walk back.'

Oscar was only half listening. 'That's good, dear,' he said. 'Would you like a drink? Venetia, can I get you another drink, darling?'

Venetia appeared, carrying her gin and tonic. 'I'm fine with this one, thanks, darling,' she said, carelessly caressing the back of her husband's neck as she passed by. 'I'd better lay the table – darling, did I mention that I saw Kathy today? And she and Don can't make it to your party?'

'Dad's ill,' Kate said, suddenly. Her voice was louder than she'd meant. The room was suddenly deadly silent.

'What?' Venetia turned to look at her daughter. 'What did you say?'

Kate gripped the side of the sofa. 'Dad's really ill. He's had a kidney transplant. He's in intensive care.'

'Oh, my god,' Oscar said, looking towards his wife. 'That's – well, that's awful.'

'I'm going home,' said Kate. 'On Saturday. To see him '

'Back to London?' her mother said. Her face was white.

'Yes,' said Kate, shaking her head very slightly, willing her mother to do the right thing.

'My god,' said Oscar. He chewed at a cuticle, nervously. 'Will he be – OK?'

'Yes, yes,' said Kate, wanting to reassure them. 'I mean – it's dangerous, but he's very lucky. I hope so –' She swallowed, as black dots danced in front of her eyes, and a wave of panic swept over her at the thought of it, her poor darling dad. 'Yes, Lisa thinks he will be . . .'

Lisa's name dropped like a stone between them. It was Venetia who broke the silence. 'You're going back Saturday? What time's your flight?'

'Nine. In the evening.'

'Right.' Venetia put her drink down; she patted her collar bone, her slim white fingers stroking her skin. 'We'll drive you. Oh, darling. How long are you going for?'

15

'Two weeks, probably,' said Kate, coming towards her. She wanted her reassurance, for her mother to tell her it was going to be OK, not just Dad, but everything to do with it. 'I'll be back for Oscar's party, of course I will – I'm just going to make sure he's OK.'

'Course you do!' said Venetia. She put her arm around her daughter, squeezed her shoulders. 'Darling, it's just – well. It'll be hard for you. That's all.'

There was silence again in the room, as Oscar looked from his wife to his stepdaughter. Kate gazed out of the window. The sunset was almost over; it was nearly dark.

'Yep,' Kate said. 'It will be hard.' It felt strange; it felt alien here, suddenly. She hated that feeling. 'I had to go back sometime,' she added, and Oscar nodded and sat back down at the piano. 'Just wish it wasn't for this, that's all.'

CHAPTER TWO

Kate had lived with Oscar and Venetia since she came to New York. She was always just about to start looking for an apartment of her own – or a studio, more likely, since renting in New York was still staggeringly expensive, even with the rental money she had from her flat in London. Still, it was ridiculous, being thirty, living with your mother and stepfather and when she'd moved to New York she'd thought it would only be a temporary measure, that she'd be moving out soon. But the right time never seemed to happen.

She and Betty often talked about getting a place together, but Betty's love life was erratic to say the least, and whenever Kate was at her most desperate to move out, move on, move away from her domestic situation, coincided exactly with Betty and her latest five-star full-on love affair being at its height, whereupon Betty would say ' . . . I think we're getting married . . . or at least, moving in together . . . in a couple of months I'd say, so no Kate, sorry . . . I can't!' Then they would break up, awfully, and Betty would be too heart-broken to contemplate anything, and Kate would have to soothe her back to sanity with a variety of cocktails all over the SoHo area, and Betty would gradually perk up and say,

'We should really look for a place soon!' and Kate would say, 'Yes!' and then, without fail, the next day, Betty would go to a gallery opening, and there she would meet Charles (public schoolboy with nappy fetish) or Johan (Norwegian bike courier) or Elrond (poet with long hair), and the whole apartment thing would go quiet for a while ... and Kate would tell herself to wait a little longer.

So the weeks turned into months, and the months turned into years. To her surprise. And still she didn't move, still she stayed in Riverside Drive.

On Friday evening, Venetia and Oscar gave Kate a farewell supper. It was early, because Kate was going out to meet Betty, and Venetia and Oscar were off to a drinks party at Alvin and Carol DaCosta's on the third floor. Venetia made quiche, Oscar made a beautiful mesclun and pomegranate seed salad. They drank a toast to Daniel, said bon voyage to Kate.

The last few days seemed to have flown by; how could it be Friday already, Kate wondered? Escaping their ministrations – 'Remember to take an *adaptor*.' 'Did you collect your drycleaning?' she excused herself, and shut the door of her bedroom slowly and sank down on the bed, wondering when she should pack.

Now she was alone, she wished, as she had done these past few days, she was going tonight, that she was already there, even though Lisa had told her there was no point in coming over till Daniel was out of intensive care; but still, Kate wished she was there, even if he didn't realize it. 'It'll give you time to sort your stuff out, before you come,' Lisa had said. Kate supposed she meant it kindly.

The truth was, really, that she didn't have that much stuff anyway. Clothes, yes, but all her books, her old things from her old life – they were all in storage in the basement of her flat in London, like her old self, trapped in aspic, while the new self gazed longingly into the window of Pottery Barn or Bed Bath and Beyond, picking out covers for imaginary cushions, towels to hang on illusory rails. She'd bought a new duvet and pillow set for her room in the sales this year and she was *still* excited about it.

Kate shook her head, smiling. She realized now, with a start, that she'd lived for nearly three years with her mother and Oscar – because she enjoyed it. Not just because they were fun – Oscar *wanted* people to be happy in his presence, and he wanted Venetia to be happy more than anyone else and, therefore, her daughter by extension. The truth was, it was fun, living with them, especially for a girl like Kate who was, as Zoe had once pointed out, old before her time anyway, and more likely to enjoy an evening around the piano singing showtunes than queuing for ages to get into a loud, sweaty, pricey club (as she saw it).

But it was also nice because Kate had got to know her mother again, after years of never really seeing her, years of her name being *persona non grata* with almost all her father's friends and family in London. Even Venetia's sister, Jane, who was much more stiff-lipped than she, and lived a life of rigid, middle-England organization in Marlow, could barely tolerate any mention of her. It was fun, living with her mother again. Especially this happy version of her mother. She didn't put any pressure on Kate to do anything she didn't want to – she was just happy to have her living there.

Still, perhaps that's why it's a good thing I'm going back, Kate told herself as she climbed up on a stool to take down her big suitcase from on top of the wardrobe. It was dusty – when was the last time she'd used it? She couldn't remember. Cars honked faintly outside: Kate looked at her watch. It was time to go. She pulled some slouchy boots on over her skinny jeans and ran out into the hall.

'You look lovely, dear,' Oscar called, spying her through the open doorway.

'Thanks, dear,' said Kate. 'I won't be too late.'

'Stay out! Enjoy yourself!' called her mother. 'Where are you going?'

'Downtown, near the West Village,' said Kate, without great enthusiasm. She sighed. She wanted to see Betty, of course, but Betty was on a matchmaking drive and tonight, Kate feared, was to be the culmination of this. Since the last person Betty had set her up with turned out to be gay, and was only going along with Betty because he wanted her gallery to show his work, Kate didn't hold out much hope.

'So, will you stay in London?' Betty wiped her fingers on the napkin and stared at Kate, who paused with a bowl of miso soup halfway to her lips. 'I bet you will.'

'Stay there?' she said, in astonished tones. 'Good god no, Bets. Are you mad? I'm going back to see Dad now he's had the op, then I'll wait till he's on the mend ok, I'll see Zoe and the kids and I'll be back on the first plane that'll take me. It's Oscar's sixtieth in three weeks, anyway. I can't miss that. Can you imagine?' Betty said nothing. 'Come on.'

'Hm,' said Betty. 'Well, I'm just saying, that's all. It's going to be weird. Three years!' She turned to Andrew, who was next to her, and gestured at him. 'What do you reckon?'

Kate and Betty had been friends since university, so Kate should have been used to her ways. Now she reminded herself, as she stole a glance at Andrew from under her lashes, that Betty – and Francesca, for that matter, so thank god she wasn't here too – always said what they thought, always had done. It was funny, really. Most of the time. She blushed as Andrew suddenly met her gaze.

'I hope she comes back,' Andrew said. He coughed, awkwardly, and was silent again. Betty rolled her eyes significantly at Kate and made nudging motions at her. Kate ignored her. She was too astonished, and pleased, at what Andrew had said, for usually he said nothing, let alone anything conclusive.

Kate had known Andrew now for a couple of months purely because, since he'd moved into Betty's building in January, Betty had wasted no time in throwing him into Kate's path. This was made easier by Andrew's eagerness to meet Kate when he heard she worked for a literary agency. For Andrew was that not-so-rare creature: the boy with a book inside him. Kate had met enough of them both in London, when she worked on various magazines, and in New York, working at Perry and Co, to recognize Andrew as conforming fairly typically to type: he was angry about a lot of things, not least the parlous state of the Great Amer-Ican Novel, and his novel was extremely difficult, both thematically and practically. He had thick hair he brushed back from his face a lot, mostly in anger. He hadn't written more than a word since he had first started talking to Kate about it. He was 'circling round the themes', he had told her, when she'd asked.

'Right,' Kate had said, politely, when she first heard this. She had glanced at Betty, who was nodding hopefully as if, a mere few minutes after their first introduction, she expected Kate and Andrew to dive underneath the table and copulate.

'Honestly, that's not exactly true,' Andrew had added with a rueful smile. He scratched his cheek. 'Could also be that I'd rather be out having a few beers after work than writing.' He smiled at her, and Kate had instantly liked him again.

She found that, over the following weeks, she alternated in the same way, not being sure whether she liked him or not. Sometimes he was really very funny, coruscatingly rude or charming about something. Other times – too many – he

21

was moody, virtually silent, as if oppressed by the weight of matters on his mind. Betty was running out of excuses, of social events to ask him to. Sooner or later Kate was just going to have to make a move, she told her. Ask him out for coffee.

As Andrew got up to use the bathroom, Betty said this to Kate, in no uncertain terms.

Kate was horrified.

'Ask him out? No, no way, Bets. I couldn't. Get him to.'

'He's not going to,' said Betty decisively. She looked around her, to make sure Andrew wasn't on his way back and hissed across the table, 'It has to be you. Come on. You've got to seize the moment. Otherwise it'll be over, and – and then what? You could have missed the chance to get married. For *ever*. How would you feel then?'

'Oh,' said Kate. 'Relieved?'

Betty shook her head. 'You are weird, did you know that?'

'No I'm not,' said Kate.

'You're like a metaphor for . . . argh. Intransigence.'

Betty worked in an art gallery in SoHo and was prone to remarks like this. Kate suppressed a smile.

'Oh dear,' she said. 'Damn.'

'Don't you want to get married?' said Betty. She stabbed at a dumpling with a chopstick. 'Is that what you want? Would you do that to me? To your mother?'

Kate stared at her in astonishment. 'You're from West Norwood, Betty. Stop talking like that. Anyway, I don't want to get married.'

'Why? Why don't you?' Betty said, but as she was saying it recognition flooded her face. 'Oh my god. Kate, I'm sorry –'

Kate held up her hand and smiled, but underneath the table her foot beat a steady tattoo against the aluminium table leg. 'It's ok! It's fine. Now –' as Andrew came back to the table, 'I kind of need to get an early night, I'm afraid, and I have to pack. Can I get out before you sit back down again?' She shot up and scooted along the plastic bench.

'Kate –' Betty said.

Kate looked up at her.

'Sure,' Betty nodded. 'Sure.'

'Bye, Andrew,' Kate said, turning to him as he stood next to her. They stood to one side against the table as a tiny Japanese waitress bustled past them, bearing a huge tray of sushi, and Kate felt the pressure of his arm against hers.

'Sorry,' he said.

'It's fine,' Kate put her bag on her shoulder. 'So I'll see you when I get back . . .'

'Let me walk you outside,' Andrew said, in a loud, rather unnatural voice. He cleared his throat.

Outside on the crowded sidewalk, the heart of the tiny Japanese district on East 12th Street, Kate cast around to see if there was a cab.

'I've got something to ask you,' Andrew said, staring intently at her in the evening gloom.

'So, thanks,' she said. 'I'll see you when I'm back –'

'Kate, Kate,' Andrew said, rapidly. 'I gotta say this now.'

'Oh,' said Kate, with a dreadful sense of foreboding. 'No, I should walk to the –'

He gripped her arms. 'Kate, let me finish.'

'No, really,' said Kate desperately, stupidly hoping that if she warded him off then what was about to happen might not happen.

Andrew stepped back. 'Look,' he said, crestfallen at her apparent horror. 'I just wanted to ask you out when you get back. Maybe see if you wanted to go for a coffee, see a movie some time. But I guess – I guess that's not such a great idea at the moment. With your dad, and all. I'm sorry.'

'Ah,' said Kate, feeling rotten that she was hiding behind her dad's kidney transplant to get out of a date she didn't want to go on. 'You're right. It's – not a good time for me right now.'

God I sound American she thought. I really must go home.

'Of course it's not,' Andrew nodded. 'Hey. When you get back, if it is a good time – call me. OK?'

'Sure,' said Kate. 'Sure.'

'I promise not to talk about the novel,' said Andrew. 'Much.'

She looked at him, into his big brown eyes, as he smiled at her in the street, the lanterns from the bar next door swaying in the breeze behind him.

'I just kind of like you, Kate,' he said. 'There's – there's something about you. You're cool. I – I guess.'

He scuffed the pavement with his toe and she watched him, her heart pounding. It had been so long since someone had said anything like that to her and, to be honest, she had thought they never would again.

'Oh,' she said, and a lock of her dark blonde hair fell into her face. He looked at her, and pushed it off her cheek, his fingers stroking her skin. Kate met his gaze, shaking her head. Something was wrong.

'Andrew,' she said. 'I –'

He bent his head and kissed her. His touch, his warm lips on hers, his hands on her ribs. Perhaps –

But she couldn't. And the force of her response surprised her, for Kate pushed him away and said, breathlessly,

'No. I'm sorry, no.'

She gave a huge, shuddering sigh.

Andrew stepped back, blinking uncertainly. He looked bewildered.

'I'm – my god, I'm sorry.'

'No,' Kate said. She was almost backing away from him,

24

she realized, trying to escape, like a cornered animal. 'It's not you. It's me.'

He wiped his mouth with his hand, almost in disgust. She smiled. 'No, really. I mean that. It's the oldest cliché in the book – but in my case it's totally true . . . it really *is* me.'

'Right,' said Andrew formally. He brushed something off his shirt. 'I'm just – I'm sorry if I offended you. I thought –'

Kate held out both her hands, still keeping him at a distance. A couple walking down the sidewalk, who didn't want to break their joint stride, bumped into her and she stumbled.

'Look,' she said, still breathing heavily, 'I'm sorry, again. It really *is* me, Andrew, and I wish it wasn't.' She looked around, wildly, and he watched her.

'Yeah,' he said, after a while. 'Betty said something.'

'What?' said Kate.

Andrew nodded, and looked at his feet. 'Hey, it's no big deal. She said some guy screwed you over. Something bad happened to you in London.'

She loved the way certain Americans always said the word 'London', investing it with a certain amount of reverence. 'You could say that,' she said. She winced, and looked up at him, not sure how he was taking all of this. 'Hey –' she began.

'It's no big deal,' he said. 'Really, it isn't.' He ran his hands through his hair. 'You wanna cab?'

'Sure,' said Kate. 'That'd be –'

Andrew whistled, and almost immediately, as if he were calling up the Batmobile, a cab zoomed around the corner. 'So,' he said. He held the door open. 'See you around, I guess.'

'Sure,' said Kate. 'Yeah. Upper West Side, Eightieth and Broadway. Thanks.'

The cab pulled off; through its greasy window she watched Andrew as he turned and walked off. Kate touched her fingers to her lips as the car sped through mid-town. She was shaking, and she didn't know why.

The traffic was light, miraculously. Please go through Times Square, she willed the cab driver. Please, go on. Out of the window the lights of Broadway grew closer and they headed past Macy's, and a sense of disgust came over her. Why had she let that happen with Andrew? Why couldn't she just have kissed him and jumped into a cab? Maybe arranged to see him when she got back? Why did she have to behave like that? What was she going to say to him, to Betty?

I'm too good at running away, she said softly under her breath. She put her head against the glass, watching the reflection of her skin as the streets rushed by and they came to Times Square. Kate loved Times Square, much to Oscar and her mother's horror. She couldn't tell them why she loved it, quite, it never seemed to make sense. She loved the anonymity of it, the adrenaline that came with it. You could be wholly yourself, a unit of one, walking on its concrete, neon-lit stage. You could stand in the centre of the traffic all day and twirl around – and no one would look at you. She loved the contradiction of it – when she first came to see her mother, and went looking for Times Square, she had spent ages trying to find an actual square. She didn't know now what she'd been picturing in her head: a stately square of London houses, with a garden in the centre, railings around the edge, perhaps? And when she'd realized this was it, this grey meeting of roads, stretched out over three or so blocks, she had laughed. It was unlike anything she'd ever seen before, it was utterly unlike London.

Twenty-four hours' time, and she'd be on the plane. Twenty-four hours' time, and her dad's stay in hospital would nearly be over. Less than forty-eight hours till she saw him again. Till she was back there again ... The lights of Manhattan flickered and flashed into Kate's cab, the theatre signs, the road signs, the bars and restaurants and clubs, flickering on her face, keeping her alert, but then, suddenly, she was very tired.

CHAPTER THREE

There was a backlog at Heathrow, and Kate's plane circled over London, coming in from the east, flying straight across the centre of the city. It was the perfect bird's-eye view. Kate shifted in her window seat, her hands resting lightly on the stack of magazines she'd been reading, and stared down at the view, craning her neck in excitement. The huge jet followed the path of the Thames, its tiny black shadow flickering through the streets and places below. The river was bluer than she remembered. She'd forgotten how green it all was, how many open spaces there were. They flew over the Houses of Parliament, glowing gold in the early morning light, as the centre of the city stretched away in front of them. Kate twisted in her seat, following the path of Regent Street all the way up to Regent's Park, the Telecom Tower, King's Cross away to the side, as they headed west.

It looked like a toytown, Legoland, and she couldn't reconcile it with what had gone on before. In those tiny streets below her, in that park there, in that tall building just beyond the river – yes, it was all still there.

The wheel on Kate's trolley didn't work. Of course it didn't, they never did. It got stuck, and whirled around on its own, and consequently the trolley made a loud, juddering noise, like a goods train thundering through the night, which caused the other passengers and those waiting to greet them to look at Kate with a stare of disapproval, as if she personally was making the noise herself, had taken a large mallet to it and bashed it repeatedly, to cause maximum annoyance to others.

Kate never understood people who said airports were full of romance or love. Not only had no one ever met her at an airport (except her mother, and that hardly counted), she wouldn't want them to meet her. Reunited with the love of your life under polystyrene ceiling tiles, strip lighting and grey upholstery? No thanks. She struggled with the trolley, flaring her elbows out to manoeuvre it around corners, trying not to let hopelessness and the strangeness of the situation overwhelm her. Taxi. She needed a taxi. A good old black London cab and she pushed on through to the arrivals hall, vaguely registering the expectant faces of people waiting as she went. Kate had learnt, now. She didn't even bother to look around. She had long given up playing that game in her head.

It was a sunny day. Warm and fresh, with a cool little breeze whipping about. It smelled of spring, of something in the air, even there at the airport. Spring had come to London, and she felt it as she crossed the tarmac to the cab rank, as a man in a blue sou'wester waved her into a cab, and nodded politely as she said 'thank you'. He helped her in with her bags, the cab driver tutted proprietorially over her and said, 'Mind your head, love,' as they both heaved the heavier of her suitcases into the back with her. She thought of JFK, of how fast it all was, how the director of the cab rank barked questions at you, of how fast the cab drivers went, manically swerving from lane to lane, talking wildly to their friends on an earpiece.

29

But although she kept expecting something dramatic to happen, for someone to leap at her and stop her, or yell at her, nothing did, and so the taxi moved off, gliding along smoothly. They reached the Heathrow roundabout, where the daffodils bobbed in the sunny breeze and the motorway opened up in front of her and they headed into London.

On a grey motorway, how prosaic, but there she was, and as the redbrick streets flew past she looked for the old familiar signs, like the old Lucozade sign, but that was gone; the blue and gold dome of the Russian Orthodox Cathedral, Fuller's Brewery at the roundabout. She stopped trying to think and simply sat there, drinking it all in, wondering how she'd got there, and most of all, how her father was, and what would happen now.

And then suddenly they were there, turning off Maida Vale, into the long tree-lined boulevard, where the buds on the elms were just visible, and they were grinding to a halt outside the red-brick building, and the bin with the face painted onto the lid was still outside. Kate didn't get out of the car. She looked around only as the cab driver pulled her bags out onto the pavement, puffing, and said,

'Alright, love?'

He opened the door, regarding her curiously. She knew he was probably thinking, Uh-oh. Is she actually a bit . . . mad. Kate blinked at him, suddenly, as if he were speaking Martian.

'Oh,' she said. 'Yes.'

'Is this where you want?'

'Yes,' said Kate, stepping out onto the pavement, though actually what she really wanted to say was, I've changed my mind, can we go back to the airport? 'Yes, it is.'

She gave him money and thanked him; he drove away, with a hand-wave out of the window. She felt like an alien, she couldn't remember how to behave. She looked down at the paving slabs on the pavement. Rectangular, scratchy dark grey, slightly cracked. It was silly. She'd forgotten what they were like here.

Shoulders squared, Kate picked up the bags, and stood at the foot of the stairs up to the hallway of the flats. A bird called in a nearby tree, a large black car hummed next to her, its engine running, but otherwise it was silent.

It's strange, the things that are stored in your brain, but that you haven't thought about for years. The black front door of her old building was really heavy, on a spring. You had to wedge your body really firmly against the door to stop it clapping shut in your face; she forgot. It banged shut behind Kate, practically trapping her with its force, as she dragged her bags into the hallway and looked rather blankly around her, at the large, beige, sunny hall, quiet and dusty in the cool sunshine.

How she was going to get her huge suitcase upstairs? The thought of lugging it to the first floor, her body already bone-tired, made her feel rather blue. Impossible not to think about the first time she'd come here, with him, impossible not to think about how it had been, the day they'd moved in, over three years ago, in deepest winter. Then the pigeon-holes had been over there; they'd moved around now. Kate peered inside the box marked Flat 4; two catalogues, five pizza delivery leaflets, four minicab cards, three Chinese takeaway menus, and a plethora of random letters addressed to assorted names she didn't know, and some bills, addressed to her, greeted her. Flat 4's pigeon-hole had obviously become the storage depot for everyone's unwanted post; and Gemma the tenant had only moved out last week. Lovely.

Kate looked down at her bags, and decided she'd deal with the post later. She stuffed the letters back in their box and pulled her suitcases across the hall. She was not usually given to moments of girlish weakness, but she was suddenly overcome with fatigue. Up till now coming back to London had been anonymous, impersonal. The taxi driver, the man at customs, the lady on the passport desk; they didn't know her. Now she was here and she was in the flat where people knew who she was. This was when it started to get . . . messy. Somewhere above her a door opened; she heard voices. Kate shrank back against the wall, like a prisoner on the run. Perhaps this was a mistake, a big mistake, perhaps she should just turn around and . . .

Suddenly there was a loud noise, a thudding sound, and boots on feet thumping across the landing, coming downstairs, several pairs of feet, she thought. Kate pushed her bag up into the nook by the bannisters and peered up. There was muffled cursing; they were obviously carrying something heavy, and she heard an old, familiar voice say,

'Thank you. Thank you very much. I'll see you later then.'

Kate peered up through the bannisters. There was a coffin coming down the stairs. A coffin. She blinked, and to her alarm an hysterical, horrifying urge to laugh bubbled up inside her, before she swallowed it down, frantically scrabbling to push her suitcase out of the way.

'Can you open the door, Fred?'

'No mate,' Fred answered. 'You've got the front, you take it.'

'It's heavy, remember?'

They were turning the last corner, outside her own flat, just appearing at the top of the stairs, and Kate called up,

'I'm down here. I'll hold the door open.'

'She's down there,' said the other man. 'There's someone down there.'

'Thanks love,' Fred said. 'We've got a coffin here, you know.'

'Yes, a coffin,' the other man added.

'Yes,' said Kate gravely, wondering if she were being filmed as an extra in a hidden-camera Pinter play. 'Don't worry. I'll stay here.'

She leant against the door, holding it flat open, and frowned at the driver, who had left the engine running, which always annoyed her. Questions ran through her head. Who was it? What did you say in the way of pleasantries to undertakers? And how did you tell someone to turn their engine off without sounding self-righteous? She caught the thought escaping into the dim recesses of her mind that she didn't think like this in New York.

It was, indeed, a coffin, sleek and brown, borne gently by its bearers to the bottom of the stairs, held only at a slight diagonal angle. She stared at it as they reached the bottom step and gingerly readjusted their load.

'Been on holiday?' Fred said politely. He nodded at her suitcase as they walked towards the front door.

'I've been away,' said Kate vaguely. 'Just got back, yes. This is – er – sad.' She gestured pathetically at the coffin. 'Who – who is it?'

'Old lady who lived upstairs. Had a husband. Nice fellow.' Fred jerked his head up, indicating where in the labyrinthine view they might live. Kate followed his gaze.

They passed through the front door and left her standing there on the threshold.

'Second floor?' said Kate, her voice faint.

'Yep,' said Fred, nodding kindly at her.

'Mrs – not Mrs Allan?'

'Yes, love,' he answered her. 'Sorry. Not the best welcome back for you, is it now?'

Kate loved him then for apologizing, as if he were personally responsible for Mrs Allan's death. She smiled at him and shook her head, as if to say please, don't worry. She followed them onto the pavement as they slid the coffin gently into the hearse – she hadn't realized it was a hearse.

'There he is,' one of them said under his breath to the other. 'Ah,' and they looked up. There in the window, two floors above Kate's, an old face looked out through the glass. She recognized him then, of course she did – it was Mr Allan. Mr Allan pressed a hand to the glass, looking down at the street, his face impassive. He was much older than she remembered.

The car drove off. Kate raised a hand in greeting to Mr Allan, not sure whether to smile or not. Once again, she wasn't sure what to do, how to behave. What did you yell up to a neighbour in circumstances like this? 'Hiya! How are you! Haven't seen you for ages! I know, I moved to New York. So, what's new with you? Apart from your wife dying?'

She hadn't spoken to them since she'd left. They'd written to her in New York. Kind, sweet Mrs Allan had sent her newspaper clippings, articles she thought she might like, but Kate hadn't written back, and the communication had dried up. Mr Allan's face now looked down at her, grey and yellow through the sun on the glass, and she waved again, uncertainty flowering within her, and looked around to realize she was standing on the pavement alone. She pointed in, towards the flats, as if to say I'm back, and looked up – but he had gone.

'I'll –' she started to say out loud. I'll see you later. Climbing up the steps, she shut the front door behind her, picked up her heavy bag and dragged it upstairs.

CHAPTER FOUR

The lock that clicked in the door, the floorboard in the hall with the big hole in it, where you could see the Victorian pipes underneath; the sunny little sitting room down the corridor with the bay windows, the radiator in a fretwork covered box. The bookshelves, still filled with her books, gaps where he had taken his books away – all these things, stored somewhere in her memory, forgotten till now. She didn't remember leaving her flat for the last time. She remembered scenes within it, though. She remembered coming here for the first time with Sean, the first Christmas here . . . waking up on a Sunday morning, in bed together, the papers, friends for lunch . . . as Kate stood in the living room, keys in her hand, and looked around, she smiled grimly. Every bloody couple cliché under the sun, like an advert for a sofa workshop or a kitchen sale.

The recent tenant, Gemma, was about her age, and while she'd left everything pretty much as it should have been, for a furnished flat, she'd moved the armchairs around. Frowning, Kate pushed them back to where she'd had them before, one next to the sofa, the other in front of the window. She leant against the window sill and breathed in, memory flooding over her with the smell of wood, of lavender, of something indefinable, dusty, earthy, cosy, the smell of her flat.

Funny that it should be so comforting to be back here. Funny. She put the keys quietly down on the table, almost as if she were afraid of disturbing someone, and took off her coat, putting it gingerly on an armchair. She went into the kitchen, noting with pleasure that the pots and pans hanging on the hooks she'd so lovingly put up a couple of months before she'd gone were still there. On the tiny little balcony that led off the kitchen door, no more than doormat-size, really, she could see the thyme and rosemary were still going strong. She opened the door, pulling it slightly, remembering how it always used to stick.

There were people walking on the street outside; families pushing buggies, people chatting outside the little row of shops down the road. Kate craned her neck to watch them, to look down, over the wide boulevard of redbrick apartments lined with trees that were sprinkled with fat, green little buds. Beyond the shops was Lord's cricket ground, a ten-minute walk, then Regent's Park, the Zoo, the canal . . . down Maida Vale, which she could just see, was Edgware Road, leading into the park, to Mayfair, into town. All just outside. She could go out now, could be in any of those places, which she'd dreamt of over the past three years with increasing frequency. She could do that, she was back.

A loud noise from the bedroom made her jump. Kate turned and ran, relishing the size of the space that was her own, now, and she saw that her suitcase, which she'd leant against the wall, had fallen over, bringing down with it her telescope. She smiled at the sight of it, memory leading her back down a path. Her telescope! She hurried over to the corner of the room, straightening it out, setting it right again. How she had loved that bloody thing when she was a teenager. While Zoe and most of her other friends had been standing outside Tube stations of an evening with their waistbands rolled up and over, to shorten their skirts, ponytails high on their heads, usually to one side, smoking Silk Cut Menthols and chipping their nail polish, Kate had been – where? Yes, at home, looking through her telescope, high up in her attic bedroom, or curled up on her ancient patchwork bedspread, reading *Gone with the Wind*, or *Forever Amber*, or some yellowing Victoria Holt novel.

'Hello old thing,' she said to the telescope, stroking it gently, brushing the light film of dust from its casing. It had been so long since she'd looked through it. She caught herself, and the memory of her teenage self, and smiled, grinning widely at how touchingly and unintentionally hilarious she had probably been. Poor Dad, she thought, gazing away into nothing. What he had had to put up with, on his own, looking after this strange, solitary teenager, who didn't understand why her mother had gone, who blamed herself for it more than anyone. Still partly did, though it was more than half her lifetime ago. Kate's hand flew to her collarbone.

The reverberations from the suitcase crash had toppled over some photos on her bedroom shelves. Her parents on their wedding day, in black and white, her mother in a dark velvet mini-dress, almost painfully young and thin, her beautiful hair swinging about her shoulders, her father, so pleased with himself – and with his wife. They were clutching hands, so tightly that even through the years and the monochrome, you could see the whiteness of her mother's knuckles.

It was stuff like that that got in the way, Kate thought, putting the picture back carefully on the shelf. Nice of Gemma to leave it out for her, but it was best put away, along with the marriage itself, and the photos next to it – her twenty-first birthday, taken by Zoe, her and Steve and Sean, hilariously awkward in suits, for some reason and – a sop to her new family – her stepmother and Dani, at Dani's christening, nearly four years ago, her half-sister resplendent in a little gown and white hat embroidered with fabric flowers that made her look like an entrant in an Esther Williams look-alike competition.

Kate turned away from the photos, frowning. She felt out of kilter once again, remembering why she was here, and she went into the sitting room and picked up the phone, calling Lisa again.

'Yes?' Lisa answered immediately. 'Hi, Kate.' She added, more warmly, 'How are you? Good flight? Everything . . . OK?'

'It's fine. How's Dad?' Kate said, running her fingers along the bookcase in the corner of the room, staring out of the window.

'He's OK. He's having a nap,' said Lisa. 'He can't wait to see you.'

'Oh –' Kate pursed her lips, shaking her head and looking down at the floor. 'Oh. I can't wait to see him. Lisa, can you give him my love? Is it OK if I come over now?'

'Give it an hour or so, if that's alright,' said Lisa. 'He's still quite weak, Kate.'

Kate turned and looked back at the picture of her parents on the shelf behind her, perfectly still. She had spent the last three years with her mother, making up for lost time; she had always known though that once she came back here, everything that she had neglected would hit her, hard. It struck her now, that she had almost become too good at what she did: shutting out a whole area of her life. She had crossed the ocean and simply closed the door behind her on her life in London. As if, for the most part, it didn't exist. As if she could.

She needed to keep moving, keep busy here. She'd go and

get Mr Allan some flowers. Yes. She turned away from the telescope and the photos, and went into the sitting room again. She grabbed her bag and left the flat, running down to the shops on the corner of the road, marvelling at the price of a pint of Rachel's Dairy Milk. She got some flowers, daffodils, bought the papers and some Marmite and some hummus and crisps. The old corner shop now sold posh President butter and had its own orange juicing machine.

Back again, as she unlocked the front door to the building, she realized how quiet it was. She climbed the stairs slowly, listening for sounds. There was nothing from upstairs, and she didn't know whether to go up now or wait till later. When had Mrs Allan died? Was it too soon?

The phone was ringing as she unlocked the door to her flat again; she ran for it, but missed the call and she couldn't work out who it was. But it reminded her who else she was here to see, as if she could have forgotten. Kate picked up her mobile, fingers toying over the keypad, and after a minute she shook her head. No, it would be too weird to speak to Zoe right now, after so long, to hear her voice – she could still hear her voice when she was going to see her later. She texted instead:

Hi. I'm back. Can't wait to see you. Shall I come round about seven? K x

Almost immediately, so that it felt she had barely finished writing the message, her phone beeped back at her with the reply.

Seven is perfect. Can't believe you're back! Can't wait! Lots of love Z x x x

She finished her unpacking, pottered around in the kitchen,

still listening to the radio in an effort to cheer herself up, and then she sat on the sofa and read the newspapers for an hour, feeling like an alien, wondering who some people were, amazed that other people were still in the news. A car went past in the street now and then; the rustle of some tarpaulin sheeting, covering a balcony on the flats opposite, drifted over every now and then; a child called out in the street, but otherwise it was eerily, ominously quiet. Normal, unremarkable, mundane. God it was strange, like she'd never left.

As Kate reached for a hair tie on her dressing table, she looked up at herself in the mirror. She hadn't seen herself in this mirror for years, and the effect was rather like coming back from holiday and seeing how tanned you'd got in the mirror you look into every day, after two weeks away. She looked – different. Older, probably. Thinner, but not in a good way. Mostly she looked tired. Her dark brown eyes were smudged underneath with circles, her dark blonde hair was longer. Had she always looked that serious? The hairbrush she'd been holding gently slid out of her hand and Kate stared at herself, silence echoing around her.

She shut her front door behind her, and as she did she remembered Mr Allan. She looked at her watch – she was expected at her dad's. Tonight there was Zoe. She would go tomorrow. The thought crossed her mind as she slung her bag over her shoulder and tripped downstairs: what else would she do tomorrow, other than seeing her father again and seeing Mr Allan? But over the past couple of years, Kate had got very good at filling in hours of time, doing not very much, lying low, staying in the shadows.

It was getting late, and she glanced into her pigeonhole again, remembering too that she had meant to go through her post. The pile of letters was still there, undisturbed, but as she peered closer something in the compartment caught her eye and it was then that she saw the letter.

A new letter, at the top of the pile.

In handwriting she would never forget, as long as she lived.

Kate Miller
Flat 4
Howard Mansions
London W9

Kate's hand froze in the air, the letter clutched in her fingers. Air trapped in her throat; she felt hot, boiling hot. How did Charly know she was back? And more importantly, why the hell was she writing to her?

CHAPTER FIVE

Daniel Miller had not been an ideal father to a teenage girl, in many ways. After Venetia left, his professional decline had been rapid: in 1990 *The Times* had said that his interpretation of Beethoven's Violin Concerto was probably the best ever – yes, ever – yet by the time Kate was taking her A-Levels, four years later, he hadn't had a proper solo recital for months. The gigs were starting to dry up, as Daniel was late for rehearsals, argued with conductors, cried in his dressing room, got drunk at lunchtimes and sometimes didn't turn up at all. When he'd had a reputation as being one of the best, if not the best, he had been – for a musician, admittedly – modest about it. Now it was on the slide, he had turned into a prima donna, sulking in the house in Kentish Town, skulking angrily, smoking furiously, talking, always talking to friends, on the phone, around the kitchen table.

It wasn't as if Venetia had been the world's most regimented mother, either; but when she'd been around there had, at least, been some semblance of order, some idea that there might be food in the fridge or water in the boiler; now, Kate and Daniel simply got used to muddling through. Dinner times were sporadic, usually set by Kate; school parents' evenings went unattended. Daniel never knew where he was going to be on any given day, or indeed where his daughter was: it was luck on his part that his only child was a shy girl, more likely to be in her room reading Jean Plaidy than out in London somewhere, raising Cain. Sometimes Kate would come home and find him talking to the postman, eagerly, angrily, about budget cuts, about society today. (The postman read *Socialist Worker* and was also angry about a lot of things.) Daniel remembered Kate's birthdays, but only after he'd been reminded by others. But he forgot to ask about most other things: when her university interviews were, when she started her exams, how she might be feeling about everything.

In other ways though, for Kate, her father was the perfect father. Kate was tall and ungainly from her teens onwards, with long spindly legs that rarely did what she told them. She was thin, flat-chested; like a stick drawing. Later, of course, she would come to see that being tall and sticky wasn't so bad; in fact lots of other girls wished they were like that. But being tall and sticky, with an always-too-long fringe, and short nails, bitten and chewed cuticles, and no social skills whatsoever, it was a long time before she could see it. She was not particularly sure of herself, much as she longed to be, much as she desperately wished she was like her charismatic father or her mesmerizing, much-missed mother, or the confident, smiling girls at school who hung around at the Tube station. She would gaze at them shyly from under her fringe as she passed them, going down the stairs to the platform, going back to her dad, to an evening of homework, of music, of conversation around the kitchen table with Russian composers, Italian singers, obtuse German conductors ... and Daniel, directing the evening, shoving his floppy blond hair back with his hand when he got excited, as young Kate collected up the plates, dumped them in the sink, drinking the dregs of the wine quietly behind their backs, alternately fascinated and bored by their conversation, as only the wistful outsider can be.

She wished she could be one of them. Not necessarily the band gathered around her father, but the band of girls outside the Tube station, gossiping about 'EastEnders', about who Jon Walker liked best, about whether Angie really got fingered by Paul at Christa's party on Saturday and did her dad know because he was really strict? Whether Doc Martens were just totally over or who was going to see Wet Wet Wet at Wembley? But she knew she never would be.

Kate thought about this, how much things had changed, as she came out of the Tube station and walked towards her father's new house. New – well, not any more, she supposed. It was a long time since the days of the house in Kentish Town. And it was years now since Daniel Miller had found himself not only a new wife, but a new career, as a recording artist doing covers of ABBA and Barber's 'Adagio for Strings', posing artfully with a loaned Strad (for the photoshoot only) in black and white, standing on a clifftop. He'd even been nominated for a Classic FM Award (and whether he had been outraged not to win or secretly relieved, Kate couldn't be sure). Just before his health had declined a few months ago he had emailed Kate to announce that his next project was a cover album of Barry Manilow's greatest hits.

She was proud of him – she was his daughter, how could she not be, having seen him at his lowest, and how he'd built himself up again? But Daniel Miller's change of career had been greeted with absolute outrage in the more traditional musical world – an open letter to him in the *Telegraph* signed by the six biggest music critics, pleading with him to pull his album of Abba covers, offers of 'proper' work, third desk in the Bournemouth Symphony Orchestra, publicized far and wide, making Daniel a scapegoat, almost, for what the more puritanical elements of the classical music world saw as the selling out of genuine talent for big bucks. Daniel had stuck to his guns, though, and his bank manager thanked him for it, and the *Hello!* interviews started, as did the chats on the GMTV sofa orchestrated by Lisa, who was herself in PR. For Lisa was behind it all, it was Lisa whom Kate had to – reluctantly – credit with turning her father's life around, even if Kate didn't love her the way she felt she should . . .

Now Daniel and his new wife and daughter lived in Notting Hill, in a cream townhouse off Ladbroke Grove, with a huge, clean, neutrally coloured basement kitchen (not a chaotic, eclectic basement kitchen) leading through to a perfectly manicured garden, artfully designed, with an enormous communal garden at the back of it. A distressed chandelier hung in the hallway; aluminium window boxes with ferns adorned the window sills; the 4x4 stood outside. In its careful independence it was virtually indistinguishable from the other houses on its exclusive little road. Yes, times had changed for Daniel Miller: until now, for the better, as he had frequently told his eldest daughter, almost daring her to challenge him on it.

As Kate rang the doorbell of her father's house, just after six o'clock that Sunday evening, she was shaking somewhat, though she tried to hide it. In her hands were some more daffodils – she wasn't sure what to bring her father, not knowing what he would or wouldn't be able to eat. And she couldn't remember him, couldn't remember what colours he liked, what present might cheer him up, what books he liked reading, these days, who was out of favour with him, who was in – though, conversely, she now knew all of those things about her mother.

The door was suddenly flung open. There, like an action heroine and her matching miniature doll, were Lisa, her stepmother, and Dani, her little sister, as if they'd been standing there, simply waiting for her to come along.

Lisa was standing with her hands on her hips, her tiny frame encased in an expensive brown velour tracksuit, chocolate Uggs on her feet, car keys jingling in her hand. Kate goggled at her rather stupidly, not knowing what to say. She stared at Lisa's beautiful, unlined face, her skin moist and tanned, perfectly buffed and cleansed and possibly peeled by a team of high-tech beauticians, and just said, blankly,

'Lisa!'

'Kate, hi,' said Lisa. Her expression was neutral. She pushed Danielle forward. 'Dani, it's your sister. Kate. Say hi.'

'Hi-yerr,' Dani spoke loudly.

'Hi, Dani,' Kate said and, bending down, kissed her.

'Hey there! Hi!' Dani said, showing her tiny teeth.

'Why've you got an American accent?' Kate said, peering at her half-sister as if she were an alien. Dani stared back at her, impassively, her curly blonde bunches bobbing slightly as she sucked her thumb.

'Kate, she hasn't got an American accent,' said Lisa. She gave a tight smile. 'Dani, we're going to get you ready for bed in a minute, OK? Then you can come back and talk to Kate.' She turned back to her stepdaughter. 'Look, it's lovely to see you.'

'Oh, and you,' said Kate. She held out the daffodils, and Lisa reached out for them. 'Um, these are for Dad,' Kate went on, as Lisa's hands dropped like stones. 'I mean, you know. Shall I show them to him?'

Lisa stared at her with something close to exasperation. 'Whatever you want,' she said. 'He's through there.'

She guided Kate with her hand on her elbow, pushing

her down the cream-carpeted hallway to the sitting room, where she said,

'Dan, darling? Kate's here, and I'll be back soon.'

Kate stood in the centre of the huge space and stared at the figure at the other end of the room.

'Kate?' came a low, raspy voice, from the sofa underneath the window, and Kate walked towards her father.

'Hello, darling girl,' he said, reaching up. Kate leaned over him and he put his hand around Kate's neck, pulling her down to him as he lay on the sofa. 'How's my Katya? Look at your old dad, eh? Bit of a shambles, I'm afraid.'

Kate hugged her dad, kissed him awkwardly, still holding the flowers. She stuck her lower lip out, unintentionally mimicking her thoughts. She was totally, utterly knocked sideways by what she saw. His face was yellow, his hair colourless, the creases in his cheeks looked like folds, and now his hands were lifeless, crossed pathetically on his stomach, like an old lady waiting for a bus. Those hands, which once coaxed sounds of pure heaven from a three hundred-year-old wooden box, the hands that were insured for a million dollars when Kate was ten – they looked flat, deflated, like the rest of him. Where once his hair had been dark browny blond like his daughter's, slippery and uncontrollable, his grey eyes snapping fire as he waved a fork at a friend, violently disagreeing about something, where once his tanned, healthy face smiled excitedly down at an adoring crowd, now did he smile gently at his daughter and pat the sofa.

'Come and sit here, old lady, come and tell me how you are.'

'God, Dad,' said Kate. 'I'm so sorry . . .'

She trailed off, and bit her lip. A tear rolled down her cheek. Daniel looked at her.

'Oh darling,' he said. 'Come on,' and he pulled her arm

so she sat down next to him. 'It's a bit of a shock, isn't it? But I'm having a bad day today, leaving hospital and all. I've been much better than this. You haven't seen me for a while Kate, that's all. Never mind, it's over now isn't it? I just have to concentrate on getting better.'

'I didn't realize,' said Kate. She felt almost dizzy with sensation overpowering her. How could this have happened, how could she have *known* this was happening to her dad and not come sooner? Forget her mercurial, vague mother; he was, without doubt, the person she loved most in the world. How could she have shut herself off so completely? She stared at him frantically, and he looked at her.

As if reading her thoughts, her father said,

'Lisa's been amazing, you know. I don't know what I'd have done if she hadn't –'

'I know, Dad,' said Kate. 'I'm so sorry I wasn't here sooner.'

'She has been brilliant,' her father persisted. He lay back on the sofa again. 'And Dani – gosh, she's quite different from you at that age. Very noisy!'

'I bet,' said Kate, smiling at him, holding his hands.

'But it's nice to have a young person around the house again. A little Katya.' He blinked. 'Ah, here she is!'

Danielle rushed into the room, in her pyjamas. 'Daddeeee!' she cried. 'I'm here!'

Her pyjamas were pink; she had a glossy, huge teddy under her arm and slippers in the shape of bunny rabbits, and she looked very small and totally innocent, her chubby legs thumping across the carpet.

Kate bit her finger sharply, the pain flooding through her, calming her down, and she looked away from her father to her half-sister.

'I like your pyjamas, Dani,' she said. 'Pink pyjamas, like the song.'

'What song?' said Dani, in an American accent.

'"She'll Be Coming Round the Mountain",' said Kate. 'Do you know it?'

'No,' said Dani. 'You're lying, man.'

'I'm not lying,' said Kate. She sang.

She'll be wearing pink pyjamas when she comes,
She'll be wearing pink pyjamas when she comes,
Wearing pink pyjamas,
Wearing pink pyjamas,
Wearing pink pyjamas when she comes.'

'*Singing aye-aye ippy-ippy aye,*' Daniel boomed loudly, suddenly, from the sofa, and Kate jumped, and Dani laughed. '*Singing aye-aye ippy-ippy aye,*' they sang together.

'*Aye-aye ippy*
Aye-aye ippy,
Aye-aye ippy-ippy aye.'

Dani laughed again. 'I like it,' she said, jumping onto the sofa. She wiggled in between Kate and her father, her warm, hot little body writhing with excitement. Kate put her arm around her and hugged her, inhaling the scent of her damp hair. She looked over at her dad, watched him smiling down at his small daughter, then up at her, and she squeezed Dani a little tighter.

'Sing it again,' Dani said.

'I'm tired now, darling,' said Daniel. 'Tomorrow.'

'Daniel,' came a clear voice from the door. 'Is Dani giving you trouble? Is she being a bad girl?'

'I'm not, Mom!' Dani screeched in a slow, high voice. 'Kate wouldn't sing me another song and she promised!'

'I'm sure she didn't mean to,' said Lisa.

'I didn't,' said Kate, sounding totally unconvincing. Lisa walked into the centre of the room, and Dani ran towards her and clutched her leg, with the desperation of a man finding the last lifebelt on the *Titanic*. Lisa looked down at her daughter.

'Ah, mum's darling girl,' she said. 'Is she tired tonight?'

'Yes,' said Dani, sucking her thumb so loudly it echoed, the sound bouncing off the fake dove-grey antique French armoire all the way across the room. 'Rilly, rilly tired. Night Dad.'

'Say goodnight to Kate, darling,' Daniel said, shifting on the sofa. 'She's come to see you too, you know.'

'She should have come earlier,' Dani said. 'Mum told me.'

Silence, like a blanket, flung itself over the room, broken only by the noise of Dani sucking her thumb again.

'Nonsense!' exclaimed Lisa, looking flustered for the first time in her life. She ran a hand over her forehead, the other resting on her daughter's head. Kate thought how tired she looked, for a second.

'Sshh, darling,' said Lisa, looking at Daniel, who ignored his youngest daughter.

'Lisa.' Her husband's voice was quiet but firm. 'Why don't you put Dani to bed, and Kate and I can catch up.'

'See you in a minute, Kate,' said Lisa, ushering Dani out of the room.

'Bysie bye, pink pyjamas,' cried Dani as she skipped out of the room, utterly unconcerned with the familial havoc she, the only person in the room related to everyone present, had wrought.

'She didn't mean it,' Kate's father said. 'She's got a lot on her plate at the moment.'

'Dani?' Kate said, smiling gently.

'Hah,' said Daniel. 'Lisa. I'm not easy at the moment. She's very . . . organized.'

She saw him now, in these new surroundings, and watched him as his hand scraped, pathetically, over the surface of the coffee table, as if searching for something to cling onto. The thought that this was the best thing you could find to say about your wife, for whom you had almost had to throw your daughter out, for whom you had worked yourself into the ground, moved houses, made new friends, gone on flashy, expensive holidays to 'network' with flashy, expensive people that you didn't really like that much, for whom you had essentially reinvented yourself, struck Kate as singularly depressing. But she said,

'I know. Yeah. She must be great to have around at a time like this.'

'Oh sure,' said her dad, and they both fell silent, the two of them sitting awkwardly in the pristine sitting room. Kate shifted on the sofa.

The letter from Charly was in her bag. She could feel it in there; humming with intent. She hadn't opened it, she didn't want to open it, knew she couldn't. She didn't know why she hadn't thrown it away. But she hadn't. Now, silent next to her father, she slid her hand into her bag again, to touch it for the umpteenth time since she had left the house.

The envelope was stiff; there was something inside it, more than just a piece of paper. What could it be? What was it? The postmark had said Mount Pleasant, the main London sorting office: that proved nothing at all.

'What's that?' said her father curiously, his voice resonant in the stillness of the vast room.

'Nothing.' Kate thrust the envelope hurriedly into the darkest recesses of her bag, way out of sight. 'Just something that was waiting for me. Post.'

'You must have a lot to deal with,' her father said. He shunted himself up slightly on the sofa, grimacing as he did so. 'Sorting out the flat, and everything.'

'Yes,' said Kate.

Daniel looked up at the ceiling, then at the floor. 'Um – while I think of it,' he said, casually, 'are you going to get a new tenant while you're here? Approve them yourself?'

Before she left for New York, her father had bought half

the flat, and as such he was entitled to half the rent. Kate skimmed her foot along the carpet. 'Not sure yet,' she said. 'I might wait till I go back, get the letting agents to do it again. I need to think about it. I mean, Gemma leaving and me coming back – it was all quite sudden.'

'Right,' said Daniel. 'Still.' He coughed, Kate thought rather awkwardly. 'We don't want to lose rent on it, do we? You don't, I mean.' He cleared his throat extensively.

'Two weeks, I'll be here, Dad,' Kate said gently. 'You won't lose that much rent, I promise. I'm sorry –' she didn't know what to say. 'I'll get onto it,' she said. 'I'm sorry,' she said again, wondering what else to say. A germ of an idea formed in her head; she rejected it, surely not. 'Anyway, Dad, you mustn't worry about that at the moment. It's not important.'

'Easy for you to say,' her father said, quickly, loudly. 'Eh? Isn't it?'

'Yes,' said Kate, realizing she had to appease him, not aggravate him. 'Of course, Dad. I'll get onto it.'

'Hm,' said her father. He breathed out, heavily, a sort of groan. 'We don't want it sitting idle. That's all.'

'I'm talking to the estate agents tomorrow,' Kate said, mentally adding this to her list of things to do. Her father groaned again. 'Dad, you OK?' She put her hand on his, it was shaking.

'Yes, yes,' Daniel said, almost impatiently. He shifted slightly.

'How long till they – till they know?' Kate said. 'Whether it's taken, I mean?'

'What's taken?' He shook his head, not understanding.

'The kidney.' It felt like a dirty word.

'Oh, I see. I don't know. If it hates me, it'll tell me pretty soon; I'll go into arrest and probably die,' he said, smiling mordantly. 'They've got me on enough different pills though;

good grief, I could practically set up a fucking pharmacy.'

'Dad.' Kate put her hand on his, which was lying on his chest. Her hand was shaking.

'Oh, Kate,' he said. 'God, it's lovely to see you, darling. I miss you.'

She looked down at him; his eyes, blue, fierce, with a flicker of their old fire, locked with hers.

'I'm sorry,' said Kate, and she meant it. 'I am so sorry.'

'No need,' said Daniel, mildly. 'I could have come to see you more, you know. But you should have come back. Dani hardly knows who you are. And she's your sister. You've only seen her once in the last three years.'

Kate had a childish, stupid impulse suddenly, to scream like Dani, but she merely tightened her grip on her father's hand.

'You know why I had to get out of here,' she said instead.

'You did the right thing,' Daniel said. 'It was right that you left, you know. I just think you've been gone too long. That girl,' he added, casually. 'Charly. It was Charly, wasn't it, the one you met in your first job?'

'Yes,' said Kate.

'Well, I never liked her, I have to say.'

Since this was patently untrue, and Daniel had always had a crush on the long-legged, tousle-haired, foul-mouthed Charly, Kate said nothing, but she smiled at him, and he twinkled back at her. 'Well,' he said after a while. 'Maybe just a bit.' He was silent for a moment. 'How's your mother, then?'

'She's well. She sends her – well, she sends her love,' Kate said, cursing herself for phrasing this so badly. What Venetia had actually said at the airport, hands clasped to chest, while Oscar struggled with the bags, was,

'Oh my god. My darling Daniel. Tell him . . . God, what? You know, he's a shit, but I still can't help loving him.'

53

'How's that gay husband of hers?'

'He's not gay. He's fine,' Kate said automatically.

'Hmm,' said Daniel, flicking back his hair, in an unconscious gesture. 'Do you or do you not remember your engagement party? When he told me he'd had a manicure specially for the party? My god.' He shook his head.

'Some men like manicures,' Kate said defensively.

'Not any men I know,' said Daniel.

'Dad!' Kate said, hitting him gently on the arm. 'You used to wear gloves in summer to protect your hands!'

'That's completely different,' Daniel said crossly. 'I was a musician, they were my tools.'

'Well, so's Oscar. He's a musician.'

'No, he's a tool,' Daniel said, chuckling to himself, coughing a little bit. He recovered. 'And he's not a musician. Arranging silly songs about farmers and cowmen is not being a musician.'

'He doesn't –' Kate wasn't going to get into the merits and demerits of *Oklahoma!* with Daniel, nor point out to him that actually it was probably the greatest musical ever written. She and her father had fallen out over this many times before. So she frowned at him, smiling too, but her frown quickly turned to alarm.

'Dad, are you alright?'

'I'm fine. Well, I'm not fine. Aarrpff.'

She looked at Daniel in panic rushing over her; perspiration covered his forehead, and he was terribly pale.

'Lisa,' she called, getting up. 'Dad, I'm going to get Lisa,' she told him, shaking free of her father's frenzied grip.

'No, don't,' he said, flashing a ghastly rictus grin at her. 'I'll be fine. When do you have to go, darling?'

Kate looked at her watch, she didn't want to look at him. 'I'm going to see Zoe, but it really doesn't matter if I'm late.'

Lisa appeared in the doorway. 'Dan? You OK?' she said, bustling forward. 'What's wrong with him?'

'He went a bit . . . funny,' said Kate. She looked down at her father as Lisa put a hand on his forehead and checked his pulse.

'Went a bit funny,' Daniel repeated. 'That's the medical term for it, I'm sure.' He closed his eyes. 'God, I'm fucking tired. It really knocks you for six, this business. And I'm so bored. So bloody bored.'

He was a man of action, used to doing, speaking, thinking, striding around and yelling. Kate could see how much he hated this confinement. He needed constant distraction, attention, to keep him stable, otherwise . . . she remembered this much from her childhood. The consequences were awful.

'I'm sure you are,' said Kate, still standing, and watching him. Her eyes met Lisa's. 'Look Dad,' she said, bending down, 'I'm going to take off and let you get some rest, OK? But I'll be back tomorrow.'

'How great!' said Lisa, smiling thinly. 'That'll be great for you, won't it Dan?'

'I look forward to it,' Daniel said, slightly inclining his head, mock-formally. He took his daughter's hand and kissed it. 'Until tomorrow, my darling.'

'Yes,' said Kate, stroking his hair. 'Bye Dad. I love you.'

'It's great to see you again,' he said, clutching his heart in a dramatic way; a flash of the old Daniel Miller, the amateur dramatics that the crowds used to love. 'So wonderful to have you back.'

She couldn't speak; she shook her head, smiling at him, as her eyes filled with tears, and followed Lisa out into the hall. Lisa handed her her jacket with an air of polite efficiency.

'So – are you getting a job while you're over here?' Lisa said suddenly. 'How did you leave it with them?'

'In New York? I said I wasn't sure when I'd be back.

55

They've got someone to cover for me, don't worry. She's really good.'

'It's not that hard to learn the skills though, is it.'

Uh-ho, Kate thought. She steeled herself for another blow.

'What do you mean?' she asked, trying to sound polite and friendly.

'You're the office assistant.' Lisa sounded exasperated. 'Aren't you?'

'Er – I –' Kate didn't know what to say.

'I'm just surprised, that's all,' said Lisa. She drummed her fingers on the stone-coloured wall. 'I never thought that's what you'd end up doing.'

'Right,' said Kate, briskly. 'OK, well, thanks, then, I'll –'

She put her hand on the door frame, and pointed vaguely towards the street, but Lisa was not to be put off. She ran her forefinger lightly over the flawless skin on her cheek, stroking it.

'It was such a shame, what happened, wasn't it,' she said, conversationally. 'Because you know. You were doing so well on *Venus*. Your dad thought you'd be editor of the magazine in a few years. Or writing a novel, or something. He always said that. He's a bit surprised, I think –'

Lisa's eyes were bulging slightly; Kate realized, with a start, that she had been dying to have this conversation with her stepdaughter for some time. Her face loomed close to Kate's, and Kate could see her pores, as Daniel coughed in the other room.

'Right,' said Kate again, nodding furiously. 'Lisa, look, now's not the time for –'

Lisa held up her hand, briefly. 'I must say this –' she began. Kate's heart sank. 'That's all very well. But I don't think you quite understand how much your dad worries about you now, Kate.'

'I know he does.'

'He feels very let down.' Lisa looked at the floor.

Kate was angry, suddenly. Angry at herself for mismanaging this situation, angry with Lisa for her insinuations, her nasty barbed comments.

'Look, I'm very tired, and so are you, much more so than me. I haven't seen you for eighteen months, or Dad or Dani. Please, Lisa,' she said, surprised at how scary she sounded, 'Let's not get into this.' Being angry made her stronger, she realized. She wasn't scared of Lisa anymore. 'I'll see you tomorrow, is that OK?'

Lisa stared at her. 'Yes. Yes, of course. Look – I'm really tired,' she whispered. 'Sorry.'

'I'm sorry, Lisa,' said Kate, feeling really uncomfortable. 'I should have been back more. To see him, and to see Dani. I can't believe how much she's grown.'

If she was expecting a more emotional moment on the doorstep, she wasn't going to get it from Lisa. She nodded, as if the apology was what she was hanging out for, and then opened the door. 'Yes,' she said. 'She's a great little kid,' as if Dani were a neighbour's child who lived down the street. 'So then, see you tomorrow, and – yeah.'

That was not how Kate would have put it, but this was her cue to leave, clearly, so she did. She stepped into the front garden, and knocked on the sitting room window, peeping over the frosted glass so she could see her dad on the sofa again. He waved at her, his face lightening, and then shooed her away, blowing a kiss, as Lisa came back into the room and stood, watching her from a distance. Kate made her escape, hurrying down the path into the crisp March night.

CHAPTER SIX

'I'm on my way.'

'Oh my God.'

'I know. Zoe, I need a drink. Put some wine in the freezer.'

'Already in the fridge love. Got some Twiglets here too.'

'Twiglets! Oh my God, when was the last time I had –'

'I know, I know. Now stop wittering and get on the Tube. I'll see you when I see you.'

'Bye. Zoe –'

'Yes love. Bye.'

Kate picked up her pace. She was going to see Zoe! Actually see her, look at her face, be in her presence. Sit at her kitchen table, see Harry, meet Flora for the first time! She was terrified, but she couldn't wait. After seeing her father, nothing else seemed as bad as that, and it was with a curious lightness of heart that she stepped off the kerb, looking around her in the evening gloom.

Zoe, Henry and Flora lived in Kilburn. When they were first engaged, Zoe and Steve had bought a garden flat in a terrace house, moving from a spacious, airy flat in Muswell Hill because, as Zoe kept saying, Kilburn was the Next Place. The Next Place that was going to go stratospheric, the new

Notting Hill/ Clapham/Shoreditch. By the end of the year, where there were roadworks and rubbish and old green Eighties council bins with white stick men on them miming 'Don't Litter', where there were dealers and a WH Smiths with old livery, there would now be potted plants. Widened pavements, tapas restaurants, and all the shops apart from the Primark and the Tricycle Theatre would have gone, to be replaced by Space NK, Carluccio, and Strada. Zoe and Steve would stroll out of an evening, to sample the delightful new Italian and friends would say admiringly, 'You live in *Kilburn*?' much as one might say, 'You live in *Mayfair*?'

Three years on, and everything else had changed. They'd bought the flat upstairs, when Harry was born. But Steve was gone now, Harry and Flora were here, yet Kilburn was still more commonly bracketed with Soweto, the Gorbals and South Central LA than Fulham or Battersea. But by then other things were, simply, much more important.

Kate realized, as she stumbled along in the dark, that she knew the route to Zoe's house from the Tube so well she could have done it almost blindfold. The broken cracks in the paving stones; there was the parking ticket machine; there was the gate that half hung off its hinges. It was so unlike Daniel and Lisa's house; it was more like Kentish Town, where she'd grown up. She ignored the lounging youth who sat on a wall two houses along from Zoe's, staring balefully at her; she even smiled quite sweetly back at him, hammering on the door impatiently, all thought of fatigue gone.

And then darling Zoe opened the door. They didn't say anything. Zoe just smiled at Kate, and held out her arms, and Kate remembered what she'd forgotten, that Zoe and Steve's house was more of a home to her than anywhere she'd ever known, that she loved Zoe more than most people in the world, probably. Zoe looked exactly the same, like a little brunette imp, and as she stepped forward and hugged her best friend, Kate felt her heart hurting, physically hurting.

'Missed you.' Zoe's silky thin brown hair muffled Kate's voice; after about a minute they laughed, and stepped back, Zoe still gripping Kate's elbows.

'Look at you, lovely girl. You're so grown-up. What's happened to my Kate?'

'Hardly,' Kate laughed, and shook herself free. She crossed her arms. 'Where are the children?'

'In bed,' said Zoe. 'Sorry,' she added. 'I knew if I let them stay up to see you we'd never get rid of them. I told them if you came round at all it'd be very very late. And I told them you wouldn't have had time to buy any presents yet, because there aren't any in America.'

'Ah.' Kate followed her in, and shut the door behind her, looking round in pleasure at the long corridor, littered with small wellington boots, a bike with stabilizers and coats, hung on various things. A birdcage hung off the umbrella stand.

It was like being home again. She hadn't realized how much she'd missed this house. Zoe gazed around rather helplessly, then clapped her hands and said,

'Right, let's get some wine. Put your coat – er, there. That's right.'

'Thanks.' Kate followed her through into the sitting room, piled high with brightly coloured videos, books, toys, cushions, and more cushions – Kate had forgotten this, that Zoe was incapable of entering one of those Cath Kidston-style lifestyle shops so beloved of her, the kind that stocked chipped enamel jugs and beautiful cups and saucers for the modern vintage home, without walking out with a cushion under her arm. She must have had about twenty. It made sitting on sofas in Zoe's house extremely hard.

'So how was –'

'So how are –'

There was a constraint in the air all of a sudden; they broke off and laughed. 'You go first,' Kate said.

'How's your dad?'

'Fine. Weak, bit shaky, but basically fine, for the moment. They won't know if it's been a success for a while.'

'Must have been great to see him.'

'Yeah.' Kate couldn't articulate it all. She scrunched up her nose, and nodded, and Zoe nodded back. She understood.

'How was the flight?' said Zoe, brushing the worn edge of the large blue sofa.

'Good, good, thanks,' said Kate.

'How's New York! I want to hear everything. How's it going?'

'How's it going' is one of the world's most annoying questions. It is not a request for specific information, more a general 'fill me in' command. Kate didn't know where to start. Trying not to sound churlish, she said,

'What do you want to know about?'

'You know!' Zoe's enthusiasm was loud, too loud. 'How's everything going, what's it like in NYC, are you liking living there. What's new?'

'Um. Well, I saw Betty on Friday –'

'Yeah? How's she?'

'She said she'd just spoken to you.' Betty was an old friend of both of theirs.

'Yeah, she rang last week, actually.' Zoe cleared her throat. 'Who's Andrew?'

'Andrew?' Kate was blank for a moment, then she remembered. It seemed years ago. The drinks, the kiss, her running

61

away . . . Andrew. She tried to picture his face, mortified, in the darkness. She felt her cheeks flame red; she raised her hand to her face. It was another life.

'He's – no-one, really,' she said. 'Someone Betty's always trying to set me up with.'

'Oh!' Zoe said, too loudly again, like this was a jolly, great conversation between two normal friends. 'Oh you!'

'No,' said Kate flatly. 'I kissed him and then I felt sick and had to get into a cab and run away. If you want the truth.'

Zoe's brow furrowed. 'Right.'

'Nothing really to talk about,' Kate said. 'Honestly.'

Zoe took the hint. 'So, then. That's – great. So, how's the flat? Did the tenant leave it in a state?'

'No, it's fine actually,' said Kate. 'I've unpacked, it's nice to be back there.'

'Yes, it must be.' Zoe ran into the kitchen, collecting the wine out of the fridge. 'Is it – er, is there a lot of stuff in it still? From . . . before?'

'Yep.' Kate took the glass she handed her. 'Most of it's in the storage area in the basement. But quite a lot's still in the cupboards in the hall. Just – you know. Books. Photos. Clothes I should have thrown away years ago. Joint stuff we had together.'

'I'm the same,' Zoe said. She waved her hands around. 'Too much stuff of Steve's around, still. It's been a while now. Why can't the bastard come and pick it all up eh?' She smiled, her eyes filling with tears.

'I know,' Kate said, inadequately. She could feel her heart, hammering away in her throat, it seemed. This was it, now. 'Look, Zo –'

'Can I say something?' Zoe interrupted her, her voice high, nervous. 'Darling. Can we just – catch up, you know? Not have some long, awful, depressing conversation that leaves us both in tears and makes us feel hugely guilty?'

'But –' Kate had come expecting that; she deserved it, she *was* guilty. But Zoe put her hand on hers.

'Look, Kate. Darling Kate.' Her eyes were bright with tears. 'Do you know how much I miss you?'

'Zoe –' Kate said, easy tears coming to her eyes. 'I –'

Zoe interrupted her again. 'This is what I mean. I miss you so much. There's so much to say, and so much I want to know about. I don't want to sit here having a maudlin conversation about all the shit that's happened. It happened. You ran away.'

'I did.'

'But I'm the one who kicked you out.'

'No, you weren't.'

They were facing each other.

After a few moments, Zoe sighed, deflated. 'It doesn't matter. Oh Kate. I was furious with you, but now you're back so, oh, please let's not waste time being apologetic and wringing our hands about it all. I want to know how you *are.*'

She sat back on the sofa, and nodded her head solemnly.

'But ' There was so much Kate could say to this, and she fumbled for words.

'I mean it,' Zoe said, almost fiercely, and Kate saw that she was struggling with emotion, emotion that threatened to overwhelm her. Kate nodded back.

'Right. Of course,' she said.

'Yep,' said Zoe, recovering herself quickly. 'Cheers, darling Kate. Cheers. Welcome back.' She stood up, and Kate followed suit. 'God, it's good to see you again.'

Their glasses, clinking heavily together in the quiet room, made a harsh, clanging sound. After they'd each taken a large sip, they both sank into the sofa and looked at each other.

'So really, how's your dad?' Zoe said first.

'Yes,' said Kate. 'He came out of hospital this morning. Um, he's OK. Not great, actually.'

'How is Loosa?'

This was the childish name she and Kate had given Lisa after her appearance on the scene, over six years ago. Loosa made them cackle for hours in the pub, at Kate's flat, and so on. Even Charly tried to claim she'd thought of it. It was less of a joke when, after about nine months together, Loosa and her dad announced they were expecting a baby and were engaged. She was Lisa after that.

'She was – er, fine,' Kate said. 'You know what she can be like.'

'Was she mean?'

'Noooo . . .' Kate grimaced, remembering the conversation. She smiled, it had been so stupid. 'Ahm, she told me I've wasted my life and I'm a disappointment to Dad.' She nodded at Zoe's outraged expression. 'Oh, and then asked me about the rent, wanted to know when I was getting someone else into the flat and I needed to sort it out ASAP.'

'What a bitch.' Zoe's dark eyes snapped fire. 'Don't worry about her. She's always been a bitch, Kate. She's a cliché – I thought they didn't make them like her anymore. Evil step-mothers, I mean.'

'Still . . .' Kate was trying to be fair. She knew Lisa had it pretty tough. And as she thought about the huge, spotless house, perfect without and within, weirdly, she felt sorry for Lisa, and Dani, just a little, and desperately sorry for her dad.

There was silence; another awkward silence. Zoe cradled her glass of wine in her hand; there was a noise from upstairs, a creak, but then silence, and they looked back at each other and smiled.

'Oh, by the way. I should have mentioned,' Zoe said after a moment, 'Mac's back.'

64

Kate looked up sharply. 'I thought he was living in Edinburgh again?' she said.

'No, he came back. He's looking for somewhere to live. He wants to move up here, find a flat closer to us, actually.' She looked curiously at Kate. 'Hey! Maybe he should rent your flat when you go back!'

'That's a good idea,' Kate said. She rummaged for some imaginary item in her bag, so Zoe couldn't see her face.

'He'd love to live in your flat, I bet. I always thought he had a bit of a crush on you.'

'Did you!' Kate waved her head around, as if this was hilarious.

Zoe nodded, her brown fringe bobbing up and down her forehead. 'Yes, seriously, me and Steve used to talk about it.' She looked at her friend curiously. 'But . . . well, it didn't work out, did it.'

'I suppose not,' Kate nodded, seemingly interested. 'So, how's his job?'

'Good, good,' Zoe said. 'He's a resident now in a hospital down here, actually doing pretty well I think. It's just – since everything happened, it's good to have him around,' she said, looking glum. 'It's nice for Harry and Flora to see their uncle. He's so good with them.' Zoe smiled. 'Oh, he's lovely. He's just a gentle giant, you know.'

'Yes,' said Kate, smiling gently at her. 'He is lovely. I can imagine he would be.'

'Anyway,' Zoe shook her head, recovering herself. 'When he heard you were back and you were coming over, he said he'd pop round tomorrow instead. He said he didn't want to intrude, you know. On us catching up and everything.'

'Of course,' said Kate. 'That's really nice of him. Still, it'd be great to see him.'

So Mac *could* be on his way over, as she sat here on the sofa. But he wouldn't come over, Kate knew it. Once he knew she was back, he'd no more pop round to Zoe's to say hi than he would eat a glass vase. And she couldn't blame him.

'So how's work?' Kate said a bit later, two more glasses down.

'OK.' Zoe swallowed. 'OK. Good, actually. They've really been great about the kids and everything. And it's a nice place to work. I like going there.'

Zoe worked as a garden designer for a picture-perfect little garden nursery near Primrose Hill. Having been a lawyer at one of the top London firms, averaging eighty-hour weeks and earning double that, suddenly three years into her job, she chucked it all in. Memorably – or this was how Steve told it – she'd told a partner at the firm that she didn't want to end up like him.

She'd trained as a garden designer, because she could afford to – and Steve was a management consultant, still working long hours and bringing home the bacon – and when they had Harry her job was flexible. It was perfect – until Steve left them and now she was struggling to make ends meet. But as she said, she'd rather struggle, working in the open air with the flowers and seeds, and pick her children up from school, than work all the hours of the day and be able to afford five-star holidays to Dubai.

'You should come and have lunch with me one day, when I'm at the nursery,' Zoe said, patting the table flatly with the palm of her hand. 'What are you going to do for the next week or so?'

'Not sure, really,' said Kate. 'I need to sort stuff out in the flat. See Dad. Spend some time with Dani, too, I suppose. And catch up with people, Francesca and all that lot.'

'How's your work going?' Zoe emptied the rest of the bottle into her glass.

'OK,' said Kate. 'Someone's covering me while I'm away. They've been really good about it.'

'Are you – what's happening with becoming an agent? Are you handling any stuff of your own yet?'

She took another swig of wine as Zoe watched her, waiting for her answer.

'Not really, no,' she said honestly. 'And I like it that way, Zo. I know it's terrible, but I loved it. I liked not having to be me any more.'

Zoe nodded.

'I thought you'd be editor of some huge magazine some day,' she said. *Devil Wears Prada*, that sort of thing. Or writing a bestselling novel.' She shook her head. 'That's all.'

'You sound like Lisa,' Kate pointed out. 'I thought you'd be a QC by now.'

'You thought lots of things would happen,' Zoe said. 'So did I. Look at us.'

The cluttered kitchen was silent; the house was quiet. Kate tried to imagine what it must be like for Zoe, alone every evening, while the children slept upstairs. Tears pricked her eyes; a painful lump rose in her throat.

'Hey,' she said, trying to change the mood. 'Do you remember your housewarming party here, all those years ago?'

'My god,' said Zoe. 'I always forget about then. We only had the groundfloor flat then. Isn't it weird, how different it was then.'

'Sure was,' Kate nodded. 'That was a great party though.'

'You wore your blue and gold dress.'

'You stood on a chair and sang "Cabaret".'

'Oh dear,' said Zoe ruefully. 'Didn't Francesca snog that Finnish gatecrasher from the flat upstairs?'

'Yes, she did!' Kate hit the table, memory flooding back.

'And – oh my god. Wasn't that the night you got together with Sean?'

She cleared her throat, as Kate was silent, drowning in waves of memory. Then Kate said,

'No, it was a few weeks later.'

'But you were flatmates, weren't you?'

'Yes, we were . . .' Kate squashed a piece of bread into her fingers. 'Yep. That was a weird night. I'd forgotten.' And she had, strangely. It had been one of those event evenings that mark the beginning of a new time in one's life and thus the end of another, she realized now. 'Six years ago,' she went on. 'I can't believe it. It seems – well, it's weird.'

'So near yet so far,' said Zoe, and Kate nodded.

Kate unwrapped an after dinner mint, and carefully smoothed the foil out onto the table. 'When did you buy the flat upstairs?' she asked. 'I can't remember. Was it after you got married?'

'After,' said Zoe flatly. 'Steve flirted totally disgustingly with the estate agent and I didn't speak to him for two days. But he got the price down by five grand, so I couldn't hate him anymore.'

Kate well remembered Steve's flirting. There was nothing she could say to this.

'Typical of him,' Zoe went on. 'Bloody typical.' She blinked rapidly. 'Anyway, what was I saying? Yes, Mac. Mac!' Kate nodded. 'You see, I always thought he had a bit of a thing for you. That night at our housewarming party, you know. He was mad about you for a while, you know that, don't you?'

Kate was silent, and then she said, 'Well, it's a long time ago, isn't it.'

'Yep,' said Zoe. 'It's just a shame. We should get you two together before you have to go back, you know.' She looked Kate over, appraisingly, like she was a prize heifer. 'You haven't seen him since – how long?'

'I don't know,' said Kate. Keep your voice light, she told herself. 'Is he –' she opened her eyes wide. 'Is he well, though?'

'Yeah.' Zoe nodded. 'He's OK. Got a bit of grey hair. Works too hard. Doesn't talk about stuff much. But he's OK. I know he'd love to see you.'

Kate looked around the bright, cosy room, feeling cold suddenly, and very tired.

'It's weird talking about this,' Zoe said, sighing. 'I never talk about it, about all of us any more. I'll have to make the most of you while you're here. It'll be a while won't it? Perhaps you'll love it back here so much you won't go back. Yay!'

'I am going back,' said Kate. 'Seriously. I love it there. I've got a new life, you know.'

'I know you have,' said Zoe. She crinkled her nose. 'You needed it. I like thinking of you leading this super-glam New York life, meeting up with Betty for cocktails, running around like Sarah Jessica Parker. Sort of means I can't hate you for not being here, Katy.'

Since her last birthday party had consisted of her mother, stepfather, and the Cohens (from down the corridor), and Maurice the doorman having a slice of cake out on the side-walk, Kate didn't know what to say to this. She smiled and nodded, sagely, as if hinting that a life full of incident and drama lay waiting for her across the ocean.

At eleven o'clock, Kate left, by then a little worse for the wine. As she was putting her coat on, Zoe opened the door and said,

'Bye darl,' Zoe said. 'I love you. It's so good to have you back.'

'It's good to be back,' Kate said and then, that moment, as she hugged Zoe, it was.

When Kate got back home, the letter from Charly was still in her bag. She waited till she was in bed, face washed, warm chunky bedsocks from Bloomingdales, which her mother had given her last Christmas, enclosing her feet. Her old bedroom smelt faintly of familiar things, Coco perfume and peonies. Outside, someone somewhere was yelling at someone else, or perhaps at no-one, and away beyond her the city flickered, lights gradually going off one by one, still at its heart never asleep. Kate smoothed her hands over the duvet and blinked, the fatigue of the day finally catching up with her as her fingers fluttered on the glue of the envelope.

She drew out a letter. A letter and a photo. It was of Charly and Kate, dressed up before the office Christmas party, their first year at the magazine. Kate winced at her ill-advised Spice Girls-era black clompy platform boots, black miniskirt, waistcoat and hair in a high ponytail, and then, almost greedily, her eyes drank in Charly, glorious as always, her long, tousled hair tumbling around her tanned shoulders, the little black dress with spaghetti straps, the gorgeous, still-covetable knee-high black suede boots. It had been so long since she'd seen her, she'd forgotten how beautiful she was, how hilariously different the two of them were.

Hilarious, yes. That they'd been friends, so close you couldn't slide a finger between them, so obsessed with each other it was almost like a relationship, so heartstoppingly sad that she hadn't seen Charly for years, that Kate rocked back against the bookshelf, as if a ray of something had just shot out and hit her in the chest. That was the effect Charly still had on her, nearly eight years on, all those years since they'd first met.

Dear Kate

It's been a while, hasn't it. How are you?
I'm fine I suppose, working hard, not.

I found this photo of you and me at the Christmas party, the year you started at Woman's World, thought you'd like to see it? What did we look like back then??!!

Kate I'm writing to say hello. Also to remind you I'm still alive. I wonder if you still care about that.

This is hard for me to write, you know I never was one for letters. I wanted to apologize. For everything I suppose. Well I thought I might as well try. Also, I'm writing because I wanted to let you know I'm having a baby. We don't know what it is yet —

Kate didn't read any more. She screwed the whole lot up, jumped up out of bed, and the cold hit her. She ran through to the kitchen, opened the little narrow french doors, and threw the letter, the photo, the envelope, out. She wondered, as if watching herself from above, why she hadn't just opened her bedroom window, or thrown it in the bin. But it wouldn't have been far away enough.

It was only when she felt something drop onto her chest that Kate realized tears were running down her face. In the dark corridor there was no sound. She crawled wearily back to bed, turned the light off, praying for a deadening sleep.

But the thoughts crowding into her brain danced there all night. She should have realized that those scenes would go through her head again, that she would dream about it all again. Back when she was starting her life as a grown-up, they all were. Look how it had turned out. She'd told

Zoe, she never thought about it, she'd practically forgotten everything.

But that was a lie. Although she didn't want it to be, it was imprinted on her brain, for always. How could it not be? And the dreams always ended the same way, with Kate realizing what, deep-down, she carried around with her every single day in New York. That she shouldn't be here. She didn't deserve to be here. That was why she didn't let herself remember.

CHAPTER SEVEN

October 1999

'Hey. New girl. I'm going to Anita's for lunch. Do you want to come?'

Kate blinked up at the vision before her, and pushed her tortoiseshell glasses slightly further up her nose.

'Er, yes, please,' she said, shocked. 'Thanks.'

'I'm going *now*,' the vision said. 'I'm bloody bored, and Catherine and Sue are going to be gone for fucking *ages* on that conference meeting thing. Let's get out of here.'

Nearly three weeks into her exciting new job at *Woman's World*, and Kate had yet to have lunch with anyone; she was too terrified. She sat on a bench by Lincoln's Inn each day at lunchtime, eating her sandwich and hiding behind a book if she saw anyone from the magazine. The offices were near Holborn, a big glass building housing all the magazines in the stable of Broadgate UK, and every morning the revolving doors sucked in these tall, gorgeous, glamorous stick-girls who strode past Kate, hair flowing in the breeze, expressionless and cool, and every evening it spewed them out again, as she flattened herself against the wall, trying not to get in their way. She spoke to her boss Sue, to Gary, the postroom boy, with whom she was insanely jolly and chatty, the way new people always are with the photocopying man, the postroom boy, the security guards. They're men, they're not bitchy, they don't ignore new people as a point of principle.

To everyone else, however, she felt miserably that she might as well be invisible. If by chance one of the tall goddesses who hustled and bustled around Catherine Baldwin, the fearsome editor, should be forced to address her with some features-related query which only she could answer, Kate heard herself replying to their careless questions in a voice rusty with lack of use, and a tone hopelessly fulsome and inane.

'Hi!' she'd squeak. 'Hi, there! No, Sue's not here! She's still out at lunch! Sorry, sorry,' she would say, practically bowing, as Georgina or Jo or Sophie looked bored and not a little contemptuously down at her.

Because it was now October, the whole new job thing had a curious resemblance to going back to school, or university. The days still dry and relatively warm, the leaves dusty and crunchy on the trees, the streets of town suddenly busy again after the dog days of August and September. They were still playing 'Everybody's Free (To Wear Sunscreen)' and 'Livin La Vida Loca' on the radio, but they sounded flimsy, summery, silly, out of kilter. The Argos Christmas adverts had started appearing on TV, even. As Kate and her new flatmate Sean walked to Rotherhithe station in the mornings, the still rising sun would hit them in the eyes, and in the evenings though they tried to deny it, it was too cold to sit outside at the pub.

Kate and Sean had been friends at university, but they were more friends-in-a-group than friends who went out for drinks on their own together. Tall, laconic, with a Texan drawl, Sean was Steve's best friend. Steve was a good friend of Kate's too. In the Easter term of their first year at university, Kate had introduced Steve to her best friend Zoe, and Steve and Zoe had been going out ever since. So Kate and Sean had spent a lot of time together in the past few years.

Still, though, Kate was still fairly surprised to find herself sharing a flat with Sean, but then lots about her life now surprised her – the fact that she was south of the river, for starters, was a shocker, as was the fact that she didn't like alcopops any more – she preferred a glass of Chardonnay. She'd been to TopShop and bought a black and grey checked miniskirt, which she wore with a black polo-neck and black tights, mistakenly in the warm, dry weather of September, but it made her feel super-mature. She did her own shopping at the supermarket, picking out Things to Cook from her new Jamie Oliver cookbook. She bought the *Evening Standard* on her way home each night and felt super-grown-up, reading it with a concentrated expression on her face on the Tube.

Three weeks into her new living arrangement and all was going swimmingly – too swimmingly, in fact, because Kate had started to dread saying goodbye to Sean each morning. He sometimes perplexed her with his constantly flirty ways and optimistic, can-do attitude, as well as intimidated her since he was, without doubt, usually the best-looking man in the room. Now, he was the friendliest face Kate saw most days and she would cling to him at the ticket barriers.

'I don't want to go to work today,' she'd say, clutching his arm.

'Hey now. Don't be silly,' Sean would say, gently prising her off him with a giant, paw-like hand. 'It's only been ten days. You'll soon make friends, Katy. You're shy, that's all.'

'They're horrible,' Kate would mutter, biting her lip. 'Don't like it. Don't want to go to work and be grown-up.'

It was true, in its way. Part of her wished this wasn't

happening, that she was back at home with her father, cheer-fully cooking stew, throwing insults at each other, listening to music. Warm, exotic – but a little bit safe, boring. Wouldn't it be easier if she just moved back in with her dad again? And never left the house, faced the real world, with all its terrifying complications that she wasn't at all good at? Yesterday, she had spilled coffee over one of the girls at work – George. George had given her what Kate could only iden-tify now as a death stare and said, 'That fucking top was *new*,' even though it was only a tear-drop-sized spot of coffee. Kate was thinking of having plastic surgery to change her appearance.

'Look,' Sean would say, punching her playfully on the arm. 'You're Kate Miller, aren't you? All you ever wanted to do since I've known you was work in magazines. Didn't you?'

'I'm not right for them. I don't fit in.'

'You got a First in English from Oxford, Kate,' Sean would say. 'You're right for anyone. You gotta see that. You're young, you're cool! Man. They're lucky to have you, OK?'

Kate would rather die than use her university education to impress people, and she refrained from pointing out that at college she'd done nothing *but* work, while everyone else was off having fun, drinking, putting on plays, drinking, sleeping with each other, going to balls, going to silly parties, drinking and sleeping with each other. She wasn't cool, she was the opposite of cool, she was . . . lukewarm. She was destined for the shadows, watching from the sidelines, not centre stage. Ugh. But Sean, whose nature was as sunny as his hair colour, couldn't see that about her, and it annoyed her.

'You'll find some friends,' he said, one Thursday, nearly three weeks after she'd started there. He patted her on the shoulder, moving her away from the ticket barriers. 'You'll love it there soon. This is your time! You're in the big wide world now, and you're gonna find your niche. I promise.'

Sean was untroubled by self-doubt. 'It's easy for you,' Kate said, childishly. She looked down at the floor, knowing she was being stupid, feeling eleven again, like she was back at school, trying to persuade her mother to let her stay at home. Sean put his finger under her chin, and she turned her face up towards him.

'Hey,' he said gently, looking into her eyes. He smiled, his tanned, kind face crinkling into lines. 'It'll be easy for *you,* Katy. You're wonderful. We all know it, you just need to know it.'

She clutched at his wrist, taken aback. 'Oh, Sean.' She was embarrassed, she didn't know why, and she smiled back at him, shyly. 'You're just saying that.'

You're just saying that. She sounded about five; Kate cringed, inside, then asked herself why it mattered, as awkwardness fell upon them. She tightened her hold on his wrist, reached up and kissed him on the cheek.

'Thanks,' she said, and she smiled at him, feeling happy, all of a sudden. 'You're right, Sean. Thanks a lot.'

'I know I am,' he said, and he was still watching her. 'Now, you're gonna be late. Have a great day. I'll be there when you come back, after a long day slaving over some JavaScript. OK?'

'OK. Bye. Thanks.'

His mouth curled a little. 'No, thank you.'

He was a flirt, such a flirt, she told herself, as Sean walked away. Kate watched him shaking his head at her over the ticket barrier, as the sea of commuters bustled past them, off with lives of their own, full of promise and exertion and interaction and . . . Oh, all the bloody things she was no good at. It was so sweet of him to try, she told herself. She stared after him. He would be there tonight when she got home, watching TV, and they'd sit on the sofa together and chat about their day and yet another day would have passed with her being shunned, like the Amish. So she'd cook him something and he'd teach her how to mend her bike, or how to rewire a plug, or something, and they'd spend the evening together, like they always did. She'd be fine, if she could come home to that life. It was a nice life. Who said you had to love your job?

But Sean was right. Because that very day, Charly decided to notice Kate.

They went to Anita's, a traditional Italian around the corner from the office. It was free of Broadgate employees, by dint of the fact it served food, in particular food that wasn't just leaves. Charly seemed to know them all, the waiters practically clapped as she slunk in, her long legs sliding into a table by the window.

'God, Sue's a bitch, man,' she said as they were seated. She pushed her small frameless sunglasses up on her head and nodded at a waiter. Her honey-coloured hair tumbled around her, she smiled at Kate, the freckles on the end of her nose wrinkling. 'Yeah, we're ready,' she said to the waiter, hovering nearby, a look of adoration on his face. 'What you having? Salad nicoise for me. No dressing. With extra olives. And a coke. Thanks.'

She flung the menu back at him without acknowledging his presence. Kate said,

'Er . . . me too.'

'The same?' the waiter said, raising his eyebrows.

'Yes,' said Kate, not wanting to be conspicuous. She handed him the menu back.

'You don't want dressing neither? The same?'

'Yes!' said Kate, trying to affect an incredulous laugh.

'You want extra olives too?'

'Oh, go away,' Charly said, batting the waiter away. 'Just bring her a normal one. Leave us alone. So. D'you like Catherine? What do you think of Sue?' she demanded, leaning in, her long, slender fingers plucking a stale roll from the basket in front of them.

Kate was taken aback by the directness of the question, and a little terrified. She hadn't imagined she'd have to speak, more that she could just sit there and listen to Charly, whom she'd noticed striding around the office, effortlessly glamorous. She never seemed to hang around with the Georginas and the Jos, the Pippas and the Sophies, she was her own separate entity. More beautiful than them, cooler than them (she had been wearing cropped trousers and heels for ages – long before Madonna in the Beautiful Stranger video, as she informed anyone who wanted to listen) – less posh than them, less fake than them. She knew it, and she didn't seem to care.

'Come on,' said Charly impatiently, and Kate was shaken from her reverie. 'Is Sue a good boss? She really annoyed me today, you know, telling me to recheck that piece on gloves for autumn.'

'Er . . . Aah,' Kate said, hating the impaired speech she seemed to have developed since her arrival at *Woman's World*. What would Sean say if he could see her? She thought about it, and smiled. 'I like her. She's nice. Bit uncommunicative – I mean I wish she'd tell me what's going on a bit more.'

'Yeah,' said Charly, nodding. 'She seems to think you'll just guess. She's OK, but I know what you mean. I used to work for her.'

'Did you?' said Kate. 'How long – how long have you been here?'

'Not long,' said Charly. 'Too long, you might say. A year. I was her assistant, now I work with Catherine and Georgina –' Kate nodded, she knew this '– and I sometimes write the editor's letter when no-one else can be fucked to do it, and I do a couple of featurettes.'

'You do the Letters Page, don't you?'

A frown passed over Charly's beautiful face. 'Yeah, and I fucking hate it. Load of weirdos writing in to tell you how to make stuffed animals out of the lint from the washing machine, or wanting you to print a picture of their grandson just cos he's done a shit that's shaped like Alma Cogan.'

'Really?' Kate was fascinated.

'Not the last one, no.' Charly shook her head. 'Barbara Windsor, actually.'

Luckily the salads arrived, saving Kate from further comment. Charly ate like a demon, shovelling food in her mouth, throwing out odd comments, inviting responses from Kate, making jokes about the office, filling her in on what she hadn't known – Barbara in Sales had slept with Fry Donovan, the new Broadgate publisher, a couple of years ago, and he'd given her a job to keep her quiet, so the rumours went, which is why Barbara giggled helplessly whenever Fry walked into the room. Claire Cobain on the subs desk threw up into Phil's yucca plant the day after the Christmas party; she'd forgotten and he hadn't realized for three days, except they all kept gagging on the smell. And Jo and Sophie weren't speaking to each other after Sophie heard Jo saying to Georgina in the loos that she looked rank in her new black patent platform boots.

All Kate had to do was throw in the occasional question, raise her eyebrows at the required moment, but Charly was a great companion, and soon Kate found herself opening up, telling her about her flatmate Sean, about her best friend Zoe, about how she'd started to dread coming into work, how she'd eaten her lunch on a park bench for the past two weeks –

'By yourself?' Charly demanded. 'Sitting in Lincoln's Inn

eating a sandwich from Prêt à Manger by yourself? God that's sad. What did you do if someone you recognized came past?'

'I'd look down at my book, or else I'd turn my head so they couldn't see me,' said Kate, and as she said it, she realized how silly it sounded. Charly laughed, her eyes wide open with surprise, and Kate joined her.

'That's the saddest thing I've heard for a long time,' Charly said.

'I know,' Kate agreed. She looked at her watch. 'We should get back, you know.'

'Yeah, in a bit.' Charly looked carelessly at her watch, then pouted. 'Let's have a coffee first. So – where were you before here?'

'Here?' Kate gestured to the building behind them. 'Nowhere. This is my first job.'

'Your first jeez,' said Charly. 'How old are you?'

'Twenty-two. I left university this summer.'

'Oh my god,' Charly said, peering at her as if she were an exotic specimen. 'And you started work right away? Didn't take any time off?'

Kate shook her head uneasily. She didn't want to disabuse Charly of the notion that she'd gone straight from university to a job, when in fact, she'd had a solitary, dusty summer at home in Kentish Town, slowly driving herself mad with the future. Her anyway-mostly-absent mother and stepfather were in the Hamptons for the summer and incommunicado, Daniel had a new girlfriend and was rarely at home; Zoe had skipped off into a Magic Circle job; so had Steve; Francesca and Betty, two of her closest friends, had gone travelling together for six months, not back till after Christmas. A few weeks ago, Kate had nearly put the phone down on Zoe when she'd told her that Mac, Steve's older brother, had just been put on some special fast-track system for the best surgeons in the country. People she hadn't even *met* were falling over each other to out-do each other, while she had whiled away the dog days of summer, saving up a trip to the newsagents each day. But that was over now, she hoped. OK, it was *Woman's World,* it wasn't *Vogue,* but it was a start.

'What's your ambition, then?' Charly asked. It was a strangely childish phrase, that; it touched Kate, though she wasn't sure of the answer. She wrinkled her nose. Charly persisted. 'What do you want to do, what's your dream job, I mean?'

It was what Sue Jordan, her new boss, had asked her, a month ago, at her job interview, and Kate gave the same answer then, as now. She looked over and above Charly, to the shelves behind the counter in the little restaurant. They were lined with spreads, old jars, tins. 'I want to work in magazines, that's all,' she said. 'I love them.'

'Really?' Charly sounded dubious. But Kate had heard it before.

'Yeah,' she said, smiling, and shaking her head. 'I was a geek all through school, and the one thing I loved that wasn't geeky was *Vogue.* Don't know why, just did.' She did know why, though; it was the entrée into a world she wasn't part of, a world she could only aspire to: glamour, style, elegance, beautiful clothes. It wasn't the posh people she was inter-ested in; it was something more fleeting than that – she supposed it was the idea of a blueprint for how to live your life. With style, flair, purpose, and organization. The cold, beautiful women in those magazines, they weren't ignored by boys, or by their co-workers, they didn't have mothers who left them, fathers who were messy and annoying. They – all of them, whether they were the writers, the models, the society people – they had black shift dresses, scented candles, fresh linen. Boughs of apple blossom in big glass vases, thick black velvet evening cloaks – that sort of thing. She loved magazines, that was all; the smell of the new pages, the sheen of the pictures, the slice of life, the answers to her curious questions about things, how other people behaved, reacted, everything. She was happy simply to observe, she knew that too.

'Well, good for you,' Charly said, sounding uncertain. 'So, you'll be wanting Sue's job in a year, then? Better tell her to watch out.'

'Oh, no,' said Kate, looking horrified. 'It's not –'

'Calm down,' said Charly. 'Don't get so worked up about it. It's a job, OK? When you've been here for longer you'll realize it's not worth having kittens about. Me, I'm happy if it pays me enough to buy a couple of glasses of wine and some new boots every few months.'

'Really? What do you want to do, then?' Kate said, curiously.

'Fuck all,' said Charly. 'I want to marry someone rich and go and live in Spain. Have a house here too, in the Bishop's Avenue. With a heated indoor swimming pool, and lots of Sophie's friends.' They both laughed; Sue had just signed off a feature that morning about the millionaires' row of houses in North London, and Sophie had spent a lot of time saying in a Very Loud Voice that she knew someone who lived there. 'I think she's reading the A-Z wrong. It's probably Bishop's Avenue in Acton, more like,' Charly had said loudly that morning, and Kate had smiled, as Sophie turned on her heel and flounced back to her desk.

'Hey,' Charly added, as they laid their money on the table. 'You been to the Atlas pub? Round the corner from the office?'

'No,' said Kate.

'It's nice. Fancy a quick drink there tonight?'

'Really?' Kate said, then corrected herself. 'That'd be great.' She looked at her companion. 'Thanks, Charly.'

'What for?' Charly slung her bag over her shoulder, and pulled out the hair that was trapped underneath it. She shook her head, and the waiters in the café watched in adoration. Like a Timotei ad, Kate thought with amusement.

'Just – thanks for asking me out to lunch and stuff,' she said, as they stepped out onto the street. 'It's weird when you start a new job. Not knowing anyone, you know.'

'Course I know,' said Charly. She didn't look at Kate. 'When I joined last year no one spoke to me for three weeks. Hey.' She pushed her hair out of her face. 'I reckon we could be a bit of a team, don't you think? Show Sophie and Jo and Georgina, those bitches, show them we've got our own thing going on. OK?'

'I'm not bothered about them,' Kate said, surprising herself.

'Sure, whatever,' said Charly darkly, and Kate wondered which one of them had incurred her wrath. 'No worries. But still, we're going to stick together. I've decided. You up for a drink then?'

'Definitely.'

'I'll see who else is around, too. Introduce you to some other people. We're going to have a great time.'

The sun was warm on Kate's hair; she felt relaxed, herself, for the first time since she'd started there. 'Great,' she said, as they turned the corner and walked up towards their building.

'Look at that loser over there, with the Beckham haircut,' said Charly, flinging her arm out so that she nearly knocked over a teenage boy who was staring at her. 'What a jack-fruit.'

The loser with the Beckham haircut was coming out

through the revolving doors. He raised his sunglasses and smiled at them. He was extremely good looking.

'Hey,' he said.

'Hey,' Kate said, then wished she hadn't.

'You never called me back, Charly,' he said, looking hopefully at her. 'When are we going out again?'

'Fuck off, Ian,' said Charly. 'It's not happening. Kate, I've got to get some gear from the postroom. See you later, OK? Atlas, straight after work? I'll come and pick you up.'

'Great,' said Kate, and Ian stared at her, annoyance crossing his otherwise perfect face.

That night, when Kate rolled back to Rotherhithe at twelve a.m., swaying and singing softly to herself like a sailor on shore leave, Sean was still up watching American football on Channel Five. As she staggered into the sitting room, Kate waved at him nonchalantly, trying to prove she was sober, and her hand flew back and hit the door frame with a loud *thwack*. Sean smiled to himself but only said,

'Good night then?'

Kate's mind was whirring, with the white wine pooling in her stomach, in her throat, in her head. Good night? The best night, that's what. She and Charly, Claire and Phil had gone to the Atlas, sunk a few drinks, then some more, then Sophie had joined them, and the five of them had played the pub quiz machine, screaming with joy when they got one of the questions right. It was Kate who knew that Chairman Mao died in 1976. She didn't know how she knew, she'd just known, and as she'd leant forward, punching the big plastic square on the machine, shouting 'Yesss!' as she did so, she felt, slightly hysterically, as if all those years of being the class swot, the one who got their homework in, the one who really never did anything bad, they were paying off. Charly had screamed, jumped up and down, and

85

high-fived Kate, and then 'Spice Up Your Life' had come on the juke box, and they'd both jumped off their stools and danced like crazy.

'I hate the Spice Girls!' Charly had shouted. 'They're fucking awful!'

'I love them!' Kate said. 'Sort of . . .' she continued, as Charly looked on at her in horror, and both of them laughed again.

Gorgeous Ian had turned up – Kate didn't know how he'd worked out where they'd be. Charly ignored him all evening, drinking beer from her bottle, cheering Kate on in the quiz and then, as they all stood around outside the pub after they were kicked out, suddenly walked off down the street with him, her hand carelessly clutching the back of his neck. Kate had been almost shocked, impressed by her total insouciance, the very *Charly*-ness of it, and then it had made her smile.

As she sat on the night bus home, trying not to acknowledge that she did feel a bit sick, she thought how great life was, how all the usual things that worried her – her dad, her mum, her sad little life, her fear that, since she split up with Tony, her university boyfriend, nearly two years ago, she would never find love again, her fear of her job, that she was just a big fat failure – all these things seemed to vanish, with the optimism of youth, and what she remembered instead was Charly's face as she bought them all another round of drinks with the winnings from the machine. Her amused expression as she said, 'You're hilarious Kate, you know that?'

'Thanks, Charly,' Kate had said. 'This is great.' She patted her arm.

Charly had shrugged. 'My pleasure.' She'd looked strangely pleased.

Kate fell onto the sofa next to Sean, put her head under his armpit, and smiled, ridiculously.

'Found some friends then?' Sean said. 'Or have you been drinking alone again?'

'Shurrup,' Kate said, her voice muffled by Sean's sleeve. 'Friends from work, nice.'

It was so cosy on the sofa, next to him; she loved Sean. 'So, where did you go?' he said, muting the sound on the TV. He turned towards her, and stretched his arms, yawning, and pulled Kate towards him. She wriggled into him, happily.

'Just pubs near the work, near the work building,' she said. They were silent together, for a moment, and she could hear his breathing, feel the rise and fall of his chest, her head against him.

'Oh, Kate,' he said, softly.

Kate sat up slowly, suddenly not feeling so drunk, knowing he was looking at her, and their eyes met.

Sean was a closed book to her in so many ways; she had known him for years, though they had never been best friends or gone out with each other. He was a genial, all-American kind of guy – the first impression, and then you realized, in his quiet, understated way, he was more British than that. His clean-cut, sporty appearance belied his more studious, careful character; though she knew him well, Kate never quite knew what he was thinking. Through the waves of cheap white wine, spirits and exhaustion, she looked at him now, blinking, wishing he would speak first, not knowing what was suddenly, now, between them. Someone more worldly-wise would have known what to do now, on the sofa, having a moment with their flatmate. They would either have leaned over and kissed him, or got up and made some coffee.

Watching him, watching his softly twitching lips, Kate wanted to kiss him suddenly, wanted it fiercely. But she couldn't. It was *Sean*, after all. Her flatmate. And she was drunk. No.

'Pfff,' she said, rather helplessly, smoothing her skirt with her hands.

It broke the tension, and Sean smiled at her. 'Oh, babe,' he said kindly, and he patted her arm. 'You're hilarious.'

'That's what Charly said!' Kate said, remembering the evening again, happily.

'So the mean girls aren't being mean to you any more?' Sean said lightly, sitting back and taking another sip from his bottle of beer.

Kate sank against the sofa. 'Oh,' she said, her eyes closing, glad the moment was over, and it was normal again. 'No, hope not.'

Sean nodded, and looked back at the screen. After about a minute, he realized that the head next to his arm was lolling, and that his flatmate was fast asleep.

The last thing Kate remembered that night was Sean's gentle shove as he pushed her onto her bed where she pitched headfirst onto the duvet. She woke up early the next morning as the late September rays were creeping into her room, the curtains wide open, having not been drawn the night before. She lay there, reconstructing the evening slowly, from its unexpected start to its slightly strange finish – had any of it really happened? Had she imagined the lunch with Charly, the drinks, the general knowledge? The night bus – and that moment with Sean, last night, had she made it up? She patted the bedside table next to her, feebly, feeling for her water glass, and then sat up slowly. Her mouth was dry, her head was ringing, she felt as if she wanted to die, but for the first time in what seemed like a really long time, Kate realized she was looking forward to the day ahead.

CHAPTER EIGHT

March 2001

More than a year after she'd started at *Woman's World*, the pic chart of Kate's friendships was clear. Charly was her best friend. Zoe was her newly engaged, other best friend. Her other friends Betty and Francesca were happily ensconced in their chaotic flat in Clapham; Betty worked in a gallery and tied bunches into her short dyed hair, while Francesca, who was a banker, and the person Kate had been closest to at university, was now extremely grown-up, wore grey suits and worked in Canary Wharf, which was suddenly where everyone was working.

Charly and Kate were still editorial assistants, they sat across from each other and helped each other, they went to the same Italian deli round the corner for lunch (where Kate happily stuffed her face with carbs and fats and Charly gingerly picked out the tomatoes in her sandwich and ate them) and occasionally got the tube to TopShop on Oxford Circus where Kate would try on clothes that didn't suit her and buy them, and Charly would try on clothes that made her long, leggy form look even more stunning and complain that nothing fitted her, and leave buying nothing. In the evenings, they went to the pub, where they gossiped and bitched about the day at work, their sometimes eccentric colleagues, and the endless fascination of the microcosm of the office.

Kate was changing; she only realized it when other people remarked on it. 'Nice work, Kate,' Sue had said briskly to her a couple of months ago, after she had written a little piece on Alma from 'Coronation Street'. 'You're really coming out of your shell, aren't you?'

The truth was she loved it, she loved her life now. She took to it like an ugly duckling to water. Now Kate strode to the Tube station in the mornings, her long legs flying out in front of her, her long hair catching in the breeze. She laughed with the mailroom boys, she said hello to Catherine the Editor with a bright smile on her face, not a mumbled, half-horrified grunt, in fear lest she might try to engage her in conversation. She loved answering the phone to random readers, calling to ask whether 'The Darling Buds of May' was ever coming back on TV again or where they could get the recipe for hot-pot that had been in last week's issue. And she looked forward to relaxing, drinking, chatting, laughing in the evenings, as she had never done before.

One Friday afternoon in March, Kate sat at her desk, trying to concentrate on the letter she was writing, whilst resisting the temptation to play with her new mobile phone, her first, which she had picked up that very lunchtime. She hadn't actually called anyone on it yet, but she had taken down everyone in the office's number, entering each one in the address book, slowly and painfully. It was four o'clock, and the office felt dead. Kate felt dead too – it had been Sophie's birthday drinks the night before, a long, messy night, culminating in Kate not getting home till two because of the vagaries of the night bus. Charly had disappeared at midnight, with a random ad exec she'd pulled hanging onto her arm. She had been in a strange, cool mood, and Kate could tell a storm was brewing.

Kate chewed on her biro and looked up from her desk, where she had been idly pressing buttons on her mobile. 'So – did you go back to his place?' she asked.

Charly was flicking through a magazine, exaggeratedly pouting. She was supposed to be checking the text for the recipe card layout.

'God, I love Britney Spears,' she said. 'There's no way she's a virgin. No way. Look.'

She waved the magazine in front of Kate.

'Fake boobs,' said Kate, glancing at the magazine.

'No,' said Charly. 'They're real.'

'They're fake!' said Kate. 'Come on! Where did they come from! She used to have no boobs at all.'

'From growing up, she's only nineteen,' said Charly, as Kate's boss Sue zoomed into view, her heels clicking madly on the thin lino. Charly carried on flicking through the magazine, as Kate turned back to her computer screen.

'Are you in next week?' Sue said, not slowing down or making eye contact with Kate.

'Yes,' said Kate, who was used to her boss. 'Why, what do you need?'

'I'm on holiday next week. Bloody half-term. Fucking Malcolm's booked that stupid riyad in Morocco. Can you do the Editor's Letter for me? I thought you might like to do it.'

'Sure,' said Kate, half standing up, like a Captain in the mess when the General pays a visit. 'Of course, Sue. Wow, how great! Thanks – thanks a lot.'

Sue stood still, several steps ahead of Kate, on her way out to the lifts. 'Great. Good one. Get it to Catherine for her to look over by Tuesday morning. OK?'

'"Thanks – thanks a lot",' Charly mimicked as Sue walked away. 'You big suck!'

'I know,' said Kate, embarrassed. Charly rolled her eyes.

'Well done,' she said, after a pause. 'Good one. I'm going to be really kind and take you out for a drink to celebrate tonight. And there's a new club in Soho just opened. Virus, it's called. We could go on there afterwards.'

Kate bit her lip. 'I can't, sorry. Steve and Zoe are having a housewarming party. Sort of engagement party thing too. It's fancy dress. And especially not after last night.'

'Ooh la la,' Charly said. 'Sorry I asked. How about just one after work instead?'

'OK,' said Kate. 'Great.' She swivelled happily on her chair. 'The editor's letter! Hurrah!'

'Where shall we go?' said Kate, as they left the office an hour later, striding out together in the dusk of the March evening. 'The Crown?'

'No,' said Charly, firmly. 'Anywhere but The Crown.'

'Oh god,' said Kate. 'Who did you do there?'

'Shut up!' said Charly, glaring at her, but smiling. 'I didn't "do" anyone there, thank you very much. It's just Phil and Claire . . .' She trailed off, chewing a strand of hair.

'What?'

'They're there tonight, heard them say it as they left.'

'So?' Kate liked The Crown. It had nice bar snacks, like mixed nuts, and though it didn't have a quiz machine, it had a jukebox, a rarity in a central London pub. And it was by the Inns of Court, tucked away on a little side-street – she thought it was rather nice, like something out of a Dickens novel. There were barristers in there, sometimes in gowns. 'Go on. I love it in there.'

'No, come on, we're going to the Atlas.'

92

'*Again*,' Kate moaned, like an unwilling child being forced to the shops on a Saturday. 'What's wrong with Phil and Claire?'

'There's nothing wrong with Claire,' said Charly grimly, jabbing the button for the pelican crossing smartly. 'Claire is great. I don't have a problem with *Claire*.'

'You – and Phil?' Kate was aghast, not because she was surprised Charly had slept with someone, but because she hadn't noticed. 'When?'

The lights changed. Charly marched across the road, impossibly fast. Kate ran behind her. 'Hey, slow down. When? Didn't you know he and Claire –'

Of course she knew he and Claire were an item, it was the worst-kept secret in the office, two best friends at work, also having an affair. It wouldn't have mattered either, except it was blindingly obvious Claire was mad about Phil and Kate could see he wasn't that into her. He was a bit of a player; nice enough, but he was twenty-seven, he didn't want to settle down yet.

But Charly didn't answer, and they arrived at the pub. The welcoming smoky fug of the Atlas drew them in and, after they had settled down with their drinks (double gin and tonic for Charly, white wine spritzer for Kate), Kate said, tentatively,

'Look, Charly, sorry. I didn't know. What's going on?'

'Nothing's going on,' Charly said, and there was a tone to her voice Kate hadn't heard before, dark, and bitter. She smiled; small, sad smile. 'Just me. Fucking things up as usual, OK?'

'So you –?' Kate made a gesture with her beer mat, waving it around, hoping it would convey the phrase *You've been shagging Phil?*

Charly tutted, impatiently. 'Yes.'

'How many times?'

'Jeez, Kate, do you want a tally?'

'Oh.' Kate nodded. 'So more than once then.'

'Yep,' said Charly, and she gave a ragged sigh. 'It started a few weeks ago, well, it started at the Christmas party. I went back to his, and we saw each other over Christmas, you know I'll do anything to get out of Leigh.' Kate nodded. 'So I'd come down to London and stay the night with him, we'd wander round town, no-one around, all that shit. It was – lovely.' Her voice cracked.

'Oh my god.' Charly never talked like this. Like a person with emotions. Kate watched her friend, she patted her arm. 'You've fallen for him, haven't you?'

'No,' said Charly furiously. 'He's a dick, OK? We were supposed to be meeting up last week and he called and said Claire was getting suspicious! He said it had been fun but we should call it a day, he couldn't have two secret office affairs going on! What a –'

Her hand clenched into a fist and her lovely face crumpled. 'Oh, Charly,' said Kate, unhappily. She didn't know what to say. She liked Phil, but she couldn't understand why he was so secretive about his relationship with Claire, either. Was it that big a deal? Was it naïve of her not to understand why he was so weird about it? She put her arm around Charly's bony shoulders, clad in slithery oyster silk. Charly sniffed loudly and caught Kate's hand.

'That's why I don't want to go to The Crown tonight. OK?'

'Yes, that's OK,' said Kate, kissing her hair. 'It's always OK. Now, we need to plan our next move. Tell him he can't get away with it.'

Charly looked at her in surprise. 'Are you serious?'

'Yes,' said Kate, feeling incredibly protective of Charly, who was so screwed up in her own, weird way. 'It's Claire I worry about now, don't you? He's just going to mess her around like he has you.' She got out her new mobile phone, her pride and joy.

'What are you doing?' said Charly.

'I,' said Kate proudly, 'am now going to send my first text message.' She keyed laboriously, for a minute. 'God, this is annoying, scrolling through. There!' she said, eventually. Charly peered over her shoulder.

I know what you did to Charlx. If you mess Claire arovnd we will tell her. Have a god eveming. K x

'Hm,' said Charly. 'The typing's a bit crap.'

'So?' said Kate, pressing 'Send'.

'Well, Kate Miller,' said Charly, admiringly. She cleared her throat, and sat up straight. 'You are turning into a bad girl, you know that?'

'Hardly,' said Kate.

'Slept with your hottie flatmate yet?'

Everyone always thought she was having a torrid affair with Sean. 'No!' Kate said, and she blushed. 'It's not – there's nothing going on. Shut up!'

'Yeah right,' said Charly, draining the last of her drink. 'In your head there is. I don't blame you, he's gorgeous. Dull as fuck though.'

'No he's not,' said Kate defensively, though Sean had in fact, this morning in the kitchen, droned on for five minutes about the new Microsoft enabling functions, while Kate held her hungover head in her hands and prayed for death. 'He's just passionate about his job, that's all.'

'Bor-*ing*.'

Kate thought back to the weekend before, how Sean had showed her how to use his new laptop, set her up with her own hotmail account and everything. They had sat side by side at the computer for hours, she listening, he explaining, their legs touching, neither of them acknowledging it. 'No,' she said, quietly. 'Not all the time.'

'He's so not the one for you,' said Charly. 'Don't shag the flatmate just because he's there and you're busy playing husband and wife. *Textbook*. I mean it.'

Kate was silent, uneasy all of a sudden. She looked at her watch. 'Let's get another drink, and then I'd better be off,' she said, after a pause.

Charly sprang up, suddenly alive again. 'These are on me, doll,' she said. 'Thanks. Thanks a lot.' She sashayed to the bar, and every man in the vicinity glanced in her direction.

CHAPTER NINE

It was after eight when Kate got back, and she was two-white-wine-spritzers drunk, which is to say not sober but not disastrous. Sean was watching TV as she barrelled into the sitting room.

'I'm late!' she cried loudly, hoping that by making a drama of it she'd get the guilt over quickly. Sean hated being late, it was the one area of flatmate life where they diverged wildly. If Kate said Sunday lunch at one p.m., she expected people to pitch up by two and to serve food by three. Sean meant lunch on the table at one p.m.

Sean didn't look up from the TV. For some inexplicable reason (Kate said it was because she was being all grown-up), Zoe had decreed that tonight was to be evening dress, and Sean was immaculately dressed in black tie. He was that kind of boy, the sort who always had nicely shined shoes and owned his own dinner jacket.

'Are you furious?' Kate said, unwrapping her scarf and throwing her coat on the ground. 'Sean, it'll take me two minutes to change, I'm sorry —'

He looked up and she saw his face.

'What's wrong?' she said.

His big blue eyes were curiously expressionless; but Kate knew him by now, knew him well enough to know something was up. 'Jenna's engaged,' he said.

'Oh.' Kate sat down next to him, and took the remote out of his great big hand. She turned the TV off. 'Oh, Sean, that's – that's crap.'

Jenna had been Sean's girlfriend all through high school in Texas, and most of university, till they'd broken up before he came back to England for his third and final year. She was, as far as Kate knew, the only woman he'd ever loved, and the circumstances of their breakup were mysterious. Sean had been really unhappy. Kate had only met her once, in their second year, when she'd come to visit. She reminded her of a girl from a Seventies perfume ad: long, wavy brown hair, flicking out at the sides, endless long legs, the shortest skirts, the widest smile. And she was nice, which was the killer. Kate and Francesca had hated her.

She patted her unresponsive flatmate's leg, feeling the hard muscle beneath the black cloth. 'How did you hear?'

Sean cleared his throat, and flicked his eyes wide open, then shut them rapidly. He did this several times. 'She called me. I was just leaving work, and she called me.'

'Are you really upset?' said Kate gingerly.

'No,' Sean said, sitting up and shaking his head. 'Hell no!'

Rubbish, Kate thought. He reminded her, fleetingly, of Charly and her earlier bravado.

'It's just – hey, Jenna was my first proper girlfriend, and I was really into her, you know. She's marrying some farmer guy called Todd. Ugh.' He shook his head again. 'He grows maize, has like thousands of acres. It's such a fucking *cliché*, man!'

Kate looked round their warm, small flat, crammed full of mementoes of their happy flatmate life together. Sean followed her gaze and she nudged him, desperately wanting him to feel better, be happy. She hated seeing him like this, it hurt her too, and it was then she realized how close they'd become. 'I know,' she said, almost desperately. 'Oh love.' She clutched his hand a little tighter and he turned to look at her, with something like surprise on his face.

'Kate –'

'Who wants to be a bloody maize farmer, eh? Aren't you glad that's not you? Aren't you glad you're here instead?'

There was a silence as they looked round the flat again, together. On the floor was a Kentucky Fried Chicken box, five bottles of vodka forming a pyramid on a shelf, several really vile lads' mags, several equally vile gossip mags, and pinned haphazardly on the wall were a poster of *The Graduate*, a panoramic photo view of New York, from Kate's last trip to see her mother, and a series of photos of Sean, Kate and their friends stuck onto cork boards. At Kate's feet were two empty beer cans. Their eyes met, and they burst out laughing.

'You know what,' Sean said, turning to her slowly, 'you're right. I am glad I'm here instead, Katy.' He took her hand, and kissed it.

'Don't be sad,' said Kate, and she gave Sean a hug.

'I'm not,' he said, and he squeezed her tight. His hand cupped the back of her head. 'Bless you, darlin'. It's just I thought she might be the one . . . you know? I thought she was the love of my life. So you can't help thinking about it.'

'I know,' said Kate, though she didn't. She had never thought Jenna was right for Sean. He needed someone . . . Well, not like Jenna, that was all, and she'd been glad when Sean had come back for their final year single, truth be told. She felt cross, all of a sudden, like the conversation was shifting out of her control. She rested her head on his shoulder, breathing gently.

'Thanks, darling,' he said, and she could hear his voice reverberating against her back. 'I feel fine, god, it's years ago now, but you can't help having a little think when you hear something like that, can you.'

'No,' said Kate, stroking his back again, and feeling a little like Florence Nightingale, doomed to tend eternally to the romantically injured. 'You can't.' She stood up briskly. 'I'm going to get changed, OK? We're going to get dressed up for the ridiculously-themed fancy dress party, we're going to look a million dollars, and you're going to have a great evening, I'll make sure of that. Get another beer. I'll be five minutes.'

'Sounds perfect, darling.' Sean settled back on the sofa. 'What you wearing?' he said.

'The blue and gold dress,' Kate yelled as she ran down the corridor to her bedroom. 'It's a special night.'

'Sure is,' said Sean, and Kate heard him cracking open another beer, as she took the blue and gold dress from the hook on her bedroom door where it was hanging. She stroked it happily.

Kate wasn't a girly girl when she was a teenager, she was more into the old-fashioned, vintage dresses of years ago. She had her old stack of *Vogue* magazines, from the 1950s and 60s that she'd picked up in second-hand bookshops and school fairs, and she still loved flicking through them, staring with envy at the girls in their effortlessly elegant cocktail dresses, in completely inappropriate settings: posing with a bough of cherry blossom, or hopping off a suspiciously empty, clean Routemaster bus.

On her nineteenth birthday, she and her father were walking through Hampstead. After Venetia left, they would often go for long walks through London, mostly on Sunday afternoons, ambling without aim through the deserted City, or along the river, or through the parks. They'd just come off the Heath, and were looking for a place to have a cup of tea. As they crossed a little cobbled courtyard, deep in conversation about what utter bastards Daniel's record company, who had just dropped him, were, Kate's eye fell on a dress in the window of a rickety old shop. It was Fifties, blue silk, embroidered all over with gold silk thread roses. Kate gazed at it, helplessly. Her father, turning around and seeing his pale, lanky daughter peering shyly into the window, had looked at her quizzically, as if trying to work out why she was looking at the dress, why would she be interested in that? It was just a dress – Daniel had never been good at empathy. Then his expression had changed.

'My god. I did get you a proper birthday present, didn't I,' he said, suddenly remembering, panic streaking across his face in case there was a repeat of That Birthday Which They Never Talked About, the one where Kate had gone to school the next morning and come back in the evening to find Venetia had left.

'Yes you did,' said Kate loyally. 'You got me the new lens for my telescope, and that beautiful box of chocolates. It's OK, Dad, honestly.'

(She had, in fact, bought the lens herself and he had given her the money, but to be fair, Daniel had actually bought the chocolates.)

Daniel breathed in heavily through his nose and pursed his lips, musing.

'Do you want that dress, old girl?'

Kate looked amazed. 'Dad! But it's a hundred quid!'

Daniel looked quickly at his watch and put his arm round her. 'Who cares! It's your birthday, darling. Come on. Let's go and try it on . . .'

Five years later, it was Kate's most treasured possession.

When she was answering those quizzes at the back of the Sunday supplements, the reply to 'What one item would you rescue if the house was burning down' was always, always the blue and gold dress. It had been her telescope, but she was a bit over that now, and it lay, gathering dust, in the back of her cupboard in the Rotherhithe flat.

She only wore the dress on special occasions. She'd worn it to her mother's wedding, to her ball at college, and she was going to wear it tonight, for no other reason than that she suddenly felt alive with happiness. First Sue had given her the editor's letter to write, and now she was off to Zoe and Steve's housewarming party, and everyone was going to be there, and . . . who knows what might happen?

Kate was at her most beautiful that night, though of course she didn't realize it. She was twenty-three, still young but much more confident, more relaxed than she'd been even a year ago, her skin clear and unlined, her dark brown eyes shining with excitement, her cheeks flushed. She was smiling as she entered the sitting room, forty-five minutes later, and as she cleared her throat lightly, and Sean sat up and tried to pretend he hadn't been asleep, she grinned at him, her evening bag cupped in one hand, the other hand holding the skirt of the blue and gold dress, and Sean whistled.

'Wow, Kate,' he said, rubbing his eyes and standing up. 'You look absolutely fucking amazing, do you realize that?'

'Oh . . .' Kate rolled her eyes. 'Be quiet!'

'I mean it,' said Sean, still staring at her. He bowed, and gave her his arm. 'Let battle commence. You're going to hook up with someone tonight, I know it. I'm going to have to make sure no one takes advantage of you.'

They moved graciously towards the front door and he held it open for her.

'Thank you very much,' said Kate, stealing a glance at him. 'You're too kind.'

'My pleasure, miss.'

'People are staring at us,' Kate said as they moved slowly down the high street towards the bus stop, Kate's high heels making steady progress tricky. Rotherhithe High Street on a Friday evening was not especially accustomed to seeing men in black tie ambling down the street, accompanied by ladies in vintage silk and gold thread.

'I know,' said Sean, loudly. 'Well let them stare. I have a broken heart and you look ravishing. Hello!' he said brightly to an old lady in a thick purple coat who was gaping in open-mouthed astonishment at them. 'Good evening.'

'Evening!' she replied. 'Ooh. Do you know you take me back in time. Back to when I was twenty, you two.'

'Madam,' Sean replied, formally, in his rich American accent, 'surely that time can only have been a matter of weeks ago.' He smiled wolfishly at her, and she laughed, delighted.

Kate laughed too, and took hold of his arm again, and they continued their unsteady progress up the hill to the bus carrying them north of the river again.

'So, Kate,' Sean said, as they turned into Zoe and Steve's road in the wilds of Kilburn, over an hour later. 'Are you looking for love tonight?'

Kate stared at the ground. 'Maybe. I'm going to take it easy this evening, anyway.'

'Still hungover?'

She stifled a yawn. 'A bit.'

'That Charly's a bad influence on you, girl,' Sean said. 'Are you feeling OK?'

'I'm not feeling great I must say,' Kate admitted. The excitement of what had happened at work, the drinks with Charly, comforting Sean, rushing to be ready – all had buoyed her up and now, nearly there at the end of the long journey across the city, she was starting to flag. She had had, after all, roughly four hours' sleep the previous night.

Sean watched her as she rubbed her face.

'You funny girl,' he said. 'Where's the Kate I know from college who used to wear her hair in a ponytail all the time and sit in her room all night, studying?'

She met his gaze, boldly.

'She grew up.'

Sean smiled lazily, looking her up and down. 'You bet she did.'

He was flirting with her; he always did this; it didn't really mean anything.

'How about you?' Kate said, bringing the conversation back on track. 'You on the pull tonight then? Drown your sorrows?'

'Oh, you bet,' Sean said. 'I'm hoping to break my '98 Exam Party Record.'

On one heroic night after their finals, Sean had pulled the prettiest girl in the bar, and snogged ten other people – including the barmaid at the pub where they'd started off.

'You're such a tart,' Kate said, as he fell into step with her, her gold high heels clattering on the ground. 'But – hey. Good luck. Here we are.'

They stood at the garden gate to the house. Sean held out his hand, solemnly. 'Hey, darlin'. Good luck to you too. May the best party-goer win. Who is Jenna, anyway?'

'Exactly!' Kate shook his hand firmly. 'Definitely.'

'And we're sharing a taxi home, whatever happens,' said Sean. 'I'm not doing that bus thing at three in the morning, we'll be taken to, like, Manchester without realizing.'

Despite the fact he'd lived in the United Kingdom for over four years now, Sean's grasp of the geography of his adopted country was somewhat shaky. He sort of thought that because everything was much smaller than the US, *ergo* everywhere was literally five minutes away from everywhere else. That is, Edinburgh was a thirty-minute drive away, not an eight-hour drive away.

He released her hand. 'Let's go in, Katy-Kay,' he said.

She was a bit flustered, and fumbled with her bag, but he took her elbow and, as they approached the front door, it flung open and there was Zoe, dressed in a Twenties flapper dress dripping with sequins, her glossy dark hair curled into ringlets.

'Hooray! You're here!' she cried. 'Now the party can really start! Woo hoo!' She called out to Steve. 'Steve, love. Kate and Sean are here. Turn the music up! I'm going to get you two a cocktail each. We've got Moscow Mules in the bath. Hurrah, you're here! Come in!'

Steve appeared behind his fiancee, his dark eyes full of pleasure. 'Well well well!' he said, clapping his hands together. 'Man!' He slapped Sean's hand. 'Kate, you look like – like a dream.' He kissed her. 'I could eat you.' His smile was enormous. 'Seriously, you two. I kept saying to Zo, the party won't really get going till you get here. And now you're here! Yes.'

Sean and Kate smiled at each other on the doorstep, proud of their party-starting status, which was acknowledged and, in Sean's case, well deserved. Sean rubbed his hands together and Kate smiled. They were good, and they knew it.

'We'll see you inside,' said Kate, and she pushed Sean towards the door again, wanting to get inside, and as she stepped forward, following him in, someone came in from the other side and she stumbled across the threshold, into the house, almost falling into their arms.

'So this is the famous Kate,' the someone said, holding her by the arm to support her. She gazed up at him, helplessly, in the dull glow of the swinging lightbulb in the hall. His open, handsome face, his dark eyes, his ready, wide smile

. . . he looked strangely familiar and yet – she knew him, but she didn't know him.

'This is my brother, Mac,' Steve said, a catlike grin on his face. 'Finally! You've never met, that's really weird.'

Mac. Of course. He looked like Steve, and yet he was totally unlike him. Steve was easy, open, laughed a lot, restless. Mac was taller, broader, his hair was the same light brown as his brother's, but closely cropped. He had lines on his forehead, laughter lines by his mouth. Kate suddenly had the irresistible urge to reach out, touch them with her index finger. She stared at him. She was glad Zoe had gone into the kitchen.

'No, we've never met,' said Mac, still looking at her. He took her hand now, and shook it. 'I know a lot about you though. A *lot*,' he said.

'Yeah, sorry about that,' said Kate, recovering herself, her eyes still on him. His eyes were green, a strange, scrubby, sea-like green colour. 'I know a lot about you too.' When she was nervous she talked too much. 'You're a medical genius, and you live in Cricklewood, which is weird, because I never thought the two would go together, except we just did an article in the magazine about people who come from unlikely places. Did you know Cary Grant was born in Redland in Bristol and he was an acrobat at the Bristol Hippodrome.'

There was silence. Kate looked down at her feet, hating her high heels, which prevented her from fleeing into the night. She bit her lip, yelling at herself inside her head. What? How? Was she *mental*? *This*, this was why she hadn't had a date in six months, she told herself.

'I did not know that,' said Mac, conversationally. 'Did you, however, know that it took ten million bricks to build the Chrysler Building in New York?'

'No!' said Kate, with pleasure. 'That's – that's wonderful.'

Their eyes met again; he smiled, she smiled, and that was it.

'Kate! Are you coming in?' Sean called from the kitchen. He sounded almost cross.

'Better come inside, then,' said Mac. So she did.

CHAPTER TEN

Two hours later, it was after midnight, and Zoe and Steve's housewarming party was an unqualified success. Zoe had made vodka jellies, of which Kate had had four. Steve was the music mixer, flipping between CDs and his LPs with the greatest of ease. They danced themselves stupid to Michael Jackson, all pretending they could Moonwalk in their narrow kitchen. At one point there were thirty people doing the conga to Perez Prado through the small, corridor-like flat, out into the garden, down the side entrance and through the front door again. Then Steve – who was a brilliant host, one who only wanted his guests to have a good time and one who didn't care about the carnage they caused to his new flat, as long as they were enjoying themselves – started making flaming B52s, and Zoe stood on a chair and sang 'Rescue Me' into a hairbrush, until she fell off and Steve had to pick her up. He threw her over his shoulder, slapping her on the bottom, and carried her out of the room, as she screamed and the others applauded.

Occasionally she would catch sight of Sean, who was drinking steadily, and wave at him or pat his arm, checking in to make sure he was doing OK. But otherwise she lost herself in a whirl of drinks, of laughing, of catching up. She kept looking over her shoulder to see where Mac was, kept thinking she saw him – had she just dreamt it? – as the party grew more and more raucous. In fact, it turned out the party was so good that when the new neighbours from upstairs – a married couple in their thirties – came down after twelve to complain about the noise, Steve thrust a Moscow Mule each into their hands and had them both dancing with Betty to Britney Spears in five minutes.

Betty was after Sean tonight. Kate could tell, and she watched her bat her fake eyelashes at him with some amusement, impressed at the way she could be so subtle and yet so obvious with him. Kate was pretty sure Betty and Sean had slept together at university and, watching them, she was suddenly pretty sure that was the way it was going to end up tonight. She stood in the corner of the sitting room, taking a breather from the dancing, with her glass curled up against her, and she saw the way Betty touched her top lip with her tongue as she talked to him, her blonde bunches wagging on each side of her head, the way Sean watched her mouth as he answered her, the way they smiled into each other's eyes, moving slightly closer. Suddenly the Sean of a few hours earlier, desolate at the news of Jenna's engagement, seemed far away. He was on a mission tonight, that was clear. Kate bit her lip, tasting blood on her tongue, and turned away, surprised at the intensity of her reaction.

'Great party, Zo,' she said.

Zoe was hugging the doorframe, using it as support, her small hands clinging to the carved wood almost desperately. 'Thanks,' she said. 'This bloody flat, you know what a nightmare it was getting it, I can't believe we're here now.' She banged her head gently against the frame. 'I think I may have to grovel to the neighbours tomorrow though,' she added nervously, glancing down the corridor into the kitchen, where through the french windows Kate could see Francesca and Steve were lying on the small lawn, singing something loudly.

'You're cute though,' said Kate. 'They'll love you. We had a thing in the magazine last week, how to get on with your neighbours. Accept responsibility, go round to each of them with a box of chocolates tomorrow and just say sorry. It'll be fine.'

'Did you meet Mac then?' said Zoe suddenly.

'Yes,' said Kate. 'Well, at the beginning –' she looked round '– I don't know where he's gone.'

Zoe shrugged her shoulders. 'Don't know,' she said. 'He's working too hard. He looks exhausted. Don't you think?'

Kate hadn't noticed anything, except how lovely he looked, and she'd never met him before, so she was hardly qualified to judge.

'Zo, Zo!' Steve yelled from the kitchen. 'Zo! Come and see! If you put shaving foam in a tupperware box and light it – look what happens!'

'Jesus!' said Zoe. 'You are such a fucking *infant*, Steve!' she yelled back, half-laughing, looking down the corridor. 'Oh, wow. That's really –' There was a loud bang. 'I'm going to –'

'Go,' said Kate, draining her drink. 'I'm going to find another glass of –' she looked at her glass. 'Don't know what that was. I'm going to find it, anyway.'

She turned around in the tiny hallway as Zoe walked away.

'Hello,' said a voice behind her, and Kate spun around. It was Mac. He was shutting the door to the spare bedroom.

'Hello again,' she said, uncertainly. 'I haven't seen you for a while.'

He scratched his head. 'I know. I fell asleep.'

'You fell asleep? In the spare bedroom?' Kate was mysti-fied. 'Can't be as good a party as I thought it was, then.'

'I'm sure it is,' he said. 'I heard Zoe singing "Cabaret".'

'Oh,' Kate said. 'Well – there was more, but perhaps you –'

'I like your dress,' he said, interrupting. 'It suits you.' He caught himself. 'I mean, I've never met you before so how would I know. But you look nice in it.' He turned away to the wall and said something under his breath, before turning back. 'Man. How – god.'

Kate smiled; she was a bit bemused. 'Thanks, though. That's really – *nice* of you.' She repeated the word uncon-sciously and then realized; they both grinned, relaxing a little more. 'It was a present from my dad. It's old, like from the fifties, I think.'

'Of course, your dad's Daniel Miller, isn't he?'

'Yes,' said Kate, vaguely pleased he should know that, that there was this old connection with them because of Zoe and Steve, even though they'd never met. It made it seem even more comfortable, the air between them.

'I heard him the other day, on the radio, talking about his new album. Some covers of songs by ABBA?'

'Yes,' said Kate again. 'Er, it's great apparently. It's just out, I haven't heard it yet.'

'Well, I've only heard bits. He was interviewed on the radio. And he was on some daytime TV thing I saw, while I was on rounds yesterday.'

Daniel had a new publicist, called Lisa, who was getting him all this new coverage. She was responsible for Daniel's new, choppy haircut, his Ralph Lauren suits, the moody shots of him gazing out of windows in dilapidated old country buildings. She called him 'Danny', too. She didn't seem to like things like long evenings in basement kitchens drinking cheap red wine (red wine stains the teeth), walks on the

Heath on cold days, or daughters who were close to her in age. Yes, Kate had met her. She wasn't mad about her.

'Yep,' said Kate. 'It's great, he'd been quiet for a while before that.' She cleared her throat to change the subject as a shriek echoed from the next room. 'God,' she said laughing. 'Zoe's absolutely trollyed.'

Mac's expression was mock-serious. 'So, what were the two of you like when you were little, then?'

Kate laughed. 'Well, Zoe was very bright and bubbly, and loud. Very loud. And I was – clumsy. And a bit moody. And not as nice as Zoe.'

He bent his head, and lowered his voice. 'Kate. I'm sure that's not true.'

'Thank you,' she said slowly. 'But it pretty much is.' There was a pause. 'How about the two of you?'

'Who? Me and Steve?' He shook his head, and crossed his arms, so his hands were wedged under his armpits. 'He was the typical annoying little brother, always bright and perky and funny and loud. Bit like Zoe, clearly.' Kate shook her head, moved closer towards him. She wanted to touch him.

'How about you, then?'

'Me? I was . . .' He was smiling down at her. 'Well, I was quite awkward, and I liked staying in my room, reading books and writing terrible poems. And looking at things under my microscope. God, this is embarrassing.' He grimaced. 'And I can't believe I'm telling you this.'

'A microscope?' She laughed, incredulously, and embarrassment flashed across his face till she said, putting her hand on his arm, wanting to reassure him, 'Mac. That's weird. I had a telescope.' Kate thought of her poor telescope, confined to the back of the cupboard. 'In fact, you've just described me as a teenager. So there you go.'

'Great minds think alike,' said Mac, nodding. 'Or perhaps not.'

112

There was a silence again; comfortable. He yawned, suddenly. 'Sorry, crap of me.' He rubbed his face; she realized he'd only just woken up. 'I've been – busy, you see.'

She remembered Zoe saying how tired he was. 'Is it work?'

'Something like that,' he said. 'Yeah.' He hummed, and looked down at her; she was tall, but he was taller. 'Let's get a drink, shall we?'

'Great,' she said, her eyes flicking up to him again. She couldn't stop looking at him, not just because he was incredibly attractive – but because she felt she knew him, recognized him from somewhere, and she couldn't work out where.

'Good kip, then?' Steve called, as they came into the kitchen. 'Feeling better?'

'Yeah, bruv, thanks,' said Mac. 'Sorry about that. Kate, what do you want?'

'That looks good,' said Kate, pointing at a bottle, simply because it happened to have liquid in it. 'Thanks.' She stole a glance at him again, to find him watching her, as he poured the wine into her glass. Strange, strange, she told herself. She had never felt like this before. So . . . in control of it, so – certain. She didn't know what was going to happen next but yes, there it was – a kind of certainty when she looked at him, into those kind, yet quizzical green eyes of his.

Mac clinked his glass against hers. The kitchen was nearly empty of guests – some were in the garden, shivering in the cold spring night, most were back in the sitting room or in the corridor, and the music was punching through the walls to where they stood. Steve watched them for a moment, scratching his face, and then he said, 'Hey, Francesca, you've met Mac, haven't you?'

Francesca was the girl Steve had been seeing right before Zoe appeared on the scene, and she turned away from her ex-boyfriend reluctantly, and gave Mac a catlike, enigmatic smile.

'Of course I have, darling,' she said. 'Hello Mac, how are you?'

'I'm fine,' he said. She kissed him, patted him on the shoulder.

'What happened to the Edinburgh job?' she asked, semi-curiously. Kate watched her, very curiously.

Mac shifted on his feet. 'The one at St Giles? It –'

'Hey! Hey!' Zoe called from outside. 'Oh god, I think he's about to be sick. Ugh! Steve! Steve, can you –'

Francesca turned away, watching through the french windows. 'Oh no,' she said, sounding bored, as Steve ran into the garden.

'You need me, bruv?' Mac called after him.

'No man,' said Steve, kneeling behind someone. 'Urgh. That's horrible.'

'Come on,' said Mac, and he put his hand on Kate's elbow. His touch sent a jolt through her; his thumb was dry and warm on the inside of her arm. 'I want to ask you something.'

Kate followed him into the corridor again and stopped short. There were Sean and Betty, locked in a grappling embrace and oblivious to everything else, including someone reaching up behind them to get their coat off the bulging coat rack. Kate looked at Sean's face, what she could see of it, absorbed in chewing off half of Betty's, and smiled to herself. Why wasn't she surprised? He was Sean, wasn't he? Always the same.

Mac didn't notice, he was looking out into the garden again, to make sure the poor unfortunate outside was OK. His jaw was set, his posture tense. But as she gave a little sigh and shook her head he looked down at her then, and said,

'What do you think about getting out of here?'

'What?' Kate said, dazed.

He touched her shoulder, lightly. 'Come back with me. Let's get out of here.'

'But it's –' Kate looked at her watch, unsure of what to say next: it was two o'clock. 'Oh.' Then she looked over at Sean and Betty again, then back at Mac. Mac, who just met her gaze and nodded.

She nodded back at him.

'Yeah,' she said. 'Let's go.'

It was dark in the corridor, by the entrance to the kitchen. He took her hand and pulled her towards him, and they kissed, their hands twining together. She could feel his stubble rasping against her skin, his tongue pushing inside her, his lips on hers, warm, dry, strong, like the rest of him.

'Kate Miller,' he said, when he broke apart from her. 'The famous Kate Miller.'

They walked past Betty and Sean; Kate had to tap them on the shoulder to let them know she was going, especially since she had a pact with Sean. 'Hi,' she said, picking a limb, hoping it was Sean's. Mac held her other hand, his fingers stroking hers. She felt warm, melting, swoony with him beside her, his hip touching hers.

Sean turned around, his eyes glazed, panting slightly. 'Kate, hi,' he said, and there was a note of irritation in his voice; Kate couldn't blame him. Behind him, Betty tried to look casually around, as if she were a prospective buyer for the flat, making a note of the ceiling mouldings.

'I'm going,' Kate said. She jerked her head, as if to indicate Mac, that this was the situation.

'What?' said Sean, quickly. 'Oh. Right . . .' His gaze left Kate's face and looked behind her, to Mac, who nodded, politely, and tightened his grip on Kate's hand. She swayed towards him, dizzy with wanting him, wanting to be alone with him. She cast a look back at Sean.

'I'll see you tomorrow, OK?' she said. 'Don't –'

'It's fine, Kate,' said Sean, and there was a sharp note to his voice. 'See you tomorrow babe.' He took his hand off Betty's bottom and squeezed Kate's arm. 'Have a good one.'

She turned away, and she and Mac stepped across the front door, and closed it behind them, and then it was just the two of them, alone.

CHAPTER ELEVEN

They stood outside on the pavement, looking at each other, the sky above them flecked with bright stars, it was a cold, clear night. The space between them was fraught; particles of tension, magnetic attraction, that Kate felt was drawing her closer to him, closer and closer. And then Mac said,

'Listen. There's something I have to tell you.'

'Oh.' Kate shoved her cold hands into her pockets. Even she knew no conversation that started like that ever ended well. 'What's that then?'

'Look,' Mac said, stepping towards her. 'I just thought I should say it before this gets —'

Kate heard herself say, 'No way. You can't dump me. We haven't even done anything yet. We only met three hours ago.'

He laughed. She liked his laugh. It was a proper laugh, from deep inside him, a warm, chuckling sound. 'No, nothing like that. You are funny. Why would I dump you?'

She ignored this, and said, 'So, what is it?'

He said, blankly, 'Er, well – it's not a big deal, because like you said, we only met three hours ago. But – before this goes any further, I thought I should say.'

'Say what?'

Mac spoke in monosyllables. 'I'm leaving, in the morning. Edinburgh.' Kate stepped backwards. 'That's why I'm tired. I've been packing all day. The flight's at midday.'

'You're –'

'I'm moving there. Got a consultancy at St Giles's, in the city. It's – yeah, well, I had to take it. And Mum and Dad are there, that'll be nice too.'

'Oh, right,' said Kate, deliberately keeping her voice light. 'Well, right!'

'Yeah,' he said, shifting his weight, from foot to foot. 'Like I said, Kate. Just thought I should say something, you know.'

'Yes, of course.' She didn't know why she was being so stupid. After all, they'd just met – it was hardly like . . . She smiled at him and stepped back again. 'So why are you telling me? Do you want a lift to the airport tomorrow, is that it?'

'Come back with me,' he said, even more softly. 'You can still come back.'

'I – I can't,' she said.

'Why not?' Mac said, a note of impatience in his voice.

'Because –' she gestured weakly around her. 'It's different.'

'You have the most amazing face, did you know that?' Mac said.

'Face?' Kate laughed, bemused.

'Yes. It's totally heart-shaped, and when you're sad about something, or thinking about something, you're totally closed off, and when you smile – you're beautiful. Absolutely beautiful. Did you know that?' He spoke conversationally, looking around him, at Zoe and Steve's low front garden wall, into the sitting room, as he said all this.

'Mac – you're mad. And a massive flirt,' Kate said weakly.

His faint Scottish burr was more pronounced; he said, grinning, 'I'm not, that's the strange thing, my dear. I'm not a flirt at all. Normally can't think of a single thing to say to a girl I like. Never normally meet a girl I like.'

'I –' Kate said. She shrugged her shoulders, helplessly.

'You're not coming, are you.' It was a statement, not a question. 'Oh well.'

'It's – look Mac, I don't know . . .'

He laughed. 'Very eloquently put. Come with me. It'll just take a minute.'

He pulled her out into the road, the middle of the road and there in the cold night air, he put his hands either side of her head and, pulling her towards him, kissed her. So she kissed him right back, wrapping her arms around him, laughing softly as she did, feeling his tongue in her mouth, his beautiful, hard, tall body against hers, so strange and yet so familiar, and they kissed for a long few minutes, until Mac pulled himself away and said, his voice husky,

'You're really not going to come back with me?'

She thought of Zoe and Steve inside, of not having said bye to them properly, of Sean and Betty entangled in the hallway, and she thought of how even though she was changing every day, growing more and more into herself, how still unlike her, Kate, it was to go off with someone like this. On the other hand, it wasn't like this was the first time she'd gone off with someone, so why was she so scared? Scared – of what? Hurting herself, of disappointing Mac, not sure why he'd picked her, thinking he must be drunk or mad or both.

'Seize the day,' Mac said. 'Never heard that expression?' He touched her forehead with his finger.

Kate couldn't help thinking of her mother when she heard that expression, it was almost her mission statement. 'All the bloody time,' Kate said. 'I'm normally just no good at it.'

'It's my last night in London,' said Mac. He looked at her,

119

that strange look she found so disturbingly familiar. 'And I like you, you like me, I know it, you know it too, don't you?'

'Yes,' she said, honestly.

'Are you the girl who usually helps the other drunk girls home? I bet you are.'

'Er,' said Kate sadly, thinking of the previous week, when she had ended up on the night bus after Jo's post-work birthday drinks, with Sophie's slumbering form slumped over her lap like a sack of grain. 'Sometimes.'

'Come on then,' he said, and he stepped forward and hailed a passing cab, which Kate found extremely impressive, and then castigated herself for doing so. She put her hand on his arm, suddenly.

'You're really leaving London tomorrow morning?'

'Yes,' he said, holding the door open for her. She stepped inside.

'Better make the most of it, then,' she said.

Kate had never actually run out on her friends before. She realized this, the next day, as she lay in Mac's arms, the early summer light flooding into his dingy, grey, boy's bedroom, stripped bare of all his possessions which had gone up to Edinburgh ahead of him. And she didn't care. Didn't care about a thing. She had given herself up to pleasure, totally, not worrying about anyone else. And it had been totally, utterly worth it. She could feel happiness washing over her, into her, like she was bathing in it.

'You don't think it matters,' she said, sitting up and stretching her arms out, yawning.

'What?' said Mac, his voice muffled, and he smoothed her hair back from her forehead, pulling her back down onto his chest, which was thickly matted with hair. He stroked her hair, and she turned her face towards him, so she was looking at him.

'That we didn't say bye,' Kate said. 'To Zoe and Steve. We just did a runner.'

'Oh,' said Mac. She stroked him, ran her hand down his body.

'Don't you care?' she said, half-mockingly. 'You're leaving them today.'

'No, not at all,' he murmured, enfolding her in his arm so she was just above him. She felt him growing hard again, against her. 'I'll call Steve, don't worry.'

'When?' Kate said, kissing him. Her hair fell over him, surrounding the two of them. As Mac kissed her shoulder, her breast, her collarbone, she pushed her hair out of her eyes and looked at his tiny, bashed-up digital clock. It was six o'clock. 'Your flight's in six hours.'

'Oh,' he said, and he turned her over so she lay beneath him, and he was over her. He stroked her hair, and bent down to kiss her again. 'We don't have much time, then, Kate Miller.'

'No, but –'

She couldn't say any more. She felt so happy with him that she couldn't burst the bubble of the night. Like asking 'So . . . will you call me when you're four hundred miles away and working seven nights a week and never coming down to London?' As Mac pulled the duvet over both of them, enclosing them both together again, Kate kissed him back and laughed happily, thinking back over the past twelve hours in befuddled, pleasurable amazement – but also a strange sense of certainty, one that she never got back again.

She went with him to the airport. After all, she told him, he was leaving London, he needed someone to wave him off. She stood in her blue and gold dress on the pavement, thanking the Lord she'd bought a black cardigan and her coat that she could wrap around herself to minimize the too-dressy slash I-am-a-prostitute look, and she watched as Mac locked up his bare flat, as he slung his suitcase into the back of the minicab. He stood back and sighed, looking up at the tall, redbrick house for the last time. It was strange, sharing all this with him, part of a life she'd never known that he was now saying goodbye to.

'Were you happy here?' she asked him.

'I was,' he said, but he didn't say more. She didn't know what he meant and there was suddenly, now, constraint between them; he moving on, she staying here, both of them not really knowing each other. He held the door open for her; she got into the back of the cab, he climbed in after her. He looked rather desolate, his face tired in the morning light and she pulled him towards her so his head was resting on her shoulder, his hand in her lap. She took it, held it tightly.

'Kate Miller,' Mac said after a moment. His voice was serious. 'God. I wish we'd met sooner,' he said, as the cab ploughed silently through West Hampstead, long grey shadows flooding the streets, early morning sunshine cutting through the gaps in the buildings. No one was around.

She said nothing, just squeezed his hand tighter. Kate still sometimes felt like a juvenile in a world of grown-ups, someone who didn't know the rules when everyone else seemed to. Here, in the back of the cab, racing through town towards the airport, she felt as if she knew what she was doing.

'I wish we had one more day, one more night,' he said, into her chest.

'Shh,' she said, and with her other arm she pulled him in more closely towards her. She kissed his rough hair, so strangely boyish, at odds with him when he was . . . such a

122

man, compared to the other men she knew, those boys from university, those boys from growing up. Mac was – he was a grown-up.

That was why he was going away, she told herself, staring out of the window, her chin resting on his hair. His life was sorting itself out, he was three years older than her, he was simply a grown-up, and she felt as if she still had to establish the most basic facts about herself.

'I wish we'd met sooner too,' she said. She fought back tears, staring ahead as they rolled on. She didn't know how to say what she wanted to say. 'It's like a bolt from the blue, this . . .' She gestured weakly, between them. 'You know?' He nodded. 'I didn't think *this* would happen last night.' She shrugged her shoulders, smiling at the way she'd thought the night might go, at her own vanity. 'Strange, how things turn out,' she said.

Mac's fingers beat a pattern on hers. 'You and your flat mate, eh?'

Kate was startled; she sat up straight. He laughed, amused at her shock. 'What do you mean?' she said.

'You and – what was that guy called? Sean? Steve's friend?' Kate nodded. 'I thought you were a couple when you arrived last night, when I saw you both on the doorstep.'

'Hah,' said Kate.

'I got that vibe off him, too.' Mac shrugged his shoulders. 'That's why I left you alone for most of the evening. Didn't want to annoy him. He looked like the sort of bloke who'd bite your ear off if you annoyed him.'

Kate giggled. 'He's not like that!' she said defensively. 'He's like a great big puppy once you know him, honestly.' Mac nodded sombrely. 'He's lovely,' she said. 'Really.'

'Right,' Mac said, without rancour. 'Well – perhaps you should have got together with him last night, then.' Kate started.

'I'm not saying –' she said, defensively. Mac held up his hands.

'I'm glad you didn't.' He took her fingers again. 'I'm just saying, I'm glad you didn't. Last night, anyway.'

'You're both very different, anyway,' Kate said, mirroring him. 'And – well, I think he went off with someone else, anyway. Our friend Betty. Not that I want it to happen, anyway.'

'– anyway,' Mac said, gently. 'Stop saying anyway. You babble when you're nervous, did you know that? And you have the most beautiful eyes, Kate, they're black when you get cross. I love them.' He kissed her. 'And I don't want to talk about Sean. I want to talk about us. About how you've made me not want to leave, and it's only one night. OK?'

'Yes, OK,' said Kate. 'More than OK.' She clutched both his hands in her lap. 'Oh, man.'

'I know.' Mac looked out of the window.

'There's no way –?'

His hand tightened around hers. 'Perhaps, you know?' He sat up straight. 'But Kate, I just don't think it's realistic. Is it?'

'Why? I'm not saying "oh no why", I mean, tell me just why it's completely out of the question,' she said bravely.

'Perhaps it's not,' Mac said. 'But I'll be working five nights in a row most of the time, and I won't be back to London for at least three, four months – and I have to find a flat, and you have –' He smiled. 'I don't mean this to sound patronizing, but it seems to me from what you say, and from what Zoe says, that you've got a pretty good thing going on in London, at the moment.'

They were turning off the motorway slip-road into Terminal One.

'No –' Kate began, defensively, and then she stopped, looking down at their hands, hers holding his. Her hard-won job, her friends, Charly, her flat. Sean . . . Sean – she wondered where he was. Suddenly she missed him, the security of their flat together. This – this was new and strange and . . . sad. It was just so damn bloody sad. She couldn't work out what Mac was trying to say, whether it was a gentle let-down or the truth. In any case, facts were facts. He was moving to Edinburgh, and it was just over two hours till his plane left. When she looked up into his face, he was staring ahead, his jaw set again. He turned away from her, to look out of the window, and then he said, calmly,

'We're here.'

Perhaps she had been wrong. Probably she had. She raised his hand to her lips and kissed it. 'Thanks anyway.'

'No,' he said. The cab driver was opening the boot of the car, loading suitcases onto a trolley. Mac's grip on her hand was painful. 'Kate, no. Thank you.'

She moved towards him, almost frantic to feel him against her again. He pulled her close. 'This is stupid,' she said, in his ear. 'Why is it like this?'

His breath was warm on her neck; her coat itched in the spring sunshine. 'Because our timing's crap,' he said. 'Look, when I get there I'll call –'

'Don't say you'll call me,' said Kate, and she put her hands on his cheeks. 'Don't take my number, don't say you'll email me and we'll have jolly banter about the weather or how hungover we are, or whatever, each of us trying to inflate it with something. Just – let's leave it.' A tear ran down her cheek; he wiped it away, gently, and then he slowly kissed her skin where it had been, as if she was the most precious thing on earth to him.

'Yes,' he said. 'I think you're right. Today. Not for ever. I'll see you again, Kate. This isn't goodbye.' She shook her head, fervently, and he said in her ear, 'I don't know what it is, in fact, but it's not goodbye.'

The cab driver cleared his throat, and the spell was broken; Mac turned, and handed him the fare, and took the trolley from him.

'I didn't think I'd spent Saturday morning at an airport with Steve's brother,' Kate said, sinking her hands into her pockets, stepping back, trying to restore normality.

'That can be our second date,' Mac said, looking down at her once more. She met his gaze and they stood utterly still, watching each other, for a few seconds more. And then he turned, saying nothing, and pushed the trolley away. The automatic doors into the terminal snapped open for him, and snapped shut again; and he was gone.

When Kate arrived home in Rotherhithe, having cried silently all the way back on the Tube, ignoring the curious glances from her fellow passengers, Sean was there.

'She's back,' he called, as she opened the front door quietly. 'The dirty stop-out's back. Yee-hah!'

The flat was still a mess; the hallway was littered with trainers, bits of Kate's bike that Sean was allegedly mending for her, old newspapers. As she stood in the hall, tiredly taking off her coat, Kate thought back to the previous evening, when she'd arrived back home from the pub, and how long ago it seemed. A lifetime really. She looked down at the blue and gold dress, stroking the silk over her stomach.

'Hi,' she called. 'How are you?'

'I missed you, darlin',' Sean said. She could hear him turning on the sofa. 'I've been waiting for you to come back so we can go and get some lunch. What an awesome night.'

'Not sad about Jenna any more then?' Kate said, half joking.

'Who?' Sean's voice was blank. 'Ha, ha. You know what?'

'What,' said Kate, longing for a bath.

'She seems a long time ago now. Like I've moved on.' He

sat up on the couch, not looking at her. 'Hey, so you wanna run and get changed? We can go and get some food and I wanna ask you what you think I should do for my birthday.'

It was Sean's birthday the following Sunday, she'd completely forgotten. 'We'll think of something,' she called, taking off her shoe, rubbing her aching foot.

Sean appeared in the doorway of the sitting room, out of his black tie, back in his normal uniform of jeans, trainers, t-shirt, a light v-neck over the top. 'Wow,' he said. 'You still look hot, Katy.' She felt even more ill-at-ease, standing there. His eyes ran over her; his fingers drummed on the door-frame. 'So I guess you did, then?'

'Did what?' Kate took off the other shoe, not meeting his gaze.

'Well, well,' said Sean. A silence fell between them, then he said softly, 'You dirty girl.'

'You snogged Betty,' Kate shot back. Sean raised his eyebrows.

'I didn't realize it was a competition,' he said, coldly. Kate felt confused; she was tired, hungry, and sad. She wanted to crawl into bed and cry, cry over someone who wasn't ever coming back, who she barely knew anyway, it was ridiculous.

'Oh, just forget it,' she said, passing her hand over her eyes. 'Let's go and get some lunch.' She smiled at Sean, giving him her most winning grin, and he recovered slightly and nodded back at her, his eyes twinkling, wolfishly.

CHAPTER TWELVE

Over the next few days, Kate didn't know why she expected Mac to call. She just did. But he didn't.

In fact, Kate Miller and Mac Hamilton didn't see each other again for nearly two years. In the intervening days, weeks, months, the night she spent with him was to become almost mythic in Kate's mind, until she came to see what it probably was – the night bridging her old life with her new life. Part of her didn't understand why he didn't call. Even though they'd said that was it, and the reasons for leaving what happened as one night only were still so clear to her, a part of her didn't believe it, didn't understand it. He would call eventually, she told herself, a couple of days afterwards, when she was missing him more than she could say. But he didn't.

A week later, with no news, Kate sort of knew by then he wouldn't contact her. It never occurred to her to call him; perverse logic told her he'd never want to hear from *her* – he'd just moved! It was in the past! They'd both agreed to leave it. He had a new life; she had to get on with hers. And so she did. Kate was always good at following instructions.

That Saturday evening, Sean had his birthday drinks, and that's when Kate finally shook herself out of the mood that had enveloped her all week. Sean knew, and Kate knew, that no one would come to Rotherhithe; instead they and their friends went to the Punch and Judy in Covent Garden, which was loud and stuffed full of people, shouts of merriment bouncing off the flagstones and stucco walls of the covered market. Kate loved Covent Garden, it was touristy and full of silly shops and stalls selling plastic brooches that no one would ever want, but it reminded her of being young, coming into town with Zoe, going to the Bead Shop and buying exotic beads for earrings that would never be made, or sitting outside in the Piazza, drinking coffee, watching magicians, feeling ever so grown-up and sophisticated. Covent Garden was like a film set; it never stopped being so for Kate, even though she was grown-up and (relatively) sophisticated now.

Just being out, being with her friends, watching Steve and Sean as they mock-wrestled in the courtyard, chatting to Zoe and Francesca, standing in a crowded, sweaty pub with a drink in her hand, Sean's arm around her shoulders, was more than enough to cheer her up. Here was where she belonged, she told herself, here in this city, with her friends, and screw anyone else who tried to make her doubt that. For damn sure! she told herself, trying to sound like a motivational trainer.

'You OK, babe?' Zoe said, as Kate returned from the bar after last orders with a drink for her and Steve.

'Me? I'm fine,' said Kate, wedging herself against Sean in the crush of the throng. 'Why?'

'I just wondered,' said Zoe, bellowing into her ear. 'Thought you seemed a bit down this week. Wondered if everything was OK.'

Steve was leaning in, nodding along with interest. 'Yeah,'

he said loudly. He cupped his hands around his pint, the way he always used to at college, as if it were a cup of tea; Kate watched him fondly. 'Me and Zoe, yeah, we wondered. Didn't we Zo?' Zoe looked at him in alarm. 'What happened with you and M-ow! Fuck!' He hopped backwards in agony, squashing several people behind him, including Sean and Betty, who were talking intently, and knocking over several drinks in the process.

'What?' said Zoe, innocently.

'You stepped on my foot! With your bloody heels!' Steve winced, as people looked at him in disgust, thinking he must be drunk. 'My god, it's like a knife through me!'

'He's such a girl,' Zoe said, rolling her eyes impatiently. 'Ignore him, darling.'

'Zoe, you – ow!'

Kate was trying not to grin. She patted Steve's back, feeling sorry for him, as a harrassed barman appeared with a towel, to mop up the drinks.

'It's drinking up time anyway,' the barman growled loudly. 'Come on, get moving.' Steve set the glasses right again, back on the bar.

'Poor Steve. What did you want to say?' Kate said, innocently.

Alarm crossed Zoe's face; she put her arm through her fiance's. 'Right then. You OK, Ste?'

She doesn't want to give me the bad news about Mac, Kate thought. That's why she's freaking out now. Like, he's got syphilis, or a girlfriend, or he's really a woman. She shook her head, realizing she must be drunker than she realized. He definitely wasn't a woman, she knew that much.

And she didn't really mind who knew, after all. It wasn't a big deal. She didn't care – she checked her phone again, pretending to look at the time, and then looked up to find

Sean watching her, standing next to her. Behind him, Betty hovered, in a hopeful way. He touched Kate's shoulders.

'You OK?'

'Yup,' she said. 'You going on somewhere?' She was tired; it showed in her voice.

Sean paused for a moment. 'Um. Not sure. What do you think, you on for it?'

'I'm quite knackered –' Kate began.

'Me too,' said Sean, quickly. 'Why don't we just head off. It's been a long week,' he said, turning to the others. 'I'm bushed.'

'What?' said Steve. 'It's your birthday, man!! You don't want to go on somewhere? How about the Rock Garden?'

'Oh my god,' said Zoe. 'No way. The Rock Garden? What are you, an American tourist from 1983? I want to go home. I've got to get up early tomorrow, we said we'd take the tiles off around the fireplace, remember?'

'Hm,' said Steve. 'No.'

'Liar,' said Zoe, hitting him again.

'God, the abuse,' said Steve, squashing her with a hug. 'Stop assaulting me, woman!'

Kate watched them, swaying slightly on her feet; she was, suddenly, really tired, and Sean's arm came around her shoulders again. 'Come on, Katy-kay,' he said. 'Let's get you home. We can have a bowl of cereal and watch my new video of *The Godfather*.'

'Plan,' said Kate. The barman was shouting again; Betty turned to leave, discontent written all over her pretty face. 'Good plan.'

They sat on the sofa, in their pyjamas, Kate eating toast, Sean with a bowl of cereal, the empty video case of *The Godfather* between them on the cushion and a collection of beer bottles on the floor. It was late.

131

'You happy now?' Sean asked, through mouthfuls. 'You been quiet all week, Kate.'

'Yeah.' Kate held the toast in her hand. 'Just – you know. Stuff.'

Sean shook his head, his eyes still on the screen. 'Stuff. Right. Like – anything to do with you being a dirty stop-out last week?'

Kate watched him, curiously. Irresistibly, she was reminded of Mac's hands, how supple and thin they were, proper surgeon's hands, how they felt on her, holding her. She gritted her teeth. 'Yes,' she said.

'Thought so,' Sean said, waving the spoon at her. He turned and looked at her, rather strangely. 'Kate, I didn't know you were that kinda girl.'

'Oh, shut up,' said Kate.

'Was he good?' Sean said, still watching her. 'Was it worth it?'

She didn't want to go over the details with Sean. 'You know.'

'I don't know,' said Sean. His jaws were working again.

'Well, it's a non-starter.' Nice and vague. 'Hey, how about you? What exactly happened with you and Betty, then? Were you a dirty stop-out too?'

Sean set the bowl down carefully on the ground. 'I didn't go home with her, no,' he said briefly, wiping his mouth. 'I thought it might –' he shrugged.

'Yeah,' said Kate, understanding that he meant it might have become weird. 'You're friends . . .'

'Well, it was late, and we were all pretty drunk.'

'Is it cool?' Kate said. 'She seemed a bit . . . weird tonight.'

'I hope so,' Sean said. He put his head on one side, unconsciously considering. 'She said, is this OK, all that.'

'You did the right thing,' Kate said wisely. 'Friends shouldn't sleep with friends, and that's why.'

She patted her thighs, and made as if to stand up. But Sean caught her hand.

'Sometimes,' he said. 'Sometimes they should.'

'What?' She turned, not sure she'd heard him right. But he shook his head at her, smiling provocatively, teasing her almost, and she smiled back, watching him, his eyes, his lips, how well she knew him.

He raised his hand to her mouth, and ran his forefinger over her lips, staring into her eyes. 'Kate –' he said. 'God, Kate –'

She was kneeling, turned towards him. His hand was on her thigh; slowly, he turned too, and pushed his knee between her legs. His hands moved, up her body, under her fleecy pyjama top. She could smell him; he smelt of shower gel, of beer; of safe, familiar things. But his eyes were glittering over her; this was unfamiliar, strange, weird, and yet of course, she told herself, it was not that much of a surprise, and as Sean slid his hand around the back of her neck and pulled her towards him, and as they sank onto the sofa, kissing with fierce passion, their teeth clashing, their arms wrapped tight round each other, they said nothing, nothing at all – what was there to say?

On Sunday morning, when Sean woke up in Kate's room, their limbs entangled, hungover, exhausted, but exhilarated, it just seemed simpler for him not to go back to his room. So he didn't. And he didn't that night, nor the next night, nor the one after that.

As Sean said, that first morning, as they lay in bed together, surprised, but not really that surprised,

'I knew this was going to happen, didn't you?'

'Er . . . yes,' Kate said. 'I did, that's what's weird.'

'I knew,' Sean said, rolling on top of her again. 'I knew, last Saturday, especially after I heard about that bitch Jenna getting engaged. I just didn't care that much. And on Sunday, after you came back from shagging Mac.' Kate patted him, gently; she didn't want him to put it like that. 'I wanted to kill him. That's when I knew.'

'That's pathetic,' Kate said, sliding her arms around his neck.

'No, it's human nature,' said Sean. 'And it's you, Katy. I don't know what you do to me, but I can't stop thinking about you. I've been wanting to do this for the longest time.' He brushed her hair back from her face with one hand. 'You feel it too, don't you?'

'Well, yes,' said Kate, pulling him towards her. 'Yes, I do.' She didn't know what else to say – it just seemed right. She looked up at him, smiling almost shyly. Sean gave a shout of delight, a cry that rang out in the small, sunny bedroom.

'God, this is a great start to my birthday, you know that?' He kissed her. 'Now, wish me happy birthday properly, and then I'll make us some coffee, and get the papers.'

CHAPTER THIRTEEN

Kate had never been the sort of girl to ask for much: she was not a princess, the type who sat with her arms folded in a restaurant, ignoring her boyfriend because he hadn't noticed her new shoes. She was the girl who was used to sitting in the corner, watching her father as he told a story, his hands suspended in mid-air, fluttering like birds over the table.

She could remember her mother coming downstairs in the evening, ready to go out and meet him after a concert, for dinner, in wine-coloured velvet, smelling deliciously sweetly of roses on a summer's night, smiling graciously at her daughter, their babysitter Magda. People would clap when her parents walked into a room after a show, or into a restaurant sometimes. All eyes were on them, they softly talking, flirting after all these years. Or screaming at each other, slamming doors, throwing things.

None of it ever involved Kate and she grew used to watching from the sidelines, through the bannisters, silent at the other end of the table, lonely at the end of the garden, happy up in her room, always by herself. She was quite happy with it; it gave her time to think, to dream, to play with her dolls, or when she was older, to read, to imagine things, to think about what she would do when she was grown-up.

When she was eight she thought she would like to live in a big house, with blue painted window-sills, in the countryside. Wisteria climbing up the walls, a little round window by the front door, a huge garden, with the River Thames at the end of it. She would have a husband, called Mr Brown, who worked in the City and carried a briefcase. And whenever she wanted, she would get a boat down the river, and sail into London.

When she was sixteen, she wanted a flat in town with a roof terrace and a window seat, and a CD player, she desperately wanted a CD player of her own. She would play Ella Fitzgerald songs on it while curled up on the window seat, gazing out glamorously at the London skyline. Someone who looked a little like Gregory Peck in *To Kill a Mockingbird* would be her lover; he would be desperately in love with her, and would turn up, demanding to be let in, shouting glamorously, 'Kate Miller, goddammit! I love you! Let me in!' (Why Gregory Peck was not allowed in wasn't a detail she troubled herself with.)

Now she was, she supposed, a grown-up, Kate had never really thought about what she wanted, in reality, from her life. She was used to everything being easy for other people; going to parties, chatting to people, kissing boys, falling in love. Kate had never found it easy. So when she realized she loved Sean, that that was what she was put on earth to do, that everything over the last couple of years – their getting a flat together, him becoming friends with Steve, even further back, him deciding to come over from Texas to England to study – even Kate's night with Mac, which had kick-started it – had led to this, well it all made sense to her and she ran towards it wholeheartedly, and the next few months passed in a haze of pleasure.

'Worrtah.'

'Wewrrterrr.'

'No. Worrtah.'

'Wawwterr.'

'Sean. No. Listen.'

'I don't want to listen. I want to do *this*.'

'Don't be disgusting. We're in public.'

'In a park. In Battersea Park. Doesn't count. Can I feel up my gorgeous girlfriend without anyone noticing? Ah, yes, I can.'

'Worrtah.'

'Can I have some worrrtah please,' Sean said, in a perfect English accent, kissing her languorously as they stretched out on the rug together. Kate reached behind her, and threw the bottle at him.

'Ouch! You bitch,' he said, rolling on top of her.

They stayed like that for a while, giggling quietly as people walked past. Kate looked at her watch. 'Oh,' she said, sitting up. 'I should get back.'

'No you shouldn't,' Sean pushed her back down again so she lay facing him. 'You should lie down and stop checking the time. It's a Sunday. You don't need to do anything today.'

'But I've got to finish that article and Sue said . . .'

'Sue said nothing. You'll finish it. Now finish off what you started here. Have another beer.'

His fingers traced her jawline; staring up at him, framed by the wide blue afternoon sky, Kate gazed into his eyes.

'I'm so happy,' she said quietly.

'Are you?' Sean said, mock-curiously. 'Why?'

She felt a rush of honesty overtake her; a desire to stop playing it cool, to tell him everything she was feeling. But there were no barriers between them anyway, hadn't been when they were friends, and now they were together, nothing but honesty between them. They were alone as much as possible; from waking tangled up in each other to rushing back from their other social commitments: drinks after work, cinema outings with friends, catch-up meals in desultory, cheap pizzerias, to their gorgeous, grubby flat, sinking into each other. Sean had not slept in his room since the night of his birthday. In fact, the only time he went in there now was to get new clothes or to dump some of his dirty clothes back in there from Kate's room, especially when they had friends coming round.

Though she was a daydreamer, in daily life Kate was a practical girl, for the most part. It blew her away, the feeling she felt for Sean. As spring flowered into summer, they didn't go away. It got stronger and stronger, and they both grew more confident, and happier.

They started telling their friends: Betty and Francesca were amazed, and a little appalled; Steve and Zoe were fascinated, dumbstruck, and then very happy for them. Sean's friends at work barely cared: in the world of IT, falling in love was akin to killing people: socially unacceptable. The one friend Kate hadn't told, the one cloud on her horizon, and it was so silly she couldn't believe she was worrying about it, was Charly. She didn't know why she hadn't. She didn't want to hear what Charly would say, hadn't seen much of her lately, either, not just because she was spending all her spare time with Sean, but also because, if she was honest, she knew what Charly was like sometimes and she didn't want to be on the end of it. She felt guilty about it, hated making excuses to Charly on account of it. She was Charly, after all. She didn't know why it bothered her.

Thinking of this now, Kate frowned, and bit her lip.

'Are you going to tell your dad, then?' Sean said. Sean

loved Kate's dad. He thought he was a real dude, a great guy. They got on pretty well, on the rare occasions Daniel Miller made it down to Rotherhithe.

'He's in Jamaica, recording his new album, with that horrible new girlfriend,' Kate said glumly.

'Who?' Sean said, almost joyously. He slapped his thigh. 'Your dad, man! He's crazy! Always some new girl on the scene, it's like a revolving door. Sorry.' He corrected himself, as Kate gave him a withering look. 'So . . . who is she? Is she a stayer?'

'Oh, I don't know,' said Kate. 'It's that PR from the record label, Lisa. Remember, she was at his birthday dinner thing.'

'The short thin one with the massive –' Sean gestured expressively with his hands. 'Yeah. I remember.'

'Dad's mad about her,' said Kate, crossly. 'He even bought her a *watch*. To say thank you for what she's done for him.' Sean raised his eyebrows; Kate flicked him. 'Don't. Ugh,' she shook her head. 'It's a holiday fling, that's all. I give it a couple of weeks. I'll go and see him when he's back and tell him about us. It'll cheer him up after he's dumped her. He likes you.'

Sean grinned. 'I like him, man. Lisa! Well.' He shrugged his shoulders.

They fell silent again, Kate lying with her head in Sean's lap, watching the sky, listening to the people around them playing in the park. She breathed in slowly, catching everything, how she felt.

'What shall we eat tonight?' she said, lazily.

'Can I ask you something?' Sean said then, kissing her on the nose. A bee droned dangerously close to Kate's ear and she sat up suddenly, bashing him.

'Ow,' Kate said, rubbing her nose. 'Ow. What?'

Sean rubbed his face; she thought it was because she'd hit him. It was only afterwards she realized it was because he felt awkward.

139

'I think . . . Gosh, I don't know how to say this.'

'What?' said Kate, feeling the breath tighten in her throat. She leaned against him. He looked into the distance, up away towards Primrose Hill. Kate followed his gaze. She could see a kite in the sky, its red and yellow tail fluttering in the breeze.

'You know the lease on the flat's up next month?'

'Yes.' Kate nodded, too vigorously. 'Er, yes. They're raising the rents, I told you –'

'I've been thinking,' said Sean, cutting across her. His voice was awkward. 'I think we should stop living together.' He breathed deeply, and sighed, like it was a weight off his shoulders. 'I think we should move in with other people.'

'Why?' Kate said, trying to swallow, fighting down the panic washing over her. 'Don't you – don't you love me anymore?'

It sounded so weak, compared to what she was feeling.

'Of course not,' Sean said. 'I'm in love with you, and I want to ask you to live with me at some point.'

'Oh,' Kate said. 'I see.' But she didn't.

'Kate,' he said. He took her hand solemnly, and kissed the tips of her fingers. His forehead, under the short thatch of yellow hair, was a little pink from the sun; so was his nose. She looked at him in amazement, still not quite believing he was here, and that this might all be about to end. 'I'm in love with you. This is all I want. But I want us to start our life together properly. Like it's special. I want to date you, take you out to dinner, stay the night at yours sometime and *then* move in together. Not just go from being flatmates in some dingy flat who got drunk and had sex one night and then never moved on. I want us to be . . . special.'

Kate blinked at him, a smile spreading across her face, like sunshine warming her up again.

'There,' he went on. 'You see what I mean. Do you?'

140

'I do,' Kate said.

'Does it make sense? That we need some time apart if we're gonna be together?'

'Well . . .' She thought of how much she was going to miss him. She saw him every day, spent every night with him, he was her world, totally, and panic suddenly gripped her as she thought about making her way in the world without him. As if he were reading her mind, Sean said,

'Hey, babe. Look at me.' He lifted her chin with one finger so she stared into his eyes. She clutched his finger, like a little baby clutching an adult's hand. 'This is a good thing, OK? We'll be glad we did it. I promise.'

She knew he was right, but she clung to him, not wanting to let him go, as the shadows lengthened in the park. Only after a while did it occur to her, when she was drunk with wanting Sean, as they swayed home together, wrapped around each other. Charly. She would move in with Charly! She gave a little shiver.

'OK, babe?' Sean asked her, wrapping his arm round her a little tighter.

'Absolutely,' she said softly. 'Great.'

'You're a weird girl, Katy-Kay.'

'I'm not!'

He pulled her up so she was sitting on his knees, and she wrapped her arms around his neck, then he kissed her, all over her face, her ears, her neck, her eyes, till she stopped crying and was laughing, shrieking, pleading with him to let her go. He could always win her round like that, could always make her fall in love with him again, all over again.

CHAPTER FOURTEEN

'*You*?' Charly said, the next day, when Kate ran into the office, eyes shining. 'Why the hell d'you think I'd want to move in with *you*?'

'Oh,' said Kate slowly. She put her bag down on her desk and took out the floppy disk with the Editor's Letter she'd written hastily the previous night, after she and Sean had got back from the park.

'I mean,' said Charly, sinking into her chair and pushing herself away from the desk with one long, shapely leg, 'you're a bit of a loser, Kate.' She started counting with her fingers, long nails passing over each other. 'You own Ace of Base's debut album. *And* "Fields of Gold" by Sting.'

'I bought them with a voucher –'

'You think little grey cardigans are the answer to all the world's fashion dilemmas,' Charly went on, lifting and then dropping the edge of Kate's beloved Whistles grey cardigan, currently the most expensive item in her wardrobe, bought with the money her mother had given her for Christmas. 'You like "Coronation Street", for fuck's sake. Like an old granny. *And* you like garden centres. I

142

can't live with someone whose idea of a good weekend is picking out trellis plants and then rushing home for another gripping instalment of what happened to Derek and Mavis.'

'Derek died in 1997, and Mavis has moved to the Lake District. They haven't been in it for years,' said Kate, trying to fight back. 'Get your facts straight. And garden centres are . . . cool! You can buy all sorts of stuff in them.'

'Jeez.' Charly stood up. 'Look, if it'll help you out, I'll move in with you.'

'What?' said Kate.

'God.' Charly rolled her eyes, looking totally bored. 'I'll live with you, Miller. OK?' She put her arms round Kate and hugged her. 'You know I'd like to.'

'Really?'

Charly squeezed her. 'Look.' She sounded embarrassed. 'You're my best friend, aren't you?'

'Right!' said Kate, pleased not just that Charly was going to live with her, but also that she'd called her her best friend. 'Yes!' She hugged Charly back. 'Ohmigod, this is so great! Do you seriously want to . . .?' She gazed anxiously at Charly, who sighed again.

'Man, I said I did, didn't I?' she said crossly. Charly didn't do overt displays of emotion.

'Great! Great!' said Kate. 'I'll just give this to Sue –' she waved the Editor's Letter at Charly '– and then let's start calling up places shall we?'

'Go on then,' Charly said in a childish voice. 'Give your little head girl swotty letter to Sue. Hey – you never said, by the way. What's happened with the Tex Mex Sex Machine? Why aren't you guys living together anymore? Finally got bored of waiting for him to snog you, did ya?'

'Oh, that,' said Kate, humming nervously, and turning

back towards her, running the piece of paper through her fingers. 'Well – um.'

'What?' Charly looked at her suspiciously. She could smell intrigue a mile away.

'Yep,' said Kate. 'Look. There's something I have to tell you.'

'No way,' said Charly. She stood behind her desk, arms akimbo. 'You're doing your flatmate. I can't believe it. Kate Miller. How long?'

Kate swallowed; she could feel her eyes bulging. 'How the hell did you know that?'

'I'm not stupid. You're shagging Sean. Sean the sheep. Sheep-shagger. Hey! You're a sheep-shagger!' Charly clapped her hands. 'Woo-hoo!'

'Charly!' Kate said sharply. 'Zip it.'

Sophie and George, who sat a short way away from Kate and Charly, looked round curiously, to see if they could work out what was going on. On the other side from them, Claire and Phil, reunited once again, studiously ignored them. Relations on their side of the office since his encounter with Charly the previous year had not been great.

'Sorry,' said Charly. She narrowed her eyes, and was silent. 'OK,' she said, after a moment's pause. 'You fucked him.'

'Charly.' Kate felt helpless; she forgot, always forgot what Charly was like when you showed vulnerability.

'Oh my god,' said Charly, stepping around her desk and coming and standing next to Kate. 'Has he dumped you? Is that why –' she looked into Kate's face, searching, and Kate felt the power of Charly's gold-flecked tiger eyes, sizing her up, seeking her out. 'No way, no way. What's going on? Don't tell me you like him, Kate.'

'I love him,' Kate said, trying to sound calm, and like it was normal, not extraordinary. 'He loves me. Our lease is coming up, so we're moving out, so we can start over properly, go on dates and stuff. He's moving in with our friend Jem. And I want to move in with you.'

'Uhuh.' Charly nodded. She was silent again, her eyes taking in Kate once more.

'So that's the situation,' said Kate, firmly.

'So you've got a boyfriend,' said Charly. 'This is shit, you're going to be a real pain in the neck, having dinner out of Jamie Oliver books with other couples and talking about property. God.'

'Yeah, right,' said Kate.

'You'd just better not have anything like that in *our* flat,' said Charly. 'Otherwise I think I'd rather stay in Leigh-on-Sea with Mum. Got it?'

'Promise,' said Kate.

'And no fucking Radio 4 in the mornings, either,' said Charly. 'I'm depressed enough already in the morning. I don't want to have to listen to John Humphrys going on about Kosovo or the rainforests before I've even had coffee. Got that too?'

'Fine by me,' said Kate.

'And another thing –' Charly began, but Sue appeared in the doorway of her office, looking rather more flustered than usual.

'Kate! Have you got the thingy –' she waved her hands vaguely '– Editor's Letter?' Already moving away, pulling down the jacket of her executive suit, 'I need it for –'

'Yep, sure, in a minute,' said Kate, looking down at the crumpled, sweaty print-out of the Editor's Letter, which she had crushed in her hand. She looked at Charly. 'What else?'

'I'm pleased for you,' said Charly. 'He's a really nice bloke. OK?' She turned back to the desk, as Kate smiled with pleasure. 'And you're in luck. I had a fling with an estate agent in December. I'll give him a call. And the beat goes on. Now, off you go to buy some matching monogrammed dressing gowns, OK?'

145

Kate ignored her and sat down to print out the letter again, as Charly picked up the phone. A minute later she was talking to an ex-boyfriend whom she'd dumped only last month and who just happened to be an estate agent for a lettings agency in Kilburn and West Hampstead. By lunchtime they had five different flats to see. Charly was, as she reminded Kate, really really good in the sack.

'You're going to share with Charly?' Sue didn't look up from her desk, but she swivelled from side to side as she read Kate's piece, chewing a pencil, her cropped blonde hair never moving an inch as her head bobbed. 'This is good, Kate. Great. I thought you had a boy you lived with? Isn't he your boyfriend?'

Confused by this non-sequential speech, Kate said, 'Thanks. Yes, he is now, actually. Er –' She scratched her head, trying to keep it simple. 'We were flatmates when we got together, so we thought it'd be best to live apart for a while, make sure we're doing the right thing.'

Sue wasn't that interested. 'Hm, hm . . .' she said, looking up at Kate, over her article. 'Thanks again, dearie. You know . . .' She stared into space. 'You're an interesting girl. Did you know? You Are An Interesting Girl.'

Kate moved from one foot to the other, not sure how to respond, she never was with Sue, who was capable of great insight and total, crushing rudeness at the same time.

'Interesting,' Sue said again. She tapped a pencil on the table, her small, busy fingers drumming a beat. 'How long have you been here now?'

'Nearly two years,' said Kate.

Sue nodded. 'I'm thinking about something. Forget it. It's just – you.'

Kate raised her eyebrows hopefully.

'You, Kate. You're such a funny mixture.'

'How?' Kate asked, suddenly impatient.

'Well. Of reserve and openness. You're so shy, you wouldn't say "Boo!" to a goose –' she made the 'Boo!' extremely loud, and Kate jumped '– but at the same time you're a very intuitive girl. You get what people want to read about. What they're interested in. Always have done. I worried you were this shy little freaky thing with her head full of books. And I'm glad I was wrong.' Sue flicked her eyes over her. 'And you look good these days too, now you've found black and stopped experimenting with tartan miniskirts. That's all. Thanks.'

'Er . . .' said Kate, brought up short. Sue waved her away, imperiously, with the pencil.

'I'm thinking about you, that's all,' she said. 'Wait to hear more.'

'What does that mean?' Kate couldn't help asking. 'Sorry.'

'OK,' Sue sighed, and looked around, conspiratorially. She was clearly bursting to tell. 'Have you heard about this start-up magazine Broadgate's financing? Have you heard of . . . Venus?' She said it in a whisper, like it was a hallowed name.

Kate shook her head slowly. 'Oh. Well . . .'

She had, of course, heard loads about Venus, but since the world of magazines was rife with gossip, and since Sophie, Jo and George were the worst gossips in the world, wildly unreliable and apt to over-embroider to the point of Bayeux-Tapestry-lengths and since Charly loathed 'industry' gossip, as it implied an interest in one's job, Kate had tried to ignore most of what she'd heard, as it was impossible to separate the wheat from the chaff. Besides, for the last couple of months she hadn't really cared either way, had just worked as hard as possible so she could get home as soon as possible to Sean.

But Venus was the secret obsession in the office. It was going to be bigger, faster, glossier, trendier, younger, more beautiful than anything that had gone before, they said. New offices, by the river, they said, being designed right now and the interiors were being done by Phillipe Starck. *Venus* was going to be revolutionary, they said, a fortnightly glossy for young women, with fashion and celebrity and gossip and interesting articles too. They said more was being spent on its launch than the combined turnover of *Woman's World, Lovely Life* and *even* the mighty *Great!* in one whole year. They said ... well, they said lots of things, all in hushed voices, in corners, which gave the already super-secretive enterprise an even more momentous air.

'You like your job, don't you?' said Sue, after a moment.

It was an unexpected question. Kate looked at her curiously. 'Of course I do.'

'Do you like magazines? Working in magazines?'

Kate said simply, 'More than almost anything. I can't believe how lucky I am.'

'You want to stay at *Woman's World* for the rest of your life, then?'

'No,' said Kate frankly. She wanted Sue to understand. 'But you know, I love it. I mean, I love working here, with everyone, but I love the magazine too. I like answering the Reader's Letters, and working out what they want to read about, and talking to people, and giving people a slice of their lives. You know, the good slice.' She realized she was talking too much; she babbled when she was nervous – she knew it. Suddenly Mac's face, saying the same thing, flashed into her mind. How strange. She shook her head, as if exorcizing his image, willing it away.

'Yes,' said Sue slowly, and Kate wasn't sure if she thought she was crazy or not. 'Thanks, Kate. Thanks a lot.' She tapped her pencil impatiently on the desk. 'And good luck with the flat-hunt. I think you're mad to move in with Charly. You'll have no liver left, no boyfriend and no money after six months. She'll steal them all. But each to his own.'

148

'You could be right,' said Kate, happily, but the phone rang, and suddenly Sue wasn't listening any more.

The next week, Kate and Charly found their flat, a sunny but tiny two-bed at the very top of a tall, narrow Victorian house, in between Kilburn and Queen's Park, near Zoe and Steve. The agent said they should say they wanted it now. It was a busy time of year, and the market was crazy. It was all happening fast, too fast for Kate. Only a week ago she hadn't known about any of this and now . . .? But Charly had been galvanized into action by the thought of leaving Leigh-on-Sea and having her own place, a place with Kate. 'Two crazy single girls out on the town,' she said when they signed the lease.

Kate wanted to say No, that's not it. But, on her first night in their flat, after Sean had helped her pack up their old flat, taken her to the new place, lugged her boxes up the stairs and then regretfully, sadly, kissed her goodbye and gone off to meet his new flatmate Jem at the pub, Kate found herself standing on the steps of the spindly redbrick house that was now her home, without any idea how she'd ended up there.

She turned back, opened the front door, and started wearily on the stairs. As she did, she heard a loud bang from the top floor, up in the roof, and looked up, cautiously – what had Charly done now? Was it always going to be like this? Loneliness clutched at her again, and as she got to the second floor she thought of Zoe, wished she could take advantage of their new neighbourly situation to pop round to their home, a real home. But she and Steve had left that morning, to visit Mac in Edinburgh. Zoe had told her a few days ago that they were going, in a very soft voice, as if she was worried about how Kate might react. Kate wasn't sure what she, Zoe, was worried about; that she wouldn't be around for Kate's first night in the flat, or was Mac still *verboten* as a subject between them, even now? She shrugged, thinking about this as she climbed the stairs. Coolly, she told herself she rarely thought of him now; she didn't need to. To remember him – it – what had happened, how she had felt . . .

She blinked. Surely that was all behind her now – she had her life, he had his, and there was no further proof needed that their night together was way in the past than this – her new life, what she was doing now, climbing the stairs to her new home.

Kate finally reached her floor panting slightly, squared her shoulders and pushed open the door. Time to get on with it, then, she told herself, and she forced herself to smile, faking a cheeriness she didn't feel.

Wheeeeeeeeeeeeeeeeeeeeeeeeeeeeeeeeeee! came a high, whistling noise from inside, and as Kate came into the sitting room, not knowing what to expect, she found Charly, a small, silver party hat sitting lopsided on her silky tawny hair, blowing a streamer whistle, with a just-opened bottle of champagne – the source of the loud bang, Kate realized – in her hand.

'I thought you might need cheering up,' Charly said, smiling at her. She handed her a glass, shaking her head, as if laughing to herself about something, and she looked happy, happier than Kate had seen her in ages. 'Welcome to our new home, Kate.'

'Hey!' said Kate, delightedly. 'That's so – you're so sweet!' They clinked glasses. 'Welcome to yours!'

'To new beginnings,' said Charly. She nodded wisely at Kate. 'Who knows what the future holds, eh?'

Kate nodded, and they each took a sip, framed by the window in the early evening light as the setting sun streamed in across the rooftops.

'Who knows,' she said, but she was thinking only of Sean, now, only of the life that lay ahead of her with him, and she crossed her fingers with one hand. 'Who knows.'

150

PART TWO

CHAPTER FIFTEEN

London, 2007

Kate woke feeling like she'd been hit by a cosh. She banged the clock radio, ineffectively, trying to turn it off, emerging from the kind of deep sleep where you feel your limbs are melding into the mattress. She blinked wearily, trying to work out where she was, fragments of dreams and memories and actual events all crowding into her mind. Coming home. Dad – Mr Allan – the coffin. Dani's pink pyjamas. She'd seen Zoe. Zoe – Mac – Sean – Charly's letter.

Sitting up slowly, Kate rubbed her eyes with fumbling, clumsy hands. Her limbs felt as if they were full of lead. Her head ached, her throat was a little sore and she didn't really feel rested at all. She looked around slowly, taking in the contents of the room, how weird it was to be here again. The grey painted chest of drawers, the long blonde wood wardrobe that was to have housed her and Sean's grown-up, business attire. He had put up the creamy Venetian blind; you could still see the black holes in the wooden window frame from the previous blind that he'd taken down.

No. No more of this. Slightly to her own surprise, Kate stumbled out of bed, pulled up the blind and opened the window. Outside a bird sang enthusiastically, chirping loudly against the faint hum of traffic and it hit her weary brain then: she was definitely back in London. She could even smell it. Coffee. She needed coffee. She stumbled through to the kitchen, remembering how the floorboards squeaked just so, how she and Sean had discussed carpets.

Kate shook her head and started hunting for something to put her coffee in. She loved opening the cupboards in her kitchen again, rediscovering the old mugs she'd left behind; the orange striped Penguin mug that said 'Pride and Prejudice'; the spotted set from Habitat her dad (or probably Lisa) had bought for her birthday; the ones with pictures of the Moomins, the old chipped mug that said 'Central Perk' on it: she'd been so proud of that one when Sean had given it to her, a month after they'd got together. She opened the tiny door onto the minuscule balcony, no more than a windowsill really. Fresh air flooded into the kitchen and she took a deep breath.

'So you're back,' she said aloud. 'It's OK. But you've got to –'

Got to what? She looked out, around her, drinking in the wet, London, petrolly, grassy smell, back inside the kitchen again. She didn't know what she had to do. Then she caught sight of the Central Perk mug.

'Got to make it work. So you sort everything out. Don't leave, feeling like you're slinking away.'

The kettle switch flipped off. She took it as a sign, and nodded firmly, ignoring the stare of the man in the flat opposite her. She came inside and closed the window, feeling properly awake, and suddenly full of purpose.

She was going to see her father later, but she had to time it right, didn't want to tire him out – or make him angry. He was not a good patient. Lisa knew enough, too, to keep Dani out of his way for a large portion of the day. That was

154

for after lunch: in the meantime, what else was she supposed to do? Kate poured water into the cafetiere, thoughtfully.

She could go and see Zoe again, or call Francesca. She hadn't spoken to her since she'd been back. But Francesca would have a go at her, ask questions Kate didn't want to answer. She couldn't quite face it, not just yet. She couldn't call in to the office and make sure everything was going OK; they wouldn't be there for another six hours. And she'd only left on Friday; what was the point? Then it struck her with force that, apart from anything else, there was nothing she needed to check on anyway. Jersey Lorraine could do that job standing on her head. Better than Kate.

Standing in the kitchen, silence crowded in on her, the strange situation of her own futility. Out there was London, the city she loved, friends she knew, and Kate felt removed from it all. And then she heard a noise from upstairs. Someone was moving around, shuffling slowly across the floor.

She felt the pull of the city, suddenly, like it was talking to her, telling her to come outside, walk around again. There was spring on the breeze, and outside she could hear someone singing in the street. She had to get up, go out, keep moving, she had to embrace this or else just not bother, slink back to New York and give up. She poured the coffee, cradling the mug in her hands as it got cold, looking out of the open window until she realized her bare arms were flesh-cold and she was shivering. She had a shower, got dressed, and shut the door. She knew where she was going.

'Hello Kate,' he said.

'Hello, Mr Allan,' Kate replied. She handed him the daffodils she'd bought the previous day and kissed him, squeezing his arm briefly. 'How are you?'

He moved out of the way to let her in, nodding his head

155

in a kind of motioning movement. She walked in. So like her flat and so utterly different, the corridor, the light, pretty sitting room, books and records lining the walls, shelf after shelf of them, another wall devoted to CDs. A breakfast bar, with stools, was cut into the wall between sitting room and kitchen, and an old speckled blue fruit bowl sat on it, a denuded bunch of grapes its only inhabitant. Everything was too tidy, somehow. The two of them stood in silence, looking alternately at the floor or out of the window, and Kate wished she was back downstairs again, not trying to be a good neighbour.

On every spare inch of unshelved wall there were album covers. Blue, red geometric shapes, faded black-and-white photos of lanky young men. 'Chappell Quartet Plays the Tin Pan Blues' proclaimed the framed album nearest to Kate.

'Is that you?' she said, pointing at the second of the lanky men in the row.

'Yes,' said Mr Allan, plunging his hands into his pockets. 'That was me. West Berlin, I think that photo was taken. Well, by then Jimmy had left, so . . .'

He trailed off.

'You've come about Eileen, I expect,' he said after a long pause.

Kate was thrown by this. She looked down, and saw that she'd put her hands in her pockets, unconsciously mirroring her host. Mrs Allan had usually done most of the talking.

'Um. I came to say hello,' she said.

'Right.' Mr Allan nodded; he didn't venture anything further, or ask her to sit down.

'I'm so sorry,' Kate said firmly.

Mr Allan nodded again. He said, without looking at her, 'I thought that was why you'd come.'

He blinked; his receding white hair moved up and down slightly as he frowned and then widened his eyes in rapid succession.

'When's the funeral?' Kate said.

'Thursday,' said Mr Allan. 'But we're actually having a cardboard coffin, not that one she left in. We both want cardboard coffins, it's more environmental.' He said this flatly. 'You saw her, yesterday, didn't you? When you were getting back.'

Again, Kate was irresistibly reminded of a Pinter play. 'Yes – I didn't know if you'd seen me. I nearly knocked yesterday –' Mr Allan bowed his head.

'I didn't want any visitors, really. Just wanted to be on my own. Get used to it for a while.'

'Right, right,' said Kate. 'Well I'm sorry for –'

He batted her apology away with his hand. 'We were together for fifty years, you know. So it's strange. We always knew one of us would be left alone, you know.' He blinked again, and looked round the flat. 'We're having people back here afterwards,' he said suddenly 'You missed Sue yesterday.'

'Sue . . . Sue!' Kate said, contexts slotting into place, her brain whirring. Sue – of course. Mr Allan's nephew Alec was married to Sue Jordan, her beloved boss at *Woman's World*. It was she who had mentioned that the flat below Alec's uncle and aunt was for sale at auction, nearly four years ago . . . 'Oh, I'm, er, sorry I missed her. I haven't seen her for –' she trailed off. 'Ages.'

'Yes,' said Mr Allan. 'And she's looking forward to seeing you, Kate. She wants to know how you are.'

Kate thought of Sue, brisk, comforting, hard as nails, always encouraging, always demanding the best. She wondered what Sue would say if she heard what Kate had spent her last week at work doing (sorting out paperclips and booking Anne Graves' flights to Bermuda for her holidays). She would be cross with Kate, and rightly so. Kate shook her head, looking back at Mr Allan. 'I've missed her.'

'I'm sure. Now, she said you'd be able to help me.' Kate nodded. 'Would you mind telling me something?'

'Yes, of course,' said Kate.

'Where can I get some food, crisps and things?' He said this as if they were extraordinary delicacies. 'You know, if people come back after the service.' Agitation was working its way across his face. 'You see Eileen is – was the one who did all that sort of thing. I was on the road, she was at home. That's how it worked. The shops at the end of the road – would they be best, do you think? I'm just not sure.'

'Yes, and the supermarket and stuff,' said Kate. She crossed her arms and rocked back on her heels. 'Look, Mr Allan, why don't I take care of all of that for you?'

To her relief he didn't protest or make excuses. He opened his eyes and said,

'Thank you, Kate. That really would be extremely helpful.' He looked out of the window and was silent for a while. 'It's a lovely day outside, isn't it? Spring really is here.'

'Gorgeous, I know,' said Kate, following his gaze. 'Actually, that's why I came up here. Apart from – well, you know I wanted to . . . er . . .' She cleared her throat. 'I was wondering. Would you like to go for a walk?'

'A walk?' he said, slowly, as if she'd just suggested joining the circus.

'Yes,' she said. 'Like we used to, remember? I need to get out of the flat. Clear my head a bit. I thought you might want to, as well.'

'Well, yes,' he said. 'Of course. I'd forgotten. You're only just back, aren't you? How long has it been?'

'A day,' said Kate.

'No, my dear,' Mr Allan said. 'How long has it been since you left?'

'Oh,' said Kate. 'Nearly three years.'

'Has it really. You never came back to visit, did you?'

'I've come back now,' said Kate, looking out of the window again.

'Eileen always said what a shame it was,' Mr Allan said. 'She thought you were such a lovely girl, my dear.'

'I don't know about that,' said Kate, embarrassed. 'She was a lovely woman, though, Mr Allan. I am sorry.'

'Well, well, well,' he said, shaking his bowed head, and a tear dropped to the ground. She looked away, embarrassed, not wanting to see his grief. He looked up. 'I'm not ready to talk about her as – as a dead person yet. So, please don't be sorry. Is that alright?'

'Yes, of course,' said Kate hurriedly, and Mr Allan continued as if uninterrupted,

'She'd be sorry to have missed you, you know. We often used to wonder how you were getting on.'

'I know, and I never wrote back to her,' said Kate. She felt as low as can be. 'She sent me newspaper cuttings, bits and bobs, you know.'

'Yes, I know.'

'I never replied.' She shook her head. 'It was so rude of me. I'm sorry.'

'No, it was natural, after everything that happened. We just wanted you to be happy, dear.'

'Bless you,' Kate said, giving him a small smile.

Mr Allan strode across to the coat rack and picked up a long raincoat. 'So how's New York? I want to hear all about it.'

Kate jangled her keys in her pocket. 'Not really much to tell.'

'Well,' he said, and he let her help him on with his coat, 'let's get going then, and you can tell me all about it.'

The daffodils were out all along the roads up to the park, in window boxes, in clumps on the ground. They walked through St John's Wood, towards Lord's, through the heart of London's apartment block land, every street lined with charming Victorian flats, with balconies, brass plaques fitted with bells, perfectly manicured gardens. The hum of the first mowing of the lawns echoed around them, as they walked further, through the wide, quiet streets, past the private hospitals, the synagogues, the little rows of shops with flats above, and down St John's Wood High Street. It was Monday morning, and the roads were almost empty in the cold spring sunshine; pensioners and middle-aged couples emerged from their blocks, slowly moving down the street, talking politely to each other.

Mr Allan walked fast, which Kate liked; she wasn't a stroller. For a man of his age he was extremely fit: tall and sinewy. They talked for a while, he asking her questions about how she'd been, she replying, and asking him questions in return, but after that they fell into silence. He didn't say much, neither did she, but it was almost as if they didn't need to. After twenty minutes or so like this, he suddenly stopped abruptly.

'Oh, we're here,' he said. 'We have gone far. We've reached the park. I was miles away, I'm afraid.'

Regent's Park. She could see it unfolding ahead of her. To their left was the zoo; ahead, the tangled bushes at the edge of the park. She could just see parts of it rolling away towards the heart of the city, gorgeous, glorious Regent's Park. It seemed so strange to her, all of a sudden, so . . . *English*. She hadn't realized how much it affected her, how overwhelming it was, now, here, to be back home, and how strange it must be for Mr Allan. Last week he wouldn't have known, couldn't have imagined in his worst nightmares that this would be his Monday morning, his wife dead. They were both silent. Without meaning to, Kate said impulsively,

'I miss New York.'

He looked up, amazement written on his face.

'You miss New York? After twenty-four hours? Oh come on. Look at this!'

He waved his umbrella at the scene in front of them, then at her. 'Come on, Kate. This is London! How can you say that?'

'Er . . .' Kate was embarrassed. 'I don't know; I just do.'

'Rubbish,' Mr Allan said, firmly. He was quite animated. 'I've lived here all my life, apart from when I was touring. I went everywhere, all over the world, Kate, we were playing when British Jazz was up there, it was the Golden Age. And do you know something?'

Kate shook her head.

'Always missed it. Always glad to be back. To see Eileen, to do our walk to the shops, to walk across Hyde Park, into Soho, to see my old band mates, listen to Dankworth or Humph in concert. Eileen and I used to do that when we were younger, you know, or we'd meet in Soho, in a café, pretend we were on a date, not a boring old married couple.

'It's the same for you, Kate. I remember seeing your father in concert at the Festival Hall, and this little girl leaving with him at the end, you were jumping up and down and holding onto his hand and your mother's, too. Between the two of them. Your mother, she was so beautiful. Red hair?' Kate nodded, and he said eagerly, 'Do you remember that evening?'

'No,' said Kate, smiling. 'I don't think so, anyway. That's so funny. I never knew that.'

'Brahms Violin Concerto.' He shook his head. 'Ah, he was wonderful.'

Kate could, in fact, vaguely remember the treat of that evening, of being allowed to come and see her father. It was a rarity, she hadn't often gone. Her mother and father had argued about it, badly. She must have been about eight. She remembered then not liking the South Bank, it was like an alien landscape, it wasn't a London she was used to. She sucked her lower lip into her mouth and bit it, whistling through her teeth, the cold air stinging them.

'He's not very well,' she said incoherently. 'That's why I've come back.'

'Ah,' said Mr Allan. He stared at her briefly. 'What is it?'

'Kidney transplant. He was very . . . he was very lucky.' Kate didn't trust herself to say more.

He nodded and patted her arm, as if she were a little girl again. 'I am sorry. We both have our sadness then. Let's cross the road.'

Suddenly Kate felt strangely at home again, standing on the side of a road, overlooking the park, with her neighbour Mr Allan. He was one of several people she hadn't allowed herself to miss since she'd left. Concern for him flooded over her once again, on this strange and awful day for him, but as she turned to ask him something, he interrupted her brusquely.

'Miss New York,' he muttered. 'I'll show you what a foolish thing that is to say. Look. There. The Regent's Canal –' waving his umbrella in the direction of the bushes '– now that is something to admire. Perhaps we should go to the towpath and see, eh?'

There was the canal; there behind it was London Zoo. Kate stood still, and heard the faint but raucous cry of something; a chimp, perhaps.

'There,' said Mr Allan. 'There's a boat. My goodness.'

There was a narrowboat just pulling into a little docking station outside the Zoo. It was so strange, she thought, that she had never known or seen this before. Mr Allan made a sound, like a cough, and Kate turned to look at him.

'I'm sorry,' he said. 'Eileen loved the canal. This boat we used to get up to Camden Lock, from Little Venice. At least once a month. She really did just love it.' His voice trembled. 'This is . . . Oh dear. Everything's awful. That's all.'

Kate didn't know what to say. She took his arm and squeezed it. 'Oh, Mr Allan.' They stood there, on the canal bank, in silence. The trees were all in bud; sun flickered on the water. It was a beautiful day.

They heard a man on the narrowboat shout, 'Last call for the boat trip please!' Suddenly, Kate heard her little sister's voice. 'I wanna go on a boat trip!'

'Mr Allan,' she said. 'Why don't we get the boat back home?'

So they sat with the tourists, and the strange old man with a camera who took notes, and a moody girl reading a book, as the narrowboat sedately glided through the water, past the vast, white stucco houses with private launches and perfect gardens, through Lisson Grove, where three crusties on an old, rather dilapidated boat were trying to start a barbecue, through the long, dark tunnel cutting underneath Maida Vale and bringing them out in Little Venice, past the café, and the spot where Nancy Mitford used to live, and finally they arrived at the lake where the Regent's Canal met the Grand Union Canal, and got out.

'This is called Browning's Pond,' said Mr Allan, as they stood on the little bridge crossing over the canal, watching the moorhens slide through the water, and the Canada geese honking overhead. 'Do you know why?'

'No,' said Kate.

'Robert Browning. He lived there.' He pointed to the houses overlooking the canal. 'See that blue plaque there? That's for him. The house is demolished now. But they named it after him.'

'I didn't know that.'

'Lots of things you don't know,' Mr Allan said. He crossed

163

the road, and they walked next to the canal. Kate glanced up at the houses, the sunshine bouncing off the creamy white stucco, the blue grape hyacinths and daffodils bobbing happily in the gardens, and felt a sort of calm within her. She laughed, quietly, as they turned the corner, and crossed the road again.

'What's so funny?'

'Nothing, really,' she said. 'Just . . . I didn't expect to be doing this on my first day back. I don't expect you did, either.'

'No,' Mr Allan said. 'Kate, I didn't. But I'm glad you're here. Thank you.'

She patted his arm back. 'I'm glad I'm here, too.'

They walked in silence a little while until Mr Allan said, 'Are you writing anything at the moment?'

Kate wrinkled her forehead, slightly taken aback by the question. It had been a longish walk; she was surprised he wasn't more tired, but he seemed absolutely fine. 'Er . . . no. Why?'

'I mean to say, what are you doing in New York?' Mr Allan said. 'Didn't you get some wonderful job out there, that was what we heard from Sue?'

'Ha,' said Kate. She had to be careful, she realized. This was the scenario she had practised for, being back in London and answering questions about her job. 'I'm working at a literary agency.'

'Working with writers, you mean? At the agency?'

'Something like that.' Kate neatly sidestepped a cracked paving stone. 'Be careful.'

'Yes, yes.' They were on Warrington Crescent, walking back up towards Elgin Avenue. The sun went in, suddenly. Kate looked up; grey clouds scudded from nowhere across the blue sky. She shivered.

'So it was worth leaving for,' Mr Allan said. 'Eileen and

I always thought you'd win a Pulitzer prize one day. Or the Booker prize. Weren't you going to be a magazine editor before you left? Sue always said you would.'

This was the thing with old people, Kate reminded herself. Their version of the past was totally unreliable.

'No,' she said. 'I loved *Venus*, but I needed to get away . . .' He was watching her. Time to roll out phase two. 'And, you know, I wanted to see Mum – she left when I was fourteen, and I've never really spent much time with her, you know . . . It seemed like a good time to go, then.'

This was her stock answer, and it always worked. It was vulnerable enough to guilt people into accepting it, and it had the merit of being true, although that was far from being the whole story. Mr Allan said,

'I'm sorry. So you're back to see your father, and that's fine with your – your employers, I suppose?'

'Yes, yes,' said Kate. 'Someone's covering my job while I'm away, while Dad's ill. I'm only here for a couple of weeks, and then I'm back there.'

'Two weeks,' Mr Allan said, sinking his head onto his chest. 'I see.' He blinked. 'What will you do about your flat?'

'I don't know,' Kate said. 'Get someone else in, get an agency to rent it out, I expect. But I'm not staying. I don't really live here any more, you see.'

'Of course, of course,' he said, and then they were both silent, walking in pace together until they were almost home.

'That was quite a walk,' said Mr Allan, taking off his deerstalker hat, while Kate unlocked the door and let them into the lobby of their building. 'Phew.'

'I'm knackered,' said Kate. 'Well done us. We must have walked – what, about three miles?'

'Goodness gracious,' said Mr Allan. He rolled his eyes and then smiled at her. They walked upstairs to his flat and Kate waited as he jangled his hands in his pockets for his keys.

'Dear Kate,' he said, as he unlocked the door. 'Thank you so much.'

'Not at all,' said Kate, almost laughing. 'Thank you – I'm so sorry –'

He brushed her condolences aside again. 'No, no. Thank you, dear girl. It was a wonderful morning. And – ah. Thursday –?'

'I'll buy the food,' Kate said. 'You don't need to worry about a thing. Now,' she said, bossily. 'What are you doing for the rest of the day?'

'Alec's coming round soon, and Sue.' Alec was a rather unlikely husband for Sue, a scholarly, quiet man who worked on the finance side of the magazine business, quite unlike his energetic, firecracking wife. 'They're bringing lunch, we're talking about – about arrangements, you know.'

'Right,' said Kate, not wanting to meet his eye, embarrassed. 'Well.' She pushed her toe along the ground, gingerly, not wanting to leave him on his own, not wanting to be on her own, suddenly.

'Don't suppose you want to pop up for a cup of tea, later, they'd love to see you, I know.'

'I can't,' she said, hurriedly. 'I'd love to see them, too – but I'll be at my dad's.'

'Of course,' Mr Allan said. 'Well, they'll be gone by six-thirty, they have theatre tickets. How about after that, maybe a glass of wine?' He made a gesture like a maître d', welcoming her to a restaurant.

'Sure!' Kate smiled. Mr Allan smiled back. Her unease vanished, and she kissed him on the cheek, and went back downstairs, to her welcoming but echoing flat. She opened the door, humming a tune Mr Allan had been singing.

But as she was taking off her coat, her eye fell on something on the floor. A letter, someone had pushed it under the door. No address this time. Just

Kate Miller
by hand.
And inside Charly had written:

Here's my mobile number, Kate. Please give me a call. Did you get the letter I posted you? I'm having a little girl. I wanted to tell you. I need to see you, please get in touch,
Charly :)

CHAPTER SIXTEEN

It was Wednesday evening and Kate had been back in London for four days. It seemed to her as if the first twenty-four hours had passed in a flash, and from then on it was almost scary how easily she fell into a routine, one she'd been sticking to for months. Like the first few days at a new school, when after less than a week a need for normalcy makes it feel like you've been there for years, not days. She'd visit her father at home in the morning, usually when Lisa was out with Danielle. On Tuesday Lisa had given her a key so that Daniel didn't have to answer the door. Then she'd come back to the flat and potter around for a while, making lists of things – *buy new pots for balcony* and *need more teaspoons* – small tasks, never big things. She didn't call the letting agent, she didn't call Zoe again, though she knew she should. In the early evening, Monday, Tuesday and Wednesday, she'd go upstairs for a cup of tea with Mr Allan, and he'd tell her about Eileen, about their life together, and they'd sort things out for the funeral. Kate wasn't sure how much of a practical help it was, but as he said, it was good to talk. She'd speak to her father again, and then go to bed, early.

She didn't go into town, didn't explore further than she'd walked with Mr Allan. She went to the supermarket, to get the food for Mrs Allan's wake, but that was about it. She was back in London, but she might as well have been in another country still. She didn't ring any old friends, or email anyone from the laptop she'd brought back with her. Francesca called several times but never left a message, and Kate simply let her phone ring and ring.

On Monday evening, she had rung her mother, but that merely served to unsettle her.

'Darling, so what have you been doing?' Venetia had asked brightly. 'Lots of fun superb things? Catching up with all your friends? How lovely.'

'Oh,' Kate said uneasily, 'Er, well . . . I saw Zoe.'

Venetia sounded insanely over-enthusiastic. 'Lovely! How is she?'

'Oh . . . Fine.'

There was a pause. Kate felt, as she did so many times, that she had never worked out how to show her mother her best side.

'How are the party plans for Oscar going?' she said, after a moment.

'Oh, they're exhausting,' Venetia said. 'I've booked us both into the hairdresser for the Saturday morning, I'm going to have rollers, you can have what you want – do you want a blow-dry? That's probably best, isn't it?'

'Um,' said Kate. 'Not sure – can I –'

'I don't need to let them know for a while, but if you could have a think about it.'

'Sure,' said Kate, biting her little finger and trying not to laugh, because her mother was funny, especially from a distance. 'And the party? All under control?'

'It is going to be ah-may-zing,' said Venetia fervently. 'Less than three weeks to go, my god. But you'll be back before then, won't you!' Her voice rose a little.

'Of course I will, Mum.' Kate tried not to sound stern. 'I said, right from the start, I've always said I'll be back in lots of time, I wouldn't miss Oscar's party, would I?'

'I know,' said Venetia, sounding chastened. 'It's just – well, you know how I feel about London.'

She made it sound as if London were a war criminal on the loose, persecuting her. 'Mum, you know, I'm really glad I came back,' Kate said, hearing a certainty in her voice she did not feel. 'It's been so great to see Dad –'

'Well, exactly. And how is darling Daniel?' interrupted Venetia fondly, as if darling Daniel were a particularly beloved old friend of hers, or her pet dog, not her ex-husband from whom she had parted on the most painful terms, and to whom she would refer at dinner with her New York friends, after a few glasses of wine, as 'that bastard Miller'.

'He's OK,' said Kate. In truth, Lisa had told her that day, with a semi-exasperated sigh, that the doctors thought he wasn't doing as well as he could be. He was a bad patient, that was the trouble. Nothing to worry about, the nurse who was to come and see him each day had said, but the transplant operation had knocked him for six – and they still wouldn't know for a while whether the body might reject his new kidney or not. It was a waiting game, and he was no good at waiting for something over which he had no control – especially his own body.

On Tuesday, she called Perry and Co, to check in with Bruce Perry. For some perverse reason, she wanted her boss to know she wasn't on holiday, she was back in London for a reason. She wanted him to think she cared about her job, didn't she?

'So it's all going OK?' she asked him.

170

'Sure thing!' Bruce's tone was breezy. 'We miss you, Kate! But we're just about managing here, you know. Don't you worry.'

'So is everything OK with Lorraine? You don't need . . .'

'Hey, hey. Kate.' Bruce's voice grew louder, as if he were closer to the phone. 'Lorraine isn't you, please don't misunderstand, OK? But she's great!' His voice grew distant again, as if he were announcing this to the office. Kate could hear someone laughing in the background. 'She brought donuts in today for everyone! Krispy Kreme, no less. What a gal. And she's changed a few things, it'll make your life so much easier.'

'Uhuh . . .' Kate said. 'Like what?'

'A few corrections to the filing system, and she's called a couple of authors to introduce herself. Personal touch. It was Doris's idea.'

Kate kicked the skirting board in the hallway viciously, then hopped in agony. God, that dwarfy helmet haired bitch Doris! She was a . . . bitch! She took a deep breath.

'That's great,' she said. 'What a great idea. Hey, I've got to go, Bruce, but I'll call you on Friday, OK?'

'No need, Kate!' he said. 'No call for it! You just focus on your dad, OK? And we'll see you soon. Soon as.'

Yes, they were fine without her, just fine. No, she told the voice that said loudly in her head, 'They're not missing you at all, are they?' That was the bargain I made with myself when I went to New York. A quiet life, no ties, no commitments. A life I can walk away from if I need to.

She just hadn't realized *how* easy it would be to walk away from it. To be forgotten, melt into the background.

And it went on. On Wednesday morning, she visited her father once more and on her way back she went to the shops at the edge of Elgin Avenue, to buy a few final things she needed for Mrs Allan's funeral tea the next day, and a

171

newspaper. She marched up to the desk and deposited her wares on the counter.

'Hi,' she said, brightly, and she realized it sounded almost desperate. She *wanted* to talk to the shopkeeper, wanted some human interaction.

But he just nodded, and shoved everything into a bright blue plastic bag, and when Kate said 'I don't need a bag' he looked at her coldly, as if she'd just been sick on the floor.

Kate said, feeling insane, 'How are you today?'

In New York, they would have known her name by now, smiled with utter delight when she walked in, have everything piled up and in her own bag in three seconds, and engaged in mundane but satisfying small talk while they made change. The strip lighting above the till hummed. A car outside revved loudly, and silence reverberated in the shop as the man behind the counter nodded, politely, but said nothing.

'Well . . . Bye,' said Kate. 'See you later!'

She walked out, her bag swinging by her knees, feeling mad, wanting to talk to herself, shaking her head. Suddenly, the spell of the last few days was broken. Wednesday stretched ahead of her, lonely hours spent in the flat she'd thought would be her first married home, and the only respite conversation with two old men, one sick, one grieving, one her father, one her neighbour. She opened the front door with a heavy heart.

And then Francesca rang.

'So, stranger,' said the voice on the phone, as Kate slid over and upright, as upright as she could get on the sofa. 'What. You've been back for practically a week and you don't call me. How kind. What's up?'

'I think I'm going mad, Francesca,' Kate said. 'I need a drink.' She paused. 'How are you? Are you well?'

'Fine,' said the reassuring voice, so cool and collected. 'I'm still at work. Give me thirty minutes. I'll meet you at Kettners, in the bar. Eight, OK?'

'Er . . .' said Kate, suddenly getting cold feet. That was the Centre of Town. She hadn't banked on having to go into the Centre of Town.

'That's my best offer,' said Francesca. 'Take it or leave it. I'm not schlepping over to you. I'm in Clapham, remember, or is your geography shot to hell now you're a New Yorker?'

'Shut up,' said Kate indignantly. 'Of course it's not. I'll take it. Eight p.m. See you in a bit. Bye –'

But Francesca had already put the phone down.

This, then, was it. The centre of town, the tawdry, pulsing, utterly confusing centre, filled with sights and smells and sounds. She had missed the pre-theatre chaos; coming out of the tube at Piccadilly Circus, Kate almost smiled at how awful it was, this centre of her beloved home city. The Trocadero, Eros, Shaftesbury Avenue – all marooned in a sea of traffic, swelling tourists, horrid, feral pigeons and the hotdog stands, with the ever-present smell of reconstituted pigs' eyelids, fried and sweating next to rancid onions. In New York the streets were wide, Times Square may have been Disney-fied but it was clean and friendly and open all night, and the adrenaline rush of walking through it was incomparable. There was order there, she never understood people who said New York was chaotic. This – this, she thought, as she walked up Shaftesbury Avenue, dodging caricaturists, lounging men in cheap leather jackets, angry white van drivers, gaggles of tourists with backpacks bigger than them, as she turned into the bottom of Wardour Street – *this* was chaos.

As she stepped into Soho, the traffic eased off. She walked past the little school and the church with its graveyard, so unexpected, down Old Compton Street, where a few brave souls were sitting out in the night air, celebrating the relative warmth of another sunny March day. Nostalgia was nudging her, the memories of evenings at Pulcinella's, or the tapas place round the corner, the Mayflower back across the road, or the Dog and Duck on Dean Street – she had spent vast amounts of her twenties in one of those places. And Kettners.

Kettners hadn't changed, she was relieved to see. It still kept its old-world, almost frowsy charm, a certain faded elegance mixed with a buzzy atmosphere, old-fashioned waiters who were proper waiters, not out of work actors who wanted to let you know they were great at every available opportunity. No, Kettners was old-school. It had been one of Kate's favourite places in London. She smiled at the girls behind the cloakroom counter and turned right, down a step, into the bar by the restaurant, where the old guy sat at a piano, singing 'Someone to Watch over Me' – it was always 'Someone to Watch over Me'. Memory and emotion washed over her, and she paused on the step, momentarily disorientated.

'Oi,' said a voice in the corner, and Kate looked over to see Francesca slumped on a sofa in the corner, her suit jacket bunching up, the shoulder pads standing up inches higher than she. Her long dark hair fanned out about her shoulders. She smiled at Kate, and patted the leather cushion.

Kate knelt on the sofa and hugged her, remembering as she did so how thin Francesca was.

'It's great to see you,' she said.

'You too,' said Francesca. 'About bloody time, too. Do you know it's been . . .'

'Two years,' Kate said. 'I know. I'm sorry.'

Francesca said, unexpectedly, 'I know you are. Let's not get into all that.' She cleared her throat and said dryly, 'Not until we've had a few drinks, anyway. There's a bottle of champagne on its way.'

The house champagne at Kettners was famous – it was cheap and good. A dangerous combination.

'Great.' Kate rubbed her hands, the excitement of being out finally hitting her.

'So. How've you been?' Francesca said, as a waiter gingerly placed an ice-bucket on the table and two glasses.

'No,' Kate said firmly. 'How've *you* been? I'm sick of myself, tell me how you've been. You look great, Francesca.'

'Screw that,' said Francesca. 'Kate, the mystery woman, comes back all of a sudden, and I'm going to spend the evening talking about loan structuring and how much I hate London Bridge, and how my boss is a total fucking pig? Idonthinkso. Come on, Katy. How the fuck have you been? Tell me.'

And, as if watching herself from the ceiling, Kate heard herself say, 'I don't think I should have come back.'

'Back to that flat?' Francesca nodded, and poured the champagne. 'I did wonder, you know.'

'Really?'

'Course,' said Francesca. '*I* wouldn't have, that's for sure. Why couldn't you stay with someone else?'

'Zoe?'

'Well, yes –'

'I know,' Kate said weakly. 'She's just got so much on. And what with everything. I didn't want to . . .'

'Yep,' said Francesca. She handed Kate a glass. Kate took it. She took a huge gulp of it, and the fizzing bubbles stung her nose, but she let them. It reminded her, as it always did, of something; what was it?

'How's she been?' Kate said, not wanting to hear the answer.

'You've seen her though, haven't you?'

'Yes, yes,' Kate assured her. 'I may be crap, but I'm not *that* crap.'

'Hm.' Francesca raised her eyebrows, and then she smiled, her serious dark eyes crinkling with warmth. 'Maybe you're not, darl. Zoe.' She took a sip of champagne. 'She's OK. You know she's back at work now?'

'She told me,' Kate said.

'It's – it's time for her to rebuild her life.'

'Two years and nine months.'

'Of course,' said Francesca. She ran her palm, flat, over her forehead, and Kate remembered that Francesca had loved Steve, long before Zoe had appeared on the scene. She had been his first girlfriend at university. Kate nodded at her, eyes narrowed.

'Hey!' Francesca said sharply, and she brought her palm square down onto the low table in front of them. The other drinkers looked around in surprise. Francesca said in a low voice,

'Look, I know Steve. I knew him. Remember? I went out with him for a whole blinking year, until you introduced him to that young harlot Zoe –' she smiled. 'What happened happened, OK? It wasn't your fault.'

Kate shook her head, the pain of tears already stinging at her eyes, in her nose. She smiled grimly. 'Too heavy. I'm sorry.'

'In what way?' Kate said innocently. 'God you're so literal. I mean . . .'

'I know.' Francesca laughed hollowly. 'Nice start to the evening, eh? I get out of work and come to meet you and it's like an evening with Verdi.'

She leant over and hit Kate on the arm. 'Look. Cheers, darling. It's just so nice to see you. You look different, you know?'

'How?'

'Grown-up.'

'That's what Zoe said,' Kate said, remembering. It didn't

sound like a particularly great thing to be. 'Don't feel it, myself. Anyway. How are you? How's the job, how's the house? How's . . . everything?'

'Job crap. Far too hard.' Francesca sighed. 'There's a squeeze on in our department. They do this every couple of years. Just fire a whole load of people, get some new better people in, then do the same in two years' time. So they know they've always got the best. We're in the middle of it now.'

'Are you . . .' Kate said.

'Please,' said Francesca. 'I made them millions last year. London's their most profitable office.'

'Wow,' said Kate.

'It's just – you know. It's hard.' Francesca blew air out from her bottom lip so it ruffled her fringe, as if she were trying to cool down. 'It feels like there's there's nothing left over.'

'After work?' said Kate, not sure what she meant.

'Yep,' said Francesca, nodding in agreement. 'You know what it's like.' Kate nodded uncertainly; she only vaguely remembered what it was like. Francesca went on, 'Work work work. And then – what? Everyone else is settled down, living out in –' she waved her arm vaguely '– Cheam. I don't know. Places outside town. I don't want that. It's just –' she gulped the rest of her champagne down, poured some more in. 'I didn't sign up for this. When we were younger, you know it's even depressing I can say "when we were younger", too – well, when we were younger, I didn't think this was the way it was going to be. Look at us now. At our friends. You remember Zoe and Steve's housewarming party?'

'Of course,' Kate said. She smiled. 'Funny, we were talking about it on Sunday. Me and Zoe.'

'I remember that evening so clearly,' Francesca said. 'Mainly because I couldn't drink that much, I was on

177

antibiotics. I remember just looking round the room at all of us, thinking how great everything was.' She laughed, bitterly. 'Look what's happened to all of us since. Zoe, *Steve*, Mac, you, me – even Sean . . .' She dropped their names in like stones, hitting the palm of her hand with her fingers each time and then she gestured around the room, and Kate shuddered, involuntarily, remembering Charly's letters, which she still had done nothing about. She took a deep breath, and blinked, pushing it all away, down inside her.

'We're scattered all over the place now, all of us, aren't we?' Francesca said. Her face clouded over, then she laughed. 'Look at us. Tell you what, let's stop being maudlin. You're back and it's wonderful to see you, babe. Tell me about New York and I'll tell you about my new bathroom. It's got heated floor tiles. If that doesn't cheer us up, nothing will.'

'My god,' Kate recovered herself. 'You're living the dream.'

'It's true,' Francesca said. 'I'm the only landlady in Clapham offering heated floor tiles.'

'How's your flatmate?' Kate couldn't remember her name, a whey-faced girl Francesca had worked with.

'Sara? She moved in with her boyfriend, a couple of months ago. I had to get someone else. Oh my god, I forgot to tell you, Kate darling – at the moment I'm lucky because I've got – oh yes? Hello. Thanks, another bottle.'

Kate nodded fervently in agreement as the waitress moved away.

'Where was I? Yes. Let's play Who Would You Do?' Francesca said. 'It's been far too long.' She shook out her hair decisively. 'God this is nice.'

'Who Would You Do?' Kate asked.

'Him,' said Francesca, nodding at the man next to them, who was extremely short, with thinning, all over sparse black hair, who was grunting slightly as he worked his way through an elaborate cocktail.

'You wish,' Kate said.

'He's your boyfriend.'

'He's *yours*.'

'How about you?'

'Who Would I Do . . . ?' Kate mused. She looked round, surreptitiously. 'Him. Actually, seriously, I would.'

They swivelled round together, again incurring the curious stares of their fellow drinkers. There, in the doorway, was an actually remarkably good-looking man, bulky, tall, something of the rugby player about him, close-cropped curly dark brown hair, an open, handsome face. He was looking round the room, and smiled at them gently, before being claimed by a rather cross-looking, short girl who leapt up and waved, her fingers wiggling in the air.

'Dom! Dom! Over here! *Dom!*'

Kate and Francesca looked back at each other, chastened.

'All right, calm down,' Francesca muttered crossly. 'Don't get your knickers in a twist, dear. Ah, second bottle. Right, my turn.'

'Who Would You Do?'

'Him,' said Francesca, pointing again at the gorgeous Dom, and both of them collapsed in laughter.

CHAPTER SEVENTEEN

After the second bottle of champagne, everything was a bit of a blur. In the file Kate kept in her brain called Things I Must Remember When Sober (a file that is neurologically impossible to access, unfortunately) she filed the fact that Francesca paid the bill, insisting she should, and the fact that she thought the waiters probably hated them both, as they got more and more helplessly giggly. And the fact that it was great to be out, to be back, to see Francesca, to laugh and have a drink and gossip and talk about things: important things, silly things – just talk. That, she remembered, though the particulars of their conversation weren't so clear.

She didn't, however, remember the following things:

What else they talked about.

What time they left.

How they got home.

The next day, she thought wearily that the difference between New York and London was that in New York it was impossible to get anyone to behave like that, whereas in London it was impossible to meet a friend like Francesca for 'a' drink and not get knee-walking, eyeball-bleedingly drunk. It *should* be possible, it just never was.

She remembered that they decided to go back to Francesca's, because Kate wanted to see the heated bathroom tiles, suddenly she was desperate to see them. This she remembered. She also remembered:

Francesca's front path had black and white tiles leading up to the front door.

They stopped at a cash-point on the way back. It was blue.

She had asked Francesca if she knew how she could find out where Charly was now. Where she was living.

But she couldn't remember the answer.

So the next morning, Kate woke up, and she was chewing her own hair, and it was half strangling her, half choking her. Her mouth felt like she'd been using it to store vinegar. She rolled around in bed, her mind a total blank, trying to remember where she was, what she'd done the night before. For a brief, hangover-induced moment, she thought with panic that her mind must have been wiped during the night, like a broken iPod. She looked at the pale, ascetic walls around her, through the window at the bare trees with buds outside, and then she looked at the wall next to her. There was a photo, and she recognized herself, Zoe, Betty, and Francesca, all in 'formal' dress, the night of Zoe's house-warming party all those years ago . . . Her arms were slung through Zoe's and Betty's, she was bent double, laughing at something Betty was saying, pulling the others down with her in hysterics . . .

Kate blinked and stared at the photo again. Yes, that was it. She was here, at Francesca's, in her room, wearing a strange small vest and some baggy boys' boxers – but where was Francesca?

Downstairs, someone was moving about in the kitchen, and Kate rubbed her eyes. She felt dreadful. She swung her legs out of bed and picked up a dressing gown hanging on the back of the wooden door. She raked her hands through her hair, clutching her scalp as she did. It felt warm. Was her blood actually boiling due to the amount of alcohol in her brain? Was that it? Kate stumbled downstairs, holding her head, her hair.

'God, I feel awful,' she said to the figure rustling the paper loudly, too loudly.

The figure looked over the paper.

It wasn't Francesca.

'Mac?' Kate whispered.

'Kate.'

Mac was looking up at her from his paper, his eyes locked on hers. He didn't move. He looked as if he'd seen a ghost.

'What are you doing here?' Kate said softly.

'I live here,' he said. His jaw tightened; he opened his mouth to say something, then shut it. His voice was deadly quiet. 'I might ask you what *you're* doing here.'

'You don't live here,' Kate said, confused. Her champagne-scrambled brain was turning over in itself, desperately trying to remember what Francesca had said last night.

'Sara? She moved in with her boyfriend, a couple of months ago. I had to get someone else. Oh my god, I forgot to tell you, Kate darling – at the moment I'm lucky because I've got . . . Thanks, another bottle.'

He hadn't forgiven her for what she'd done. Had he? Kate forced herself to look at him. She looked at his hands first, how one of them was clutching the side of the paper so hard it was in a fist, the paper crumpling around it, like a rosette, and he threw it on the table, and stood up. He was tall, she always forgot how tall. She took a step towards him, not allowing herself to look at him. The two of them stood there in silence. Memories of the last time she'd seen him came rushing at her . . . but she pushed them away. No, she didn't let herself think of it any more.

Vaguely, somewhere else in her head, Kate heard the sound of the shower, in another corner of the house. It recalled her to her senses, and she finally looked straight up at Mac, and it was then that she felt it. She was almost felled by the venom in his eyes, the anger, the disgust, that he felt for her. Kate backed away, quailing under the force of his stare.

'I do live here,' he said. 'Temporarily. I'm looking for a place.' He collected himself, as if he didn't want to give too much away to her. 'Anyway. Why the hell are you here?'

She couldn't think of an adequate reply. 'I didn't realize you lived here. I was out with Francesca last night. Sorry . . .'

'Fine.' He looked out of the window, collected himself for a moment. 'Francesca's in the shower. Do you want some tea?'

'Oh, yes, that'd be –'

'Kettle's just boiled,' he said, and went back to the paper.

'Thank – thanks,' Kate said, and she went forward timidly to the kettle. Her head was pounding, and her heart was beating. Ghosts everywhere, she thought. Can't escape them. She looked up at the clock. It was eight o'clock. She'd told Mr Allan she'd be with him at nine.

'Shit,' she said.

Mac ignored her.

'I've got to go,' Kate said, retreating back up the stairs to the sitting room. 'Something's – I'm supposed to be somewhere.'

'Sure you are,' he said, looking up at her briefly. His tone was careless, almost conversational. 'You'd better be off. You're good at that, aren't you? Running off.'

Kate felt something inside her release, with a ping.

'I didn't mean to,' she said, turning towards him, all fear gone.

'What?' he said, surprised. His head jerked up and she noticed the grey hairs at the sides of his head, at his temples.

'It wasn't my fault, Mac.' She was calm. 'I mean, it was my fault, but – I've paid for it. I know you hate me. I know I screwed up.' She cleared her throat.

'What are you talking about?' he said.

Kate stared at him, almost with exasperation. 'Mac! You know what I'm –'

'No, I don't,' he said, his voice almost vicious. 'You see, Kate, you've screwed my life up not just once but – yeah, actually, a couple of times. In every way. So when you troop in here and say you're oh so sorry, I'm not sure for which of the several ways you've managed to ruin things you're apologizing.'

She tried to swallow, but she couldn't. 'Listen to me. I didn't mean . . .' she began, but he started laughing.

'Oh, that's a big consolation to me,' said Mac, still holding onto the newspaper. His eyes were cold, cold green and unflinching. 'You didn't mean to. Wow. Is that supposed to make everything better? Look, Kate, just forget it. I don't want to have this discussion with you. OK?'

'It's not OK,' said Kate. 'You – me – we . . . that . . . everything that happened.' She pulled the paper swiftly out of his hands. It sliced one of his fingers, such was the speed with which she did it. Mac breathed in sharply, and stood up. He moved towards her, and Kate actually thought for one moment he was going to hit her. 'Everything that happened,' she said, leaning towards him. Fight it. Fight fear with fear, she told herself, dragging up some strength from she didn't know where, suddenly conscious of her dressing gown, her shorts, her skimpy top. They stood, facing each other, the tension palpable.

184

'I'm never going to not think it was your fault,' he said simply. He pressed his finger to his other palm; she saw blood where she had cut him. 'That's all. It was you, Kate. After everything that happened, we could have made it better, you and me.' For a brief second she saw tenderness in his eyes, and she knew he remembered it the way she did, and it hurt her so much more than she'd thought it could. 'But you went and broke it all over again. And that's why I'll never, ever not think it was your fault.'

She hit the side of a cabinet, her bones smacking hard into the wood. She winced, and he fractionally winced with her.

'You don't know what you're talking about –'

Mac ignored her, carried on as if she hadn't spoken.

'You ran away *again*,' he said, exasperation all over his lean, tired face. She thought how much older he was looking. 'God. God –!' He half-turned away. 'You never even wrote.'

'I did write, Mac, I did,' she said, justifying herself, and it sounded so weak.

He waved it away, and turned to her, his eyes so full of pain she could hardly bear it. 'My god! It's like a nightmare. All of this is a nightmare, and it's because of –'

Francesca appeared at the top of the stairs leading down to the kitchen. 'Ah,' she said, casually, doing up the buttons on her black city jacket. 'Morning – Kate. I'm hideously late. Gosh, you look awful.'

'Francesca –' said Kate, but Francesca carried on,

'Look at this nice surprise, eh? I meant to warn you who my –'

'She's going, anyway, don't worry.' Mac flicked his fingers dismissively at Kate. 'She's got things to do.' He took a deep breath and winced, and then he turned back to his paper.

That was when Kate snapped, backing away from him, sudden tears sprouting and streaming down her face.

'Why don't you understand?' she screamed. 'Do you think it was easy for me? Mac, there was *nothing else I could do*!'

Running up the stairs, pushing past an astonished Francesca, she fell into the bedroom and pulled on last night's clothes. Barely a minute later, she ran down the stairs again. Francesca was standing in the hallway.

'What on earth's going on?' she said.

'I've got to –' Kate sobbed, her eyes puffy. She wiped her nose. 'I'm going, please don't – sorry, darling.'

'You and Mac?' said Francesca, her brow furrowed. 'Wowsers. I always wondered. When did –?'

Mac appeared in the corridor, his bulk blocking the light from the kitchen. He touched Francesca lightly on the arm, his eyes never straying from Kate's face.

'Let her go,' he said, bleakly. 'Please, Francesca.'

'Just wait, Kate, I'll walk to the –'

'No, no,' said Kate, breathing in, and trying to smile like it was all OK. 'I'm late, I really am, I have to go –'

And she ran out into the street, pulling the door shut in Francesca and Mac's faces. It slammed loudly behind her. It was cold and grey outside, the sky a uniform blanket of cloud. Ghosts. The ghosts in London were everywhere.

CHAPTER EIGHTEEN

Kate blinked back fatigue and hangover. The Allans' sitting room was hot and crowded, and the exertions of the morning – getting back from Clapham, running around trying to get everything ready by the time the mourners returned from the crematorium, chatting, pouring drinks, soothing, handing things round: she hadn't stopped rushing and moving since she'd left Francesca's, four hours before, and now she was ready to drop, heartsick, champagne-soaked and miserable. Especially now, when she'd seen darling Mr Allan enter the room, back from the crematorium, pulling his black trilby off his head, pushing his fluffy white hair back from his face, which was crumpled with grief. Pain, screaming, horrible pain was etched into every line, it filled his eyes, and he suddenly looked much, much older than Kate had ever realized him to be. He had smiled at her, just a little smile, and said,

'Dear Kate. Ah. Here we are back again then.'

She'd poured him a glass of wine, as his family started streaming through the door, followed by the Allans' friends, his old jazz buddies, creaky-looking musicians in checked shirts and cords, neighbours from the building – Kate realized with a start how few people she'd ever known here, how she and Sean had never really bothered to get to know anyone apart from the Allans.

Now, an hour later, the room was full, stuffy and throbbing slowly with the buzz of good conversation and emotion hanging over the assembled throng. Kate was feeling worse and worse. Why had she put on a woolly top? She swayed slightly, trying to focus on those around her, and turned to find a serious, rather elongated man staring at her. She blinked and looked again. She knew him – how did she know him?

'Ow!' Fred Michaels, singer with the Chappell Quartet, and Mr Allan's oldest mucker, was wailing in the kitchen. 'Oh! Look, my finger's burnt!'

'Oh, Mr M, I'm sorry,' Kate cried, squeezing past the throng and rushing into the kitchen. 'You should use *oven gloves*,' she said loudly to him.

'I'm not bloody deaf,' said Fred Michaels. 'Keep your voice down. It's a wake for the deceased, not an Iron Maiden concert,' he added, as the old man next to him sniggered.

'Good one, Fred,' he said.

'Thanks Frank,' Fred replied. 'Ho, ho.'

'Leave her alone,' said Mr Allan, coming into the kitchen. He put his arm around Kate. 'She's doing a brilliant job, absolutely brilliant.'

'Er, thanks,' said Kate. She tugged her straggly ponytail tighter, rather distractedly.

'Where are the plastic cups?' Mr Allan said.

Kate handed them to him. 'Are you OK?' she said.

'No. But I will be,' Mr Allan said. He blew air out of his cheeks, in a low, whistling sound. 'Oh. My sister's just asked me to go on holiday with her.'

'She mentioned it to me,' said Kate, nonchalantly flicking at the kitchen surface with a tea towel. 'So – are you going to go, do you think?'

He waved his hand towards the window, where it was grey outside. 'Think I might, you know. Just for a couple of weeks. The only question is,' he said, his arm tightening around her, 'Are *you* going to be OK without *me*?'

She could feel his comforting, bony arm around her, his fingers pressing into her shoulder, and the kindness of the gesture took her by surprise.

'Well,' Kate said, looking at the ground so he couldn't see how close to tears she was, 'if that's your only question, then you should definitely go, don't you think?'

'Hm. Maybe.' He kissed the top of her head. 'Thanks, sweetheart.' He nodded, and then poked Fred. 'Are you ready to do some singing?'

Fred nodded, 'Absolutely,' as Frank said,

'I'll just go and get the sax.'

'Ssh please,' Fred said, five minutes later, and the crowd packed into the room was silent, and the only noise was the faint roar of traffic from outside, where the windows were still open.

'This is for Eileen,' he continued. 'Gram, do you want to say anything?'

But Mr Allan simply shook his head.

'I want to say,' said Fred, and his voice was very quiet, Kate had to strain to hear, 'I want to say that I was there when they met, I was there by their side when they got married, I was there to see them through years of happiness together and Gram –' he turned to his friend, who had his head bowed, holding his trumpet tightly to his chest, 'I'm glad we're all here now with you. Here's to Eileen. This is her favourite song. This was her favourite song.'

He nodded to the rest of the group. Kate leant against the kitchen door, her hands in the pockets of her apron, resting her tired head against the wooden frame, and he started to sing, in a husky voice, the old standard, 'That's All'.

When Kate went back downstairs at about six o'clock, her face was swollen and aching with the effort of not crying, of smiling kindly, of soothing, patting arms, clearing up. Suddenly her sitting room looked huge with just her in it, where his had been packed to the rafters with people, friends and ghosts, and memories. Here all was white and safe and clean and it was different, weird. She looked around the room, undoing her apron tiredly. She sniffed, loudly.

'Hello?' came a voice from close by, and Kate jumped. It was from the other side of her front door.

'Hello?' it said again. 'Kate, are you in there?'

It was a woman's voice. A woman's voice she knew.

'Hi. Kate?' said the voice again.

'Who is it?' she said cautiously.

'Kate, it's Sue. Sue Jordan.'

Sue Jordan – of course. How could she have forgotten. Kate flung the door open as fast as she could.

Sue's face broke into a smile at the sight of her but she didn't move. She simply nodded.

'Here's the reason the circulation of my magazine's a disaster.'

'Why?' Kate said, stepping forward and hugging her.

'Went downhill after my star girl left, didn't it?' Sue said, squeezing her briefly.

'I'm so sorry,' Kate said.

'For what?'

It really was Sue Jordan standing in front of her, like a package from the past. She hadn't changed much since the day she'd interviewed Kate for the job, seven and a half years ago. She had a neat sandy bob, was dressed in a sensible grey suit, with a large, stiff black handbag over her shoulder.

190

She had smile lines at the corners of her eyes, Kate had always noticed that, because Sue never smiled at work, well hardly ever. She used to think it must mean Sue smiled a lot at home.

Sue was smiling at Kate now. 'You'd forgotten all about me, hadn't you,' she said.

'No –' said Kate. 'Of course not, it's just –'

'The context. I know,' said Sue. 'Completely out of context. I knocked on your door on Monday after we'd been to see Graham, but there was no answer.'

'I must have been with Dad,' said Kate. 'Sorry.'

'Don't be sorry, silly girl,' said Sue, and she stepped forward, breaking an invisible wall of some kind, reached out and gave Kate a hug. Just a quick one, but a hug nonetheless, and the unexpected physical contact from her, from Sue, brought a lump to Kate's throat. 'I'm sorry I didn't see you in there –' Sue jabbed a finger upwards '– I was late, had to stay at the crematorium to sort a couple of things out. I could see you, talking to people, and handing that lovely food round, you are wonderful. But I kept missing you, and it was so crowded – I thought I'd do best to come down after it quietened down and catch you then.'

'Come in, come in!' Kate said.

'I won't, actually,' said Sue. 'Alec's in the car with Graham, we're taking him off for a meal in town. At the French House. It was his and Eileen's favourite. His idea, you know.'

'Aaah,' Kate said. 'Well – it was –'

'Kate.' Sue stepped back, and looked at her shrewdly. 'You're back now, aren't you?'

'What?'

'For good, I mean. You are staying this time, aren't you?'

'No,' Kate said, shaking her head. 'Just a couple of weeks, till my father's better, I've got to get back to New York after that.'

'Hm,' said Sue. 'So you're not interested in getting back into magazines, then.'

Kate looked up from paint-flicking, carelessly. 'What?'

'Well, you remember Sophie?'

'Yes,' said Kate. 'Sophie, of course.'

'Well, she was writing a column for *Venus*. "Girl About Town". Intrepid girl struggling through the concrete jungle, kind of thing.' Sophie was a hearty, walking-boots kind of person. 'But she's just announced she's fallen in love with some bloody Moroccan geezer from Essaouira, and she's moving there to live on the beach and sell sea shells, or something ridiculous.'

'Sophie?' said Kate, pleased. How unexpected people's lives were, especially those you hadn't thought about for so long.

'Kate,' said Sue. She cleared her throat and faced up to Kate. 'Listen. Write me five hundred words. About what you love about London. Say you've just come back to live here.' Her eyes shone. 'That's even better. Girl returns to the big smoke after two years living in New York. Her impressions, all that. What she likes about London. Yes. And come in for a chat with me about it. Tomorrow. No, not tomorrow. Um, let me think. Tuesday.' She rolled her eyes. 'Look, I want you to do it.'

'Her column?' Kate was being slow; her brain, she realized, was dehydrated, exhausted. She could follow Sue's ideas, but she was about a minute behind them; she'd forgotten how fast she thought.

'Yes. Her column. Like I say –' Sue repeated herself, slowly. 'Write me five hundred words, email them over on Monday. It's a sign, all of this –' she waved her arms, briskly, and cleared her throat again. 'I always thought you were the best. You are the best. I want you back, Kate.'

Kate swallowed; the lump in her throat was giving way

to a feeling of tightness in her chest. 'But I've got a job,' she said, smiling at her old boss, politely. 'Sue, that's – wow, that's amazing, but I've got a job.'

She hoped this would knock it on the head. But Sue fixed her gaze on her, and plunged her tongue into her cheek. There was silence between them.

'No you haven't,' Sue said eventually. 'I don't know what you're doing out there, but don't call it a job.'

'Actually, it's –'

'You're the assistant, Kate.'

It had been a long day – a longer night and day. Kate hugged the doorframe, tapping the wood with her fingers. 'What's wrong with being an assistant, Sue! That's a dreadful thing to say!'

A car horn sounded outside. Sue wrapped her scarf around her neck. 'Look,' she said. 'You're my girl. You've been my girl since you were that baby giraffe with long legs and big brown eyes looking terrified at your interview, what was it – eight years ago? Now, I know what happened to you was shit, it was awful, and it must be awful being back here. But you belong here, Kate. You just have to get used to it. Can't you see that?'

'I don't belong here,' Kate said. 'And I certainly don't belong in magazines.'

'That is the biggest rubbish of all,' said Sue. 'Look at you, your life is straight out of a magazine! You've got enough material from your life to be still writing copy fifty years from now! Don't you understand, Kate, every girl is basically like you. Every *Venus* reader, especially.'

Kate laughed. 'I bloody well hope not, for their sakes.'

'Not that,' Sue shook her head, impatient that Kate didn't get it. 'They all think they're useless, or they've screwed their life up, or their relationship with their parents is awful, when are they going to have children, they don't know what

193

they want to do with their lives. They should have married X. They let Y get away. They don't have enough money for Z. We're all the same, you know, it's just different versions of being the same.' She looked Kate up and down. 'Except you've always been skinny. I kind of hate you for that.' She buttoned up her coat. 'Right. You'll have a go at it, then?'

'Yes,' said Kate. 'Yes, I will. I'll email it on Monday.' Her eyes were shining. 'Thanks, Sue.'

'Thank me next week, dollface,' came the reply. 'Now I'm going. But thanks for today, you're a star.'

Kate shut the door behind her and, irresistibly, started to laugh. She didn't know why, but she couldn't stop. And then she stopped laughing, and stood up to her full height, thoughtfully. Squaring her shoulders, she went into her bedroom to unearth her old stack of *Venus* copies. They were there, underneath her beloved telescope, fifteen or so of them and at the top, the first issue, with its classic, Fifties-style type, its pretty and stylish shades, the girl on the front running to catch a bus on Piccadilly, wearing TopShop's newest spring bell-shaped raincoat, in apple green linen. She had loved that cover, loved everything about what they were trying to do ... Kate gingerly moved the telescope out of the way and crouched down, thumbing through the slippery, shiny covers, marvelling at them, what *Venus* represented to her. Where had that Kate gone?

CHAPTER NINETEEN

May 2003

'But I mean come on, he's *gorgeous*!' said Juliet, the Fashion Editor, stroking the silk of a top she'd brought in to show the meeting that polka dots were on their way back in. 'He's like an older Marco Pierre White. Except not mad. God, I love him.'

'Did you see him comforting that shit flute player girl from Italy last night?' said Jo, the Art Director.

'I know!'

'Who is he?' demanded Sue Jordan and Priscilla, the supersucky News Editor and Deputy Editor said, immediately,

'Daniel Miller. He's on that TV show, *Maestro!* It's like Pop Stars. He's gorgeous, Sue.'

'Daniel Miller?' said Sue. From her lofty position at the head of the table she called down to Kate. 'Hold on. Let me just ask our lovely Features Editor something – Kate, isn't he your father?'

Kate, who had been staring out of the great glass windows across the river at the South Bank during this conversation, turned back to the group. She smoothed a fleck of imaginary lint off her grey Joseph suit, her most expensive clothing purchase ever.

'Um, yes.' She scratched her hair with a pencil, and hummed nonchalantly. 'I suppose he is.'

'What?' said Tom Price, the publisher of the magazine. 'Daniel Miller's your father? My god!'

'Are you shitting me?' said Juliet. 'Kate Miller. Daniel Miller. Oh my god!'

'Wow!' said Priscilla, trying and failing to look pleased for Kate at her genetic heritage, which had given her these inadvertent brownie points.

'He's your *dad*?' said Nicola, the deputy features editor. 'Why didn't you *say so*!?'

Kate thought back to eighteen months ago, before the show had been commissioned, and how close Daniel had come to having to sell his house and move into a flat in Acton. 'It didn't exactly come up.'

'Why doesn't he like being sent chocolates?' Nicola demanded. 'There was an interview with him in *Good Housekeeping* and he said he hated being sent chocolates. That's so weird! But sexy of him!'

'He's diabetic,' said Kate in quelling tones. 'He can't eat sugar. It's really bad for him. People are always sending him presents after recitals, and so forth. Right. Shall we move on?'

And so forth? When was the last time she'd said 'and so forth'?

'Wow,' said Priscilla. She drummed her square nails loudly on the glass surface. 'This is great, Kate. Can you get us an interview with him? And tell him not to go with anyone else? Oh my god!' Her eyes lit up. 'He's divorced, isn't he? I read it in *Hello!* last week,' she told the assembled faces around the table, who were gaping with interest. 'His wife ran off with someone. Isn't that true?'

'She's my mum,' Kate said sharply. 'And she didn't *run off* with someone. She –' She was extremely thankful when Nicola interrupted.

'Well, I know he was devastated! Is he looking for love? Perhaps that's the angle! We could fix him up with someone!'

'Hm,' 'Mmm,' 'Ooh, that's a good idea,' various people murmured, not without bitterness, as if Kate had organized all of this merely to advance her career.

Kate clutched her big, square notebook, hugging it to her. It was quite funny, really, to think how the fortunes of the Miller family ebbed and flowed, resulting in this completely ridiculous conversation. She was almost laughing; she wished Charly or Zoe was here to hear it. Sean wouldn't get it, she thought to herself, bless him. He'd be outraged on all their behalfs. 'Right,' she said, feeling sympathy for the very first time with celebrities who complain about how misrepresented they are. 'First, that's my mother you're talking about and she didn't run off with someone else. She left Dad because it wasn't working.'

'Why?' said Priscilla, fascinated.

'Oh.' Kate was flummoxed. 'Well, I don't know why, actually. It just wasn't working.' They looked blankly at her. 'I was fourteen,' she offered. She didn't say, *it was the day after my birthday, and I didn't see her for over a year afterwards.*

'Mmm.'

'Plus, it was thirteen years ago,' Kate pointed out. 'It's long-passed water under the bridge. They're the best of friends, now.'

Since last week her father had referred to her mother's request for him to send her their wedding album (she'd just got into scrapbooking) as 'another demand from Satan's bitch minion' and then roared loudly 'GOD! I hate her!!' This was not at all true but, for now, here at this meeting, it would have to suffice, because she certainly wasn't going into the whole long drama with them.

'And what about your poor dad?' Juliet's eyes were like saucers. 'That's sad for him, though. Is he still on his own?'

Kate thought of the sopranos, the violin students and fans who'd littered his bedroom and the rest of the house after Venetia left, whom Kate had had to fight past on her way to school in the morning. It was like running the gauntlet every day – one never knew if Natalia from Moscow, or Briony from Colorado, might be trying to be domestic in the kitchen, making coffee for their hero, and catch her on the way out, plying her with insincere compliments, pumping her for information, how best to snare her father. Kate had to be polite to them, but it made her uncomfortable. She much preferred the constant stream of good friends, old compadres, who filled the house, always had done, filling it with music and laughter and expensive red wine, late into the night. The question was ridiculous, in any case. Her father, on his own! It was almost laughable.

Then she thought of his life since he'd met Lisa, how all of that had gone, how her home, the spindly house in Kentish Town, had been sold, how order and beige colours had entered his life. Someone had written of Daniel Miller in the *Observer* a couple of weeks ago that he was a marketing exercise now, not a musician, and Kate couldn't help but agree, secretly. It had taken Lisa six months to move in, a couple of months after that to get pregnant, ten months to get her old friends from GMTV where she'd worked to meet him, and a year later he was back in the studio, recording *Daniel Miller plays Glen Miller*. And now he could afford a wedding where his wife wore Temperley couture and the guests were each given a small silver violin charm engraved with Lisa and Daniel's initials and the date as a memento. Kate shook her head.

'He's not on his own, no,' she told the assembled meeting. She coughed. 'It's his second wedding tomorrow, actually.'

There was astonishment around the table. This was news.

'Wow,' said Tom, still unnaturally fascinated. 'Is someone taking the photos? Have they got a magazine deal?'

'No,' said Kate, holding her pencil. 'At least, I really really hope not. Otherwise I'll have to wear a yashmak.'

'Don't you mean a burqa?' asked Priscilla, faux-kindly.

'No.' Kate put her pencil back down on the table.

'Sure you do, Kate.'

'A burqa's a whole garment thing. A yashmak is just a veil, er – it's mainly worn by Muslim women, usually Turkish,' Kate heard herself say, and then she groaned inwardly.

'How *do* you know this stuff!' Priscilla trilled. 'You're like a fat old man in a pub quiz! Oh Kate. You are funny.'

'What, because she knows something else beyond how much combined weight the Spice Girls have lost this week?' said Juliet, unexpectedly and Kate looked at her in surprise and smiled.

'Right, right.' Sue patted the glass desk with a gesture of finality. She nodded kindly at Kate. 'That's all for now, then,' she said. 'Let's meet on Monday as usual and Kate – enjoy the wedding.'

As Kate gathered up her things, her Filofax, her ideas book, the latest issues of the magazine, Sue followed her out, towards her office.

'You OK about tomorrow?' she said, as Kate reached her desk. 'Just wondering.'

Sue was not given to sentiment or overt displays of affection, and Kate turned back to look at her, smiling with gratitude. She was Features Editor, only because of Sue, and it was the most unimaginable, thrilling, exciting thing.

After the weeks and weeks of interviews, the secrecy surrounding the whole thing, she had finally left *Woman's World* to be Deputy Features Editor in time for the launch of *Venus* in early 2002. But the original Features Editor, Alice

– who was more of the Fashionista school and believed in claiming every single cab, and once even her own husband's birthday dinner, on expenses – had not lasted until the launch and so, just before Christmas 2001, Kate had been promoted to Features Editor.

Thinking of this now, Kate patted Sue's arm, lightly – the two of them were rare in the *Venus* offices for not going in for displays of affection. There was a lot of surplus airkissing; Sue didn't like it much. Nor did she like anorexic models, hugely expensive photoshoots in Miami to get a shot of a model against a white wall, overpaid, irrelevant columnists, or fashion itself, really. It was why Broadgate had hired her to head up the magazine. They wanted someone with a fresh eye, someone who could keep costs down, and someone who could assemble a team of young people who *did* know all of that.

'It's going to be great,' she told Sue. 'It's not like I can't wait and it's the best day of my life, but you know . . . I'm really happy for Dad. Lisa's turned his life around.'

'I'm so glad,' Sue said. She looked around Kate's small glass office. 'It must be weird, that's all.'

'Yeah, it is a bit.' Kate was always honest with Sue. 'But Sean's coming. And Zoe and Steve – our best friends, you know. They got married last year, you remember you got that wedding company to provide the free sugared almonds?'

'Little Zoe, with the black hair.' Sue was pleased. 'Ah, lovely. How is she?'

'She's very well,' said Kate. 'She's pregnant, in fact, so she's really well.'

'Well, it'll be good for you to have a gang of your own there.'

'And Charly's coming,' Kate added, mischievously.

Sue looked mock-horrified. 'Right. A gang indeed.'

'She's wearing black, and she told my mother on the

200

phone last night that she'd scream "No!" during the speeches if she wants her to.'

Sue genuinely looked horrified this time. 'Oh dear god, she is something, isn't she. What did your poor mother say?'

'History doesn't relate,' said Kate, laughing. 'But I expect, knowing Mum, she'd love it if it was all about her instead.'

She could tell Sue didn't know whether to laugh or not at this and she waved goodbye and scurried, relieved, back to her own office. Kate turned back to her desk and picked up the phone. Sean was staying at hers tonight before the wedding, and she wanted to make sure he'd remember to bring everything. He hated staying over, much preferred it if she came to his, and would doubtless forget something. On her desk were the layouts for the next issue's Quiz: WHO'S IN CHARGE OF YOUR RELATIONSHIP? YOU OR HIM?

'Hah,' said Kate, putting her heels up on the desk as Sean's phone rang. She swung herself round to look out of the window again, and caught her reflection in the glass. That was her, that girl in the grey suit with the smooth hair and the office. How weird. She sighed with something like happiness, waiting for Sean to pick up the phone, and gazed out across the river. The spring view of the city from her office window really was lovely.

CHAPTER TWENTY

The next morning, the day of the wedding, Kate climbed back into bed, handed Sean a cup of tea, and said happily,

'It's going to be a lovely day. Not a cloud in the sky, it's already warm and it's not even eight!'

'So why are we awake then?' Sean grumbled, putting his mug of tea on the side table, turning over and pulling the duvet over his head.

Kate sat up in bed and sipped cautiously, testing the heat of the tea, letting her cold feet warm up a little under the duvet. She hooked a foot over Sean's leg and took another gulp of tea.

'Aaah,' she heard herself say, as if she were sixty and not twenty-seven. 'Ah.'

There was silence.

'Sean, is your shirt ironed?' she said, tentatively.

'Yes,' Sean rumbled, deep underneath the duvet.

'Because I could always just run over it again with the iron.'

'It's ironed,' Sean said. 'Shh.'

Kate wanted everything on her side to be perfect. She was Daniel's daughter, she had to keep the Miller family end up. She didn't want people looking at her and smiling, whispering to each other: 'His daughter, the one who had the mullet and was obsessed with Sylvia Plath – she really did turn out rather strange, didn't she?' No, she wanted her father, all his many friends and colleagues, and all of Lisa's family, to be proud of her. Briefly the thought crossed her mind: what if she'd had to go on her own, single, or go just with Charly, Zoe and Steve, what if she didn't have Sean? Truly horrible to have to go to that alone, your father's glamorous second wedding to the mother of his new child. Thank god for Sean, she thought again, and she put down her mug and snuggled down next to him.

'Sorry,' she whispered, pulling the duvet up and around her. 'I'll let you sleep.' She was tired, too; her new job was exhausting, juggling it with everything else. She put her arm around Sean, but he was snoring lightly and even though she wanted to sleep again too, she couldn't. Instead Kate lay there for another hour, blinking, staring up at the ceiling from underneath the duvet, thinking.

After a while she started to hear strange noises, banging, clattering, furious muttering, coming from the sitting room and the kitchen, and she winced every time one was particularly loud, not wanting it to wake Sean. It grew louder, and louder, as the hour wore on. Charly was up, and getting ready. It was a big operation, requiring a lot of noise, and a lot of equipment, at the end of which (Kate always thought, but never said out loud) Charly looked *exactly* the same, only more terrifying, and less sweet-faced than she looked when she was in her pyjamas, wolfing down toast, and swearing at the TV, or in hysterics over a video, or lounging around chatting on the phone. That was when Charly was at her most beautiful, Kate had come to see, but Charly had no idea.

There was a loud bang and a muffled, expletive-laden rant began.

'What's that?' said Sean, blearily, turning towards Kate. She pushed herself against him, hoping he'd pull her into his big, warm, morning embrace, but his arms were crossed on his chest and he was still half-asleep.

'Only Charly, sorry,' said Kate. 'She's so noisy. Don't worry. You should be getting up soon though . . .'

'She's doing it deliberately, stupid cow,' Sean said. He rubbed his face. 'Blaghh.' And with that, he dozed off again, and Kate sighed. Of course she wasn't. Probably . . .

Because Charly couldn't stand Sean. Kate tried her best, but it was too much like hard work after a while, too awkward.

'I just don't get you,' Kate said to Charly later that morning, after Sean had gone out to pick up Zoe and Steve, and the two flatmates were left to get ready. Anticipation, and irritation, made Kate bolder with her than she would normally have been. 'Do you really think he's that awful?'

Charly was sprawled out on the sofa, which was covered with an old batik cloth. She was dressed from head to toe in black, even black boots. It was the height of summer. Her long, tousled caramel-coloured hair hung over the arm of the sofa. Kate looked at her in the mirror, as she was drying her hair. Charly's perfect, tilted nose wrinkled.

'Look, Kate darling,' she said, in her husky, Cockney voice, 'I know he's not the Devil. Or a kiddy-fiddler. OK? I just don't like him. Got it? I don't bloody have to, do I ?'

She lit another cigarette and roughed her hand through her hair.

'But why,' Kate said in a small voice, still holding the hairdryer in her hand.

'I just don't.' She exhaled, and then turned to look at her. Her voice softened. 'Look, darling. I'm sure he's fine. I just think . . . he's . . . well, he's such a fucking *boy*.' Her voice was contemptuous.

'A boy?' Kate said, thinking of how big Sean was, how he dwarfed everyone and everything, how small she felt when she was with him, in his arms. 'Are you mad? He's the size of a house, for starters. He rowed for his college!'

'I'm sure, babe,' Charly said. 'But he's still a little boy.' She paused, and looked at Kate from under her lashes, obviously considering how far she could go, whether she'd already gone too far. 'That's what I think, anyway.'

'So you think he's a bit childish,' Kate persisted, hoping that now she'd got her talking, she'd tell her more. 'Has he pissed you off? Was it when he came as a baby to our fancy dress party?'

'Yeah, right,' Charly said drily. 'He pissed me off by dressing as a baby at our party. No, look, darling.' She sat up on the sofa, blowing her fringe out of her eyes, and curled her long, coltish limbs beneath her. 'I'm just being a bitch. I'm sure I'm just jealous, or something. OK? He's nice, I'm very happy for you.'

'He's nice,' Kate repeated slowly.

'He's nice,' Charly said again. 'But I don't see you with him for ever.' She said slowly, 'I'd have thought you'd be living together by now, and you're not, are you?'

'That's –' Kate fluffed out her hair. 'We need to talk about it.'

'Right,' said Charly. 'It's been over two years now, dollface. What's holding you back?'

'Shut up,' said Kate, determined not to let Charly annoy her today. 'I like being your flatmate too much, that's what's holding us back. He keeps begging me to, and I just can't face life without you.'

'Oh haha,' said Charly, falling over and waggling her legs in the air. She seemed more cheerful. 'OK. I'll try with him I promise. I hope you'll be buying some godawful house in the suburbs sometime soon. Is that it?'

'OK,' Kate said. She didn't want to say what she was thinking, which was that she kind of pitied Charly, actually, for simply not getting it. She didn't know how to explain it to her. But Charly's glare told her the discussion was over, and Kate kind of loved her for admitting she was a bitch, that she was jealous. Perhaps, after all, that was all it was.

The doorbell buzzed. Charly bounced to her feet. 'Come on, Katy,' she said, throwing her arms around her. She took the hairbrush out of Kate's frenzied grip. 'Your hair's fine. Let's go, OK? We're going to be late for Mr Loverman. I promise I'll be nice. Why would I spoil the Millers' big day, eh? It's going to be great.'

Kate wasn't so sure. Not long after she had arrived at Holland Park, Kate realized her father's wedding wasn't so much a celebration of the sanctity of marriage as an excellent networking opportunity for all of Dad's acquaintances and the spurious semi-celebrities he'd met now Lisa was by his side managing his second climb up the slippery slope of fame. From the moment their car drew up ouside the Orangery, the restaurant where the reception was being held (Daniel and Lisa having been married that morning, with only Lisa's sister and brother-in-law present), Kate was assailed by old friends of her father's looking for other old friends of his.

'Kate darling! Where's Boris, have you seen him?'

'Hello Kate! How are you dear? Have you seen Elizabeth?'

'Do you know if it's true she's moved to the Beeb?'

'I hear Michael Ball's coming, is that true?'

'Woo,' said Charly, as they tramped across the still-soft grass in the blazing April sunshine. 'Michael Ball, how will I contain myself.'

'This is hilarious,' said Steve, who had his arm round Zoe. 'Kate, all these years of me thinking you were the world's squarest girl and now look at you. You're the daughter of a sleb. You're going to be in *OK!* talking about your boob job soon if you're not careful.'

'She's not square,' Sean said, loyally defensive. 'She's gorgeous.'

'You are a bit square,' said Zoe, not unkindly.

'Thanks, oldest friend,' said Kate. 'That's nice.'

Zoe smiled at her. 'I didn't mean it, you know what I mean.' Kate looked down at her friend, tidy and chic in a green dress that made her bump look even bigger. She was due in a fortnight. Zoe smoothed her hair behind her ears.

'Where did that come from?' said Kate, pointing to her stomach.

'I know,' said Steve, turning his hands palm outwards, as if in total amazement. 'Seriously, it seems like only last week her stomach was almost entirely flat, and now – look at it!' He stroked his wife's bump. 'I think it's a boy.'

Anything Steve told you was always pretty unreliable; they all laughed. 'I'm sure it's a girl,' said Zoe.

'Me too,' said Kate. Sean shifted his weight from one leg to the other.

'Me too,' said Charly. She lifted her hair with one hand and threw it carelessly behind her, as if it were a separate entity. 'You're carrying quite low. That's what that means.' Kate looked at her quizzically. 'Yes, I do know what I'm talking about,' Charly snapped. 'OK?'

There was a pause; they all nodded, as guests drifted by. Steve clapped his hands together. 'Anyway! So, Kate's really square. I remember, the first time I met Kate in our college bar, and –'

'This story is complete rubbish,' said Kate, crossly. 'You always tell it and it's rubbish! I never said that!'

'She told me that she was only going to stay for one drink, because she had to go back to her room and rearrange her cassette collection,' Steve finished triumphantly, smiling fondly at Kate. He rubbed his face with delight, his green eyes flashing mischievously, and Kate shook her head at him.

'God, you look just like –' she began, and then stopped, quickly.

'Who?' Steve said. He was looking at Zoe, his hand still protectively on her stomach, as someone pushed slightly against them.

'No one,' said Kate. Sean nudged her.

'Go on, who?' he said, curious.

'Nothing,' said Kate. She noticed Charly, opening her mouth and shutting it, with desperate gratitude. 'Anyway. I deny that story ever happened, and Charly, I certainly don't need any input from you on this.'

Charly nodded. 'Yeah,' she said, smiling at Steve. 'Do you know we won the inter-company pub quiz two years in a row when Kate was on our team. There was this question about some totally obscure medievalist poet or something, and no one had ever even *heard* of him, but Kate knew when he'd died!'

'George Herbert was Elizabethan,' Kate said. 'And he isn't obscure.'

'Oh my god,' said Charly, as Zoe and Steve laughed. Sean came to her defence.

'Hey,' he said crossly, not quite looking at Charly. 'Don't be mean. I don't have a square girlfriend.'

'Hello, hello hello!' came a ringing voice from behind them. 'Well, what's all this!' Daniel appeared, between Sean and Charly. He slapped Sean on the back. 'Welcome, welcome!' he cried, cheerily. Several people turned towards him, and smiled.

'Hello, Daniel,' said Charly politely, kissing him. 'Congratulations.'

'Ah, thank you Charly,' said Daniel, appreciatively, running

208

his eyes over Charly's black, sexy form. Kate rolled her eyes. 'How's my beautiful girl?' He kissed Kate.

'Dad,' she said, kissing him back. 'What a lovely day.'

Through the great glass windows of the restaurant the sun poured in as the guests spilled out onto the lawns and manicured gardens. Around her, men in linen suits and women in little jackets, their best chiffon and high heels chattered, laughed, drank – it was like something out of a lifestyle magazine, Kate thought; she could have used all of it in the magazine, no models required. Most of the people here were perfectly coiffed. And if they weren't, they looked 'distinguished', like they could get away with it.

Sean shook Daniel's hand and Daniel slapped his back again smartly and slipped into his wedding patter.

'Ah, Mr Lambert. Sean! Good man. Good to see you, thanks for coming.'

'Thank *you*, Mr Miller,' Sean said, slapping his hand in a bear-like grasp.

'Sean, I've told you before. It's Daniel.'

'Of course, Daniel,' Sean said, smiling. 'Sir.' He slid his arm around Kate's waist, and she caught his hand in hers. Daniel watched them.

'So proud of you, darling,' he said, with a catch in his throat, and Kate thought how far they'd come, and what he might be thinking of on this day, and she kissed him again.

'I'm proud of *you*, Dad, darling,' she said.

Kate watched Daniel, smiling at someone over her shoulder. His thick, greying dark hair was swept back like a lion's mane, his great hulking body tailored and tucked in a navy blue suit, immaculately cut, with a pink silk tie and pink rose buttonhole. He looked exactly how Kate knew he'd want to: sleek, sophisticated, attractive, young for his age; no trace of the poor little Polish boy who'd arrived here after the war, who remembered having no shoes (or claimed to), whose parents changed the family name so Daniel would escape persecution from his peers at school. Kate watched him, with pride, trying to feel happy for him on this day.

After the ceremony, and as the day wore on, Kate realized she was having fun, and she blessed Lisa, for once, for her thoughtfulness in letting her bring some of her own friends. There was only one cloud on the horizon, though: that afternoon, a few drinks down, Charly really did make an effort to talk to Sean, but Kate could tell it was a lost cause. Kate realized, as she watched the two of them inside the Orangery, that the reason she didn't like him was simple – Sean didn't like her. And Charly was used to everyone liking her, especially men. She fought them like a cat, treated them like dirt – but they still wanted her. Kate was used to seeing men's eyes glaze over when she was together with Charly, and it was never because of her. Charly's pert little breasts, her tousled hair, her snub nose, her look of disdain: they fell for it, like so many toy soldiers.

But Sean just didn't get it. During the party, Charly flicked her hair and tried her best to charm Sean. She even told some of her best jokes about the magazine, including the one about the lady who'd turned up with her collection of knitted dolls stuffed with fluff, embroidered 'Kate' on the front.

'She'd been writing to Kate, ringing her up, she was a complete nut-job, and only Kate was nice enough to speak to her ... And there she is, with these stuffed dolls, but Kate's out of the office, and Josephine, that's the new editor, just said, "You'd better take care of it, Charly. Kate's *your* best friend after all. When's her birthday? You can give them to her as a present!" And –'

'Good grief,' Zoe said under her breath, rolling her eyes,

and Steve laughed and stepped back. He put his arm round Zoe, who patted his chest, and they walked away. Charly watched them, her eyes narrowing, an indefinable expression on her face, and Kate knew how much it hurt her, other people's happiness. Because being Charly was a great thing, of course it was, it had to be, but sometimes it must be pretty damn miserable.

Kate had thought about it a lot, especially since they'd been flatmates. She thought Charly must get pretty lonely at times. She wasn't as hard as she liked to think she was. Charly herself didn't realize the ways in which she was strangely kind — making endless cups of tea and bullying Kate into wearing clothes she wouldn't normally dare, or strangely funny – her impressions were uncannily accurate, and she had a pitch-perfect recall for people's idiosyncracies of speech which made Kate helpless with laughter. It was weird, these days, though. Charly was still at *Woman's World*, and Kate didn't know the people she talked about sometimes. They had less in common, less to talk about, than before. Sometimes it felt as if their bills at home were what bound them together most, that they were growing apart, and Kate hated that.

'Kate!' Charly hit her on the arm.

'Sorry, I was listening, really,' Kate said. 'What did you say?'

'I said, he's nice, isn't he?' she said, jerking her head at Steve.

'Yes, very nice,' said Kate severely. Sean's hand snaked around her waist, and she leaned into his embrace. 'Very nice indeed.'

'Oh, get over it,' Charly said crossly. 'He's totally vanilla, I wouldn't go there, Kate.' She tossed her hair, remarshalling herself. 'Hey, you two? Fancy some champagne? I'll get us some more drinks.'

She went towards a waiter, but turned back, a smile frozen on her face. 'Kate!' she hissed. 'She's coming!'

There, gliding over to them in a haze of cream chiffon and silk, was Kate's new stepmother, Lisa, with a smile like a Cheshire cat and a forehead smooth as a new apple, entirely wrinkle-free.

'Hellooo,' she said graciously, holding out one hand to Sean, who took it, rather bemused. 'Hi Kate,' she said more quickly. 'Having a good time?'

'Yes thanks,' Kate said. She kissed Lisa on the cheek. 'Congratulations, Lisa.'

'Ooh,' Lisa said, stepping away. She batted Kate lightly with her hand. 'Don't get makeup on me! Look at my ring!'

Steve rolled his eyes in amazement at Zoe, who hit him sharply on the arm. He turned towards Lisa. 'Hey, Lisa. You look absolutely beautiful.'

'Thanks, Steve!' Lisa said, pleased.

'Thanks a lot for having us,' Steve said, in his easy, polite way. 'It's been so great.'

'Well, congratulations to you, too!' Lisa stroked Steve's shoulder; he looked a little alarmed. 'I haven't seen you both since you got married. Bringing back memories, eh?' She looked across at Kate, then back at Steve and Zoe, whose mouth was set in a straight line but who was nodding, fervently.

'Well,' Steve said. 'We got married in a registry office and had a knees-up in the pub round the corner, so not really. The whole thing cost about fifty quid. So for us, this is like a dream wedding.'

Absolutely none of this was true, but he couldn't have said anything better. Lisa looked absolutely over the moon. She grasped Kate's hand, and Kate took her cue from that.

'Congratulations,' she said, admiring the peanut-sized diamond on her finger with the new band next to it, studded with smaller diamonds.

212

'It's white gold,' Lisa said proudly. 'It's very original.'

'Yes, very,' Kate said.

'Ooh, look. There he is!' she cooed, and Kate looked up to see her dad approaching.

'Hello again darling,' he said to his daughter.

'Darling,' Lisa said. She fingered his tie, and then patted it, proprietorially. 'Want you to come with me and say hi to Gabi. She's here with Cole, you know, from Funicular, the production company? She says you've ignored her all day . . .' she ran her hands down the front of his shirt, stood up on her tiptoes and bit his bottom lip and Kate gazed at her, literally speechless that she thought it was OK to do that in front of Kate, in front of everyone.

'Sure,' said Dad, squeezing her bottom, creasing the silk in his hands. He turned away amiably. Kate shook her head at her friends.

'Man . . .' Kate began, but Zoe, rubbing her friend's back, said quickly,

'Shush. No point crying over spilt milk.'

Kate watched her father and his new wife walk across the lawn, him genially following her as she held him by the hand. Lisa's sister Clare, who was the babysitter for the day, handed Lisa sixteen-month-old Danielle, decked from head to toe in white taffeta and lace, like it was her own wedding day. They stood under a tree, the three of them, and some people started snapping photos, this perfect little family unit, so happy and beautiful, on this lovely day. Kate knew it would hurt in a little, small way, but she was surprised by how winded she felt as she watched them. She recalled her parents' wedding day photo, the one she still had, her mother so fresh and free, her father so tall and virile, both of them looking so young, as if they were on their way to dinner, not to the registry office. It was so easy to imagine the whole thing had never happened, now. That her mother, that she,

213

had never existed. That this was the real wedding, the white wedding, and she, Kate, was a ghost girl.

'You OK?' said Sean, softly in her ear.

'Yes,' she said, turning to face him. He wrapped his arms around her.

'I love you,' he said. 'You look beautiful.'

'Thanks,' she said, wishing they were alone again, but as Sean pulled her towards him and they stayed like that, clinging to each other, she was watching her father and Lisa, with Danielle.

CHAPTER TWENTY-ONE

Charly and Kate climbed the stairs to their flat wearily. Charly was carrying her shoes in her hand, and Kate was more than a little unsteady on her feet. It was one-thirty, and Kate reckoned they'd been drinking for nearly twelve hours. She stabbed ineffectually at the lock with her keys, and finally the two of them fell into their sitting room. Kate put the door on the latch. The smell of the dusty flat, filled with sunshine all day, washed over her. She sneezed, flopping onto the sofa.

'There's a message,' said Charly, grabbing a sticky, old bottle of Limoncello from the fridge. She neatly shut the door with her bum and sashayed back into the room, carrying two glasses as well. 'Woah,' she said, pressing 'Play' on the flashing answer machine with her elbow. 'Here you go.'

She handed her a drink. Kate lay horizontally on the sofa. Her eyes were tired, they felt sticky. The cotton of her dress was creased, it fluttered on her stomach as Kate breathed in and out. She watched it.

There came from the machine an indistinct crackling sound, then murmuring, then the sound of people talking, glasses clinking, all very Ambassador's Reception.

'*Darling* . . . . *Darling Kate, hello darling. Hello!*' A whisky-smooth, low woman's voice floated across to her on the sofa.

'Oh, fuck,' said Charly, moving back into the kitchen. 'First wife alert.'

'Sssh,' Kate said wearily, sitting up.

'*Darling girl. It's your . . . What? No, Oscar. I won't sing. You are awful! Darling. Stop it! I'm talking to Kate. No, no more to drink for me thanks Dick. Oh, go on then, just one.*'

'Argh,' Kate said, running her hands through her hair. 'Argh. I can't bear it.'

'*Darling, how are you? It's your mother, wanting to know how you are.*'

'Why does she refer to herself in the third person?' Charly said. She was leaning against the kitchen door, swigging Limoncello and trying not to laugh. Kate smiled fondly at the answering machine.

'And why does she call me "darling girl"? I haven't seen her for nearly a year and I'm twenty-seven. Bless.'

'*. . . I remembered it was your Father's Second Wedding today. I thought you'd find it hard so I thought I'd call. I love you darling! And hope it went gorgeously well, darling. Call Mummy tomorrow. I guess you're not back yet. I'm at Dick's! We're having cocktails with Vance and DJ! Oscar sends love! Come visit New York soon darling, I miss you.*'

There was thirty seconds more of background chatter, then silence.

'She's mad,' said Charly. 'God, your parents are both mad.'

'She's not mad,' Kate said. She wasn't in the mood for Charly's needling. She took a sip. 'She's just a bit – well, she's a bit tipsy for starters, it is Dad's wedding day after all . . .'

She shrugged her shoulders slightly helplessly, trying to work out how to explain her mother to a stranger, how you

216

could love someone who brought you up and then abruptly left you, whom you honestly believed loved you more than anything, but who was capable of just shutting you out when she wanted. Still, she was the only person, other than Zoe, who could understand what today had been like for her, Kate. Suddenly Kate missed her desperately. She knocked the sweet, viscous liquid down her throat in one go. It had been a long day.

'God,' she said. 'I'm knackered, I might –'

Suddenly there was a noise in the hall, and Charly screamed. 'Shit!' She jumped. 'Oh my god! The door's open! Who the fuck's that –?'

Sean appeared in the doorway.

'What the fuck?' Charly demanded. 'How did you get in? What are you –'

She looked at Kate, accusing.

'I left the door on the latch,' Kate said. 'He's staying tonight, hope that's OK.'

Sean had gone via Zoe and Steve's to collect a laptop that needed looking at. Kate could have sworn she'd mentioned to Charly he'd be coming round. It wasn't *that* much of a shock, anyway, for God's sake. He was round the whole time.

'Hi,' said Sean, unperturbed.

'Oh,' said Charly. She stared at him, disdain so clearly written on her face that Kate withered with embarrassment at her. 'That's fine.'

She stepped forward, and Kate thought she was going to leave, but then she reached for the bottle. 'Have a drink,' she said. She filled her glass and handed it to him, biting her lip as she did, staring up at him again.

'That's OK.' Sean waved his hands at her. He looked down at Kate, on the sofa, and came over, crouching down. He ran his hand lightly over her stomach, pushed her hair back, kissed her forehead. 'Big day today. You tired, babe?'

217

'Yes,' Kate said.

He shook his head at her and mouthed, 'No'. Kate sat up.

'I'm going to bed,' Charly announced, and put her drink down, hard on the table. 'Night, Kate.'

'See you tomorrow,' Kate said, still looking at Sean.

'God, she's a bitch,' said Sean, and he kissed her, pushing his tongue insistently into her mouth. 'Why's she such a bitch?'

Kate pushed him away, bit his ear, wanting to bite all of him, eat him up. 'She's not,' she said softly. 'She's just –'

Sean's hand was inside her dress, on her breast, touching her. 'You're gorgeous, babe. Kate . . .' he trailed off, then said, as an afterthought, 'She needs a man. She needs a good fuck.'

Hazily, as he stroked her, as he kissed her harder, undid her dress, pulled her up, Kate thought of the stream of men, mostly unknown to her, who appeared in the sitting room the morning after a night with Charly. Spanish exchange students. Burly plumbers. Posh, polite boys. Angry, surly men from the magazine, who lusted after her for ages and realized they'd been used and were about to be blanked. She often ran out and left them. Kate had to make them breakfast.

'She doesn't, believe me,' Kate whispered. 'But . . .'

He pulled her into her room, and Kate knelt on the bed, and he pushed the door shut, violently. His eyes were glazed, slightly impersonal almost, and Kate realized they were both a bit drunk.

'I wanted to ask you something,' Sean said suddenly. 'I've been thinking about it for a while.' He bit her shoulder. 'Oh Kate . . .'

'What?' said Kate, looking over the room to where a pile of clothes lay. She ought to tidy them up. God, it was huge, and she didn't even recognize half the clothes in it. She was

218

tired, she wanted to sleep, and she knew that was a bit crap. *Venus* had a problem page, but it didn't have the answers to the problem of when you were a bit exhausted and not in the mood for it.

'*Dear Marie. I love my boyfriend, and we've been together for three years, and honestly I can't imagine life without him, but you know sometimes you just can't be bothered to talk to him and you don't want to have sex with him? Is that normal? Does that make me a terrible person?*' No, *Venus* went more in for the answers to questions like '*Dear Marie. I'm thinking of getting my clitoris pierced. Do you have any safety dos and don'ts?*'

'. . . marry me?'

'Hm,' Kate said, still chewing her lip and looking at the washing. Damn it, half that pile of clothes was Charly's! Lazy bitch. Kate sighed crossly.

'Kate, are you listening to me?' Sean said, pulling away from her and staring at her.

'Oh . . .' Kate blinked. 'Yes, yes of course I was.'

'Were you really?' he said, smiling kindly at her. 'I don't think you were, were you? What did I just ask you?'

'Um . . .' Kate said. 'Something about the wedding?'

'Kind of,' Sean said. He rocked back so they were both kneeling, facing each other on the bed. He took her hands and clasped them. 'Kate. I just asked you to marry me.'

'What?' Kate said, her eyes flying open. 'What did you just say?'

Sean coughed, and closed his eyes. He took a deep breath; she saw he was shaking.

'OK . . . I said, you silly, gorgeous girl, will you marry me, and make me happy, and carry on being crazy shy beautiful Kate with me for the rest of our lives?'

'Oh – my god,' said Kate. 'Oh my god – Sean . . .'

She clutched his hands tightly, staring into his face. It was weird, she thought. Every girl spends their whole life wondering what their proposal will be like, and when it comes . . . it doesn't feel like a proposal, like the most amazing moment of your life. It just feels like . . . well, two people having a bit of a casual chat. Perhaps she should get Marie to do a column about it in the next issue of *Venus*. *'How it feels when it feels a bit underwhelming.'* Of course, it wasn't underwhelming though. It was Sean, of course it was the most amazing moment of her life, so Kate leant forward, leant in towards him, and she kissed him and said,

'Yes. Yes, darling. Of course I will.'

He sighed, breathing out deeply, and she realized how tightly wound up he was.

'I talked to your father just now,' he said. 'Caught him before he went off with Lisa.'

'I bet he was grateful to you, holding up his wedding night,' said Kate. Sean frowned.

'Hey! Don't. I knew I wanted to do it today, you know?'

'Oh, Sean,' said Kate.

'I saw you . . . you and your dad, talking to him, and you looked so beautiful, standing there with a glass in your hand, being yourself, your amazing self and I was so proud of you,' he said, his eyes burning with emotion, liquid with unshed tears. 'Kate, I knew I was gonna do it. Your dad was hilarious.'

'I bet he was,' said Kate. She was trying to picture herself as the girl Sean had watched and to whom he had known he was going to propose. She had felt like a stranger in someone else's life all day, and it was strange that he had felt the opposite. But then, she knew that was how she and Sean worked, that he made her feel part of the world, less of a loner, a fruitloop. He showed her the life she should be having, opened the door to things for her, and she loved him.

'Is that what you came here tonight to say?' she said, almost shyly, not knowing what came next in situations like these.

'Well – yes,' he said, speaking softly into her hair. 'Of course it was. And now it's done. All over.'

All over, all done, of course.

CHAPTER TWENTY-TWO

September 2003

Kate didn't want a big white wedding. She was pretty unsure about the idea of receptions, cakes, big pouffy white dresses, and all that, in general. And she certainly hadn't wanted an engagement party, but Sean had been really keen.

Afterwards, neither she nor Sean could remember why they had selected a bar on a cobbled side road off Old Street, clear across town from a) their respective flats b) their friends' flats c) where they went out d) everything else. But at the time it seemed like a good idea, the upstairs room of a bar-cum-pub with new dark shiny floorboards, fuschia flock-patterned wallpaper on one wall only, a steel and glass chandelier and a host of stroppy, Hoxton-fin-wearing bar-staff who were anxious to let you know that, actually, they were really training to be an actor/studying film/doing a degree/recording an album. They did this by looking askance at anyone who ordered a drink and by loudly dropping names to each other as they turned to the wall to make the drinks.

'They said it was like Almodóvar.'

'I'm meeting this guy who knows this girl Pam who worked at the National Film School.'

'Apparently it's too meta-textual. Yes, what do you want? A mojito? We don't actually do cocktails. Have a look at the bar list please.'

Kate was wearing emerald green silk T-bar shoes, which were making her uncomfortable but happy, and a caramel-brown silk shift dress with huge pockets at the sides, which Juliet, the fashion editor at *Venus*, had been sent the day before. She'd given it to Kate, with a kiss. 'Wear it tomorrow!' she'd said. 'It was made to be worn, not hanging around our sample cupboard for weeks on end. Come on! It's your night.'

As she waited to be served at the bar, Kate thought of how kind Juliet had been, how kind everyone was, and she looked around her, at the crowded room, humming and buzzing with people she loved. There were Zoe and Steve, Betty, Francesca, Bobbie, Jem, and her old gang from *Woman's World*, Sophie and Jo and George, in a corner with Charly who was holding court, and Sue Jordan and her husband Alec, and all the lovely new people from *Venus*, Claire and Juliet and Tom – even Priscilla was being nice. Perhaps it *had* been a good idea, after all.

But she hadn't wanted all the attention. They had decided they weren't getting married for at least a year, until they'd found a place and Sean had left his job and found something better. On the subject of the party, Kate had ummed and aahed through the summer, through all her friends' congratulations, as other things took precedence. Sean had rung his mother in Texas about her engagement ring, which he wanted to give Kate. Zoe had her baby, Henry, always known as Harry, and she and Steve bought the flat upstairs, meaning they owned a House, and had a Baby, both of which were great, but really scary. Betty got a job in New York, and had a leaving party, which took the pressure off Kate, she'd thought, except everyone at the party sided with Sean and kept saying, Why aren't you having an engagement party?

Then Sean was given the perfect piece of ammunition because, in early September, Venetia rang, and announced that she and Oscar were coming to London in a couple of weeks. One of Oscar's musicals was transferring and they were spending a month in town. Was she having a party, because then would be the perfect time?

So . . . they were having the party. And now here they were, together again – and Kate never got to say this word, it was weird, rolling it around in her head – her parents. Her father and Lisa, her mother and Oscar, and it made her love Oscar more than ever that he, normally content in the shadow, was taking the conversational lead, gently flirting with Lisa, his hand always present on Venetia's back, just letting her know he was there.

Lisa was laughing at something Oscar had said, sliding her fingers carefully between the blow-dried locks of hair that framed her face, when Daniel leant forward and said something to Venetia, in a low voice. Kate watched, absolutely fascinated, as Lisa caught Daniel's hand and held it behind her. He clutched it tightly. But he was looking at his ex-wife, and she at him, and they were smiling into each other's eyes, like a couple of teenagers.

Kate hadn't seen her mother since she and Sean had visited her in New York, just before she'd started her job at *Venus*. She always forgot how beautiful Venetia was. She didn't look anything like Kate, despite Oscar's frequent avowals. 'You could be *sisters*! Sisters, I tell you! Venetia, I can't believe you have a grown-up daughter!' It was true that Venetia looked much younger than her ex-husband, however – but that was because she was, and it shocked Kate to see them next to each other, to realize just how big the age gap was between her parents, how young her mother must have been when she married her father.

The last time Kate had seen her parents together, was on her fourteenth birthday.

She leant on the bar and felt very grown-up, for a moment, as she watched them. It was strange, thinking they were her parents, when it had been so long since she'd thought of herself as part of a family, member of a unit. Very strange. It made her feel funny; like she didn't know herself again. She looked around for her fiancé – what a weird word, again, all these weird words she was having to say, parents and engagement and fiancé and found him, in the corner of the room, laughing loudly with his buddies, in that trumpeting way men in groups have.

His eyes met hers and she looked mock-annoyed with him, then shook her head as he waggled his fingers, motioning something and mouthing, 'Do you want me to come over?' But she was quite happy here, she realized, standing on her own, at the corner of the room, relatively unwatched, anonymous, for a few moments at least.

'Yes, what can I get you?' An unsmiling barman flicked a glance at Kate, jolting her back to reality.

'Did you just tell someone you weren't doing mojitos?'

'Yes, that's right.' The barman looked hugely, hugely annoyed to be so questioned in this manner.

'Um – sorry. You're supposed to be,' said Kate. 'When we booked the room they told us we could have three different cocktails. That was one of them.'

The black-haired Hoxton-finner didn't blink. 'We can't do them now. It's just beer and wine.'

'But we paid for free cocktails for everyone.'

'Well, there isn't any.'

'Any what?' said Kate, staying calm.

225

'Mint?' he said, a sneering tone in his voice.

Kate turned so she was facing him, and rested both her elbows on the bar. 'Here's the booking confirmation, and here's my credit card,' she said, and she smiled politely at him. 'I'm sorry if you don't have any mint, but either go out and get some, or give me the deposit back. Otherwise I'll go downstairs and talk to your manager.'

He didn't even snarl, he simply accepted the will of the greater force, in the dog-eat-dog world of new London, turned, and went downstairs. Kate breathed out, and wished he'd got her a drink before he left.

'My god,' said a voice behind her, in an amused tone. 'Look at you. Who the hell are you?'

Kate froze. She knew that voice. She would know it anywhere.

'Mac!' Kate said, with genuine pleasure. She stood on tiptoe, flung her arms around him, and he hugged her, tightly. She could feel her heart, hammering in her chest, as he clutched her to him, briefly. She hoped it wasn't obvious. Don't be flustered, she told herself. You knew he was coming.

'Hey,' Mac said, releasing her and stepping back. 'Thanks for letting me come.' He rubbed the back of his neck. 'I'd booked the flight already, didn't realize it was tonight – you know.' He looked awkward.

'Don't be silly!' She smiled at him, assuming the easy, carefree note she had told herself she was going to adopt with him. It was easier that way. 'You're staying with them, you could hardly have just sat in by yourself with Harry and the babysitter.'

'I could have, actually, he's with my parents, they're the babysitters,' he said. Kate watched him as he spoke. 'God, how on earth are you, Kate? I haven't seen you since – when was it?'

'Since the wedding,' she said. 'Nearly a year.'

'We only seem to meet on momentous occasions,' he said. 'Housewarming-cum-engagement parties, weddings – and now look what's happened since I've been away.'

The bartender took this opportunity to appear again, slamming a mojito down on the counter with an injured air.

'Mint's on its way, I'll add it in a minute.'

'Thanks,' said Kate. 'Thank you very much.' She smiled politely at him as his eyes narrowed in suspicion. 'Cheers,' she said, turning to Mac and raising her glass. He clinked it with his own, looking curiously at her.

'The Kate Miller I used to know would never have done that,' Mac said. He leaned against the bar so he was facing her. He touched her arm lightly. 'The Kate Miller I knew hardly used to say boo to a goose.'

'Rubbish,' said Kate, and she laughed. 'The Kate Miller you knew you knew for one night.'

'That's not true. We spent the morning together as well, if I remember rightly,' he said, conversationally. Kate looked around, anxiously, not wanting anyone to hear. He followed her gaze and shook his head, smiling. As if he knew what she was thinking.

He had no idea, really though. No idea how, when she had heard Mac was down in London for the weekend, *this* weekend, and had to be invited to the party, how it had shaken her to know he'd be there on this night, the very night she'd resisted having for months. He had no idea that she sometimes thought of him, late at night, lying in bed alone when Sean wasn't there, or when he was next to her, breathing heavily, moonlight falling into her tiny bedroom. That she wondered how he was, was he OK, was he happy, not working too hard? Strange, so strange, to feel such tenderness, protectiveness, towards someone you hardly knew. She wondered what might have been. Not every day, of course not . . . but she wondered. And he had no idea, she hoped, how it felt to see him standing in front of her now, tall and rangy, with his cropped brown hair, his bitten nails, his deep green eyes.

Kate shook her head, willing away the thoughts inside there. Keep it light, remember what you told yourself. She glanced round casually, checking for Sean. 'Do you think anyone ever worked it out?' she asked, curiously. 'Us, I mean.'

'I never told anyone,' he said quietly. 'Did you?'

She was silent for a moment. 'I didn't,' she said. 'Well, Sean. But he doesn't count.'

'Doesn't he?'

'You know what I mean,' she said. 'It was – it's in the past, isn't it.' She sounded rather prim, like a schoolteacher, and she hated it. She felt uncomfortable.

'Heartless woman.' Mac banged his fist theatrically on the wooden surface of the bar. It broke the tension. She stared at him, helplessly, and laughed. 'You started going out with your flatmate and now you're marrying him, just to prove a point to me. Whereas I had to move to a cold inhospitable city with no friends and hear second-hand from my own brother about how much in love with Sean you were. It's all about the pointscoring with you isn't it, you young hussy. I know the real reason for this farce of an engagement party.'

'Oh dear,' said Kate, laughing again, and standing on one foot, then on the other. 'I'm very sorry.'

'I'll forgive you,' he said, with that old, strange stare of his that she remembered. Silence enveloped them as they stood together. 'Everything else OK, though?' Mac said, quietly. 'Sounds like it.'

'Brilliant, thanks,' she said, turning to him, her face alight. 'Just brilliant.'

'I'm so glad,' Mac told her. He squeezed her arm, his big

hand wrapping itself above her elbow. 'It all worked out for the best, didn't it?'

'Yes I think so,' said Kate. 'I think so.' She watched his profile, allowing herself to stare once again at that wide, generous face, the hint of stubble on his jaw, the shadows under his eyes. 'Anyway – how are you? Zoe mentioned you might be moving, is that true?'

'Back down here? Not sure. Just had an offer from a hospital in South London.'

'Wouldn't you miss Edinburgh?'

'In some ways,' said Mac. 'Not in others. I haven't decided yet, that's why I'm down this weekend, seeing them again.' Kate nodded. 'I love it up there, but I'm a bit lonely, sometimes, you know? Since Alice and I split up.'

'Alice?' she said stupidly.

'My ex.' Mac turned suddenly to the barman.

'Your ex. I didn't know –'

'What,' he said. He turned towards her suddenly, his eyes searching her face. 'You didn't know I had a girlfriend? Ever? There have been others, you know, Kate.'

She didn't know why his tone had changed, suddenly. 'I know, Zoe told me –'

His eyes flashed at her. 'Ah, did she? And you've been eating yourself away with jealousy, I know.'

One foot, the other foot, feeling uncomfortable. 'Um,' she began. 'Well, I hope you move down,' she said.

'I'm not sure,' he said, finishing his drink in one gulp. He wiped his mouth with the back of his hand and stood there, looking at her. 'I'm not sure it's the right move yet.' He paused. 'God, Kate, I'm sorry. But it's so good to see you.'

'You too,' said Kate, her heart racing again. 'Really – you too. I'm glad, you know – it was awful that we never did . . .' She trailed off, not knowing how to go on, afraid to go on. The cosy world she was cocooned in, this bright and friendly party, her parents and their spouses talking easily over there – all of it seemed skewed, false, unreal, all of a sudden. She didn't know why, didn't know why. Gathering herself together, she took a deep breath.

'I'd better go and find Sean,' she said.

'Yes,' said Mac.

'So I'll see you later.'

'I'd like that,' said Mac. He cleared his throat. 'Hey. I really need a drink. Mojito, large, lots of mint when you've got a minute, please,' he said to the barman.

'Coming right up, mate,' said the barman, and Kate slumped back against the bar.

'God,' she said.

'What?' Mac asked.

'I hate you,' Kate said. 'He didn't listen to me, he completely ignored me. I have no bar presence. And you come along and say "Jump," and he says, "How High."'

'You're doing just fine,' Mac told her. 'I heard you. You sorted him right out. That's why he's scared witless,' he said, and he nudged her, so she turned and stood next to him, watching the barman frenziedly chopping mint and crushing ice, before he swivelled around to hand the drink to Mac, who took it with a nod. 'Thanks, mate,' he said.

'No worries,' said the barman. 'Madam, can I get you another one?' Kate hestitated, looking sideways towards Mac. He smiled, blankly, like the moment was over, and said, kindly,

'Go off and find your fiancé, Kate Miller. I'm going to stay here.' He pushed her off and she tottered, staggering slightly in her high heels towards Sean, who stretched his arms wide open when he saw her.

CHAPTER TWENTY-THREE

Three hours later, the bar was still rocking, the mojitos were still flowing, and Kate was not sober. She had smoked a cigarette, which she never did. She had kissed Sean in front of everyone, which she also never did. Most importantly she had extracted a promise from Sean that they would buy the engagement ring together, and that she wouldn't be wearing his mother's. Sean had a rather sweet, slightly dubious idea of giving Kate his mother's engagement ring, which Gerda Lambert couldn't wear any more now her fingers were so bloated with water retention. Kate didn't want her engagement ring to be hers as the result of water retention. She felt there should be more of a quest for it. Not a Lord-of-the-Rings scale quest, but still, a bit more.

And all these lovely people were still there; her mother and Oscar were working the room, chatting to all her friends. It was so great to see it, to be in the same room with her again. She missed her mother. And Lisa was sitting on Kate's father's knee, whispering into his ear, like they were teenagers. Jem and Bobbie were in the very obvious stages of pre-snoggage, Kate could tell – all around was love, love and nice things.

She hadn't seen Charly for a while; she'd said hello when she'd arrived, with the others from work, and then gone off to a corner with them, where she had ensconced herself. Kate's eyes roamed around the room, searching for her. She couldn't see what she was up to, but that was probably a good thing, so she went back to her drink. It was empty.

Sean was behind her, their backs were touching as they talked to different people. She could feel his warm, comforting bulk behind her, the side of his hip nestling in her back. With an effort Kate stood up straight and wandered back to the bar for another cocktail, knowing she had probably had enough, but what the hell. It was her engagement party, after all! she told herself, and as she looked up she saw Mac, weaving his way towards her.

'Hey!' she said.

'I was looking for you,' he told her, with an old expression on his set face.

'Why?' said Kate. 'Come with me, come and get another drink.' She was suddenly heady with euphoria. Feeling free, invincible, like nothing could harm her, she shook her head, smiling directly at him, too close to him, looking into his eyes, knowing she'd had too much to drink, knowing she was flirting with him and she shouldn't be, it was her engagement party, for Christ's sake. She pointed at Sean, who had Francesca pinned up against the bar and was making her scream with laughter at something, and turned back to Mac, who was watching her intently. She met his gaze. It was oddly unsettling, knowing him so well, not knowing him at all, and the way his suddenly-flinty eyes bored into her, coldly.

'Don't marry him,' he said.

Kate blinked. 'What?' she said.

'Don't marry him, Kate. He's not right for you.'

'Mac –!' Kate didn't know what to say. She shifted her

weight, the emerald green high heels gleaming in the dark of the bar as dimly she registered how much they were hurting.

'I'm just going to say this once, and you'll hate me for it,' Mac said, looking around him, as if he were checking out the bar, the other people in it.

She felt totally sober, suddenly. 'Perhaps you'd better not say it, then.'

'I have to,' Mac said. 'Don't marry him. You're doing it for the wrong reasons.'

Kate blinked, mystified – it was like he was talking a foreign language. For the past few months, all she'd heard was congratulations, expressions of joy, attention – attention that for once she liked, that she sought out, basking in the warmth of the approval and pleasure that their engagement news brought them. She even liked discussing the wedding now, she'd got used to it. Dressmakers, caterers, estate agents, registrars, shop assistants, solicitors: an army of people was being mobilized into place, to see to this next stage of Kate's life, her grown-up life with Sean.

And here was someone saying all of this was wrong, and she could barely recognize the words, let alone process them. Kate stared at Sean, who had his arm around Francesca. As if he knew she were watching, he turned around slowly, and smiled at her, moving his hand onto his heart.

'And what makes you say that?' said Kate, trying to sound like Lady Bracknell. He looked at her, and said nothing. 'Seriously, Mac,' she went on, softening her voice. 'I don't know what you mean.' She felt as if she were trying to reason with a lunatic.

'Congratulations again, darling!' Lisa appeared, pushing Mac slightly out of the way; he stood aside, smiling politely, but still looking intently at Kate. Lisa pressed her cheek against Kate's, a glass of champagne clasped to her chest.

'Great party!' she trilled. She called across the room, 'Daniel, here's your daughter! The bride-to-be!' Then, 'Ooh, Kate. I've got so many questions I want to ask you!'

Kate had never seen her so warm, or genuine, and again, she was confused. She smiled gratefully at her stepmother, and clasped her hand. 'Oh, Lisa, that's lovely – thank you, but –' she looked around for Mac, not wanting to let him get away from this conversation, wanting to put him straight. 'Lisa, give me one minute, will you, I'll be over?' She waved at her dad. Looked at Mac who looked back at her, unsmiling. The party had an unreal air, the colour, the drinks, her shoes, the laughter – it was like a fairground ride, everything distorted, nothing what it seemed, and she suddenly hated it, wished she wasn't here.

'Of course,' said Lisa, beaming at her. 'We're over here – your dad's waiting for you, remember! And your mother – I love your mother! – I think they're going in a minute . . . Ooh look, there's Sean come to say hello – hello Sean –!'

Her voice receded into the background chatter as she tripped away and Kate and Mac stepped together again, as if she hadn't been there.

'You were saying,' said Kate, her voice low, her head suddenly clear.

'Look, Kate, this isn't a cloak-and-dagger meeting.' Mac sounded impatient. He pushed a cocktail stick along the surface of the bar. She watched him. 'I'm not – I'm not doing this to be dramatic about it. I'm being honest. Do you get it? Don't marry him. Just trust me.'

'Why shouldn't I marry him?' Kate was bewildered.

'Do you honestly think he's the man for you?' Mac said, his voice close in her ear, swooping suddenly low, and she felt her stomach tip over, full of the doubts and desires that she kept hidden away. 'Do you honestly think so, Kate? Because if you do then I'll just go away, but if you . . .'

He trailed off and their eyes met.

She put her finger to the lapel of his jacket, gingerly. 'That night we met . . .'

'Yes.'

Her heart was in her mouth. 'I thought – I felt like I'd known you for years.'

'Did you?'

'Yes,' said Kate, recklessly. 'I thought you were . . .' She looked straight at him. 'I thought I could fall for you.'

'Me too,' said Mac, his voice low.

She took a step back. 'And then you – you casually mention you're moving to a different *country* the next morning.' He was here, she was really saying this to him. 'I – I kind of hated you afterwards, you know.'

'I know. Our timing sucks,' he said. 'I nearly called you half a dozen times. I couldn't stop thinking about you.'

'Why the hell didn't you then?' she said, almost hissing.

'Believe me, not a day goes by when I don't wish I had,' he said, fiercely, close to her ear. 'You didn't either, you know.' She shook her head, closed her eyes. He was right. 'But it just seemed so – random, so out there, to call someone you've only met once and tell them that you think that they're –'

She stopped him, and gently put her hand on his. *The love of your life.* 'Yes,' she said simply. 'I know.'

'And then a couple of months later I found out you'd been having a thing with Sean anyway, and I wasn't that surprised, I thought it was on the cards.'

'I know,' she said again.

'I wish you hadn't.'

'I know.'

'I should have called you.'

She breathed out in a rush. 'Oh, Mac. Maybe. Maybe you should.' She wished she hadn't said it.

'It's too late, isn't it.'

Now Kate breathed in, closing her eyes, which were suddenly heavy. The smell of him – the feel of his skin on hers – his face, his arms, the two of them together, entangled in each other – how intense it had been, almost terrifyingly so, and then how normal, strangely normal . . . She opened her eyes, slowly.

'It's too late . . . Mac, I love him.'

'Don't do it, Kate.' He caught her wrist, and poison was in his voice, she caught it and it scared her.

'Why shouldn't I love him,' she said fiercely. 'Be more . . .'

'Specific?' he said, almost laughing. 'Kate. Come on.' He turned away, bowing his head and was still for a moment. Kate looked up, to see if anyone was watching her, and there was Sean and her father, clapping each other on the back, and she wished with all her heart she was there next to them, not in the middle of this.

'Oh god,' she said, quietly, not sure what to do next.

Suddenly, it was as if the tension had been cut, slackened. Mac shook his head, and said something, softly, to himself. She turned to him.

'This was wrong,' he said. 'I'm going to go.' He kissed her on the cheek, and she breathed in, quickly. 'Kate, I'm sorry. I shouldn't have said all that.' He stopped. 'Do something for me, will you?'

'Of course!' said Kate, already sounding cheery, though she felt anything but, and she wished she could sit down with him and talk, talk properly.

Behind them, Bobbie screeched as someone spilled part of their drink over her. It was Charly, sashaying over, a smile on her face, to Sean and Steve. She touched Sean on the shoulder.

'Hey.'

'Hey, Charly,' Sean slurred.

'Just wanted to say congratulations,' said Charly. She peered up at him, making an effort. 'OK?'

'Sure,' said Sean. 'Thanks a lot.'

'I'll see you soon. Yeah?'

'You will,' said Sean.

'Are you off?' said Kate, turning to her friend.

'Yeah,' said Charly, a fake smile of regret plastered across her face. 'I'm going to meet Jag in town, we're going to a club.'

'Cool,' said Kate, who had no idea who Jag was. 'Look, thanks for –'

'No worries,' said Charly, awkwardly.

Steve said, 'Are you getting a cab, Charly?'

'Yeah,' Charly said, flicking her long fringe out of her face. 'Zoe's gone already, so I'll come part of the way with you if that's OK. Cool.' He downed his pint, and coughed slightly.

'Smooth,' said Sean, smiling at him, turning towards him so they blocked Charly out.

'I'm going now,' said Charly.

'OK!' said Steve, faux-dramatically. 'Keep your knickers on!' He kissed Kate goodbye. 'Darling, that was a great great party. You're a star, you know that? Zo said if you had one you'd love it.' He slapped Mac on the back. 'See you later?' He didn't ask him if he wanted a lift. 'Right, come on, dollface, let's be off.'

Charly scowled at him.

'Bye Charly,' said Sean, and he stalked off to the other side of the room, as Charly pushed her way out, with Steve following, and Kate was left standing alone again. She turned back to Mac and saw him watching her intently, his expression more serious than it had been.

'Sorry, Mac,' she said. 'What was it?'

The question sounded harsher than she'd expected.

237

'Look,' he said, and he jerked his head over at Steve's disappearing form. 'It's . . . It's Steve and Zoe. Look out for them, will you?'

'Um, sure,' said Kate. 'I do. You know that.'

'Zoe, yes. I mean both of them. Spend some time with them. Just do it. Especially Steve.'

And with that gnomic utterance, he kissed her again.

'Take care of yourself, Kate Miller,' he said. She watched him go, her mind racing.

Of course, there was no doubt that Sean was the man for her, of course, but if she had to choose, as the magazines she worked for or read were constantly asking her and women like her, would she choose that one night with Mac again, or a lifetime with Sean, and what she and Sean had together?

Kate shook her head at the thought, watching the scene around her, her friends so happy for her and Sean. Ridiculous to even ask the question, and that was what sometimes irritated her about her job and the world of magazines. She spent all day working on the illusion that women could have it all, when the reality was much more complicated. Making promises, an easy sale for £3.20, the new body, new man, new job and new house that you wanted were all yours for the cover price alone.

Her eyes were on Sean and he turned around, almost as if he knew she was looking at him. Kate snapped out of her reverie with a start.

'You OK?' Sean mouthed, flexing a hand towards her.

'I'm OK,' she said nodding at him. She watched Mac at the end of the bar, saying his goodbyes to people, saw him push open the door into the dark, rainy night. She was glad he was gone, and she felt angry, too. How could he say that to her? The more Kate thought about it, the ruder it was, in fact, and she threaded her way through the crowd, who smiled kindly at the bride-to-be as she made her way towards her fiancé. Yes, that was what it was. Her engagement party. Her fiancé. Her life.

CHAPTER TWENTY-FOUR

Planning a wedding, Kate discovered, was – like so much of life – not quite how it seemed in the magazines. In her time she must have written at least ten articles on the subject of being a blushing bride and how to organize the perfect wedding, but now she was planning one of her own, well – it was all rather different, and she didn't quite know what to think about it.

For starters, she didn't *feel* like a bride. Kate wasn't the sort of girl who'd grown up dreaming of a big pouffy white dress, of a cake, of bridesmaids decked out in cherry pink, of co-ordination and happy families. For starters, her family had been effectively obliterated when she was fourteen. The lime-light was left for her father and his genius, his fans, his amazing, wonderful life, and her mother and her beauty, her grace in every situation, her hysterical dramatic gene. And like basic genetics, the combination of these two people had produced one child, a daughter who actively ran from the limelight, to whom the thought of doing a first dance in a marquee in front of two hundred people was as terrifying as having to sing karaoke in front of people. It never occurred to her that she might have inherited anything from either of them.

That was what she liked about Sean: the limelight was his when they were out together. He was the genial, loud, funny one, the storyteller, the buyer of drinks. When they were alone it was different, they were the two of them, but out together he was the centre of attention. Kate liked it. She had her friends, she had a job where people listened to her, so what if occasionally she wished Sean would let her tell the story about the time they were on holiday in Crete and an unexploded mine went off in the garden next to their hotel? She'd been there, not him, she was the one who . . . Anyway, that didn't matter, it was great.

The wedding was going to be in September, they'd finally set a date and, with a lump sum Venetia had given them as an early wedding present, they'd found the perfect flat, in a red-brick mansion block in Maida Vale. Her boss Sue had relatives in one such block, and she'd happened to mention to Kate that there was an auction about to take place on the flat below them as it had been foreclosed on. It was on the first floor; it had big bay windows, shiny glowing parquet floors, and the lobby was imposing and cavernous, with a great big heavy black door that squeaked loudly on huge old wire hinges and snapped shut after you like a trap. They moved in five days before Christmas, unable to believe they were finally there, in their own place.

On their first night they drank champagne, each sitting on a cardboard box, looking round at the bare but strangely cosy flat, and Sean clinked his glass against Kate's. His legs were between hers. With his other hand he tugged the dusky pink scarf wrapped around Kate's throat.

'We did it,' he said. 'Can you believe it?'

'No,' said Kate. She grinned. 'I can't. At last. At last!'

He knelt on the floor in front of her, looking up at her with his impish, big generous smile, his arms on her legs. 'This time next year,' he said, resting his head on her chest, 'we'll have a big tree, and presents underneath it, and we'll have been married for four months. We'll be an old married couple by then.'

'It's weird, isn't it.'

'It's not weird, that's what's so cool. It's great.' Sean kissed her. 'Look, we'll have all our Christmas cards lined up on that big windowsill there. And we'll have the sofa here, with a big otto – what's it called?'

'Ottoman?'

'That's it. A big ottoman to put our feet on, and we can build some shelves here, what do you think?' Kate nodded, watching him with pleasure and trying not to cry at the same time. She didn't know why. She was tired.

'We can put photos on the shelves, us on our wedding day. And you with your dad when you were little, and me and Doug on the baseball team. And we'll have the computer here, and a desk for all your important office stuff, and the dining table can go here, and we'll have all these dinner parties, you know?'

His enthusiasm was infectious. Kate could feel her face lighting up as she looked at him, the way she always did. 'Go on,' she said. 'What else?'

'What else. Hm . . .' Sean frowned. 'Well, next Christmas – on Christmas Eve, maybe – we'll have Steve and Zoe round, with Harry and the new baby.' Kate nodded, a cloud momentarily passing over her sunny world, the champagne suddenly tasting vinegary. 'Perhaps Betty'll be back from New York. Francesca and Pav –'

'If they're still together.' Francesca was enjoying an overwhelmingly obsessive, secretive relationship with the trader next to her at work.

'If they're still together.' Sean patted her knees, moving closer in towards her, so she could feel his breath on her neck. 'Who else?'

'Charly,' said Kate carefully. 'You forgot Charly.'

'Screw Charly,' said Sean, almost crossly. 'I don't wanna talk about Charly. Not tonight.' He squeezed her shoulders, hard, and stepped back from her, tension suddenly thick between them. Kate watched him, angrily, hating the fact that their perfect night was being spoilt with this. The newly familiar feeling of hating things, hating Charly, this girl who had once meant so much to her, was inching its way into her mind again, and it was horrible. She didn't want to feel like this, in their safe, beautiful new home together.

They were perfectly still in the centre of the room, a beam of light from the shadeless bulb hanging over them. Sean opened his mouth to say something, then didn't, and Kate was afraid, suddenly.

'I need to tell you something,' she said, her voice small. Sean nodded. 'Mm-uhm. What, honey?'

'It's about Charly.'

It had happened three days ago, and even admitting she held the memory seemed deceitful, as if she were lying to Zoe, deceiving her herself . . . She and her ex-*Woman's World* colleague Sophie had been visiting Georgina and her baby. Georgina had, slightly to everyone's surprise, not least Claire's, married Phil from the office (Charly had definitely not been invited to *that* wedding), and they were living in Hampstead, in a beautiful little house just off Keats Grove, behind the shops near the Heath. Sophie was a hearty type, now working for an off-the-beaten-track guide book publisher, who specialized in holidays through bits of the Amazon jungle that no human had ever been to before. It was she who'd suggested they walk across the Heath towards Gospel Oak station.

'Fresh air,' she'd said briskly, as they emerged from the once-chilly-now-frazzled Georgina's house into a baby-free zone and each breathed an internal sigh of relief. 'Do us good. Phew.' She blew her short brown hair off her face. 'Glad to be out of there, aren't you?' she said, slightly as if they'd just emerged from battle. Georgina, a super-efficient dynamo in the office, didn't seem to understand why Ned, her sweet baby, didn't want to organize himself in the same way her computer did, and wouldn't stay silent when she wanted him to. All in all it had been a rather disheartening hour or so, and Kate and Sophie had both felt they were in the way. They were discussing this, and skirting by the Ponds, when Kate suddenly clutched Sophie's arm.

'What?' said Sophie.

'Nothing,' said Kate. 'Thought I was going to slip, that's all. Sorry.'

Her heart was beating, she was red hot, she pulled her hat off, unwound her scarf and pretended to be listening as Sophie carried on telling her how *she* would deal with the apparently very simple demands of having a baby. But she wasn't listening. No, of course not.

There, ahead of her, standing by a bench, facing each other, were Charly and Steve. She knew it was them, of course it was. He was holding her elbows, as if trying to restrain her, contain her, and she was yelling at him, her face angry, dirty with rage. Her beautiful brown hair was underneath a black crochet hat, a matching scarf wound round her neck, her long long legs still in her Charly wardrobe of jeans and high-heeled boots.

Kate watched as she broke free of his grasp and angrily kicked at the metal leg of the bench. She didn't know what to do; they were walking towards them.

'Ohmigod,' said Sophie suddenly. 'Shit.'

'What?' said Kate.

'It's Charly. Having some massive barney with some bloke.

Oh god.' Sophie turned to Kate. 'Look, I know she's your friend and everything, but . . .'

'What?'

'I really can't face her, seriously, not while she's in the middle of that, too. No way.' She grabbed Kate's arm. 'Let's cut through to the pond, go round the side. We'll miss them.' She shuddered. 'Sorry, Kate. I'm being horrible. Do you mind?'

'No,' said Kate hurriedly. 'Of course not.'

Steve was talking back to Charly. He tried to take her hand, to pat it, and Charly broke away, sobbing. He gripped her shoulders; she couldn't see his expression, but she knew his voice, its pale undertones floating over to her. Kate tried to hear, but she couldn't. And she knew what the conversation was, anyway. Of course she knew. She'd known Charly for four years. And then she heard just a snatch of what Steve was saying, a horrible, terrible confirmation of her worst fear as Sophie, her hat concealing her face, pulled her away.

'It's got to stop, Charly. I'm sorry.' The thing that was to haunt Kate was Charly's expression, of total, utter, blind – what was it? Intoxication? Obsession? She didn't know. She only knew that here, crying like a madwoman, was Charly and, at home, looking after eighteen-month-old Harry and newly pregnant again, was Zoe. They were her two dearest friends. They had been.

Tears were running down Kate's face as she finished the story, and Sean wrapped his arm around her, enfolding her in his big, bear-like embrace. He kissed her hair.

'Don't worry, darlin',' he said, his voice soft. 'It's nothing to do with you, honey –'

She broke away. 'Of course it is,' she said, angrily. 'Sean, they're my two best friends.'

'I know,' he said. He wiped his hand across his forehead. 'And Zoe – little Zoe. Man.'

Kate's voice cracked. 'Steve's going to be your *best man*, for god's sake – what am I supposed to do?'

'Nothing,' he said, putting his arm around her again and drawing her close, till her breathing subsided. 'Nothing at all.'

'I can't just do nothing,' Kate said, pulling away from him, turning around the room.

'I'll talk to him,' said Sean, holding out a hand to her. 'It's gonna be fine, Katy. It's nothing. I know it's nothing. I don't want you worrying about it, OK? Come here.'

There, in the cold but brightly lit Christmassy flat, Kate suddenly felt fear for the future, a sensation she hadn't felt since she'd got together with Sean. As if the life she and Sean and all her friends had built for themselves was just a house of cards, flimsy, impermanent. Kate had spent years searching for structure, order, security. Here, in her new flat, in her husband-to-be's arms, a John Lewis catalogue on the table beside them, she suddenly felt in the midst of chaos, as if the wallpaper might start peeling off the walls, the china jump off the counters and smash, and the lights, suddenly, go out.

CHAPTER TWENTY-FIVE

July 2004

'Steve's got a day off today, you know,' said Zoe, sitting with her feet up on another chair outside a café in Smithfield. 'He said he might go round to yours, see Sean.'

'What?' said Kate, startled. She put down her menu, blinking at Zoe in the sunshine.

'Do you know where Sean is?' Kate's face was blank, and Zoe said patiently, 'The bathroom tiles in your flat. He's doing them today, isn't he? Steve's helping him.'

Kate stared at Zoe. It went into her head, this nugget, another little piece of information. Kate wished she could connect them all in some way; but her brain didn't seem to be working, lately.

They weren't doing the bathroom tiles for another couple of weeks, Kate knew. The tiles were delayed, some problem with the manufacturers in Italy, due to Sean's incredibly precise tile requirements, which had driven Kate practically up the bathroom wall itself. Plain white from IKEA was absolutely no good, no, they had to be from some tiny artisan shop near Modena, cut to the same dimensions as some

Japanese designer from the Sixties. Kate just couldn't have cared less. Having grown up with parents who barely knew one end of a hoover from another, Kate had learnt to be practical to survive, and it surprised her to realize just how good she was at organizing their finances, sorting out their tax returns, organizing the wedding, though actually, that didn't interest her as much as other things did. Sean laughed at her, he thought it was funny he was marrying a girl who was more interested in tax returns than bathroom tiles or fonts for wedding invitations. He quite liked all of that, he told her.

He did, too. It surprised her, to realize what a homebody Sean was, to see how subtly both of them were changing. He wanted to be an old man with his pipe and slippers, sitting by the fireside. Kate couldn't see big, strong Sean in slippers, at all – he was always doing something, always up before her, out getting supplies from somewhere, and yet more and more he wanted to stay in. He was out so often during the day for work, going to other offices, in meetings all over town, so when he was off he wanted to be with her and he liked her to be there with him, though these days, Kate's job took up a lot of her time, and it was sometimes a real struggle to get away from the office, from the parties, the launch for a new fragrance, the preview of a new film. As she did better in her job, she became less of a homebody; the opposite of Sean. Sean had enjoyed doing up their flat so much, she found it really quite touching, though his zeal for home life was sometimes a bit overpowering, as if he'd tried on the coat for size and found it was too big but wanted to keep it anyway.

'We should think about moving out of town in a year or so, though,' he'd said, a few nights ago, as Kate was sitting on the sofa in her pyjamas, tapping away at her laptop, making some last-minute changes to an article she'd done.

Kate peered at him. 'What?' she'd said, not really taking it in.

Sean was squatting on his haunches by the fireplace, a palette knife in his hand. He'd found some antique ceramic tiles which exactly matched the period of the flat, and had removed the dull Seventies grey-green tiles around the fireplace, to replace them with burgundy, floral charming ones. Now she watched him, fondly.

'I said.' Sean heaved himself up. 'We should really think about moving out of London in about a year or so.' He put the palette knife in his toolbelt; Sean loved his toolbelt.

'Why?' said Kate, trying not to sound rattled. 'We've only just moved in here.'

'We don't want to raise kids in the city, though, do we?'

'What kids?'

'The kids we're going to have, Kate.' Sean sat down next to her. 'Hello?' He patted her arm. 'Don't freak out.'

'Oh,' said Kate. 'Those kids. Yes, but – Sean, I don't want to move out of town.'

'I'm not raising kids here in the city,' said Sean. He sounded affronted. 'Do you really want to do that? Wouldn't it be better to be in a house? In a cul-de-sac? They can ride their tricycles, and . . . and stuff?' he finished, rather vaguely. 'Wouldn't it be nice to live in an actual town?'

'We already live in an actual town,' said Kate. 'I thought you liked it here. You've never said . . .'

'Darling, calm down. This is way in the future,' he said, putting his arm round her, and pulling her close. She could hear his heart beating, as she rested her head on his chest. 'We won't be in this apartment forever, will we? Or are you saying you want us to stay here for the rest of our lives, never move, never change anything, live here for fifty years, just like the Allans upstairs?'

He always did this; got her to agree with him by taking

the piss out of her, driving her arguments into the ground with gentle hilarity. She couldn't argue with him, never had been able to. He was like Teflon Man, nothing stuck to him, he just got on with it and did his own thing. Usually, she loved that about him.

'I'd like to be like the Allans,' she said. 'They've got a great life.'

'No, they've got a stupid life,' said Sean, sitting up. 'They should have realized the profit on their place years ago. Don't they realize the market's going to bottom out and they could have got a great little cottage in the country somewhere?'

'I've never asked them,' said Kate, moving away from him. 'But maybe you should run up there *now* and make sure they're aware of that.' She poked him gently. 'Calm down! Last week you wanted us to start going to the local church, now this. Is it the wedding, is that what's making you freak out and act like Mr Suburban all of a sudden?' He swung round towards her. 'It doesn't matter,' she said softly. 'I don't need a house in Epsom somewhere to be happy with you. I'm happy here now.'

He frowned, looking annoyed. 'Kate, that's not what I mean. You know that.'

'I don—'

'Hey. *You're* the one freaking out about the wedding. Ever since we got engaged, you've become Ms Career Girl in the City.'

She inhaled sharply. 'What the hell do you mean by that?'

'It's like you with your job these days. It's like it's the only thing that matters to you. "Ms Miller? Ms Miller?"' he said, imitating a receptionist on the phone, a high, silly voice.

'This is stupid.'

'That's what Sue's assistant called you when she rang about the car to the airport. "Is Ms Miller there?" Since when were you a "Ms"?'

'I don't know!' Kate ran her hand through her hair. 'You're being ridiculous! Who cares if I'm Ms or Miss or Mrs or whatever? Why should it matter?'

'Because you're marrying me,' he said. 'You're going to be Mrs Lambert.'

'I know, but –' Kate sketched something with her hands, a helpless gesture. 'Sean, don't be like that –' She reached forward; he had stood up, and she caught his leg. 'I can't wait to be Mrs Lambert, honestly.'

'Really?' he said, turning round and looking down at her. She met his gaze, solemnly. 'It just feels like – it's your job first with you, then organizing the wedding, then Zoe, then the flat and stuff, and I come about fifth on the list.'

She didn't know how to reassure him; all of those things were true, because she did them all for him. He had urged her to work that hard, to make them the money that would keep them afloat, that would pay for not just the tiles from Modena, but the honeymoon in the Maldives and, she supposed now, the house in the commuter belt, with a drive to park the car in, and a mantelpiece to put the framed photos of the honeymoon in the Maldives on. They were on a treadmill, and Kate realized they didn't know how to get off.

'Sean –' she said, moving her hands up his body, pulling him towards her. 'Sit down, darling.' He sat down. 'You are first with me, you know that, don't you? Always first.'

'Of course I do.' His face softened. 'It's just –'

'Let me finish,' she said, holding up her hand. 'Look, I want to be with *you*, I want a marriage to *you*, not so I can say "my husband's over there" to people at parties. That's why we're doing this, isn't it? Because we want to be together.'

She said it in a funny voice, like the old Prudential advert, but Texas-raised Sean didn't get it, and he looked blank for

251

a moment, before his expression cleared. 'Sure,' he said. 'Forget about it.' He leaned in towards her, and kissed her, moving her arms, breaking up her defensive body language position. 'We are together,' he said after a moment, his voice muffled in her hair.

Kate sighed. She was so tired, after a long day on the magazine, where there was a new drama every day. She wasn't sleeping, much, stymied by various things. She hadn't called the caterers to finalize the menu, nor spoken to Lisa about Danielle's little dress (Lisa was insisting on Daniel's new album of Westlife covers being played at the reception and Danielle being a bridesmaid. They'd compromised on the latter). And always, at the back of her mind, was Charly. Steve and Charly. She had absolutely no further evidence, no sign that anything was amiss. Was she going to upset pregnant Zoe over what Sean was convinced was just a misunderstanding? Threaten everything, lose Steve's friendship – because how could it be otherwise – when she wasn't really sure?

The trouble was, she couldn't stop thinking about it. Her mind ran in a circle, around and around, always coming back to the same thing: was that why she hadn't seen Charly for months? Was that why Sean and Steve didn't play their weekly game of pool any more? Was that why Zoe seemed strange with her now, like she was on her best behaviour? Everything led back to it and it seemed to her, Kate, as if she was the only person who could do something about it, and yet the only person who shouldn't. She was like a rat, caught in a trap, and she honestly didn't know how much longer it could go on like this. Her brain wasn't working properly. She was losing weight, too much weight. People kept saying it was pre-wedding nerves. She knew it wasn't.

'Did you speak to the photographer?' Sean said softly, running his hands over her shoulders, his lips on her jaw.

'No,' said Kate, twisting towards him, hoping to distract him further. 'I will tomorrow. Forget about that now.'

'OK.'

'OK.'

'So the tiles are going up today, are they?' Zoe said, sitting up and leaning closer, recalling Kate to the present.

Kate shook her head, as if the thoughts inside it were buzzing loudly, and looked around her. She and Zoe were by Smithfield Market, sitting outside in a café that overlooked the vast wrought-iron building. They could hear the shouts of traders, finishing up for the day, echoing behind them as they sat in the sunshine, smiling politely at each other.

'I suppose so,' Kate shook her head again, trying to work out what was bothering her. 'I thought it was later, but . . . perhaps they arrived early. That'd be cool.'

'Nice of Sean to give Steve the key. I wouldn't trust him with . . . anything,' said Zoe happily, as she patted her tummy, and lifted one foot up onto the slatted chair opposite her. 'Look. Harry does this when he's hungry.' She made circular movements on her rounded stomach. 'God, I'm starving. Shall we order?'

'Yep,' said Kate. 'Let's. Let's do that.' She gazed around, suddenly feeling sick. Sick to her soul, with something that was beyond her control. It couldn't be true, could it. *Could it?* Steve wouldn't . . . Charly wouldn't . . . Kate tried to focus.

'So,' Zoe was saying. 'What have you got left to do?'

'For the wedding?'

'*Yes*, for the wedding,' Zoe said. 'I know you're the least bridal bride in the whole world, but you must have *some* things left to do.'

'Not really,' said Kate. 'Dress, fine.' She would be wearing

253

a beautiful dress she'd found in Fenwicks. It was pale blue. 'Registry office booked. Venue booked, band booked.' Lisa had taken care of the venue, a disused church hall round the corner from their flat, on Shirland Road, and her father had, very kindly, after the CD debacle was cleared up, offered to find a good band for the wedding, coming up trumps with the Frank Walden Band. There was two months to go, anyway – Kate didn't see what the fuss was about, personally. She kept thinking she should be in a flap, but it was like she was watching it from a long long way away, and she simply couldn't get worked up into a mountain of stress about it. It'd be a party, she and Sean had decided. A great big fantastic party. Sean was more nervous than her, she thought. His family was coming over, whereas she had virtually no family. And he was more one for the big occasion. When the registrar, attempting small talk, had asked which of them was going to cry, both Kate and Sean had pointed at Sean and said, in unison, 'Him/Me'. As the registrar simpered, batting her eyelashes at Sean, who was nodding and smiling, he'd added, self-deprecatingly,

'I'm just a real sucker for the whole thing. I – I can't wait, you know?'

'And I'm dead inside,' Kate said to Zoe. 'She looked at me like I was a total witch.'

'Rubbish,' Zoe said briskly, putting her menu down and squinting at her friend. 'I can tell you Harry is really, really excited. I think he thinks a wedding's something to do with the police. He keeps shooting imaginary things when I talk to him about it, I don't know why.'

'Hah,' said Kate, pretending to study her menu.

'Steve says he's got an unhealthy interest in weddings for a three-year-old. Well, he says *I've* got an unhealthy interest in weddings too, and he's right, Kate, but oh, I'm just so excited!'

A waiter walked past; a pigeon landed nearby; a car hooted in the background. That was when it suddenly hit Kate, it wasn't a flash from the skies, a thunderbolt. It was one ordinary moment passing into another, but it changed everything. She put her menu down, staring thoughtfully at Zoe, not caring if she was being odd. This was her best friend in front of her, the girl she had grown up with, who had been more family to Kate than her actual blood relatives, really. She had to know what was going on, had to take control. She realized that, now. No more of little Kate in the shadows, waiting for Sean to sort everything out for her, for them both. He had failed her in that, she had to admit it. It was time for her to do something, though it terrified her.

She stood up.

'I've got to go,' she said suddenly. She picked up her bag.

Zoe looked up at her in astonishment.

'What?' she said. A curious expression crossed her face.

'I've – conference call,' Kate said, recent memory giving her inspiration. 'The Americans. I forgot. Shit I'm late,' she said, unconvincingly. She met Zoe's eyes, bent down and kissed her. 'Don't get up, darling,' she said, patting her best friend on the shoulder. 'Stay there. It'll be OK.'

'Kate!' Zoe was shouting. 'Kate? Don't go! Come back!' Her voice was incredulous, worried. 'Kate! Listen to me –!'

But Kate ran off, through the cobbled Smithfield lanes, down Cowcross Street, past the boys with tousled fins and the girls in ponchos, past the coffee shops and little restaurants, gathering pace as she went, brushing City boys out of the way, running now as she slammed her pass against the ticket gate and ran onto a train, not caring about work, about Zoe thinking she might have gone mad, just knowing now she had to get back to the flat, to stop them, because she suddenly knew that's where they'd been meeting, and it was down to her to stop it. Her alone.

Half an hour later, as Kate ran up the stairs at Maida Vale station, panting, and flew across the road towards the flat, she was no clearer about what she would do when she saw them, and doubt was starting to crowd in on her mind. Come on, Steve wasn't a cheat! He wouldn't do that to Zoe, to Harry, to the baby. He just wouldn't!

And then she saw it, outside her and Sean's building. Steve's car, a little red MG, which he had bought over Zoe's protestations, her arguments that they needed a family car. There it was, like a little shiny cliché, parked slap bang in front of the front door. Kate almost gasped at the audacity of it, and rage overtook her, rage and bile. Her clumsy, shaking hands stabbed the key in the lock.

She slammed the door and ran, taking the stairs two at a time.

She slowed down as she got to their flat, caution getting the better of her. Stealthily, smoothly, with murder on her mind and her teeth gritted, she slid the key in smoothly, opening the door so quietly she knew anyone inside wouldn't have heard her.

Perhaps there was no one in there, she said to herself. I must have got it all wrong, stupid me, and just as she thought that she heard something, heard a noise from the bedroom, the door of which was ajar. Kate took a step forward. The muscles in her throat had closed up.

Steve . . .

Oh god. No. No no no.

There she was, on the bed, moving slowly up and down, her hair falling about her shoulders, down the creamy pale, skinny back. Kate would know her anywhere. She was moving up and down on top of him. Kate stopped short at the door. But she still didn't see it. Then he sat up, pulling her down towards him, his face greedily gobbling between her breasts. He groaned, shaking his head. She moved against him, tilting her head, and Kate saw his face.

It wasn't Steve.

CHAPTER TWENTY-SIX

Steve's voice came behind her as she stood at the door. He was out of breath, she registered it vaguely. She could hear him, as if he were underwater, or far, far away.

Kate ... Kate, it's ...

It wasn't Steve in bed with Charly, her best friend.

It was Sean.

Sean's hands pressed on Charly's hips as he exploded into her, with a great, bellowing moan. Steve grabbed Kate's hand and pulled her away, but she wouldn't move. Why couldn't they see her, why didn't they notice, why didn't they *stop*.

'Shit. *Shit,*' Sean said suddenly, and Kate looked at him, realizing he'd seen her, standing in the doorway. 'Kate. *Kate.*' He groaned again, as Charly ground herself against him furiously.

'It's *Charly*, you *twat,*' she spat into his ear, as she collapsed again. 'Charly.'

He pushed her off him – she tumbled backwards, gracefully, onto the bed, turning around and looking lazily up, breathing deeply, her tousled hair falling over her perfect naked body. She stared up at Kate.

'Fuck,' she said, her eyes dilating. 'Fuck.' And then she

breathed in again, and closed her eyes, shuddering slightly, running a hand through her hair, grabbing onto it. Sean got up, pulling his boxers on.

'Kate, Kate,' he said, stumbling towards her. 'Shit.'

It was so strange, seeing him awkwardly naked, having just come inside Charly a few seconds before, fumbling with himself, his clothes: Kate backed away, like he was an embarrassing drunk on the street. She bumped into Steve, who caught her.

'Come on,' he said. She turned around in his arms.

'I thought it was you,' she said.

'I know,' said Steve, his face red, his green eyes watching the figures behind her. He breathed in, squeezed her arm. 'Zoe called me. I guessed you must be coming here. I was on the phone to her in the car and you ran past . . .' His eyes were full of sympathy. 'Oh, Kate.'

'I thought it was you,' she said again, as Charly pulled the duvet over her body.

'I know you did,' Steve said. 'But there wasn't much I could do about it, was there?'

She pointed at him. 'But you've been seeing her – I saw you –'

'I've been seeing her to get her to stop doing it, stop both of them,' Steve said, shaking his head. 'It's me, Kate! How could you think I'd do that –'

'Oh my god,' Kate said. Bile rose in her throat. She swallowed it back, but it choked her. Sean pushed her into the bathroom next door. Her bathroom, with the tiles they were waiting for. 'Get away from me,' she said, backing away from him. She turned, and was sick. Sean and Steve stood at the bathroom door, watching her. It was bright and sunny in there, her huge beautiful bathroom that she loved so much. Kate frowned, thinking abstractly to herself, as she heaved and was sick again. Stupid thoughts flew into her mind, silly

259

questions. Her head spun. What would happen to the bathroom now? She couldn't come back here again, she was sure of that.

'Kate, I'm sorry,' Sean said, when she stood up, a few seconds later. His hair was standing on end, almost comically; he was shaking his head. 'You – I'm sorry. I love you. This means – oh shit, seriously. I don't know how it happened.'

How to stand, to face him, to behave in this awful, ungodly situation? She didn't know, couldn't work it out. And Charly – she was still in there, in her bed.

She stood up straight. She wiped her mouth, breathing as calmly as she could. Her neck, throat, chest felt constricted, like she might pass out.

'Get out of here,' she said, without looking at him. 'I don't want to see you again.' Moving down the corridor, she looked through the door at Charly lying there still, curiously expressionless, and that's when Kate lost it. She could feel herself as it happened, it was a most strange experience. She marched into the bedroom, aggressively upright, standing straight, and she walked over to the bed. She grabbed Charly by her long hair, wanting to hurt her, kill her. Murderous rage swept through her. She dragged Charly off the bed, screaming, 'Get out! Just get out, you evil, *evil* bitch!'

She had hold of Charly's hair and she was shaking it up and down, and Charly's head, imprisoned by Kate's steel-strong fingers, was waggling around underneath her. 'My god, Charly, I always knew you were cheap, but – this! THIS! You COW! Get OUT!' And she flung her away from her, as far as she could, away. Charly tumbled onto the floor.

'You fucking bitch!' Charly screamed, suddenly alive, scratching at Kate, her long talon-like nails scratching Kate's arm, but Kate felt invincible, suddenly. She marched over and grabbed Charly again, not thinking, not feeling. Charly was tripping over herself, bashing into the doorframe, as Kate swung her from side to side, wishing she could swing her around the room, rip out her hair, break every bone in her body . . . Adrenaline pumped into her, coursing through her veins, making her feel light-headed. She could have killed her. She could have killed him . . . and all the time Charly was screaming at her, screaming torrents of abuse, filthy, black-hearted words close to her ear, as she scratched, clawed like an animal. Oblivious, Kate opened her front door and flung her, still naked, out into the landing and Charly screamed as she banged against the bannisters and nearly fell back, over the stairwell. For a second she hung there, as if she were going to fall, but then she bared her teeth, her dark eyes glittering at Kate, and, righting herself, she smiled.

'I always knew he was mine, darling,' she said clearly. Kate shut the door in her face as she rushed towards her and leant up against it, breathing hard. Sean and Steve watched her, in horror, rooted to the spot. Charly started banging on the door.

'Let me in!' she screamed. 'Let me in, you silly, stuck-up, pathetic little bitch! He's mine! He has been for months — years, if you want to know. I can have *whoever I want*, Kate, you *stupid* little girl, why didn't you ever see that?'

Sean was slumped in the hallway, his head in his hands. He didn't even look at her, he didn't seem to be able to. Kate started shaking. She had to get out of there, but she didn't know how. Steve pushed her out of the way, gently, and as he opened the door to let Charly in, Kate dodged past her, her feet flying down the stairs, down, away from that flat, away away away. She heard Charly's hiss, and the patter of following footsteps behind her.

'Kate!' Sean shouted suddenly. 'Come back!' No, she wasn't going to catch her up. No, no no. Kate ran into the hall, flinging the door open. She daren't pause for breath, had to keep going, had to had to. The steps behind her were getting closer, and Kate ran out on to the street, hair flying behind her, like a crazed, mad woman, like the hounds of Hell themselves were after her. She could feel Charly gaining on her, all the time, and she kept on running, towards the shops, towards safety, she didn't know where.

She kept on running as she reached the main road, and there were footsteps behind her, pounding, and they spurred Kate on, more and more. The lights were green, she could see them, but the lights were green for the traffic, not for her, and she couldn't see it.

There was a loud chorus of horns, people jamming their hands onto their horns to stop her, and there was the screeching of brakes, and Kate came to and slowed down in panic, just as someone started shouting.

'Kate! Kate, get out of the –'

As she turned she could see a great big bus approaching, and someone pushed her with all their force, so that she flew across the road and fell to the ground, on her back, and from there she saw what happened next. She saw the bus driver's look of horror, heard the desperate braking of the bus right next to her, as Steve, who had pushed her out of the way and saved her life, was hit.

Kate's leg and arm were covered in blood, where she had fallen to the ground and skidded. She rose to her feet and ran back to him, as people starting piling out of cars, rushing over to the man lying in front of the bus, his neck at an unnatural, strange angle, his body sprawled out in the middle of the crossroads. They watched her, almost not daring to come too close.

'Steve?' she croaked, in a hollow voice. 'Steve? No. No. *Steve?*'

CHAPTER TWENTY-SEVEN

Should Harry come to the funeral, was the question everyone asked. He was fifteen months old. He wouldn't really understand what was going on, he was simply too little. Would Steve have wanted him there? It was the question everyone asked because it was an issue about practicality and, in those black, horrifying days before the funeral, when there was nothing to do and everything to do, and there were no answers to why this had happened, practicalities were what kept everyone in some kind of sanity.

Zoe didn't know. She said she wasn't sure. When Kate asked her, looking into her face for some kind of direction, some sign that she was absorbing this, what had happened to her family, she saw nothing, only a sort of blankness, as Zoe rubbed her pregnant tummy, and shook her head.

'I don't know. You decide.'

Kate couldn't decide that, though. She turned to Steve's mother Mary, who had arrived that morning. 'What do you –'

'I think we'll think about it later, dear,' said Mary, in her Edinburgh-accented voice. 'Zoe, why don't you go and have a lie-down? You must be tired, what with all the arrangements this morning.'

Zoe hadn't slept since Steve had died three days ago. Because even saying Steve had died, it was so horrible, so totally alien, it was words that didn't go together. But she was docile, easily led now. She raised her hands in silent protest, as if to say, This is pointless, and got up heavily from her chair in the kitchen. Kate followed her through to the sitting room.

'Do you want some water, a cup of tea?' she said, looking around the room as Zoe sat down on the sofa. There were photos of them together everywhere, photos of Steve and Zoe on their wedding day, Steve and Mac laughing, their arms round each other. One of his ties was hanging off the bannisters. Kate wanted to make Zoe go outside, stand on the front doorstep for five minutes so she could tidy all of it up, remove every trace of him from the house, so Zoe wouldn't have to see his presence everywhere, how recently he'd been with them. An ice-cream van trundled slowly by out on the street and Harry, out in the garden, called out in pleasure at the noise. Kate rubbed her eyes, wondering again how things could be so prosaic, how life could be carrying on in its normal way when this had happened. Things kept striking her; like how Steve would never see his new baby. She would never know her dad. Harry would forget things about his father that he knew now, because he was too little to carry them with him. A trail of sweat trickled down Kate's back. It was so hot, disgustingly hot, it shouldn't be like this, now. It should be snowing, or raining, winds should be howling. They shouldn't be wearing vest tops and flip-flops while they discussed what kind of coffin Steve should be buried in. Everything was the wrong way round now, everything, Kate didn't know where to even begin, and that's why they focussed on the practicalities. Who was going to make the sandwiches for afterwards. Should Harry come to the funeral.

Interrupting Kate's thoughts, Zoe said quietly, 'Actually, can I have a glass of water?'

'Of course,' said Kate hurriedly. 'I'll get it, now. Do you want some food? You should —'

'No,' Zoe said.

'But you haven't —'

'I don't want food,' Zoe repeated, with that edge of steel that Kate had seen in her these last few days. 'I'll eat later. Not now. OK? Can you make sure Harry's OK, Kate?'

'Yes, of course,' said Kate, going into the kitchen. 'Just stay there.'

Mary was staring out of the window, into the garden, watching her grandson, playing with his grandfather and uncle on the lawn. She turned as Kate came in.

'Does she want some food?' she asked.

'No,' said Kate. 'She says she'll eat later.'

'Right,' said Mary. 'Right then.' She turned back to the window, her fingers stroking the glass. Kate poured the water.

'What are we going to do?' Mary said quietly, almost to herself. Her eyes were hollows, sunken into her face, her skin a pale, papery colour. She looked old, all of a sudden. 'Tomorrow. After it's over. What are we going to do?'

Kate nodded, because she didn't know what to say.

'Perhaps we should stay down here.' Mary nodded to herself. 'Move down and help Zoe. Oh my god. What will she do?'

Kate came over and stood by her side at the window. She touched her arm, gently. 'Her mum's here, and I'm here, Mary, I know it's —'

But Mary wasn't listening to her. 'Mac's saying he should have taken that job. He says he should move back here now, get a place nearby,' she said, almost conversationally. 'Perhaps that would be best.'

Kate watched Mac, out on the lawn, and he looked up as if he could hear them, and stared straight at them. He pointed at them to Harry, who was only just walking, unsteady on his feet. Mac clutched his nephew's arm and they both looked at Kate and Mary. They were, in that moment, so like Steve, the same quick glance, the same hair colour, shape, that it struck Kate like a blow and she steadied herself, holding onto the kitchen surface. She thought she was going to be sick. A mug rolled over, into the sink, with a clatter.

'Are you OK, dear?' Mary said briefly, flicking a glance at her before staring out at the window again.

'Fine, sorry,' said Kate. 'Just – yup.' Her arm was hurting, the injuries down one side of her swollen, bruised body throbbing with pain.

They were silent again, and then Mary said, 'I need to talk to Jim. I just don't know what we should do.'

Kate carried on looking out of the window, swallowing, breathing slowly. She looked down at the sink, full of mugs, and ran some water, as the kitchen door opened.

'Hi,' said Mac.

'Hi!' said Harry, who was holding onto Mac's hand. 'Mum!' he said, pointing into the sitting room, and he ran off towards her.

'Hello baby!' came Zoe's voice from the other room. She sounded so tired, her voice was cracking. Kate turned the tap on full blast. The hot water hurt her hands.

'How are you?' said Mac, turning the kettle on. 'Need a hand with the drying?'

'Thanks,' said Kate, handing him the tea towel. He stood next to her, and picked up a glass, glancing at her as he dried it.

'You alright?' he said, nudging her. 'You're very pale.'

Kate swallowed again. 'I feel a bit sick, that's all. It's nothing.'

He looked her over, appraisingly. 'You should take it easy, Kate. Your body's had a shock. Those are nasty,' and he gently touched her arm, which was scribbled over with deep, brown-red grazes, bruises, half-bandaged up. 'Don't try and do too much.'

'It's fine,' she said, gritting her teeth. She didn't want any sympathy.

Mac watched her. 'So, is Sean moving out today then?' he said, in a low, easy tone.

He uses this tone with his patients, Kate thought to herself. Make them feel secure. Gently, quietly, kindly, make them feel better, even when it'll never be better. He had arrived early on Saturday morning and she had not seen him cry, had not seen him anything other than composed, organized. He had taken charge of the funeral arrangements, he sat by Zoe and stroked her hair as she tried to sleep, he held his father when yesterday he'd broken down. She didn't know how he could do it. How can he be asking me things, when his world has fallen apart, completely collapsed. She stared at him.

'Sorry,' he said. 'You probably don't want to talk about it.'

'It's not that,' Kate said, shaking her head. She moved towards him. 'Mac, how can you be so –'

Mac looked down at the surface. 'Don't ask me about that,' he said. She bent her head, trying to see his face. 'I mean it, Kate. Please.'

'Sure.' She nodded, and touched his arm, fleetingly. 'I'm sorry.'

He shook his head back at her. 'No, I'm sorry. I want to do it this way.'

'Yes,' she said. She took her cue from him. 'Sean, yes. He packed up yesterday. I'm not sure how he's getting his stuff out.'

It was as if they were talking about getting a wardrobe through a door, down the stairs. 'You haven't seen him?'

'No,' Kate said. 'I didn't want to –' She trailed off. Sean had called, four, five messages on her phone each time she checked, alongside all the others from everyone else, each one sadder than the last. She had to listen to her messages, it might be friends calling about the funeral, about Zoe. But mostly they were from Sean, imploring her to listen, begging her to see him, crying about what had happened. But what could she say to him? She couldn't even cling to him, comfort him. He was the one person she blamed more than herself: she couldn't see him. She shook her head. 'He's ringing all the time, he wants to know what's going on. It's pathetic of me but –'

'Hey,' said Mac softly. 'It's OK.'

'No, you don't understand –' Kate began. Tears welled up in her eyes, she could feel something in her chest, a physical pain that hurt her when she thought about why this had happened, how it had happened, and why she was still here when Steve was dead. Steve's hands, pushing her out of the way, pushing her over hard onto the ground, so that she was alive now, standing here, now.

Why was she alive, why was Sean? Why was he allowed to live, when Steve was dead, his body cold, lying in the morgue in the hospital down the road? She didn't know. She didn't know where Sean would go now, where he was. Zoe needed her here – to field the phone calls, make the sandwiches, play with Harry, run to the shops. So that was where she'd be. Kate didn't need to be at home. After all, it didn't matter what happened to her now. She shook her head, willing the tears away.

'I'm sorry, I shouldn't have asked you,' said Mac.

He was so kind. She wished she could put her head on his shoulder, give in to it, but she couldn't. 'It's my fault,' said Kate. She cleared her throat and gritted her teeth, before she spoke. 'Sean's been in the flat today and yesterday. I think he's moving in with – with her. He doesn't have much stuff. He's cancelling everything, too.'

'Your wedding.'

'Yes,' said Kate. The idea of a wedding now, *her* wedding, seemed farcical. She turned towards Mac. He was holding a mug in his hands, twisting the towel around it, over and over, looking down at her. 'Can we not –'

'Of course,' he said. 'I understand. When are you going back there? Later tonight?'

'Yes,' said Kate. 'Zoe's giving Harry his bath in a bit, I'll go then. We should get an early night, all of us.'

'Yep,' Mac nodded. His mouth was set. 'It's going to be a long day.' He shook his head, smiling at the mundanity of his words. 'Jesus Christ.' He put the towel down with the mug.

'Oh Mac,' she said.

He gazed at her, his eyes glazed, drunk with pain.

'I can't stand it,' he whispered suddenly, closing his eyes, and he bent over, as if grief was crippling him. She put her arm around him, in the sunny, bright kitchen. He put his hands on his knees, and made a low, choking sound, his body shaking. Kate rubbed his back, not wanting to break the comfort of physical contact, not knowing what else they could do, any of them, now, other than hold each other and try to make it through the next hour, and the hour after that. Then the next day, then the day after.

It was Zoe, calling from the sitting room, who broke the moment. 'Hey, can you come through? I mean Mac, can you come through?'

'Sure,' Mac said, clearing his throat. He stood up, his tall, broad frame blocking out the sun from the garden, and wiped his eyes with the balls of his palms. Kate went ahead of him, to give him a little time to gather himself.

'Hi darling,' she said. Zoe was on the sofa, with Harry lying next to her, his eyes wide open.

'Where's Mac?' said Zoe.

'Just coming. Do you need anything?'

'I wanted to ask him something,' said Zoe.

'Right,' Kate said. 'Are you hungry yet –'

'For god's sake, Kate, stop asking me if I'm hungry all the time, OK?' Zoe ran a hand through her lank, lifeless hair. 'I'll eat when I want to.'

'I'm sorry,' Kate said, stepping forward. 'Zo, sorry, I just want to make sure you're –'

Zoe said blankly, 'Look, Kate. It's great you're here, and everything, but you can't make it better, OK?' She nodded. 'So don't try.'

'I'm not trying to make it better, I just want to look after you.'

Zoe gazed at her, biting her lip. 'Especially *you* can't make it better. Kate.' She spoke slowly, like she did to Harry. 'That's all.'

When Kate walked to the bus stop later, and waited for the bus, as she had done every day since it had happened, she marvelled again at how unreal it was to be doing this, another day gone by like this, dealing with his death, the collapse of everything around them. The bus arrived five minutes later, and she got on and sank into a spare seat. The bus was always full of people at this time, coming back from work, children from school, people heading into town. She wanted to stand up and tell them all what had happened, what grief and pain she had left behind in the little house down the road. She wanted to ask the people on the bus if they could make sense of any of it, of how it could have happened. But she couldn't. It was the same route that the bus that killed Steve had taken. On the first day she had walked for a while, she couldn't bear the idea of getting on that bus. But she realized it just didn't matter what she did or didn't do, and no one was going to see or care about it anyway.

She felt as if she were becoming invisible, as if parts of her life were becoming invisible. When she got off at her bus stop, she looked around for a sign, terrified that she might see them again. The trees were still in the evening light. There was no other traffic on the road. She got back to the flat, and climbed the stairs, trying not to feel dread, but praying he wasn't still there.

He wasn't. His stuff had gone. Four years together gone in an afternoon. The flat was exactly as she'd left it, no tidier, no messier; it was just that half the things in it were missing. Half the clothes in the wardrobe, half the books and the DVDs and CDs. No toothbrush in the bathroom, no dressing gown on the back of the door. And it didn't hurt, as Kate gazed round her flat, she tried to make it hurt but it didn't, not compared to everything else now, in this strange new world they were all coming to terms with.

She almost didn't see the note; it was on the mantelpiece, which was cluttered with invitations, photos of them all, before this happened. It was written on the back of a bill and this, somehow, made Kate angrier than any of the rest of it, that Sean would say goodbye to her like this, scribbling a few words on an electricity bill.

Kate

Believe me I am so sorry for what has happened and the way it has happened. I never meant to hurt you. I still love you – but I don't expect you'll believe that.

Look, it's been made clear to me that I shouldn't come to the funeral so that's why you won't see me there. But I hope I see you soon, to explain some things. In the meantime, I'll be thinking of you all tomorrow. You know, he was my best friend.

S x

CHAPTER TWENTY-EIGHT

At nine o'clock the next day, Kate came out of the flat, blinking in the harsh light of yet another relentlessly sunny day. The funeral was at noon. Mac had said he would pick her up to take her to Zoe's. He waved to her from the car as she stood on the doorstep checking for her keys and she waved back, as two figures appeared in front of her, their outlines almost black in the glare from the early morning sun. She was hot already, even though it was early. She was wearing long sleeves and a long skirt to hide the injuries. She didn't want people to see them, the cuts on her legs, over her shoulders. Underneath the black cotton, her skin smarted with pain, and sweat.

'Hello dear.' It was Mrs Allan. 'I'm glad we caught you.' She took Kate's hand.

'Oh, hello,' said Kate.

Mr Allan kissed her on the cheek.

'Are you just off to Zoe's, then?' he asked. She nodded. 'We spoke to Sue yesterday. It's the funeral today, isn't it.'

He had the *Guardian* and the *Telegraph* under his arm, and Mrs Allan was clutching a string bag, with some tomato juice and milk in it. The promise of a normal, ordinary day in their flat, reading papers, eating toast, being with each other, as they had been for decades and decades. Mrs Allan stroked Kate's cheek, her silver bobbed hair rippling as she did, and she said softly,

'We're here all day today. Just so you know. Alright? You be off now, but we'll be here later.'

'That's –' Kate began.

'I know you might not want to see anyone when you get back, or you might. All I'm saying is,' she said firmly, 'Graham and I are here all day.'

Mr Allan pointed at Mac, sitting in the car behind them. 'I suppose you'd better go. I'm glad we saw you. We haven't seen much of you since it happened. I came round to the flat yesterday and Sean was there, clearing up.' He looked at his wife. 'He said you'd been at your friend's most of the time since it happened.'

Kate nodded, not knowing what to say. She was almost glad to know he had been there, that she hadn't dreamt the note, the only sign of him she'd had.

'Let's go for a walk tomorrow,' Mr Allan told her. 'We haven't been for a walk for a while. I'll come and find you. Sue said she'd signed you off work for as long as you needed.'

Work. Kate blinked, trying to see Mac, in the car across the way. Work seemed like a different universe. The idea that people went to work, that she had her office and a desk and a view over the river, that she had a job she went to, a life before all of this? It was mad, unbelievable, like everything else. There was Mac, waiting patiently to take her to the funeral. And the idea that this funeral marked a point in time after Steve's death, that things would change again after, suddenly hit her.

'OK,' said Kate. 'Thank you. Thanks a lot.'

'We're here, that's all we wanted to say,' he said again.

Mrs Allan hugged her. 'You'd better go.'

She smelt of parma violets, of wool; comforting, secure. Kate hugged her back, not wanting to let go, but she did, waving goodbye as they opened the door to the flats. Then she walked down the steps, towards the car.

'All OK?' Mac asked her as she got in.

'Thanks,' she said. She looked at him. He looked like he hadn't slept at all. He was so pale, the circles under his eyes so blue, he looked almost ghostly. He was suited and his short hair was neat. He was impeccably shaved, except for a longish cut on his jaw. She pointed at it.

'You OK?'

He touched it, quickly, and shook his head. He put the car into gear and they drove away. Kate saw the Allans were still on the steps of the building. They were waving, and she couldn't understand why.

The church in Willesden was full to bursting; the noise of subdued conversation rustling through the building, like dry leaves in the wind. As Kate walked to her seat, people she knew, had known, for years and years, people she and Zoe had grown up with, people she and Steve had been at university with, all stared at her, curiously. She heard someone say, in a whisper, 'That's her.' Kate kept walking, she did not look around.

She was on her own, having left Zoe and Mac outside. He was a pallbearer, and she was walking behind the coffin. They had their roles, they had to talk to the vicar about it. About when and where and how, on this summer's day in North London, in a church that no one apart from Zoe had ever been into. Kate sank into her seat, and someone took her hand. She looked up in surprise. It was her dad; she'd forgotten he and Lisa were coming. He kissed her. Lisa reached across him and grabbed her hand.

'Babe,' she said.

'Darling,' Daniel whispered in his daughter's ear. 'This will be awful. Don't try and fight it.' He put his arm around her and squeezed her tight. 'I'm here, Kate.'

Kate sank against him, as the big doors at the back of the church swung open and the vicar called out to them from the threshold,

'Could you please all stand.'

She knew she would have to turn around, to see the procession coming down the aisle, Mac and Zoe and Steve's parents. Mac stared ahead, the coffin on his shoulders. His jaw was set, firm, but his Adam's apple was bobbing up and down with the effort of swallowing, and a film of sweat covered his forehead. Zoe seemed calm, eyes downcase, but halfway to the altar, she looked ahead for the first time, at the coffin, seeming to see what it really was. Kate watched her in alarm as her face froze. She stumbled, almost tripping, and there was a gasp, as Mary and Jim Hamilton held her up, and Zoe's mum behind stepped forward to hold her. Her face crumpled, her composure gone, and it was unbearable to watch.

And when they had set the coffin down, Mac slid into the seat next to his sister-in-law, and he pulled her towards him, her head on his shoulder, as she sobbed quietly, and the vicar started talking about Steve. From the row behind, Kate saw how Mac's fingers dug, hard, into Zoe's bare arm, trying to contain her as she sobbed, her shoulders heaving.

'It's OK,' he said, into her hair. 'It's OK.'

But it wasn't, of course it wasn't.

Mac gave the eulogy. They didn't know who else to ask; his parents' friends didn't know him as well as they all did. Steve and Zoe had loads of friends, but it was too much to ask one of them to perform this, this horrible task. Steve had spent so much of his life, from eighteen to twenty-eight, with Zoe, just the two of them, and she couldn't do it.

As Mac got up and walked to the front of the church, he left a gap next to Zoe, so she was on her own, on the end of the row, totally by herself. She was so small, her stomach already so big, sitting there on her own at the front of the church, her husband's coffin ahead of her. Kate reached forward and held her hand, and Zoe clutched it, her nails digging into Kate's palm. She was humming, quietly, as she cried, and it filled the silence of the vaulted ceiling as Mac fiddled with his notes, composing himself, his jaw set. Eventually he looked up at the congregation, with what seemed like an almighty force of will.

'Our hearts are broken today,' he said simply. 'Steve died last week. He was far too young, and all I can say, on behalf of Zoe, Harry, my parents and myself is that it's broken our hearts. I don't really know what else to say, because I still don't believe Steve is gone, and so to talk about him in the past tense seems completely crazy. He was my little brother, who stuck a pea up my nostril when I was five because he wanted to see how far it would go. I had to go to hospital to have it removed. He stole my bike when he was thirteen and trashed it, and then tried to pin the blame on me. He stayed up all night with me the night before I got my A-level results and I couldn't sleep. Last year he came all the way up to Edinburgh just to have a pint with me, because we hadn't seen each other for a while. He made me an uncle.' He paused. 'He was my little brother, but he was a bigger man than me, than most people. He was my big brother really, I suppose.

'And he and Zoe – their life together, the home they built, their family – it was just a pleasure to see it, to be a part of it. They didn't just have the best parties, they had the best life.'

Zoe bent over as far as she could, rocking in her chair and sobbing piteously. Kate looked around, looked up at

Mac, and then she got up out of her seat, pushed past Zoe's curled-up form, and sat down next to her in her row. She put her arms round her, and Zoe put her head on her shoulder, tears literally flowing down her cheeks.

Mac nodded, looking at her, and he took a deep breath, and then went on.

'So I don't know what to say to you all today, now that life has gone. Now that their baby daughter will never know her dad, now that Harry will grow up without his father. And for all of us who thought that Zoe and Steve, their life together, their house, represented everything we most wanted – it represented home to all of us, even if it wasn't our home – that's all over now, and I honestly can't see how we will ever smile again.' He was about to break down. His fists clenched at his sides.

'So perhaps we – Zoe, Mum, Dad, Harry – perhaps we have to take refuge in remembering him with pleasure, and being grateful that we had him in our lives, grateful that he met Zoe, that they had Harry, who's the spitting image of his dad. Grateful that he was here at all.

'But to be honest, I can't see a way to do that yet. Because, like I say, our hearts have been broken.'

CHAPTER TWENTY-NINE

It was Betty who planted the idea in her head. She had come back from New York for the funeral. They stood by the french windows watching Zoe talking with Mr and Mrs Hamilton in the garden, her hand on her back, as if it were aching, Harry sitting at her feet. Mac stood next to them, tall, rigid, watching Zoe all the time. Kate could just make out Mary's soft voice rising gently above the hubbub that rippled through the house.

'They seem so lovely,' said Betty quietly. 'I can't believe I'd never met them before.'

'I know,' Kate said. She watched the group, unwilling to tear her eyes away from them. 'Oh, Bets,' she said.

Betty's hand slid into hers. 'Babe,' she said.

'How's she going to cope?' Kate said bleakly. 'I just don't know what you do with something like that –'

'I don't know either,' said Betty. 'She's Zoe, though. She will cope. I suppose if you have the children, you have to.'

'Yes,' said Kate, realizing there was truth in this. She held onto the wooden frame of the door.

'Hey, Katy.' Betty's voice was still soft. 'How about you? How're you doing?'

'I'm fine,' said Kate. 'I'm not, but I'll be fine.' She pushed some cakes towards Betty. 'Here, have one of these.'

'I don't mean like that,' Betty said. 'I just think this must be much harder for you than most people realize, darling.'

'I don't know,' Kate said, through her tightened throat. 'I don't think about it like that. It's not about me.'

Betty looked at her with surprise. 'Right.' There was a pause. 'Only, sorry, I meant, because he saved your life. Because he pushed you out of the way.' She closed her eyes, shaking her head. 'Sorry, that's so crass of me.'

Francesca was standing next to them, talking to an old family friend of Steve's parents. Now she turned towards them. 'Betty, don't,' she said, under her breath. She nudged Betty. 'Hey Kate, those cakes look nice.'

Kate looked from one to the other of them, then down at the plate of fondant fancies, which she had bought that morning. They looked gaudy, celebratory almost, stripes of yellow and pink, chocolatey and delicious. Her skin crawled, nausea and heat swept over her. The wounds on her body stung; she prickled, ached in the heat. She wished she could tear her top off, scratch the scabs away.

'You OK?' Francesca asked.

Kate looked around the room, filled with people, all making desultory conversation, all watching other people over their shoulder. She whispered, almost to herself, 'I feel like – like I'm disgusting.'

'Look –' Francesca began.

'You mustn't feel guilty,' said Betty.

Mrs Allan had said that to her the day after Steve had died. She'd brought her down a cake, made her yet another cup of tea, held her hand. Her father had said that to her the previous night on the phone, when he'd rung to tell her that he and Lisa were coming to the funeral. Even Zoe had said it to her, the day after it had happened. Kate still shuddered to think that Zoe had felt she had to say it.

'I don't feel guilty,' said Kate. She clutched her left arm, where the cuts were worst. But it wasn't true. Things were starting to come together in her tired, battered head.

Watching her, Betty said, 'Perhaps you should get away for a bit. You should come to New York, visit your mother, maybe. Have you thought about that?'

'I don't want to leave Zoe,' said Kate.

Francesca stroked her hair. 'You can't be there for her the whole time,' she said. 'She'll have to get on with it. Mac's here, isn't he? And her mum, and his parents.' Kate's eyes rested on the group in the garden again, and her throat rasped with the pain of not crying.

'I kind of think maybe you need to leave her alone for a while,' Betty said, after a pause. 'You know.'

'Oh.' Kate nodded. 'Perhaps you're right,' she said.

'I think that's a good idea,' Francesca said, nodding, like they'd already discussed it and thought it was a good idea.

'Come and stay with me,' Betty said. 'Or with your mother.'

'What about my job, and the flat,' said Kate, slowly. 'I can't just leave them and go away.'

She watched Betty closely, wondering if she realized just how much she wanted her to have the answer to all of this.

Betty said, 'Oh babe. They've signed you off work for two months. Don't you remember?'

'Oh yes,' said Kate, wondering how she could have forgotten. She smiled at Betty, as if trying to let her know she wasn't mad.

'I spoke to your mother last night,' Kate's father said, his voice gentle in her ear as he came up to stand close to her. Kate started.

'Really?' she said. Her parents never spoke, normally. But this was not normal.

'Yes,' Daniel said. He stared down, into his drink. She thought how much older he looked, suddenly. When had he grown older and when had she not noticed? 'She phoned first thing. You know, she was thinking of coming over for the funeral, to be here for you. She loves Zoe, you know that. And she was so fond of Steve.' He nodded.

'She didn't need to come over,' said Kate. 'It would have –' She trailed off, thinking of her mother suddenly, how lovely it would be to have her near, to see her. She remembered her very clearly now, stroking her hair, reading her stories, laughing delightedly at her when she was little, how comforting she was, how Kate knew everything would always be fine when she was around, until suddenly she wasn't. She had never really felt that way again with her mother, after she left – the wound she left was too deep. But there in the hot, sunny sitting room, with everyone dressed in black, Kate missed her mother with a force she hadn't known before, hadn't known it was possible to feel. To see her there, her long red hair, her warmth, her smile. She looked at her dad, and clutched his hand, not able to speak all of a sudden.

'So he moved his stuff out, then?' Daniel asked, grimly.

'Yep,' said Kate. 'It was all gone when I got back yesterday.'

'And what have you agreed about the mortgage?'

'Dad! – I don't know,' said Kate. 'I don't want to talk about it.'

'How long will you be off work for, do you know?' Daniel asked, gruffly.

Kate watched him, wanting only to stay calm. 'Look, Dad – it's too soon to think about all that stuff. It's not about me, about Sean and everything, at the moment. It's about Zoe.'

'I know, darling,' Daniel said. 'But –'

'Please Dad, let's not talk about it.'

'I only want you to start thinking about yourself now,' Daniel said. He sounded stern. 'I'm your father. Your father, Kate. So I worry about you. You have a flat you have a mortgage on and you're signed off work for however long, and you have a fiancé who's done the dirty on you and buggered off. And the funeral's over now, it's a week since – since Steve died. I'm just saying, you need to think about these things. Not now –' he said, holding up a hand as Kate's eyes flashed and she started to speak, '– but you need to think about them at some point.'

'No,' said Kate. 'I'm only thinking about Zoe at the moment. Her and Harry, and the baby.'

Daniel looked at her. He put his hand on her shoulder, and turned her slowly so she was looking out into the garden, where Zoe and Mac were talking together, and Mary was holding Harry. He looked so like his father, Kate took a deep breath.

'Kate, listen to me,' Daniel said quietly. 'You can't stay here with Zoe and make everything magically better. It's not like that. It won't mean Steve didn't die. It won't mean it wasn't your fault.' He corrected himself. 'It wasn't your fault, in any case. But you have to let them get on with it. You can be the best friend in the world – but you'll only ever be a friend. You're not Mac. You're not her baby. You can't bring him back, either. And you have to consider –' He came to a stop.

'What?' Kate said.

'Nothing, nothing,' Daniel said, and he kissed his daughter, patted her shoulder. She winced, as his hand settled on her bruised skin. 'Here's Lisa. Darling, we're going now, got to pick little Dani up. I'll phone you tonight. Do call your mother.'

'Yes,' said Lisa, unexpectedly. 'Call her.' She turned to Daniel. 'We'd better go and say bye to Zoe.'

People watched in vague curiosity as they made their way across the room – Daniel was recognizable to a lot of people now. Kate gazed unseeingly at them too, as they smiled consolingly at Zoe, and kissed her, and kissed Mac and Jenny, Zoe's mother, as Lisa and Daniel kissed them all, holding hands as they did. She was alone on the other side of the room and even in the heat of the day suddenly felt extremely cold.

There is a sense, at a wake, that some people are clinging onto it, as the last stage in a recognizable process. Because after that, the period of unreality is to some extent over, and you have to get on with your life in some way. People lingered at Steve's wake for ages, until the evening, until it was getting dark. The group of them who had spent their twenties in this house, first the ground floor flat, now the whole house, stayed the longest. Betty was staying at Francesca's that night, Jem and Bobbie and the others were just down the road, and as the packed throng thinned out, Kate found herself in the kitchen again, unloading the dishwasher, with Zoe.

Zoe's mother had put Harry to bed and he was fast asleep, having been alternately bewildered and excited by the events of the day. Zoe had been for a nap upstairs, but she hadn't slept and had come back down.

'There's some soup in the fridge,' Kate said. 'Do you think people will want –'

Zoe looked out from behind a cupboard at the group of people left. 'Give it a while, if you're all still here in a bit I'll heat it up.'

'I can do it, don't worry.'

'Let's see,' said Zoe. 'I'm pretty tired now anyway, so hope-fully everyone will have gone soon.'

Kate shut the dishwasher. 'Do you want me to get people

moving?' She wiped her hands on a tea towel, and hung it carefully on the hook by the sink. Zoe was watching her as she did it.

'It'd be great if you were all off soon, to be honest.' She wiped her hand over her forehead and gave a great, ragged sigh. 'I'm not going to go hysterical again. I'm just really, really tired. I'm sick of all these people being here.'

'Of course,' said Kate. 'You must be. It's just we don't want to leave you on your own, you know?'

And Zoe looked at her directly. 'Yeah. But actually, Kate, I'd quite like to be on my own at some point.'

Kate took the hint. 'Look, I'll have a quick word with everyone. Are Mac and his parents – are they staying on?'

'Yes,' said Zoe. 'Just everyone else.' She flung her hands up in the air and gave a little, defeated moan of despair. 'Is that OK.' It was a statement, not a question.

Seeing as how she knew the contents of Zoe's fridge better than anyone at the moment, Kate said, ticking off things with her fingers, 'Zo, you're low on milk, and cheddar, and veg, and those little pots that Harry likes. Shall I pick some up tomorrow and come over first thing? We can –'

'No, thanks,' said Zoe, quite loudly. She corrected herself instantly. 'I mean – sorry, Kate. I don't need you to come round tomorrow. Steve's parents are leaving and we'll have stuff to sort out.'

'Oh, right,' said Kate. 'I'll call you in the afternoon then. Perhaps I can –'

As if it was in slow motion, Zoe shook her head. She didn't say anything, she just looked at Kate, and a tear ran down her cheek, as she rubbed her stomach again. Her eyes were shining with tears, her hand was on her back, and she stood there, silently, shaking her head, as Kate watched her, understanding dawning.

Eventually, Zoe just whispered, 'No, OK? Please, Kate. You need to leave me alone for a while.'

Kate stepped back, and nodded. She knew, she kissed her best friend's cheek, her heart cracking as she turned away. 'Of course. I love you. OK. But soon. I'll see you soon.'

Zoe nodded too, not meeting her gaze.

Five minutes later, they were all outside, on the pavement. The others went to the pub, to carry on the wake, talking about Steve, remembering the good times, like Mac had said. But Kate went home. She tore off the black cotton dress, the long cardigan. There were spots of blood on her skin, where the scabs had shifted, opened up again. She ran her fingers over the knobbly, rash-like bumps they formed, over her tired, bruised skin, as she sat on the sofa in her sitting room, staring at nothing in the darkness, for hours. She had seen the look on Zoe's face, heard the tone in her father's voice. She knew now that what she had said to Betty and Francesca earlier – well, it was probably true. She was to blame, she was disgusting, she should not be here, she should not be here at all.

CHAPTER THIRTY

So that was how it happened, that Kate left London. One sunny, dappled day in early September, just as the leaves are at their brightest, and the sky above New York is so blue it seems to bounce off everything around it, Kate found herself pushing a trolley through the airport terminal at JFK, past the baggage reclaim and passport control, where a moustachioed customs officer said with a strangely kind expression on his face, almost like he knew the importance of it, 'Welcome to New York, miss.' She smiled at him blankly, unable to believe she was there, that she had made it this far, that she was away from the flat, away from the piles of paperwork, away from her friends' questions, her workmates' sympathy, the sly looks of neighbours in the hall, the horror on people's faces when she went outside before the scabs had healed, revealing her arms, cut up, shredded. All of that, behind her now.

The automatic doors into the main terminal shuddered open as she emerged into the big glass atrium. Kate looked around, but she should have known that she wouldn't need to. Because there, standing in front of her, waving a placard that said 'MY DAUGHTER KATE!' was her mother, and as

Kate ran towards her, pushing the trolley out of the way as she embraced her, she started crying, and once she started, she couldn't stop. Venetia pulled her into her arms and kissed her. 'My little girl,' she whispered. 'You're here now. It's OK. It's OK.'

When Kate woke up, it was late the next day, nearly ten o'clock. She looked around the pretty, white bedroom, perched on the corner of the apartment. It was strangely quiet, except for the noise of the birds singing loudly outside – she'd forgotten how loud they were, how many there were. She sat up and looked out of the window, over Riverside Drive to the park. A man was chatting to a friend, both out walking their dogs on this glorious September afternoon. Other than that, it was silent. She felt nothing. She stared out of the window, and then around the room. It was clean, small, empty, blank. She thought of the possessions she'd boxed up and put away at her flat, of the new person living there now, who would call it her own home. It was three o'clock in London. Juliet would be sitting in Kate's old office now, doing Kate's old job. Gemma would be moving into Kate's flat, perhaps she'd have unpacked even now. And Kate felt totally at home, for the first time in weeks. Perhaps months.

In the other room, Oscar started playing the piano. Kate listened. It was 'I Remember You'. She did. She always would. She lay back on the bed, watching the ceiling, just listening to the music, simply enjoying the feeling of calm that washed over her. She was safe. She was at home, she was away from London. She didn't even have to think about going back. Perhaps she would never go back.

When, a few months later, Zoe had her baby girl, Flora, Kate sent a baby bag and a hamper, and a card, and Zoe never replied. Kate told herself that it was because she was busy with the baby, but she wasn't quite sure.

But Zoe did email her the following spring. She was chatty, sweet. Flora was fine, Harry was fine, they were all fine. Francesca said she was doing brilliantly. Mac, with whom she was in contact most frequently, kept her posted, sent her pictures, told her little snippets. He never reproached her, never made her feel bad about running away to New York. He never really commented on anything at all, nor could she expect him to. Her father was an infrequent correspondent, but he came occasionally to New York and she saw him then, which was almost better.

For more than two years after she left London, it was almost as if Kate Miller had hardly existed there at all. It was her home town, her life was there but now it was all gone. She tried to pretend she didn't miss it but sometimes – like once when she was in the Frick Collection, and she turned to see the Turner scene of the Thames at Mortlake Terrace, or when she heard Venetia laughing at comedy programmes from Radio 4 on Oscar's computer, or just sometimes, when she was walking down the grey, chaotic, tarry, streets of New York, chewing on a bagel, drinking her coffee and she thought of home, of the green parks and the grey skies and the people she loved, most of all – sometimes, it was almost unbearable.

She didn't consider herself as damaged. She thought she'd coped with what had happened, and what happened afterwards. Kate had come close to the edge, and she couldn't let it happen again.

PART THREE

CHAPTER THIRTY-ONE

Kate rang the doorbell of her father's house, smoothing down the fabric of her dress, nervously. It was just after eight, and she was due at the *Venus* offices to see Sue at ten. She shivered on the front doorstep in the cold March morning; it may have been a week now since she'd come back to London, during which she'd been round to her father's every single day, but it still felt weird, each time.

Lisa appeared in the hallway, and Kate watched her through the glass. She didn't make eye contact with Kate until she'd opened the door.

'Hi, Kate,' she said, kissing her step daughter on the cheek. 'You're here, then. I was wondering where you'd got to.'

'Hi,' said Kate, refusing to get ruffled. She was too exhausted to rise to Lisa's bait; the previous day she had written and rewritten her five hundred words for Sue so many times her brain felt like it wasn't working properly. She had finally emailed it over late last night, but she had slept badly, her dreams full of scenes she wanted to bury, then lying awake, mind woolly, thoughts circling inside her head like they were trapped there. Once she had woken because someone had been shouting at her; it had

293

taken Kate a while to realize it had been her, calling out in her sleep. It was still dark. She was glad Mr Allan wasn't there; she knew he would probably have heard her otherwise.

Mr Allan had left the day before, to go on holiday with his sister. 'Break a leg,' he'd told her, as he climbed into the cab. 'I'll see you when I get back, dear girl. What will I do without you?'

Kate hadn't wanted to say that she'd probably miss him a lot more. Besides her father, he was the one constant in her London life, more so than Zoe or Francesca, the one person she'd seen every day. Now it was just Dad, and Lisa and Dani of course, but it was her father she came to see. Somehow, Mr Allan's departure, and her completing the article, threw all this – being at her dad's – into even sharper relief. She felt awkward, uncomfortable again, like she had a week ago. It was just nerves about this morning, she told herself, and she stepped over the threshold.

'You look nice,' said Lisa, tonelessly.

'Oh, thanks,' said Kate. 'I've got a meeting –'

But Lisa had already turned and walked towards the kitchen. 'Your father's through here,' she said, briskly.

There was an atmosphere in the kitchen as Kate entered behind her stepmother. Her father was there, and she was surprised to see him fully dressed, sitting at the table impatiently whipping through the pages of the *Times*, an untouched pile of toast by his side.

'Hello Dad.' Kate bent down and kissed him. He smiled politely, and Kate looked enquiringly over at Lisa, who was loading the dishwasher.

'He's fine,' she said, calmly. 'He's been like this all morning. He's not hungry and he won't eat anything. He wants to go out. I've said it's far too soon.'

Daniel looked up, and ran a hand through his thin hair.

'I'm not a child; don't talk about me as if I weren't here,' he said, in a clear voice.

'Hey Dad. It's great you're feeling better, though,' said Kate.

'Thank you, darling. Thank you for coming to see me.'

'That's OK.' Kate tapped the kitchen table. 'Hey. Dad, I've got a sort of an interview today –'

Lisa slammed a cupboard door shut, and dropped something in the sink, with a loud clatter, and Daniel winced.

'Now. Listen, Lisa –' he said, trying to contain his irritation, but Lisa turned round, with a sneer on her face.

'Daniel! We're not having this discussion! I'm not doing this for my own amusement, believe me! You are Not Going Out, and that's that,' she finished, slightly hysterically, and stormed out of the kitchen.

'I was going to ask you to keep it down, dearest,' Daniel said loudly after her, his voice high, and cold. 'God, that girl,' he said, turning to Kate, shaking his head, and she was worried to see the expression on his face. 'You know, she's wonderful, but my god! So temperamental, so – bloody . . .'

Kate wanted to say a variety of things, but instead she said, 'I expect she's just tired, you know. She's had a lot on her plate, with Dani and you being ill, and everything . . .'

'I know,' said her father sadly, and it made her want to hug him, suddenly. 'I'm awful. I've been awful to her. She's so good, and I've been –' He trailed off, looking out of the window into the handkerchief-sized garden, where the wind blew roughly, shaking the tree perching on the corner of the neat lawn.

A small disloyal thought flashed through Kate's brain, that her father was actually enjoying all of this, enjoying being an invalid and maudlin and the centre of everyone's attention once again. She shook her head, and slapped her hands onto her thighs. Feeling like the supervisor in an old-people's home she said, in a loud, cheery voice, 'Well! So how are you feeling today, anyway?'

'Fine, fine,' said her father, brushing her away with his hand. His tone was still irritable. 'Just fucking bored, that's all. No one's been to visit me, not a bloody soul. It's as if I'm dead. Shows you who your friends are, doesn't it? And I've got work to do, arrangements for the Manilow album – no one cares.'

'I care, Dad,' said Kate, carefully. 'And I've been to see you, haven't I?'

'Oh.' Daniel nodded kindly at her. 'Yes, that's true. You don't really count, though,' he said. 'I mean, outside the family. You know, *others.*'

Kate said, patiently, 'Hey, I'm sorry Dad. This is the worst stage, I think, you're feeling better but you're still not that well. Shall we sit down in the other room and just chat instead?'

His eyebrows waggled together, undecided how to play this offer, but eventually he said, gruffly, 'Sure. Yup, sure, let's go through.'

They climbed the two steps up to the living-room-cum-dining-room, Daniel moving slowly, and suddenly Lisa appeared from the large, spotless cellar, where the surplus fridges and freezers for their household of three were stored, clutching Dani's lunch box. She looked flustered.

'Look, Dan, I just thought of something,' she said. 'Why don't you and Kate walk Dani to school? Kate can make sure you're OK, and I can run to the dry-cleaners.' She said this last sentence in a rush.

'Why do you need to go to the dry-cleaners?'

'Um. I forgot to pick up your DJ,' said Lisa, avoiding her husband's eye.

'What?' Daniel said sharply.

Lisa said, 'I'm sorry. I forgot, I forgot, OK? With everything that's happened.'

'I asked you to pick it up ages ago. I never know when I'll need it, Lisa, you *must* remember things like this!'

'Oh, don't sound so bloody patronizing,' said Lisa, and she ran her hand across her brow, baring her teeth at Daniel. 'It's not like you're going to be needing it any time soon, is it?' Kate watched her, alarmed at the expression in her eyes, and tightened her grip on her father's arm.

'I will!' her father shouted, in a weak voice. He sounded like a petulant child. 'Shut up! You don't know anything, anything! I will!'

'OK Dad, OK,' said Kate, patting his shirtsleeve. She remembered, with a flash, her mother doing the same thing. Patting his arm, talking him back down to normality, telling him it was OK, she was sorry.

'I'm sorry, darling,' said Lisa, seeing he looked really alarmed. 'Look, it's no big deal. I'll run and get it now, you two take Dani to school. You can have a little walk, it'll do you good, don't you think?'

There was a rumble upstairs, and a thundering sound, and right on cue Dani ran furiously downstairs, hanging onto the banister with one small hand. She jumped the last step, onto the ground, and looked face-up at her father, beaming, then at Kate.

'Hey there!' she said loudly. 'Kate! Hey there!'

'Oh,' said Daniel. He turned away, and said grumpily, 'She's doing it again. That stupid voice. She's doing it again.'

'Hi Dani,' said Kate, feeling sorry for Dani, having to live with these two. 'How are you? I'm going to walk you to school with Dad, is that OK?'

'Sure! Sure!' Dani jumped up and down, and grabbed the lunch box off Lisa. 'Let's go!'

'Bye, darling,' said Lisa, holding her wriggling daughter's

head in her hands, as she bent down and kissed her hair. 'Be good for Kate. I'll see you later, yes? Have a lovely morning. Goodbye, Daniel.' She looked at her husband, a curious expression on her face, something like triumph. 'Do you have anything to say?'

'Why should I?' said Daniel, still secure that the balance of power was his. 'I'll see you when –'

Lisa turned away; in a low voice she said, 'Just forget it. I'm sorry about the dry-cleaning, darling. Just be careful.'

Daniel was mollified. He furrowed his brow. 'No, darling, I'm sorry. I'm a horrible old man. And you're wonderful to put up with me.'

'I know I am,' said Lisa. She crunched her keys together. 'Oh, darling.' She kissed her husband softly on the cheek.

'Have a nice day,' Dani said, hitting the banisters and the wall alternately with her hands. Lisa opened the door and they trooped out in single file.

'We have to walk slowly, for Dad,' she told Dani. 'You OK, Dad?' she said, looking back at her father.

'Never better,' Daniel said, grinning. 'I'm so sorry for being such a bastard this morning. I just find it very frustrating, you know?' He pushed his fringe out of his eyes.

'You must do,' said Kate. 'Maybe you should get Lisa a present? Should we stop and get her some flowers?'

But Daniel wasn't listening. 'Ah, it's wonderful to be outside,' he said, breathing deeply in. He coughed. 'The old lungs, still not quite up to scratch yet,' and he thumped his chest, hard. 'Aah.'

'Dad, be careful,' said Kate, but Daniel was enjoying himself. He spread his arms wide, on the quiet street, and nearly stumbled over a cracked paving stone, before correcting himself. He said, casually,

'So, Kate. Tell me, have you spoken to your mother again? How is she?'

298

'Ah,' said Kate, taken aback. 'She's – she's fine. Dani, what have you got there?!'

Dani was fumbling in the big plastic wallet that passed for a school satchel, and from this she removed a blue plastic cartoon shark, its teeth bared, its face contorted in an expression of hatred.

'It's my Migmog,' she told Kate. She patted the toy, and made a soft cooing noise. 'She's my friend.'

'Ohhh-kay,' said Kate. 'Oh. He's nice.'

'*She!* She's a *she*!' Dani boomed, waving the shark alarmingly close to Kate's face, and Kate veered towards her father, feeling like she was jackknifing between two lunatics, both of whom were her blood relatives, she realized to her surprise.

'Sorry!' she said, irritably.' *She!* OK!'

'Is she – well?' said Daniel, continuing as if nothing had happened. 'Is she happy?'

She didn't really know how to answer this question. Of course her mother was well, of course she was happy. She was relentlessly positive, upbeat, a show-off showman, with the starring role in the miniseries of her own life, with the devoted Oscar at her side, living in a beautiful apartment in the most citizen-friendly city in the world.

Tramping slowly alongside her father, here back in London, Kate didn't know how to explain it, quite, to him. For she had come to see that, in the time she'd lived with her in New York, her mother was more of a mystery than she could have supposed. She still didn't know lots of things about her, really, little details like what her favourite film was, to the big things, like why she'd left her husband and daughter. Why she'd run away, and Kate knew she *had* run away, just like her daughter sixteen years later. And now, glancing quickly at Daniel, shuffling along beside her, his breath visible in the cold morning air, she couldn't see them together, couldn't remember what they'd been like. He seemed so much older, so . . . thin in spirit, somehow, whereas Venetia was overflowing with life, and energy, and lots of other things Kate didn't really understand. It seemed mad they'd ever got married, had a baby. Had her. They were her *parents*, it was strange. Kate blinked rapidly, her mind whirring.

'Well, you know what Mum's like,' she said after a while. 'Always the same old Mum.' She shook her head, smiling at the memory of Venetia's beautiful face as she solemnly recited 'May the road rise to meet you', standing and raising her glass to Kate the night before Kate had left for London, her still-thick glossy red hair falling around her shoulders. Oscar had looked on in wonderment, and when she'd finished he said reverentially, 'Isn't she the best?' Venetia sank gracefully back into her chair, as if she'd just sung the title role in Aida, not read a poem out loud.

For a moment Kate was back there, in the warm, quiet apartment overlooking the Hudson, the fire burbling in the corner, the books lining the walls. Safe, tranquil, easy. She shook her head at the memory, smiling. 'She's wonderful, just the same as ever. The life and soul of the party. You know what she's like,' she said again.

Daniel looked surprised. 'Oh.' He furrowed his brow.

'Oh?' Kate was curious.

'I don't remember her like that at all,' he said, and he looked old, confused, for a moment, and fear flashed through Kate. She clutched tightly onto Dani's hand, feeling the soft, plump fingers tighten in response. She wished they weren't talking about this, and sought to tie the conversation up again.

'You know, though. Mum's so –' she cast around for the word '– well, she's such a free spirit, isn't she? Always has been.' She semi-chuckled, as if to involve her father in the gentle joking, the way she did with Oscar, back in New York, for Oscar saw through his wife's faults and loved her for them anyway.

Daniel said strangely, 'She wasn't like that when we were together.' He trailed off, and said after a while, 'Perhaps she was – perhaps I remember that in the beginning.' His pace slowed, and he shook his head, looking down at the pavement. 'She wasn't, really though, not when you were growing up, when we were still together.' He flicked a glance at Dani. 'But it was very difficult, by then.'

Kate tried to remember something of her parents together but, as ever, she drew a blank. She could remember the house, her exercise books from school, the nativity play when she was small – but she couldn't remember her parents together, what they were like, how they *were* with each other. It was somewhere in her brain – she just couldn't get to it. The only memory she had was from Mr Allan of her leaving the Royal Festival Hall with her mother and father, she eight years old, holding happily onto each of her parent's hands. Them together: it just seemed hilarious, impossible.

The last time they'd seen each other was at her engagement party, three years ago, and they'd behaved like old friends. A little *too* much like old friends, in fact. Lisa had spent the whole week Oscar and Venetia were over looking like she was sucking a lemon. Kate often remembered the way they'd looked at each other that night: like they got each other. Simple as that. Like there was no one else in the room. She'd never looked at Sean like that, she knew. Knew it now, hadn't known it then. Oh, she'd loved him, but she'd never really understood him, the way she knew her parents understood each other. But when she thought about it, how understanding someone, like the way they got each other, the way she and Mac got one another, proved nothing, really. Got you nowhere.

So she said nothing. And Daniel said, matter of factly,

'You know, Kate, all this makes me think.'

'Think what?' Kate said, looking around her, trying to see if they were nearly there.

'About your mother.' He cupped his hand into a point. 'Bah. Never mind.'

'What?' said Kate.

'I said never mind. Did she even ask how I was?' Daniel pushed his hair out of his face.

Kate thought back to her conversation with her mother last night. 'I expect he's malingering, like he *always did*,' Venetia had said, and at the time Kate had thought that was a rather harsh judgement call on a man recovering from transplant surgery but now, having seen her father this morning, she could kind of appreciate her point. She thought she'd better change the subject, and looked down at Dani, who was completely silent, chewing her plait. She bent down towards her. 'Where's your school, Dani?'

'It's just across the road, Kate, we're nearly there,' Daniel said, a little faintly. Traffic whizzed past them, and Kate turned to him. 'Why don't you sit here, Dad?' she said, gesturing to a bench. 'I'll drop her off. Just wait a second.'

She and Dani crossed the road, and stopped outside the school gates; people looked enquiringly at Kate. She crouched down, looking into her sister's face.

'You've got really blue eyes,' she said, in surprise.

'Blue eyes,' said Dani. She patted Kate's cheek.

'What colour are my eyes?' Kate asked her.

'Brown eyes!' said Dani with pleasure.

'Yes. Yours are beautiful,' said Kate.

Dani tugged Kate's skirt. 'But I'm tall. I hate being tall,' she confided, suddenly.

Kate felt her heart contract, at this little thing thinking she was tall. 'You're still small,' she told her sister.

'I'm not,' Dani said, shaking her head firmly. 'I'm the

tallest girl in my class, the boys call me Daddy-long-legs, I hate it.'

'Well,' said Kate, thinking for a moment. 'They just wish they were tall like you, that's all. I was very tall when I was your age, tall and spindly, and it was very useful, do you know why?'

'Why?' said Dani.

'My mum could always spot me in the playground,' said Kate. She wasn't sure this was going to seal the deal for Dani, who looked unconvinced, so she added, with more zeal than she'd meant, 'And Dani, I promise you. You'll grow up and you will be so glad you're tall. It's the best, honestly You can wear boots and baggy tops and you don't look like a dwarf. Or a woodcutter.'

'Ah?' said Dani, looking utterly confused.

'Never mind,' said Kate, hurriedly. 'I *promise* you, please trust me. Aren't supermodels tall?'

'Yes!' Dani looked more cheerful, to Kate's chagrin, and she bent down and kissed her sister again.

'Wish me luck for my interview today,' she said.

'Good luck,' said Dani. 'Can I have a present, please?' She held her skirt and put her head on one side, trying to look coyly adorable. Kate stood up.

'Hmphf. Don't push your luck, love,' she said, and she kissed her sister again. 'See you soon, Dani, you go into school now, OK?'

'There's Olivia. Bye!' Dani said and then, with the remarkable callousness of extreme youth, turned around and ran inside, shouting, 'Hello Mrs Bateman!' as she did, having entirely forgotten about Kate.

Kate brushed her skirt down again and watched her sister disappear through the doors of the school, feeling strangely bereft, and she looked at her father, waiting for her on the other side of the road. He looked tired, and she ought to get him home. She checked her watch; it was just before nine. She felt strange, being so dressed up, early on this cold, windy day. Strange and nervous; what if Sue hated the piece, what would she do then? She'd done it now, she told herself. No going back, and she didn't really want to.

'I'm coming, Dad,' she called, as she waited to cross the road.

Besides, she had something to prove to herself. She was pissed off. Finally. In her bag she had the letter she'd got that morning. That made three now.

> Kate
>
> It's been over a week now, I don't know why you haven't called me. Look I know you hate me. Just wanted to ask you though didn't you ever see you had it coming to you? So smug and grown-up with your FIANCE and your FLAT and your amazing wonderful fucking job. You left me behind in the dust, darling, didn't you? I thought we were friends and you just ditched me when you found something better.
>
> I know you think I must feel guilty. I DON'T. OK? The reason I keep writing is, look Kate, I just need to tell you something. So get in touch. We need to sort some things out.
>
> Charly

CHAPTER THIRTY-TWO

'Shall I tell you what's wrong with this, then?'

The great glass office was the same; the ornaments on Sue's desk were the same. There was even the same poster up in the kitchen, a yellowing Health and Safety notice about what to do if someone was choking. Underneath it, someone had written *Leave Them Alone. They're Probably Bulimic.* Kate had never known if they were serious or not. She still didn't. The layouts for Sue's approval were the same, piled high in Sue's tray; Kate could see the marks scribbled all over them. But still everything at *Venus* felt different, Kate most especially. It was like it was with her parents. She couldn't remember being in those meetings, telling people what to do and she most especially couldn't remember leaving that life, going home to Sean, in their flat. Kate sat in front of Sue, who was holding a printout of her article. Her fringe was falling into her eyes; she blew it away, nervously.

'Go on then,' she said, torn between being completely humiliated and suddenly, inexplicably, wanting to laugh.

'Right,' said Sue, grinding her jaw. 'Here goes. "It was the advent of the canals which, coupled with the arrival of steam engine power to England, hastened the Industrial

305

Revolution and helped enable the greatest – and most contro-versial – Empire since Roman times."' She fixed Kate with a baleful glance. 'And that's one of the more interesting bits. The rest of the time it's all about the good old days during *rationing*! Rationing, for Christ's sake! This is a fun, inform-ative lifestyle magazine for young women. This is supposed to be a charming, funny column about one young woman's experience of London. It's not a slideshow evening with Isambard Kingdom Brunel and Dame Vera Lynn!'

'I like Dame Vera Lynn!' Kate protested.

'Honey, I love Dame Vera Lynn,' said Sue. '"A Nightin-gale Sang in Berkeley Square" was the first dance at my parents' wedding. I love the woman, I have nothing but love for her. That's not the effing point, OK?'

'Don't swear about Dame Vera Lynn,' Kate said.

'Kate.' Sue shook her head. 'Can you not see what I'm talking about?'

'Yes.' Kate bit her lip. 'I know, I know.'

'You're a young Londoner. Act like one.'

Kate was shaking her head. 'Sue! I'm thirty, I'm not that young.'

'Oh for god's sake, ridiculous girl. You see that's the trouble.' Sue was practically banging the table in frustration, half leaning over towards Kate. Kate couldn't decide if she was going to slap her or hug her. 'Kate, Kate. You're young, you're still really young. Half these op-ed pieces or lifestyle columns or whatever – they're written by forty-five year olds pretending to be thirty.' She calmed down a bit; her voice softened, and this time Kate really did brace herself. 'I was wrong, after Aunt Eileen's funeral, what I said to you.'

'What was that?'

'I told you to grow up. I was wrong. You don't need to grow up. You need to stop behaving like an old lady. You bought *doilies* for Eileen's wake, you were handing round mini-quiches! And those disgusting wet crisps, oh I could cry. Look. Eileen hated doilies! So does Uncle Gray! So do you!' Sue was practically screeching. 'Kate, when I poached you to come to *Venus* with me it was because you were everything a modern girl was supposed to be! You knew the key pieces from every prêt-à-porter collection that year *and* your favourite book was *Middlemarch*! You were the modern girl par excellence!'

Kate, fascinated at this description of herself, was nodding along, rapt to the staccato rhythm of Sue's speech. 'You're not a doilies girl!' Sue calmed down a little. 'It's like you've stopped bothering to engage with the real world around you. Do something wild for once. Sleep with someone you shouldn't. Dance on a table! Stay up all night! You're becoming an old lady, and you're still a young woman.'

Kate raised her hand, as if in a classroom, to make an Important Point. 'Er –'

'You are. Let me finish.' Sue waggled a pencil at her. 'Living with your mother and stepfather, for example. What's that like?'

On the verge of defending herself, crossly, Kate was suddenly, irresistibly reminded of her last Saturday before she'd left, when Oscar had held an impromptu piano party, and Mrs Da Costa and the Cohens from down the hall had come, and Maurice the doorman (practically, she was realizing, her best friend in New York) had popped by to say hi and sung, brilliantly, 'Makin' Whoopee', and they'd all had gin fizzes, made by Venetia, and Kate and Oscar had duetted to 'Baby It's Cold Outside'.

'Oh, my god,' she said, the scales falling from her eyes.

'And what have you done since you got back? Seen anyone your own age?'

I don't like people my own age, Kate wanted to say. Instead

she said, crossly, 'Of course I have. Don't be so silly. I've seen Zoe – and –'

'Zoe? The one on her own with the kids?'

'It wasn't like that, Sue, we needed to catch up, and –'

'Well, whatever. Woman in a semi-detached making jam and wearing a tabard, that doesn't count, alright? Anything else?'

'Um – I've seen Mr Allan,' said Kate.

Sue's eyes were twinkling, now. 'Yes, of course. But he's almost younger than you, dear. He's gone off to Mallorca, most likely he'll join a band and stay there, playing to 18-30 holidays. Who else?'

'Well, I see Dad and Dani most days. And Lisa –'

'Who's Lisa?'

'My stepmother.'

'How old?'

Kate considered this. Lisa was mysterious about her age, but Kate remembered her fortieth had been mentioned as having possibly taken place, a couple of years ago. 'She's about forty-two.'

'Right,' said Sue. 'So, apart from me, and my recently widowed uncle, and the mum with the kids, the person closest to you in age you've been hanging out with is your stepmother. And *that's* why this article doesn't work.'

More than just the article. Kate's head sank to her chest, but then suddenly snapped up again.

'Wait, wait!' she said. 'My friend Francesca. I saw her.'

'OK,' said Sue, her eyes lighting up. 'What's Francesca do?'

'She's a banker.'

'Cool. Where did you go?' said Sue, practically rubbing her hands together.

'Er . . . we went to Kettners.'

Sue looked crestfallen. 'God. Established 1964 or something. This is depressing. And that's it?'

Well no, Kate wanted to say to this, I also saw Mac, who I think is very likely the love of my life, but he told me he actually kind of hates me, and then I ran out screaming into the streets like a mad woman and *that* is why the food at the party was not particularly well-prepared, must you keep going on about it?

Oh, plus, Charly, your old assistant, remember her? Well, she's writing me letters that keep turning up delivered by hand to my flat. And they're scary.

If you knew what I'd seen the day Steve died, if you'd spent the last three years knowing you were responsible for his death, if you'd been told by his widow, your best friend, that it might be best if you leave them all alone and go, if you knew all of that, perhaps, you'd understand why I like hanging out with Mr Allan and hearing about the night he played with some old legend at the 606 club, or singing Dean Martin songs with my stepfather, or walking my four-year-old sister to school.

Instead, Kate reached across the glass table, and took the article back. She tore it up and threw it in the bin.

'Point taken,' she said. 'I'll rewrite it. You'll have it by the end of the week.'

'That's my girl,' said Sue. She stood up, and shook Kate's hand. 'Now go out and get yourself drunk. Or go to a club somewhere. Pick up someone.'

Kate laughed. 'Jeez, Sue! If I still worked here, I could have you done for harrassment, you know.'

Sue ushered her out of the door. 'You don't work here,' she said, handing something to her assistant. 'Book Orso for lunch, will you? Thanks.' She pushed Kate gently in the back. 'I'll walk you to the lifts.'

As they walked through the white and grey, light and airy offices of *Venus*, Kate noticed how much busier it was, filled with more things. Backlist issues lined the shelves; filing cabinets were scuffed; she recognized hardly any faces. The magazine was three years old now, it was practically a senior citizen in the marketplace.

'Look,' said Sue carelessly. 'That's Rachel.' She pointed towards Kate's old office.

'She does my old job?' Kate said, looking at the small, perky blonde girl gesticulating on the phone to someone. She looked up, saw Sue, and waved.

Sue waved back. 'No, darling. You did her job. Once. So get back to your desk and get on with it. You can do it.' They were at the lifts. She kissed Kate briefly on the cheek. 'I'll look forward to getting the piece again,' she said. 'Let's sort this out this week, otherwise I'll need to look at other options.'

Kate nodded. 'Fair enough,' she said. She stood up straight, feeling like someone was challenging her for the first time in years. 'That's great, Sue.' She put her hand on her arm. 'Thanks a lot.'

'Alright, alright,' said Sue, backing away. 'This isn't a Celine Dion video. Don't get yucky on me. Just email me when you've done it. Tomorrow?'

'Definitely,' Kate told her.

'And remember. Enjoy yourself.'

Kate walked across Waterloo Bridge, the wind whipping her hair around her face, ignoring the thoughts jostling for position in her head. The Thames was grey and choppy underneath her, the sky matching it above, and she turned and looked out at the South Bank and the London Eye, across to the Houses of Parliament and the white Shell Mex building with the huge black clock above a balcony where Churchill used to stand during the Second World War, watching the German bombers tear up his capital city. She stood for a while, thinking. About the meeting, about her dad. But mostly about the letters from Charly, how angry she was with Kate. It was weird, Kate had never really realized it before, that someone who appeared to be that strong and beautiful, so in command of her own life, could actually be so – was weak the word? No, probably not. She didn't know what it was with Charly. But, weirdly, she realized as she looked out across the river, she didn't really care that much any more. When she thought about her dad, Zoe, Dani – making things right with Mac, even – the lives and loves of Charly and Sean didn't concern her in the way they used to. She turned, and walked across the bridge. When she reached the other side, she pulled out her phone and dialled.

'Hi, Francesca,' she said. 'It's me. Kate.'

'Mysterious Kate Miller,' said a wry voice on the other end of the phone. 'Last seen running out of my house in hysterics a week ago. She lives.'

'Sorry to call you at work. Can you talk?'

'Sure, for a minute,' said Francesca. 'I'm glad to hear from you. I was starting to think you were D.E.A.D dead. What happened last week, for god's sake?'

It was a high-risk strategy, but Kate decided to go for insouciantly forgetful. Barely a couple of words in she realized it was a mistake. 'What, oh, after we went out? The next day at yours?' Her voice was getting higher. 'Oh, you know, don't you remember? I had to go, my neighbour's wife died and –'

'Good grief,' said Francesca, her smoky voice sounding amused. 'You're as bad as he is.'

'Who is?'

'He. Mac. The two of you.'

The two of you.

'Oh really, why?' said Kate, trying to sound politely interested. 'What's he said?'

'He's said nothing,' said Francesca. 'Said he wouldn't

discuss it and I wasn't to ask him about it. Thanks for making the few free moments of leisure I have at my home full of tension and stress.'

'Oh god, Francesca,' Kate said. 'I am sorry, you know that. And I should have called you. I've been a bit crazy, and – you know.'

'Well, I don't know,' said Francesca. 'That's the point.'

'Look,' said Kate. 'It's in the past. It's to do with old stuff. I promise it's nothing for you to worry about and I shouldn't have behaved that way. It was – childish of me. Old lady with doily-ish, maybe.'

'Eh?'

'Nothing,' said Kate, hurrying on. 'Nothing. Look, are you around tomorrow night? I've got a freelance job.'

'That's great, Kate!' Kate could hear the pleasure in Francesca's voice. 'For who?'

'Sue again,' said Kate. 'It's for *Venus* – look, I'll tell you all about it. I've got to do it tonight, for tomorrow. Can we go for a drink then, to celebrate me finishing it?'

Even walking down the street, Kate could hear the hesitation in Francesca's voice.

'Um,' she said after a while. 'Look, I was supposed to be seeing Zoe, and –'

'Well, that's fine,' said Kate. 'Isn't it?'

'Yeah, it's just – I was going round to hers for supper.'

'Oh,' said Kate, not sure how to play it. She was crossing into Covent Garden, her feet wobbling on the tricky cobbles, passing the Punch and Judy, where Sean had his birthday all those years ago. 'Well –'

'Look, I'm sure Zoe'd love it if you came, it's just – Mac might come. I mean, he says he can't, he's working, but he was going to maybe pop by, perhaps I should tell him not to –'

Kate was suddenly a bit cross at Francesca assuming this

way and that. How did she know what Zoe would or wouldn't love? Zoe was her best friend, wasn't she? And she and Mac were grown-ups, weren't they? Uncertainty made her defensive.

'Francesca look, I'll talk to Zoe,' she said firmly.

'Does she know? About you and Mac, I mean?'

'No,' said Kate. 'It's complicated. I mean I don't want to talk to her about it. I mean . . . he may have told her, I haven't.' How she wished she could tell them both.

'I thought you told each other everything,' said Francesca. 'Oh.'

Kate opened her mouth to say something and then didn't. The truth was, she and Zoe didn't talk about anything much, these days, both before when she was in New York, and now she was back. She'd seen her a couple of times since she'd been back, that first night at her house. It was fine, of course it was fine. But it wasn't great. Somehow she'd thought, naively, that it would be when she came back. But she didn't want Francesca knowing that.

'Listen, I want to see you, and I want to see Zo again, I haven't for a few days. Me and Mac, it's in the past, it's fine. If he turns up, it's fine. Honestly! I promise you we can be in the same room without it being awkward. I'm not Duck-face, you know. And –' she corrected herself '– anyway, he's not an ex.'

'That's almost exactly what he said!' said Francesca. She sounded almost impressed at their psychic synchronicity.

'Did he?'

'Yep,' Francesca said, firmly. 'Tomorrow, then. That's great. I really want to see you again.' And then she added, 'But god, Kate. What did you do?'

Kate stopped, and a car hooted at her. 'I – what do you mean?' She ran to the other side, so she was in the Piazza, under the shelter of the church.

Francesca's voice was kind, but she said, 'To make him hate you that much. What on earth did you do?'

Kate stared out across the square, where a magician was rather gloomily plying his trade to some unenthusiastic schoolchildren. She turned away from them, towards the door of the church. 'Good question,' she said quietly. 'I messed him around. You could say I broke his heart.'

There was a pause. 'When?' Francesca said. 'God, I knew it. When?'

'It's a long story – I'll explain it sometime.'

'You don't have to explain anything, babe,' said Francesca. Kate could hear typing in the background, and she knew her slot with her was coming to an end. 'See you tomorrow.'

'Thanks,' said Kate.

'What are you going to do today?'

Kate thought of Charly's letter, one last time. *You always were a bit of a loser.* Fuck her. 'Oh. I'm going home to work. I'll give Zo a call too. See you later.'

CHAPTER THIRTY-THREE

'I hadn't been on the canal since I was eleven,' Zoe read carefully. 'And now that, after a walk in Regent's Park and then a nice cup of tea by the canal, would definitely be my idea of a great day out in London. Perhaps you could hop in a cab and go to Fortnum and Mason's for tea. Even though I'm grown-up, I think it's the simplest things that often provide the most satisfying memories. I like this day out because it's perfect if you're by yourself, or if you've got children, or you're visiting London for the weekend, or even on a romantic date, and when I was in New York it was what I used to dream about. I'd love to know what your suggestions for your own great day out in London would be. Until next time, love from Girl About Town.'

Zoe lowered the paper. 'Very good,' she said. 'Wow. I never even knew about the canal boat ride. Or that those men in the clock are Mr Fortnum and Mr Mason. How did you know that?'

'You know me,' said Kate. She tapped her head. 'I'm a repository for useless information.'

'The only person who enjoyed General Studies at school.

315

I'd forgotten.' Zoe put the article down. 'Well, you're brilliant. Look at me now. I am a Satisfied Customer. There you go.'

'Girl About Town doing her job, you see,' Kate said, taking a sip of wine. They were sitting in Zoe's back garden waiting for Francesca, pretending it was July and not April, as a watery sun shone onto the lawn and Flora and Harry kicked a ball around. The garden was denuded still of greenery, but everything was in bud, and the daffodils and grape hyacinths were out in force, spiking up through the black earth. A bird sang a lazy evening song in a bush nearby, and across the fence Kate could hear another family chatting loudly, the kitchen door swinging open and shut as people raced in and out.

'So you wrote this in . . .'

'A day and a half.'

'And when do you hear back from Sue?'

'Tomorrow.'

'So you've only been back for two weeks and already you've got yourself a job. Wow.'

Kate loved Zoe's gloriously positive spin on everything. 'It's not a job,' she pointed out, leaning forward to offer Zoe another crisp. 'It's one column. And she'll probably hate it.'

'So will you do more?'

Kate thought of the job Sophie had had, the retainer fee Sue had mentioned to her, twenty-six columns a year plus ten articles, more money if *Venus* went weekly, which they were currently aiming for. It wasn't big bucks, but she had worked out – just casually, back of an envelope sort of thing – that it would be enough to cover her mortgage and bills, and have enough left over for the occasional glass of wine and trip to Zara. If she was going to stay here, which she wasn't. But if she was, she could. She had options. That was weird, all of a sudden.

She was lucky, she knew it now. That was luck, but when she thought about it, how it had happened – because Mrs Allan had died and had a funeral and so she had seen Sue again – a cloud passed over the sun. She said,

'I don't know. I think I'd like to. It's just weird,' she took a deep breath. 'I wish it hadn't happened because of Mrs Allan.'

'Oh Kate,' said Zoe, as Harry appeared in the kitchen, holding a muddy bulb of some description. 'You have to learn to take the good – Hey, Harry, that's great! Have you been gardening?'

'Yes,' said Harry. 'Look.' He held the bulb up even higher so it swung round, bashing Kate and Zoe in the face and spraying them with mud.

'Well, I'm proud of you,' Zoe said, half to Harry, half to Kate. 'Hey. Love, tell me. How's your dad?'

'Better and better, they say he can drive in a week or so. He's getting dressed and going out every day now. Just for a little bit, you know, but it's good.'

Taking another crisp, Zoe cracked it loudly in her mouth. She looked at her watch. 'Francesca'll be here in a minute. I'll put the supper on. Tell me, is Loosa still driving you mad? How's Dani? Still a bit awful?'

Kate felt an increasingly familiar stab of loyalty to Dani and Lisa. 'They're fine,' she said. 'Actually Lisa's not that bad, you know. And Dani – she's pretty sweet.'

She had played with Dani that afternoon, in the communal garden of their pretty little road, soaking up the sunshine, enjoying the warmth. Dani had got filthy, and Lisa hadn't even complained, saying it was good for her to get out of the house.

It was a beautiful spring that year. It came early, shining through the windows first thing in the morning, pushing the buds into leaves, gilding people in sunshine and warmth.

317

Kate couldn't remember a spring like it; she had forgotten how green, how spacious and leisurely London was, how white and graceful its buildings, how nice it was to walk around. She thought it was funny when Londoners complained about the pace of the city, how frenetic it was. Yes, it was a huffy, self-important place, yes, London was messy and chaotic and often depressing, but it was a welcome respite from the non-stop anonymity and adrenalin of New York. She hadn't realized it before, she knew it now.

And London in springtime was beautiful, especially this spring. Later it would rain for all of June and July, the weather humid and unreliable, and people would snap at each other and be miserable about it but now, when it was April and the skies were beautiful, clear and warm, with the blossom frothing on the trees and daffodils and forget-me-nots in the parks now, now it was a happy, refreshing place to be.

It had changed her, she realized now. She'd been back for eleven days. She was sleeping well, for hours and hours, sunshine pouring onto the parquet floors of her flat. More and more she felt at home there, pottering around by herself. She put flowers in jugs, opened the windows, whistled as she made her tea in the morning. She checked the post for Mr Allan and watered the plants in his flat, she saw her father every single day, she sorted out the rubbish in the kitchen and the old chest of drawers in the sitting room. She had sat at her bureau desk writing and rewriting Girl About Town articles, scratching her head till she was happy with them. Sue was right, she was an old lady. She ate carbs and drank wine and did other things she would never have dreamt of in New York, where everything for her had to be under control, her own world.

Still, though, she left things untouched. Still the letters from Charly, three of them, piled up unread, and still the letting agents remained untroubled by her, and still she did not call Perry and Co, she said to herself that, now the article was over, she'd do it tomorrow, the very next day, and the letting agents, and she'd ring Charly, summon all her strength, and tell her to Fuck Off, she didn't want to see her, she didn't wish her any harm but she didn't want to know that her child was coming into the world, the child of a person like Charly. Watching Zoe's children running around on the lawn, Kate nodded to herself, reminding herself of why it was so, why she couldn't –

'Oh, Mac rang earlier. He *is* popping over tonight,' Zoe said, suddenly, standing to get some more wine.

'What?' said Kate, sitting up with a start. She had totally forgotten Francesca had mentioned he might. 'He – what?'

'He wasn't going to.' Zoe was picking up stray bowls of crisps; her back was turned to Kate. 'Don't know if Francesca said, he might be coming or not. Well he is. He wants to see the children. He's got a present for Harry.'

'Why?'

'He's their uncle, Kate,' Zoe said slowly to Kate, as if she were a mental patient. She flicked a look at her friend and stood up straight with a sigh. 'Oof. I'm knackered. Do you think those vitamins you take to make your skin better actually work? I'm chewing down about fifty a day and I'm still always getting this spot right here on my chin, right – can you see it? Right here. Look,' She jabbed at her chin with her finger. 'What's the blimming point?'

'Yep, yep,' said Kate, waving her concerns aside. 'Keep taking the vitamins. Great for you. Zinc in particular. Er – Zo? Does he know I'm – me and Francesca are coming over?'

'Yep, course he does,' said Zoe. She stared at her. 'He asked. He's only popping over, he said he won't stay. We'll just have to persuade him.'

Kate nodded, trying to look enthusiastic about this,

whilst mentally bemoaning the fact that 'popping over' was an entirely British phenomenon. You didn't 'pop over' to someone's apartment in New York. God no. You met at a restaurant or a bar nearby. You were organized about it. Even if you were hanging out with someone, you organized where and when you'd be hanging out together. Why couldn't Mac have said right from the start that he was either definitely coming or not coming? Why was she still unable to think about him, at this very minute on his way towards her, without feeling like someone had literally laid her heart on a table in front of her and sliced it in two?

'Uncle Mac coming!' said Flora, poking Kate solemnly in the leg.

'Yes, he is,' said Kate. Kate was almost pathologically fond of Flora, having only met her for the first time a week ago. She was like a very small version of Zoe, who was already pretty small, from her black hair down to her big, determined feet, which were rarely encased in shoes and, like their owner, had a mind of their own.

'Yay!' said Flora, raising herself onto the balls of her feet and then down again, which was her version of jumping.

The doorbell rang, and Zoe went to answer it. 'That'll be Francesca,' she said. Harry ran towards Kate and Flora ran back onto the lawn, like a relay race. Kate watched them playing in the garden – they looked like Steve, both of them, so much it hurt. She caught an expression on Harry's face and was reminded of the time, early on at university, when she'd caught Steve returning home drunk, with Sean and Jem, not long after he'd started going out with Francesca, though he'd promised her he'd see her in the bar. He had the same expression on his face then: fear mixed with guilt, the result hilariously adorable, only he could get away with it.

'I won't tell anyone,' Kate had said, feeling a bit guilty herself – and not sure now what Zoe would say if she heard this. Francesca appeared in the kitchen, and waved. Kate said briskly, 'Right, let's go in and wash your faces, so you're ready for your uncle.'

'Why does he want us to wash our faces?' said Harry, clearly not sure whether to trust Kate.

'He . . .' Kate chewed her lip, and took Flora's little hand in hers. 'He thinks that should be part of the law, too. Having a clean face or else. Um . . . ask him about it when he gets here.'

'Are you going to wash your face too Kate?' Harry asked, pertinently.

'Very much so, of course,' Kate said. 'Come on then.'

They went back into the house, all three strangely subdued.

'God. Fucking buses,' Francesca was saying, as they entered the kitchen through the french windows. 'I fucking hate them.' She pulled her dark, silky hair out of the neck of her coat, and then took her coat off. 'Fuck! That hurts. F –'

'La! Lalala!' Kate sang loudly, grasping the children's hands. 'Oh, lalala!' she shouted, practically running past Francesca with them.

'It's OK,' Zoe intervened, as Flora and Harry peered in front of Kate's legs and looked at each other, as if to say, Help, everyone here is insane. 'Harry, you know what Francesca said was a bad word, don't you?'

'Yes,' said Harry. 'Really bad, you should not say it.'

'I know,' said Francesca, nodding at him. 'Tell me something else, Harry. Where's the wine?'

'OK,' said Zoe, shaking her head at Harry. 'Ignore Auntie Kate and Auntie Francesca. Auntie Kate is pretending to be Mary Poppins, and it's scaring the bejesus out of me, and

Auntie Francesca gets cross when she doesn't have wine nearby. She is an old lush.'

'Hm?' said Francesca, picking at a thread on her suit jacket.

'I'm going to put *The Little Mermaid* on,' said Zoe, and the children shouted with glee. 'You can watch it *for thirty minutes* while we talk and then I'm going to put you to bed, and Uncle Mac will come and say good night to you. OK?'

Flora nodded, but she'd nod at anything. Harry said, 'Yep, OK.'

When the DVD was playing, and the three friends were sitting around the kitchen table, a few minutes later, Francesca produced a bottle of champagne from her ruck-sack, clad in a chiller jacket.

'I had a big deal today,' she said. 'Finally went through. So let's celebrate.'

'Wow,' said Zoe, getting up to fetch some glasses. 'This is great! Congrats. What was it?'

'Germans,' said Francesca briefly. 'There –' as she eased the cork out of the bottle without so much as a murmur. 'Zoe, take that – Kate, that's yours.' She poured herself some, too. 'Ladies. A toast.'

'Yes,' said Zoe.

'To each of us. Here's to me,' Francesca said, her dark eyes glittering above the champagne glass. 'I deserve every last drop of this beautiful fizzy liquid.' She took a sip. 'Wait. Now, to you, Kate. To your article and you being back here. You're not going back to New York, we're going to start a campaign to keep you here. In fact, this is the campaign's first meeting.'

'OK,' said Kate, nodding and smiling, watching her glass, bubbling gold.

'And finally Zo, here's to you. Thanks for having us over. And here's to you especially because you're wonderful.' She smiled. 'Now, I know you've probably told Kate all about it but you'll have to tell it again because I want to know. How was the date?'

Zoe made an urgent 'ssshhh'-ing noise.

'The *what*?' said Kate, reeling.

'Didn't you tell her?' said Francesca, pointing her champagne glass at Kate.

'You went on a *date*?' said Kate. 'And you didn't *tell me*?'

'It's not *that* big a deal,' said Zoe crossly. 'Stop staring at me as if I've got two heads. It was a date. Big deal.'

'Do the children know?' said Kate. The other two turned to look at her.

'Have you lost your mind?' said Francesca. 'Why are you being so weird? Now,' she said, turning back to Zoe, 'did you wear the blue and grey wrap dress?'

'Yes, and you were so right about wrap dresses being my thing,' said Zoe, excitedly. 'Thanks a million. I always thought, with my boobs and stuff – you know, bad idea, but they're perfect, aren't they! They just keep everything –'

'Hold on!' Kate said. 'What the hell is going on? You had a date? Who with?'

'He's –' Zoe picked up her glass and took another slug. 'He's called Diggory. He's a landscape gardener. He works at the nurseries with me.'

'He's called what?' said Kate.

'Diggory. Like the boy in *The Secret Garden*,' said Francesca helpfully.

'Seriously?'

'But his friends call him Digg.'

'One g or two?'

'God, I don't know!' Zoe rolled her eyes, impatiently. 'That's not the issue, ladies!'

'So did you snog him?' said Francesca.

'Wait,' said Kate. 'Back up. Where did you go?'

323

'Well, we went to a pub near work, off Primrose Hill.' Zoe's eyes sparkled; Kate watched her, uneasily. 'It was funny, actually, because there weren't any seats.' She laughed at the memory. 'Ah.'

'Then what happened?' said Francesca, who was starting to look bored.

'Oh, then we got some seats,' said Zoe. 'A couple left. By the window, so –'

'I don't care about the frigging seats,' said Francesca. She banged her hands on the table. 'What was he like? What was it like? Was it weird being on a date?'

'Super weird,' said Zoe. The others nodded, sympathetically. 'But, you know, I just told myself it would be weird going on a date with anyone who wasn't Steve. Of course it's weird. But I just pretended it wasn't weird, and tried to get on with it. Not let it take over the evening.'

Kate sat down, suddenly. 'Wow,' she said, running her hand through her hair. 'That's huge. Good on you, Zo.'

Zoe sat down beside her, her face pleading, almost. 'Oh Kate, I'm sorry I didn't tell you, I really wanted to, to ask your advice and all that, I just – I just didn't want to make it into a big deal, and if you tell people it becomes a big deal, you understand, don't you?'

You told Francesca, Kate wanted to say. I wish you could confide in me. But instead she said brightly, 'Totally, of course!'

'So?' said Francesca. 'Then what happened?' She poured them all more champagne; Kate knocked hers back, as fast as she could.

'Well, we stayed there for ages, just chatting – you know, about work and stuff, it's really easy when you've got things to talk about already,' said Zoe, and her sweetly serious face was heartbreaking. 'Diggory spent lots of time in Australia, he's got all these really interesting ideas for irrigation systems

– as that's going to be the next big challenge in garden design in the next few years, of course.'

'Of course,' said Kate and Francesca, nodding.

'And then – well, I was a bit reckless, and I got a cab home.'

'Zoe Hamilton!'

'Did anything happen?' Francesca said.

'Nooo,' said Zoe. She looked from one to the other. 'You know. Not yet.'

'Sure, sure,' they both said. 'Not yet,' Francesca added.

'Well, good for you, Zo,' said Kate. 'That's great. Did you say you'd see him again?'

'Oh, er . . . yeah,' said Zoe. 'We're going to Hampstead Heath this weekend with the children.'

'Fast work,' Francesca muttered.

'Well no. It's someone at work's birthday and they're having a picnic on the Heath, so there'll be lots of people we know there, and lots of children – you know. It'll be great. He's met them before, at Jool's wedding party, a few months ago, anyway.'

Zoe had always looked the same to Kate – a little, energetic, determined, unassuming ball of life and fun. But since she'd got back, Kate had thought Zoe was starting to look tired. Run-down. Weary of the hand life had dealt her. Now, looking at her friend, she saw a sparkle in her eyes she hadn't seen since – well, since that fateful day they'd had lunch, nearly three years ago, when Zoe was pregnant with Flora, so soon after Harry, and Kate was engaged to be married. Look at them now, she thought. Look at Zoe, having to go out on dates. It was still wrong, she would never not think that. Kate cleared her throat, angrily.

'Look at us now,' Zoe said, like she'd been reading Kate's mind. Their eyes met and they gazed at each other, in a moment of clarity, and Zoe shook her head at her friend.

Something shot through Kate like a bolt of electricity. It made her want to bang the table and shout that life was bloody unfair.

Francesca, sensing the mood needed lifting, got up and got a bottle of wine from the fridge.

'Mac'll be here soon,' she said, in a not-so-subtle reminder to both of them. 'Is he eating?'

Zoe jumped up. 'The food!' she said, smacking her head. 'I've got to start cooking!'

'Thank you,' said Francesca, as Zoe rushed out and ran down to the cellar. 'We could be here all night, otherwise. I can't stay late either,' she said. 'I've told Mac I'm going early.'

'Right,' said Kate, still staring into space.

'So I'll be leaving before Mac, is what I mean,' Francesca added.

'I get you,' Kate said.

'So Mac'll be going home on his own,' she said.

'Yes,' said Kate. 'Thank you. I wish I could work out what you were saying. It's all smoke signals with you.'

'Shut up,' said Francesca, aimiably. 'I'm only trying to help.'

'I know you are,' said Kate. 'Sorry.'

'Go on,' said Francesca, as the sound of crashing and muffled curses drifted up from the cellar, where Zoe was trying to locate something. 'While she's gone. Tell me what happened between the two of you. She doesn't know, does she?'

'No.' Kate bowed her head.

'Can't believe that.'

'Like I said . . .' said Kate. 'There's a lot of stuff we don't talk about anymore.' She gestured, vaguely. 'Look at Diggory. *Digg.*'

Francesca ignored this. 'So what happened?'

'I stole his stethoscope and he was furious.'

'*Kate.*'

'*Francesca.*'

'I give up,' Francesca said. 'All I'm saying is, you don't hate someone that much without still feeling something for them. The opposite of love isn't hate, it's . . .'

'Indifference, I know,' Kate said.

CHAPTER THIRTY-FOUR

The doorbell rang at eight; Mac was always punctual. Zoe was hunting for a spare knife and Francesca had Flora on her lap; she made to put her down and stand up, but Kate was quicker.

'I'll let him in,' she said. 'I'll say hi. You stay there.' She brushed Flora's cold, baby-smooth cheek with her hand and went inside.

He registered no surprise when she opened the door. 'Hello,' he said. He bent forwards and kissed her on the cheek.

He was dressed in a suit and tie. When she'd seen him at Francesca's, he was in trousers, an open-necked shirt, which was how she always thought of him. He looked formal now, buttoned up. And tired.

'Francesca told me you were back because of your dad,' he said, unexpectedly, his soft Scottish accent hitting her in the solar plexus. 'I'm sorry. I didn't know he'd been ill.'

'Thanks,' she said. 'He's much better now. The operation was a couple of weeks ago. It's looking OK, touch wood.'

He nodded. 'That's usually enough time to know. That's good. How are you?' he asked, loosening his tie and putting his satchel-style briefcase on the floor. His voice was pleasant. She watched his hands.

'Oh, er,' Kate said, not sure how to contain her surprise at this, a semi-cordial exchange, 'I, I am well, thanks. And you?' She felt like a Dickens character in a TV adaptation. 'Are you well?'

Mac looked at her in some surprise. 'Yep. Fine.'

'Good. Good!' Kate said, as she shut the door. 'They're this way,' and she gestured towards the kitchen, which was the only direction one could possibly go anyway.

'Thanks,' said Mac. A smile flickered across his lips. 'This way we go, then,' and he followed her into the kitchen.

'Hey, Mac,' said Zoe, who was licking her fingers.

'Yo, flatmate,' Francesca waved her wine glass at him, over Flora's semi-somnolent head. 'How are you?'

'I'm fine, fine,' said Mac, suddenly awkward in the halogen lights, still in his trench coat. Standing next to him, Kate could smell the fresh air of outside still on him, in the warm fug of the kitchen.

'I brought some wine,' Mac offered, and he handed it to her, watching her, and Kate took it, and said, 'Thanks. I'll – put it in the fridge,' and she smiled at this faux-domestic scene, it wasn't hers, and he smiled back, and the ice was broken a little further. He was going to be nice, he'd obviously made up his mind. Very well, good for him, she told herself. She would happily do the same.

He took his coat off. 'Harry's upstairs?'

'Yes,' said Zoe. She nodded at her daughter. 'This one won't go to sleep.' She saw he was holding a bag. 'Is that for Harry?'

'It is. It's a doctor's kit. We do them at the hospital. He wants to be a doctor.'

'Just like his uncle.'

'Absolutely,' he said, and he looked away.

'Mac?' called a small voice from upstairs. 'Hello!'

'Hey, Harry,' Mac said, slightly raising his voice. 'Be up in a minute.'

'Have some wine,' Zoe said. 'I'm going to take Madam here back up to bed.'

'Ooh, I'll come with you,' said Francesca suddenly, as Zoe scooped Flora into her arms and the three of them set off upstairs.

'Sure,' said Mac. He moved towards the dresser on the side, pulled open a drawer and took out a corkscrew; he knew his way around this house. 'You want some wine?' he said.

'Sure,' said Kate, watching him, unable to believe the luxury of being in the same room as him again. 'Where are the . . .'

'Glasses. Here.' He took a bottle of chilled wine from the fridge and it was a screw-top; he smiled again, the corkscrew in his hand, and it broke the ice a little further.

There was silence in the kitchen, then. It was just the two of them, standing with the corner of the table between them. Kate put her hands awkwardly in her jeans pockets. He did the same.

Clearing his throat, he said, 'Look, Kate. I don't want to get into it again, but – just to say, I'm sorry about last week.'

Because Kate thought about him all the time, she couldn't instantly recall what was different about last week. 'What?' It took her a moment to process what he was saying, and she blinked, slowly. He watched her.

'I thought you were supposed to have a brilliant journal-istic brain,' he said. 'Last Thursday, whenever it was, at my house. I was vile to you. I'm sorry, Kate. I wasn't expecting to see you, that's all. Whatever's happened between us. I'm sorry. I shouldn't have spoken to you like that.'

Kate bowed her head. 'You should have,' she whispered. 'I deserve it.'

'No you don't,' he said, moving slightly towards her. It was so quiet in the kitchen, she could hear Harry and Flora upstairs, Zoe talking to them soothingly. He took her wrist. His skin was warm on hers. 'You don't deserve it, Kate, you've – you've been through enough already.'

Kate didn't allow herself to cry much, these days. She wasn't an attractive weeper, anyway. Tears didn't tremble on the edge of her glossy black lashes and drop to the ground as her big dark eyes filled with water, like they did in books. No, her nose went red, her eyeballs bloodshot, she got swollen lids that wouldn't go down for days, and rough, raw patches underneath her eyes. Partly because, on the extremely rare occasions when she did properly cry, she really went for it. It was silly. He was only being nice to her. But the niceness was the very thing she'd been missing and she could feel her throat swelling up, tears pooling in her eyes.

'Don't,' Kate said, and she smiled.

His hand on her wrist was suddenly tight. He dropped her arm as if he were holding a poisonous snake, and picked up two glasses of wine. The tension between them was as strong as ever, and as Kate went over to the sink, spotting a knife and washed it, all the time she was aware of him behind her, she was apprehensive.

'Anyway, I am sorry,' Mac said, with his back to her. 'It made me think. We should talk about it. About last year.'

'Not now,' she said, as Zoe's voice was heard from upstairs.

'When, then,' said Mac, wearily. '*When*, Kate? That's the trouble with you and me. Mainly you, I have to say.' He smiled, grimly, but she couldn't smile back. 'Our timing bloody sucks.' He rubbed his face; she saw again, with concern, how tired he looked. She wanted to get him to sit down, make him supper, take care of him. But she mustn't.

They heard Zoe and Francesca on the stairs.

'Later,' said Kate. She set her jaw, turned to look at him, and he was standing under one of the spotlights in the kitchen. She clutched the back of the chair.

Don't get a taxi home with him, she told herself. *Don't sleep with him.* Don't open all of that up again, don't hurt him, don't hurt yourself. She turned around, as if he'd spoken those words out loud to her. He scratched the sandy-brown stubble on his cheek. His face was expressionless but his eyes were on her, flinty, grey-green, stormy.

'Ah, Kate,' he said, simply. 'Damn you.' And, leaning back on her hands, against the chair, watching him too, Kate knew. She was terrified, exhilarated, at the power he still had over her, at how much she wanted to give in to it. She couldn't.

'Mac, Harry's asking for you, if you —' said Zoe, slightly loudly, as she came into the kitchen.

'I'll go now,' he said instantly, and went upstairs.

Zoe made pasta bake and they sat in the kitchen and ate, leaving the french windows to the garden ajar, so they could hear the birds singing in the trees outside. Mac was upstairs for a while to say goodnight to Harry, and give him his doctor's set, which he'd forgotten before, and Harry tried to get up and put it on.

Then the four of them stayed around the table till ten, when it was time for Francesca to go — she had to be up early for a meeting at eight.

'I'm going,' she said, standing up, pushing herself away from the table. She looked at Kate, significantly. 'I'm going to leave you to reminisce over times gone by.'

And then it was just the three of them, late into the evening, long after they'd cleared everything away and they were left with wine glasses and the windows were closed against the night. They talked of everything – but mostly, they talked about Steve. How he'd mended Kate's desk chair at university, and the next time she sat down on it it cracked beneath her. How, on their wedding night, he had had a nightmare about Zoe trying to kill him and woken up screaming 'No, Zoe, no!' How he had broken Mac's calculator-ruler, by flicking rubber Disney characters off it till it snapped in two, then put it back in Mac's drawer, hoping he wouldn't notice. Just saying Steve's name was hard for Kate and at first, she found it impossible. She never talked about him. Who in New York had known him? Hardly anyone. She had liked it that way, at first, and now, here, these last few days, around the table with her friends, she started to realize that she might have been wrong, like she was starting to wake up again, from a long sleep.

Still, long after Harry was asleep again, Flora would not go down, and she sat up in her small person's chair, staring round impassively and munching clods of earth she'd managed somehow to bring inside from the garden, which occasionally fell into her mouth. As Flora banged her spoon, and tried to stick some more mud into her eye, eventually Zoe said, with resignation,

'Oh, Flora love – don't do that. It's mud. Dirty. Don't eat it.' Then, turning to the other two grown-ups: 'She's like Just William. I don't know what to do about her. She's going to grow up and have boiled eyeball sweets in a horrible paper bag in her pocket. I know it. She'll be one of those weird gummy women you see waiting at a bus stop wearing a dirty burgundy nylon mac.'

Flora banged her head with the tray that lay on the table. Her face scrunched up and she screamed.

'Oh god,' said Zoe. 'She's gone. I'm sorry,' she said, scooping a wailing Flora into her arms. 'She's really really tired, I should put her to bed –'

Mac stood up, pushing his chair out. 'Let me help.'

'No,' said Zoe, firmly, pushing her hair back with her hand and trying not to look harrassed. She smiled brightly. 'Honestly, it might be best if she sees you going, she'll understand the night is over. God, she's awful.' She clutched Flora closer to her; Mac watched them both, and then said,

'Of course. Anyway, Zoe, love. We'll put the stuff away and – god, it's late.' He looked at his watch. 'Let me just –' he put his wine glass by the sink.

Kate looked at her watch, it was twelve-thirty. 'God, I'm sorry Zo. I had no idea it was so late.'

'Neither did I,' she said, holding the wriggling Flora in her arms. 'She just won't sleep like other babies, she likes the nighttime. Just like her mummy and her daddy I'm afraid. Look, you two, just go, OK? I should put her down now and I can put some plates and a few wineglasses in the dishwasher afterwards.'

'Well –' Mac looked uncertain, but Zoe shooed him along. 'Come on, seriously.'

He bent down and kissed his sister-in-law and his niece. 'Bye, girls,' he said, his voice soft. He grabbed Zoe's arm lightly. 'I'll see you on Sunday. Thanks Zoe.'

She looked up at him, grateful, her eyes sparkling. 'Oh Mac. Thank you . . .'

Kate hung back but stepped forwards then and kissed her. 'Bye, Zo. Thanks so much, so much, it's been a lovely evening.' And it had been. She squeezed Flora's little arm. 'Bye Flo. Be good.'

They were almost pushed out by Zoe and, as the door shut quietly behind them they shivered on the street, the two of them alone again, in the cold, clear night.

She knew that she was going to go home with him. It was inevitable, the way it always is, she had known it from the

moment he touched her wrist, how powerful the connection between them was. But neither said anything as they
walked towards the main road. Kate could hear Mac's
breathing. She turned quickly, and saw the black outline of
his profile in the moonlight. She wrapped her arms around
herself and stepped a little way away from him, so they were
walking in parallel, a metre separating them, along the quiet
street with its cracked pavement slabs, jammed with cars.

Did he remember this was where they first kissed, all those
years ago, after the housewarming party? It had been March
then too. Did he remember this was the exact spot they had
caught the taxi back to his flat? Did he replay it in his mind,
did he know how often she had? They stood in silence,
waiting for a cab to arrive, and when it did they both stuck
their hands out.

'Where to?' the cab driver said.

Kate didn't look at Mac. He held the door open for her.

'Maida Vale, then on,' he told the cab driver, who nodded
as Mac shut the door.

They settled down in the cab, and silence fell.

'So, how is work, Mac?' said Kate. Perhaps an interesting
conversation about the merits and demerits of the NHS might
help smooth out the spiky atmosphere.

She felt his eyes on her in the darkness, knew he was
smiling at her, and she turned to meet his shadowy gaze.

'You always were terrible at awkward silences, Katy,' he
said.

'No I'm not.'

'You are. You always crack first.'

Don't kiss him.

'Well . . .' The wine was going to her head; she sat up
straight against the hard leather of the cab seat, trying not
to smile. 'It's an only child thing. Social pressure, you know.'

'Hm,' he said, moving towards her. She could see his face

in the grey night. She was cold, hot, every part of her was tingling, and now she was smiling, as his lips were next to hers. 'You shouldn't worry about that,' he said, and he kissed her. 'Oh, Kate.' His voice was hoarse, now. 'I don't like you for your conversation, you know.'

His lips on hers, how she remembered them, the rasp of his day-long stubble on her cheek, her lips, his strong, supple hands on the back of her head. Kissing Mac had been her downfall before, because kissing him was overwhelming, as if she'd never been kissed before. The strength of her physical response to him floored her, like it always did, and they were back in the old game again, and to give herself up to it, to simply enjoy him, was a pleasure the like of which she hadn't had since she'd walked out on him before.

She pushed him away. 'I can't,' she said. 'I really can't.'

He held her head in his hands. 'Come on, Kate,' he said. 'It's one night. You're going back in a week.'

'But last time . . .'

'I'm over it,' he said. He brought her hand to his mouth, kissed her fingers gently. 'Aren't you over it? Come on. Haven't you been working hard, don't you deserve this?'

'Not if it's going to . . .' she began, but he kissed her again.

'I want you,' he said. His breath was hot on her eyes, her lips. 'And you want me. Don't worry about the rest, Kate. It's all in the past.'

Just to know that at the end of the cab journey was her front door, her hallway, where he would push her against the wall and press himself against her, so that she clung to him in the darkness, her arms wrapped around his neck, to stop herself falling down. Just to think that beyond the hall was her bedroom, where she would see him naked again, feel his body on top of her, pushing inside her, and then wrapped around her at the end of the night so that she might wake up in the early hours of the morning and turn

336

gently to see him asleep, the harsh lines that criss-crossed his face wiped away.

One more night with him. Never mind the realization that how much she missed him would be almost more pain than the pleasure that lay ahead of her now. Just once more, as they kissed in the cab, making its way silently and sedately through the moonlit streets of town.

Sue's words, the day before, rang in her ears. Do something wild. Stop behaving like an old lady. But for the first time, since she'd come back to London, Kate had that feeling she'd had so long ago: of standing at the edge of a precipice, about to jump off, bringing destruction with her as she fell. The idea that Mac was with her was extraordinary – Mac, with whom she shared a secret history that only the two of them knew about, that they kept from their friends, it wasn't over.

'OK,' she said, and she kissed him back. They were nearly home. Yes, she told herself, as his hands moved over her, as he kissed her more insistently, as she desperately wished they were alone. Just enjoy this one night. Don't think about the past. Don't think about that last lie, the last betrayal.

INTERLUDE

The previous summer

Summer 2006

'Kate?'

She was sitting at a table in a pretty French café just north of Grosvenor Square, pushing the padded tissue coaster around with the tips of her fingers. The quiet Mayfair bustle of a summer's afternoon, fading into evening, was soporific. Kate stared at her arms, thinking how brown they'd become, which was strange when she was outdoors so little these days. The bangles on her hand jangled as she shook more sugar into her cup of tea. She breathed in, the smell of rich heat rising from the ground, tarmac, cars and sweet, harsh, pollen, hitting her.

The US Embassy was closed: of course it was. July Fourth, why hadn't she realized? So stupid of her; a sinking, metallic feeling of dread had assailed her as she'd drawn closer to the square and looked for the line of people that usually ran down the side of the unlovely, humourless building.

'Come back tomorrow, miss,' the scary guard had told her, clutching his AK 47, his face expressionless.

'But –' Kate began. 'I'm only here for two days, I've come specially to get my visa renewed. I've got to get back to the

341

States. They promised they'd stamp my visa again and I could come straight home again.'

'Miss, you'll have to come back tomorrow. I'm gonna have to ask you to step away now.'

Kate was used to the humourless precision of American security now, after twenty-two months there, nearly two years, she knew it exactly. But here, on this beautiful English summer's evening, the trees dipping and whistling around the long, elegant square, it seemed totally incongruous, and she had smiled at him, without really knowing why, and stepped away, as requested.

One more day, she told herself as she trailed up towards Oxford Street. One more day here, and you can get back, and no one will know you're here. Her mother and Oscar were up in the Hamptons for two weeks, they would never realize she'd gone. Luckily Perry and Co was closed not just for July 4th but for a week, most unusually, while Bruce escorted their cash cow, Anne Graves, back to Ohio, to receive an honorary degree from the university and to spend some time at her cabin there. Bruce had closed the office as a reward to his loyal co-workers, he had told them all, not because he was a control freak who hated not being there if others were there. Kate wondered what he thought he'd be missing if he left them all to it for four days; more of Doris's interesting stories about her husband, Mikey? Nancy the book-keeper's weekly complaint about her book club's choices? The tension wrought by Perry and Co's temperamental aircon unit?

One more day here, she said, as she sat down for a coffee, gratefully resting her tired limbs. No one knew she was here, except Betty, who had driven her to JFK, told her she was crazy, but was going to pick her up in two days' time, when this visa mess was sorted out. In, out, clean, precise, and no one need know she was here.

No one.

'*Kate*? Is that you?'

She heard the voice again, but still she didn't move. She looked down. It couldn't be him, surely. Perhaps he'd just walk on, leave her here, alone, unseen, perhaps she could still get away with it . . .

'Kate.' A tall figure, looking down at her. 'My god. It really *is* you.'

She glanced up, shielding her eyes against the sun, knowing what she would see.

It was him. It was Mac. Shock ran through her, instantaneous; her heart started thumping. She put her hand to her collarbone, pushing her chair away from him, at the same time astonished at her own visceral response to the sight of him. He laid a cool hand on her arm.

'Don't go.'

'I – I –' Kate swallowed, mastering herself again. 'My god.'

She stood up, awkwardly, facing him. He was so tall, she'd forgotten that. Everything about him was so familiar, like opening a locked door stuffed full of memories, all bursting to come out. She didn't know what to say.

He stretched his arms out, briefly, as if he was going to hug her, and as she took another step back, almost frightened, he shook his head and folded his hands under his armpits, defensively. She saw he didn't realize he was doing it.

'It's been a long time,' he said, softly. 'Kate, where did you go?'

Kate cleared her throat, wanting to speak, but nothing came out. She looked round at her fellow patrons, who were watching with ill-concealed interest. How different from New York, where she and Betty had last month had a loud, drunken shouting match in the Village about Betty's useless boyfriend Troy, and no one had appeared to see them, let along notice them.

'Sit down,' he said, his voice gentle. He touched her shoulder with one finger, and she sank gratefully back down into her seat. Mac was looking at her, his eyes searching her, as if he couldn't quite believe she was really there. Kate blinked slowly, terrified of what he could say to her, not knowing what to say herself, and he followed her, pulling up a chair.

She stirred the teaspoon around her empty coffee cup. 'So – so you're down here now?'

'I moved back, got a residency at St John's. To be closer to Zoe. You know.'

'Yep.' Kate nodded, staring without seeing at the ground. 'Why are you here?'

'Visa,' she said. 'I had to leave and come back. I'm only in town for a day.'

He flashed a glance at her. 'Right.'

He ordered a coffee; they sat in silence for a while. Then he said,

'You stopped answering my emails,' he said.

'You stopped sending them,' Kate said.

Mac rubbed his palms together. 'I didn't think you wanted to hear any more. I don't blame you. You're Kate, though. You just pushed it all away instead.' He said this without emotion.

'I didn't,' said Kate hotly, though he was telling the truth, she knew it. 'I didn't know what else to do. I couldn't stay.'

'Why not?'

Zoe's words still echoed in her head. *Please. Kate, you need to leave me alone for a while. Please.*

'I just couldn't,' she said. She said, honestly, 'I was to

blame. I still think I was. And I know Zoe did too then. I had to get away. I didn't know what I was thinking then, really.'

'You were too –' He shook his head. 'Oh, Kate. So you left and never contacted her again,' Mac said, drumming his fingers on the aluminium table, looking at the ground. She noticed the grey collecting at the temples of his sandy brown hair. 'Or me. I just don't understand how you found that easy to do.'

She looked up at him swiftly, tendrils of hair falling about her face. 'Don't say that,' she said, her voice sharp. 'That's a ridiculous thing to say.'

'Couldn't you have talked to someone else then?' Mac said, his voice low. He put his hand in her lap, steadying her writhing fingers. 'Talked to someone, without running away like that.'

There was a pause, a break which spooled into a silence between them, so long that Kate could hear sirens in the background, roaring down Park Lane, the sound of sirens that she'd probably never forget. She took a breath, trying to explain, and then slumped down into her seat again. Her eyes were stinging, and she was so tired.

'What?' he said.

'There wasn't anyone, was there?' Kate said. 'No one, really. Well, Francesca – but she was so upset about Steve, she couldn't help me. And it wasn't fair to put all of that on her.'

'Come on,' said Mac, slightly impatiently. 'Your father?'

'Dad,' said Kate. 'Yep, right.' She tried to imagine what would have happened had she really tried to talk to her dad about it all, in those ghastly, endless days after Steve died and Sean left. Somehow, being with them, her father's new family, highlighted how dreadfully alone she was, and she'd realized after several awkward, disjointed conversations and offers of help, half-hearted offers of accommodation, that she'd rather face up to it by herself than blanket it in the new, neutral, perfect house in Notting Hill into which they were about to move. Except it wasn't facing up to it, it was running away, but again, fight or flight: she had chosen flight.

'Excuse. Miss.'

Someone was tugging at her sleeve; she looked around, at a Japanese tourist, with glasses and sunhat wedged firmly onto his head, his wife standing next to him, opening and shutting a guide book in Japanese.

'Diana palace nearby?' said the husband. Kate looked at Mac, who shook his head impatiently, not understanding.

'Oh,' Kate said, recognition dawning. 'Diana's palace. Where Princess Diana lived?'

They nodded. 'Please.' The wife jabbed her fingers at the guidebook.

'It's called Kensington Palace, and you need to get on a bus, or a tube, and go to . . .' she trailed off, realizing they had no idea what she was talking about. The people at the next table stared at her. Mac stared at her, amusement crossing his usually unreadable features.

Kate gave him a sharp look. It occurred to her that she was a tourist, just like them, after all. She took the guide-book out of the woman's hands and the woman tensed, looking nervous, as if she thought Kate might steal it. She found a map at the back of the book.

'Here,' she said, and she took a pen off the table and drew a cross by where Kensington Palace was. 'Bus. Top of road.' She pointed in the direction of Oxford Street. 'Numbers? You know numbers?'

'Bus,' said the husband, nodding enthusiastically. 'Bus, yes.'

'Ten,' Kate said, pointing again. 'Ten. Bus number ten.' She was almost shouting.

'She was a beautiful lady,' said the wife, carefully.

'Diana, yes,' said Kate, nodding. Mac looked alarmed.

The woman's face lit up. 'Beautiful lady. Queen of Hea—'

'Yes, she was, thanks,' said Mac, impatiently, patting the husband, to whom he was nearest, on the arm. 'Good luck!'

They moved away, saying thanks as they left, and Mac turned back to look at Kate, shaking his head.

'I'd forgotten that about you,' he said.

'What?' she said, smiling.

'You're like a girl guide. A grown-up girl guide.'

'Charming,' said Kate. 'That's not very sexy.'

'Oh it is,' said Mac, raising his eyebrows, and laughing. She joined in, shaking her head, but then he said, suddenly serious, 'So, you were about to tell me why you ran off. Did a bunk.'

There was a cool breeze blowing down the street, refreshing and calm. Kate let it wash over her, calming her down, and she looked at Mac.

'Look, I had to go. That's the truth. Don't bother hating me for it. You couldn't hate me more than I hate myself.'

He was silent for a long time, looking at her, and still he held his hand in her lap. It was so comforting, the kind of solid, kind comfort that Kate hadn't really felt for months and months. She knew Mac must despise her, blame her, loathe her, but somehow still, there at the table, her hand in his, in the shade of tall Mayfair red brick, she felt safe.

'You poor thing,' he said after a while. 'You poor bloody thing.'

'We'll just walk, then,' he said, checking back to make sure they'd left nothing behind. She liked that about him, his precision in everything, the way he managed to do it without fussing. It was a process, part of a process, like giving an

347

anaesthetic or removing a tumour or mending a tear or scrubbing up.

'Don't you have to –' she asked.

'I don't have to be anywhere,' he said. 'Neither do you, so why don't we just walk for a bit? Where are you staying?'

'Hotel in Bayswater,' she said.

'You're not staying with your dad?'

'He's away.' She was lying, she didn't know why. 'No one knows I'm here. Mac, I don't want –'

'Sure, sure,' he said, softly. 'It's fine. I think you need to tire yourself out if you're going to sleep tonight, anyway. Let's just – walk, shall we?'

'OK,' said Kate. 'Where shall we go?'

'The park,' he said. 'Let's go to the park.'

'So tell me, what you've been up to, then,' he said, as they walked into Hyde Park, and Kate saw the vistas of paths open up before them, of trees and buildings far in the background.

'It's a pretty short story,' said Kate. 'A boring story.'

'OK,' he said, easily, and he shot a look at her, and then carried on walking. She could hear the shouts from Speaker's Corner. There were the people just out of the office, relaxing in the evening sun, resting their heads on their backpacks, reading papers and books. There was the long, yellowy green meadow grass, never built-upon, never constructed and moulded into a park out of rock like Central Park. This was the parkland that Henry VIII had hunted on, that Lady Emma Hamilton had ridden over, where sandbags had been laid in the First World War. She smiled, thinking what a very tacky, touristy thing to think that was.

It was just she knew it, she knew that over there was the Serpentine, with boats floating on the still surface, and the Albert Hall, and the Albert Memorial, spun out of gold and marble, ridiculously over-shiny, and she knew that over *there* were the formal gardens, and Kensington Palace, and the spot where Tyburn stood. She knew all this, because she'd grown up here, and it was her home, and she missed it, she missed it so much it hurt, and she missed *this* – walking along with someone, just chatting. About things that mattered.

'Tell me how Zoe is instead,' said Kate. 'And Flora. How's Flora?'

Zoe and Steve's daughter was now eighteen months old. Mac smiled. 'Beautiful. Looks just like her mother. She likes things with mud,' said Mac, as they walked down towards Park Lane.

'Mud?' said Kate.

'Yes, eating mud. Harry keeps striding out to the garden and trying to shove handfuls of earth into her mouth. Zoe's in despair, she doesn't know what to do. She ate a worm last week.' She turned towards him. His green eyes were full of laughter, though his expression was as serious as ever. 'Flora ate a worm, I mean.'

'Obviously.'

'Does Harry remember –' Kate trailed off.

'About his father?' Mac said, gazing into the distance, where a group of friends were playing a noisy and erratic game of frisbee. 'Harry remembers him. He asks where Steve is.'

'What do you say?' Kate asked him.

'It's tricky. You have to be honest, but not too honest. Zoe's been amazing . . .' He trailed off. 'She's incredible, that girl.'

She's my best friend, Kate wanted to say. I know. I know. But she had forsaken that right, the right to an opinion about Zoe, or any of them.

'She tells him that Dad's not coming back, that he's gone

349

to heaven, but he's watching them all and he'll always love them.'

It was so simple.

They walked in silence for a while, until they reached the Serpentine.

'You know,' Mac said suddenly. 'They've got each other. They're still a family.'

Kate nodded gratefully, unable to speak, and he watched her. She stared out, at the wind ruffling the water, the cars trawling slowly across the white stucco bridge, at the landscape of London sloping out in front of her.

'Love. That's what they've got. Lots and lots of it. Sounds corny but it's true. They may not have a dad, but there are so many people who love them, you mustn't worry too much.'

She reached towards him, and squeezed his hand in silent gratitude, for telling her about them, for falling back into silence again, and they walked on, down to the south of the Serpentine, over the bridge towards the gates of the park. They walked in silence, past ice-cream vans, past children playing, past tourists enjoying the sun. The shouts from unsteady novice sailors echoed across the water, and the afternoon sun flashed and glittered on the surface. They were small, insubstantial, in the large, open space, where the green met the sky.

They kept their hands joined, their fingers entwined, still saying nothing, asking nothing from each other, not knowing what was going to happen. But, walking through the park as the shadows lengthened, as the day turned to summery, sunny evening, Kate felt more at peace, happier, more herself than she had since the day Steve died.

That night, after he'd dropped her at her dusty little hotel in the backstreets behind Paddington, unlooked for and unloved, she had let herself into her tiny room, little wider than its double bed, and got undressed, knowing she would never sleep. In the bed, Kate clutched the duvet cover, which was too big for its duvet. Lying there in the darkness, she could hear the sounds of London around her. She was less than a mile away from her old flat, her old life with Sean, her old happiness, and now a girl called Gemma was living there and she was here, in this hotel, waiting for tomorrow when she could get her visa stamped and get out of here. She was only a couple of miles from her father, her step-mother and her sister – what were they doing, on this summer's evening? She hadn't seen them since before Christmas, last time they'd been in New York. Kate was inclined to agree with her mother, whose version of their marriage was that Daniel wouldn't notice her unless she was standing in front of him waving, but still . . . Sudden guilt ate into her, mixed with fear of discovery, that she was losing control of the plan she'd thought was so tight. Perhaps she should just go –

And yet in her mind was the memory of Mac, rooting her to this place. His tall, broad frame, his clear eyes on hers, his serious face, so often dark, smiling at her in her distress. Mac, who was picking her up from the Embassy and taking her for a late lunch. He was due to go off on holiday early the next day. Mac, who was her only friend in London, who had held her hand, who . . . understood. Better than anyone, though she couldn't explain why. And in the midst of these contradictory thoughts Kate, who was more exhausted than she had realized, simply drifted off to sleep, and in that tiny, shabby room, badly-soundproofed and unloveable, she slept through the night, a deep and dreamless sleep.

'So, you live with your mum and Oscar – and you see Betty, and the people at the office. And that's it.'

'Yep.' Kate bent down to pick up a stone from the gravel path in St James's, where they were walking.

'That's *it*?'

'Well, and friends of mum's, and Betty's. And sometimes we have a work event.' Kate realized she was sounding defensive. 'It's just that . . . that's the way I want it.'

'Of course.' It was a statement, not a question. She looked at him, marvelling yet again at the restfulness she felt when she was with him, so extraordinary when she thought about him, what they had been through together.

'It's lovely here,' Kate said, sighing. She threw some gravel back onto the ground and looked around. They were walking down the Mall, which was strangely quiet in the summer's evening, the only real traffic that of knots of tourists, making their way down the red road towards the Palace. Along the wide avenue, the trees swayed in the wind. Up ahead of them, the white backs of the private clubs of Pall Mall, each its own palace of privilege. Kate had never walked here when she'd lived in London, you generally didn't, really, and looking up at the man next to her, she still couldn't quite understand what she was doing here.

'Do you ever hear from Sean?' Mac said suddenly.

'No.' It surprised her how quickly the reply to the question came. As if she'd been expecting it. He stopped and looked at her, and Kate stopped too. 'Never. Do . . . do you?'

He said easily, 'They've moved to East London. He emailed me, about a month ago.'

'Oh right,' said Kate.

'Do you know what Charly's doing?'

'I don't, no,' she said, and her voice was a little wavery, a little uncertain, but she was doing it, saying it, talking about these things without freaking out, and that was something, she supposed. 'I wouldn't have been in touch at all,

352

but I had to send Sean some money, you know, when we bought him out of the flat.'

'We?'

'Dad.' Kate gave him a half-smile. 'Dad and Lisa. They bought Sean's share. Bless them. Turns out the Daniel Miller album of Westlife covers was a great idea. Shows what I know, eh.'

'That was kind of him.'

'Very kind,' said Kate. 'They were great about it. Lisa said she knew I should never have got engaged to him.' She laughed, shortly. 'Hindsight's twenty-twenty, isn't it.'

'Yes,' said Mac reasonably, 'but no one wants to hear it at the time, do they.'

'It's true.' Kate watched a seagull, circling above St James's Park.

'Oscar said the same thing to me that evening, you know,' he said.

She didn't understand. 'What evening?'

'The engagement party.' They crossed the wide road, leaving St James's Park behind them. A bike appeared from nowhere, out of one of the side alleys leading onto the Mall, and zoomed towards them. Mac's hand shot out and he grabbed Kate by the arm. She pulled away from him, angrily.

'Sorry,' she said. Something crossed Mac's face, like irritation, exasperation. Kate saw it, knew it for what it was, and couldn't blame him. Perhaps this had been a mistake, she told herself, and started planning exit strategies to get back to her hotel, go to sleep.

'What did Oscar say at the engagement party?' she asked.

Mac looked around him. 'The same thing I said.'

'I – what?' Kate shook her head. 'I don't remember.'

'What?' Mac said, mockingly. 'You really don't remember?' and he took her by the elbow, gently guiding her into Marlborough Road, the small street that led away from the Mall

353

past St James's Palace, up towards Piccadilly. It was quiet, no tourists, and suddenly they were in the shade. She blinked, unaccustomed to the darkening light.

'Oh,' she said, recall of the evening rushing back to her now.

'What did I say, Kate?' he said, and there was amusement in his voice, something else, too, something she couldn't define.

'You told me not to marry him.' She had said it.

'Ah.' Mac nodded, as if she'd just pointed out an interesting statue. He shoved his hands in his pockets. His expression was unreadable. 'Oscar told me he didn't like him, and he was allowed to say that because they were fellow countrymen. I love your stepfather. They may be fellow countrymen but I've never seen two more different people.'

Kate wanted to get back to the matter in hand. 'So –'

'Well, we had a chat about it. I was a little the worse, or the better, depending on which way you look at it, for the alcohol, you know. But he seemed to me to be making perfect sense. I agreed with him.'

'Well, you were right,' said Kate.

'I was,' Mac said. 'I think I actually told you not to marry him.'

'So you did.' She turned her hand upwards, palms open. 'You see.'

'I do see,' said Mac. 'I did tell you that.'

It was hard to ask, but she had to. 'Did – did you know?'

'About Sean – and Charly?'

'Yep,' said Kate. She never knew, because she had never wanted to know. 'Did you know?'

Mac stuck his hands in his pockets. He looked deadly serious. 'I knew – they'd been sleeping with each other. Steve had asked my advice about it. Sworn me to secrecy. He didn't know what to do.'

354

'Oh,' said Kate.

'Sean was obsessed with Charly, you know?' Mac said gently. 'It wasn't love. It was – infatuation. It was a physical thing, that's all. Steve was trying to persuade him to give it up. Give her up. But she was obsessed with him.'

Kate didn't want to hear any more. 'OK.'

'Just one thing,' Mac said. 'Honestly, I think he loved you. He did really want to marry you. I just think he was in too deep, and he didn't know how to get out. Until –' he shrugged, and smiled a painful, twisted smile. 'I have to believe that, don't know why. Otherwise it's as if Steve had been completely wasting his time, and that bastard ruined the lives of all the people I love, in one day.'

There was a pause.

'I know,' Kate said, desperately wanting to hug him. She breathed in deeply, and looked up at him, then over his shoulder, breaking the tension between them. 'We should go.'

'Kate –' he said, his voice low.

'Excuse me,' a voice behind them called. 'Can you please tell me where is Princess Diana's palace?'

A small family was standing behind them, the father waving a badly folded map. 'Londres' was written on it in large letters; the wife was wearing a tee-shirt that said 'Paris'.

'Oh my god,' said Mac, under his breath. 'Over there,' he said shortly, pointing towards Buckingham Palace. He turned back to Kate. 'Look, Kate –'

The father was not convinced. 'There?'

'Yes,' said Mac.

'Rubbish,' said Kate. 'Look –'

'Is this where she lived when she died?' the wife asked Mac, looking anxious.

'Yes,' said Mac, firmly. 'Kate. I wanted to say something to you,' he said, turning back to her.

355

'Wait,' said Kate, unable to help herself. She was watching the wife, whose expression was near-fanatical. 'No. Not really. It was Kensington Palace.'

Mac looked at her, his eyes wide open, and shook his head.

'Here,' said Kate, pointing to the map. 'That's where.'

'Is this where the flowers were?' said the woman, nodding emphatically.

'Yes, where the flowers were,' said Kate.

'Did you see her?' the husband said.

'Er, I did actually, once,' Kate said, memory flooding back to her.

'You saw Princess Diana!' The woman clasped her hands.

'Yes,' said Kate, with enthusiasm. 'In High Street Kensington.' Mac groaned quietly by her side. 'In Marks and Spencer. It's a shop.' The woman nodded furiously.

'She – she was very beautiful.'

'Oh, she was,' said Kate, clasping her hands. 'You know, I think she was probably a bit mad, but gosh, she was lovely.'

'Queen of Hearts,' the woman told her, fervently.

'You know,' Kate said, stepping towards her. 'It was –'

'Right!' said Mac, taking her elbow. 'Have a lovely time,' he said, bearing Kate off in the other direction and smiling at the tourists, who called 'Thank you!' loudly after them. They walked in silence a little further, a constraint suddenly upon them. They stopped outside St James's Palace, which glowed almost rose-pink in the sunset, and a slight breeze blew across Kate's face, her neck, through her hair.

'Ah,' said Kate. 'I hope they find it.'

'Mm,' said Mac, looking wrathfully at their retreating backs. 'They should pick their moments better.'

'We're here, aren't we?' she said honestly. She put her hand on his. 'We're here. That's all that matters.'

She turned away from him for a second, looking up at St James's Street, the great Regency stage set, towards Piccadilly. He was standing directly behind her, and they were quiet, though Kate could feel his eyes on her.

He bent and kissed her bare shoulder, and she felt his lips on her skin. He slid his arms around her waist and he kissed her again, kissed her back and her hair, gently. She held his arms, wrapping her own around his, so they were snaked together in the shadow of the palace and no one, not the passing tourists, not the guards standing to attention outside, not the couple in evening dress hurrying towards Pall Mall, paid them any attention, as they stood there in silence, holding each other, both watching the evening scene in front of them.

Eventually she loosened herself from his grasp, and swivelled round to face him, to meet his eyes, his face, the face of the man she knew so well. He opened his mouth to say something, but Kate knew she had to speak first.

'You're lovely,' she said, her hands on his chest, as he pulled her tightly towards him. 'I've missed you.'

'Eloquently put,' he said, and kissed her on the mouth, and she wrapped her arms around his neck and kissed him right back.

At four o'clock the next morning, in her tiny, rabbit-hutch of a room, he ran his hand over her stomach and pulled her towards him. Pushing her hair out of her eyes – for it had wrapped itself around her face, like candy-floss – he kissed her again and said,

'Would it be alright with you if I didn't go away on holiday?'

The strange thing about Mac, Kate felt, was how none of it was really a surprise, a revelation. With Sean, she'd never really felt she'd known him, even through the mundanity of their shared lives, their long time together. Here, she just knew what was going to happen. She had known he wasn't going on holiday anymore, known it from the moment they kissed. She ran her hand over his shoulder, down his arm, and took hold of his fingers.

'Fine with me.' She smiled at him in the darkness. He took a deep breath.

'When do you have to go back to New York, Kate?'

It was Thursday. Thursday, and she had to be back for work tomorrow. She had to leave later today.

'I – I don't know.'

'Tell me.' He clutched her hand.

'Tomorrow night,' she said quickly.

There was silence. She could hear a siren outside in the street, rushing towards the hospital.

'And what if you were to lie?'

'Lie?' she said, not understanding. She moved closer towards him; they were on their sides, facing each other.

'Say . . .' his voice was soft in her ear. 'Say there was a problem with your visa and you had to stay here a bit longer.'

'I couldn't do that,' she said immediately.

'Of course you couldn't,' he said, rushing to agree with her. His voice was light. 'It's just that I've been in love with you for five years, Kate. I was sort of hoping perhaps now . . . maybe . . . before you screw everything up again and fly back to New York to hang out with your mum and an assortment of embittered writers and crazy old couples in your apartment block . . .' he was whispering in her ear now, so softly in the dead quiet of the bedroom, his lips tickling her skin, 'Well. I was hoping we might have some more time together. For this.'

'For this?'

'This.'

'What is *this*?' she said, desperately wanting him to tell

her the answer, but he cut her off as she finished the sentence.

'We'll worry about all that later. Let's just say it's imaginary, it's an interlude. Who cares what happens afterwards?'

But she knew he didn't mean that.

'Stay, Kate. I love you. Don't go back. Stay for just one more week.'

'OK,' she said, ignoring the hammering in her chest. 'I will.'

'Do you want to?'

Like someone had sucked all the air out of her lungs, Kate felt her chest, her heart, cave in, as if she were swooping down low over something, losing her senses. She blinked, trying to steady herself. She put her hand up to his cheek.

'More than you could possibly imagine.'

We'll worry about all that later. I love you.
More than you could possibly imagine.
I've been in love with you for five years, Kate.
Five years, Kate.
Stay, Kate. I love you.
Stay.
OK. I will.
Stay.

When they weren't in bed, they were walking through the park, and when they weren't in the park, they were sitting in a cafe somewhere in between the park and her hotel, Bayswater, or Marylebone. In the dog days of July, no one bothered them. Apart from crowds thronging Westminster Abbey or Madame Tussauds or the Tower of London, the city was empty. They went to the Turbine Hall at the Tate Modern early one morning, but it was crammed with people and they only wanted to be with each other, so they walked along the river instead, ducking behind into the old wharfs around Blackfriars Bridge, along by the Oxo Tower. They went to Borough Market and bought pies and cold lemonade and picnicked, on the benches outside Southwark Cathedral. They walked along Marylebone High Street, weaving in between pubs in tiny mews streets, they sat outside eating Lebanese food, hummus with diced lamb and pitta, they walked along Clerkenwell Road, stopping to drink cold glasses of rosé in elegant bars normally stuffed with workers – the city was theirs, no one troubled them, and they troubled no one.

No one at all, except themselves. Zoe was away visiting Mac and Steve's parents in Edinburgh, Francesca was on holiday with some friends in Italy – oh, the luck. She'd established via email that her father was in the recording studio, Dani and Lisa were with Lisa's parents in Cornwall. It was her and Mac, that summer, and she didn't know what was going to happen but for once, cautious, sensible shy Kate, Simply Didn't Care. All she cared about was him.

His laughing, kind eyes – how could she have thought they were cold?

His easy, quietly authoritative manner: the hotel tried to overcharge her when she extended her stay, until Mac stepped in, his negotiation technique far superior to Kate's (which was to be flustered and furious), and she ended up paying almost nothing for the tiny, happy little room that became their whole world.

The way he laughed – properly laughed, with helpless gulps and shouts that consumed his whole frame, when she told him a story that amused him, about Betty's new boyfriend, or about the old days, or something that had happened to her in New York.

How in his sleep he sometimes sighed, so deeply, and seeing him in repose, strangely vulnerable, almost broke her heart. She wanted to look after him, to protect him, to make sure he wasn't ever hurt again, especially by her.

His hands on her body – she watched them moving over her, watched him, his face, and knew she would never be happy again unless he was by her side. And, as the days moved into a second week, and they stopped lotus-eating and realized they were going to have to make a plan of some sort, the dreams came back.

She'd had them before, after Steve died, all the time, and only going to New York made them stop.

She would dream she was back somewhere they'd been that day – in a tiny little Italian restaurant in Soho, eating sage and butter ravioli, kissing Mac in between bites and drinking red wine. And Charly would appear at the table next to her, and then Sean. Or they would walk past the window and stare in. They never said anything, just watched her, smiling, demonically. And she never knew when they were going to appear, sometimes the dream would last for ages, and only then, at the end of revisiting the lovely walk she'd had with Mac through Battersea Park, would Charly suddenly walk casually out from behind a tree, her long hair ruffled in the summer's breeze, and Kate would awake, sweating, terrified. And another memory of a beautiful day with Mac would be ruined. She couldn't sleep, and he didn't notice, and he couldn't help her, and she started to hate him for that.

She ignored it for a few days, the voice in her head that dripped poison into her ear, but she knew it was only a matter of time before she admitted it.

Admitted that if she really loved Mac, the only way not to hurt him, now, was to go.

It grew hotter and hotter, as August drew near, and now they had spent nearly two weeks together, barely a moment apart, other than lavatory breaks. Or when Mac had to go back to his flat to pick up more clothes. Their tiny, bare hotel room and the London of tourists in the summer was their world, and though someone cleaned the room each day, clothes, shoes, possessions were flowing across it like water by nighttime, when they lay asleep, the covers thrown off, Mac's arm draped over Kate.

Yes, Kate would decide, as she lay by his side, watching him during those stuffy, airless, dark nights. He does love me. She knew that.

But Kate also knew that, while Mac thought he'd forgiven her, it was only a matter of time before he started to hate her for it, to blame her for the death of his beloved brother. For making her best friend, his sister-in-law, a widow – all these things. It would happen: it was a way off yet, but it would happen, and it would gradually poison everything – that's why she'd left London in the first place. She had tried to separate herself from it all. She had put an ocean between herself and what had happened and now, it was starting to catch up with her.

In the last few days of their time together, Kate slept less and less, and Mac's arm across her body, over her shoulders, weighed down more and more, and the dreams became more and more regular, and the weather grew humid and frayed her nerves even further, and he was crowding in on her, more and more. She could sense him clinging on to her, even as she tried to push away, knew he was reaching out to her for reassurance because he felt her rejecting him. He would kiss her, draw her towards him, open her legs to let him inside her, and she let him, wanting him desperately, trying not to cry with love for him, even as she wished he'd just leave her alone, alone. Alone, a unit of one, so she wasn't bothered by him and how he made her feel.

So she had to leave.

The question was how. And when. And one night, her thirteenth night back in London, it came to her, suddenly.

'Ill? Your mother? How – what do you mean?'

'She fainted today. She was in Saks. She banged her head, she's unconscious.' Kate stood on the other side of the bed, trying not to panic. 'There's a flight at seven. I've spoken to someone at Virgin, I'm on it.'

Mac had gone back to his flat, to pick up more clothes, check his post, his messages, run some errands. He had left her there, in their cardboard world of the hotel, promising he'd be back by three, and he was, to find that everything had changed, to find Kate surrounded by clothes, her eyes red, curiously withdrawn from him.

He ran his hands through his hair. 'My god, Kate. That's awful.' He came round to her side of the bed as she stuffed her meagre, much-worn clothes into her bag; every one had a memory now.

'What did Oscar say?'

'He said to come home. He'll meet me at JFK.'

The black cotton broderie anglaise sundress; she had worn that when they hired a boat on the Serpentine, Mac rowing, Kate reading him Sherlock Holmes stories, and covertly giving him sips of illegal wine.

She watched him hugging himself, his hands shoved under his armpits, his body language tight, panicked. 'But what do they think . . . Do you want me to speak to him, to someone at the hospital, find out what's going on?'

'God, no. No, Mac, please. I just need to get home. They think she's going to be OK, that it's just concussion, but . . .'

The polka-dot navy and white shirt she had worn the night it rained, five days ago; drenched, soaked to the soul, they had given up trying to stay dry and had run back to the hotel, his white t-shirt virtually transparent, her hair like rats' tails, both laughing silently, almost hysterically.

He was shaking his head, his eyes full of damned sympathy, concern, emotion for her. She hated it, hated him for feeling like that, herself for making him feel like that. He moved towards her, and put his arm around her.

'Oh, Kate – darling . . .'

That skirt, the one she had worn the first day she saw him; she bit her lip, bowing her head over the bed, as he released her and took her hands in his.

'I wish you weren't going. Shall I come with you?'

For a second, Kate leant against him, allowing herself to indulge what it would feel like to say yes. To just breathe out, and give in. To say, yes, come back with me, actually, stay with me, let me stay with you. I love you, I want to be with you, to stay with you forever. Love me, let me love you.

She rolled all these words around in her mouth, unspoken. But she had to go, and when he found out how she had lied he would start to hate her, and by the time she came back to London again, he would properly hate her, think she was a lunatic, and her work would be done.

Two years of pushing everything down, deep deep down inside her, of guilt and mourning, not just for her friend's death, but for the lives she'd left behind, were finally catching up with Kate, she knew it. And now it pleased her to be mad. That's how miserable she was.

'I'll come with you to the airport,' Mac was saying.

Kate ran her hands through her hair. 'No.'

'Of course I will.'

'No,' she said. Her voice surprised her. She turned to him. 'Please, Mac. Can you just take me to Paddington, put me on the Heathrow Express. I hate airports so much. I don't want to say goodbye to you there. Please.'

It was true, the only true thing she'd said since he'd got back, and he didn't realize it. But he nodded, bewildered.

'Of course.'

She waited till she was on the train. He even got on with her, put her bags on the rack, having charmed the guard into letting him through the ticket barriers. She tried not to cry as he kissed her, told her he loved her.

'I'll be over as soon as I can,' he said, kissing her hair, the way he had done the first time they'd kissed, outside St James's. 'I'll call you. Call me when you get there, but I'll call you.'

'Sorry, sir,' said the kindly guard, who'd let him climb onto the train with her. 'We're about to leave. You'll have to get off.'

He stood up. She didn't stand up. She just said,

'I'm sorry.'

He looked at her, puzzled.

'Bye,' she said. 'Mac –' She held out her hand.

'I've written you a letter. It'll explain everything.'

'This train is about to depart. Please stand clear of the closing doors.'

'In the drawer by the bedside table. At the hotel. I'm sorry.'

He looked even more bewildered, as the doors closed, and Kate sank back into her seat, not looking to see if he was watching, not knowing. She was shaking so hard she thought she was going to be sick, and the train pulled away, gliding seamlessly out of the station, and she didn't look around once.

Dear Mac

Mum's not ill, I made it up because I had to leave. I'm sorry.

I can't be with you, not in the way you want. It would

have been nice, but it just can't happen. After everything that's happened but especially because of Steve. Can't you see that?

I expect you'll hate me now, but don't feel bad about it. After everything I've done to you it would be weird if you didn't.

You'll never know what these last two weeks have meant to me. In another life I love you.

Kate

PART FOUR

CHAPTER THIRTY-FIVE

Kate woke after five, and lay in the darkness of her flat, staring at nothing.

How long, she didn't know, but after a while, she realized Mac was awake too. He was breathing heavily, half-asleep, but he wasn't asleep. She knew it because she wasn't either, and she remembered how well he used to sleep back then, last summer, while she lay awake, praying for the sunrise. She didn't want to move, though, to move things on, she wanted to stay there, in his arms, feel his body next to hers, their legs entangled, caught between being asleep and awake, this state of security and the next state of uncertainty, for as long as possible, until dawn slid through the slatted blinds.

She turned over, so her back pressed into his chest, and his arm slid around to hold her. Kate blinked in the darkness, her eyes aching already with fatigue. Why had she let it happen?

Because it was always going to, a little voice inside her head told her. *Because the two of you have unfinished business.*

She blinked again, staring at the crumpled edge of the duvet.

Because you're lonely.
Because he understands.

But he didn't, that was the trouble. He pushed into her space, he brought back the past, he invaded her, he upset her, every single time. And she even more so with him. It was like an old scab, she had decided. They were bad for each other, yet they couldn't stop picking at it, opening it, because of everything else it covered.

Mac moved against her, drawing her closer into him, so there was nothing between them. She could feel him against her thighs, his muscles against her back. He sighed, she didn't know whether it was conscious or not. He kissed her shoulder, gently, the back of her neck, and stroked her arm, and was still again. They were quiet, in the dark room, and Kate stared out again as a cold, heavy tear streaked onto her pillow. This, this tenderness was what got to her the most. This was why she'd left London. The agony of complication, of entanglement.

And then Mac spoke.

'You're awake, aren't you?'

Kate cleared her throat. 'Yes.'

She rolled over and rubbed her eyes, in an effort to look more half-asleep than she actually was. In reality, her mind was whirring, flipping over possibilities and endings like a pinball machine, but she said, after a moment,

'You OK?' She leaned in and kissed him, somewhere on the chin. He didn't react, or reply, in any way. 'Hm,' she said, and closed her eyes again, jokingly. 'Hey. You OK?'

He put his hand on her neck, and pulled her towards him. 'Yeah. Just thinking.' He kissed her back.

'About what?' Kate said. He was silent again. 'What?' She pushed him. 'Hey. Don't go silent on me. About what?'

'Your flat,' he said. 'I finally get to see your flat.'

372

Of course. 'You've never been here, have you.'

'No,' he said. 'You were with Sean – and then, afterwards
. . .'

Afterwards.

'Do you like it so far?' she said softly into his ear, as he
drew her towards him. 'Do you like what you've seen?' She
touched him, in a way she knew he liked, that only they knew.

'Hm?' He pushed her away but then he sighed, laughing
softly. 'Oh, Kate.'

'I'm looking for a new tenant,' she said, moving into him,
wrapping his arms around her, feeling calmer as he responded
to her.

'That's strange,' he said. He nibbled her ear. 'I'm looking
for somewhere to rent.'

'I remember,' said Kate. 'We should talk. I could do you
a discount. Mates' rates.'

'Mmm. Kate's mates' rates.' He kissed her, on the mouth,
her neck, her ear. 'Only – I don't think we're mates,' he
said. 'Do you?'

'I'm sorry you feel that way,' said Kate, rolling on top of
him, smoothing her hands over the muscles in his shoulders. 'That'd solve all my problems.' She kissed him, running
her hands through his short, scrubby hair. He froze.

He lay still beneath her, then he pushed her off him,
gently. 'Nice. Always the same.'

'What?'

'You're really going back there again, aren't you?'

Kate had the feeling of being out-manoeuvred. She rubbed
her face, pushed her hair out of her eyes. 'What?'

'New York. You're really going to go back. Again. Aren't
you.'

'You know I am,' she said. He pushed her hand away.

'Screw you, Kate,' Mac said. He sat up. She stared at him,
astonished. 'God. You never want to face up to it.'

'Mac –!' Kate said, sitting up too, turning into him, leaning on one hand. 'You were the one last night saying it was a one-night thing! What the hell –'

His face was furious. The words wrenched out of him. 'Of course it's not a one-night thing!'

'Don't shout at me,' she said, furious. 'Don't shout. You *said* this was a one-night thing! And I said we shouldn't do it again, it would hurt too much and you were all "No, Kate, give in to it, it's only one night", and here you are blaming me because I'm leaving in a few days – *God*, Mac, you're like the reverse of one of those stupid dating books!'

'What do you mean?' He looked at her, coldly.

Kate knelt in front of him, suddenly hating her nakedness. She wrapped the corner of the duvet around her body. 'Why are you doing this to me, trying to force me into a corner, when last night you made it clear this was only for one night?'

'Look, this was never about one night. Stop trying to sound like a lawyer, Kate. Stop avoiding the issue. The issue is you. You always run away.' He gestured. 'The first night we spent together.'

'I didn't run away then!' Now Kate was practically shouting herself. 'You ran away! You shagged me and then went to bloody Scotland and never called me!'

'I didn't need to, did I?' He threw the words in her face. 'You were fucking your flatmate a week later, what did it matter?'

She put her hands over her eyes, wanting to block it out. 'That's not true –' she said.

'I even turned up to your engagement party, I told you not to marry him,' he said, throwing the words in her face.

'That's what I mean!' Kate shouted. 'You're being ridiculous! It's always on your terms, Mac, what was I supposed to do with that? Leave him, in front of everyone, just because

374

you appear out of *nowhere* after two years and start drunk-
enly hinting at some dim and dark secret? I thought I loved
him! I thought this was it!'

'It wasn't, though, was it,' he said grimly.

'Exactly,' she said, shaking. *I never loved him the way I loved
you. Never.* 'So don't you dare make me feel guilty about it.
You bastard.' She turned away from him, but he carried on,
ignoring her.

'Kate, you even ran away after Steve died, and I thought
you were the only one who could help me through it.' He
banged his fist on the mattress. It made a deadening,
whooshing sound.

'You really thought that?' she whispered. 'But I was the
last person who you'd –'

'And last year, when we had everything, you did it again.'
Mac rubbed his face, scratched the shadow on his chin.
'Everything. I told myself you were damaged, you'd had a
hard time, that – you know, perhaps it was worth one more
try. And now, when we're here in bed together, and I'm
actually thinking well, despite everything we said last night,
isn't it clear now, isn't it obvious we're great together, and
you turn around and offer to rent your fucking *flat* out to
me.'

'Oh,' she said. 'OK.'

'I don't get you, Kate.' He was standing by the bed,
watching her. 'I just don't get you.'

'No, you don't,' Kate said. 'You think you can fix everything, and you don't understand you can't.'

'What does that mean?'

She climbed out of bed, naked, her back to him, and
pulled on her blue velvet dressing gown. Standing in front
of him, she said,

'I ran away because I needed to work everything out
myself. I know it was crap of me. But that's the way it was.'

'But Kate – it didn't need to be like that,' he said, bewildered.

'It did.' She rubbed her nose. 'Mac, listen to me. I'm the one who should have died that day. Not Steve.'

He winced. She hated, hated saying this to him. 'It's not like that.'

'It is,' she said, moving closer towards him. 'He pushed me out of the way. He saved my life. Did you forget that?'

'It doesn't matter,' he said, but she heard the note of hesitation in his voice, and that was enough for her. 'Kate, what happened happened. You have to accept that.'

'I have accepted it,' she said. She was quite calm. 'Now I'm back I can see I'm getting used to it. But that doesn't mean I don't feel guilty about it every single day. Don't you see, that it's impossible? For us to be together? There are some things in the past that just can't be overcome. You'll love Steve, and Zoe, for the rest of your life. But if it hadn't been for me, your life would have been completely different. Better.' She put her hand on his chest; he caught it, held it there. 'I wish I could change that. More than anything else. But it's the truth and you can't change it, no matter how you look at it.'

His hand tightened on hers. 'You can't look at it like that, Kate.'

She whispered, 'I do, though. I do. You have a choice. Your brother, or the girl who was responsible for his death.' Her throat was dry; she couldn't swallow.

Was it getting lighter in the room, or was she imagining it? They stood there, perfectly still, neither wanting to move, to choreograph the next step. His hands were always warm. She could feel his heart beating in his chest. She prayed that he would understand.

'I don't understand,' he said, finally. He opened his fingers; her hand dropped to her side, heavily. 'I've tried so hard with you.'

She hated the way he boxed her in, like those nights at the end of the summer when she couldn't sleep, trapped under the weight of him, and the weight of her feelings for him. 'What are you looking for, some kind of reward?' she said sharply.

'Why do you always push people away?' he said, pulling on his shirt and buttoning it up swiftly. 'Why don't you want someone to look after you? To care about you?'

'Don't patronize me,' she said, angrily. 'You know it's not about that. This is about you trying to sort everything out, your way.'

'What's wrong with that?' He pulled on his jacket. 'You've got a damned funny way of looking at things, Kate. I'm trying to help you.'

'You've got a damned funny way of helping,' she said, bitterly. He was facing her again, there were only a few inches between them. 'Don't be such a hypocrite.'

'How am *I* a hypocrite?' he said.

'Because you come back here with me and we have sex and it's great and we *know* it's a one-night thing, and then you start making me feel horrible again,' Kate said, her voice thick. 'You always do. You always do.'

'That's called life, Kate!' Mac said furiously. 'That's what life's like! You can't lock yourself away for ever. You can't put your heart in a safe somewhere and hope no one touches it, comes near you! You can't sleep with me just for some human contact without having the fallout afterwards.' He put his hands on his forehead, kneading the skin with his knuckles. 'My god. This is crazy.'

'I think you'd better go,' Kate said.

'I'm going,' said Mac. 'Don't worry. I've learned my lesson with you, Kate. Finally.'

She picked up her house keys, lying on the dresser, and caught sight of the post. She had picked it up when they'd got back the previous night, stumbling around each other in the hall, his hands inside her coat, pulling her towards him, the promise of the night ahead intoxicating them both. She had held the letters, crumpled in her hand, thrown them down as they came in . . . She snatched up the pile again.

Kate Miller
Flat 4
Howard Mansions
London W9

'No . . .' she whispered, stopping herself.

'What?' Mac said. He looked at her. 'What is it?'

'Nothing,' Kate said, snatching the letter up. 'Bills.'

He looked curiously at the envelope in her hand. 'I know that writing. Who's the letter from?'

'*No-one*.' Her stomach hurt.

Mac sighed softly. 'God Kate, you just won't change, will you.'

Charly was writing to her and she was the one who was getting stick for it. No. Not again.

'It's from Charly,' she said. He took the letter out of her hand. 'She's been writing to me.'

'She – what?' He froze, the paper half-opened.

'She's having a baby. Mac, she's –'

He was watching her. 'She told you that?'

'Yes,' she said. 'She's pregnant. That was the first letter.'

'What do the others say?'

She was cold in her dressing gown, the night was still black, and there he was, dressed, ready to go. She wanted him out of the flat, now.

'Kate, what do they say?'

'It's my problem,' she said. 'Let me sort it out.'

Washed up, single, living with your mummy. I always said you were a bit of a loser, didn't I?

'Forget it,' Mac said again and the sound of his voice was

awful. 'You're right. It's too complicated, all of it. This is over. I'm sick of trying to mend you.'

'*I don't need mending*!' Kate shouted, nearly screaming. 'I'm not one of your fucking patients! Just leave me alone!'

'Well, I will, then,' he said. He picked up his bag and turned towards her. 'You were right Kate. I can see it now. This would have been a disaster. Thanks for proving me wrong – 'he shook his head at her. 'It took a while, but I'm glad you were right.'

She heard the front door close gently. It wasn't even light, and he had gone. Kate turned off the light, crawled back into bed, to find she was shaking, juddering from head to foot. She was freezing cold, and now she couldn't stop shaking, even if she'd wanted to. The letter was still in her hand. The light from the blinds in her room fell in stripes over the words, shafts of black and white on the difficult, messy handwriting.

Kate
You didn't call me, Kate. I've written four times now and nothing. And I bet you're wondering how we knew you were back, aren't you? Wouldn't you like to know WHO TOLD ME. Well, if you won't even have the courtesy to ring me I'll have to do something about it. I'll have to come and see you. Don't worry, I've got the address, see you soon.
Charly

CHAPTER THIRTY-SIX

When the morning finally arrived, Kate was still freezing. She hadn't bought enough winter clothes and she hopped around the flat trying to stay warm. At the bottom of the cupboard, beneath some of her old trainers was a squashed black felt hat. She pulled it on, gratefully, and sat down in front of her computer. She was bone-tired, but she reasoned it was no more nor less than she deserved. Kate knew, with a certainty born of experience, that it would be a few days after what had happened last night, early that morning, before it would start to hit. At the moment, she just felt numb.

She poured herself some coffee and opened her emails. In amongst messages from Kate Spade about their summer collection, enticing offers from Amazon that promised her thirty per cent off a box-set they thought she'd want but she found vaguely insulting to be offered (what had she bought recently that made them think she'd like even one Jeremy Clarkson DVD?) and entreaties from disenfranchised Nigerian aristocrats were hidden three emails. If she wanted a wake-up call, she got it.

The first email read:

> Dear Kate,
> I trust your father is recovering well; please pay him my respects. I have left several messages on your cellphone and sent you numerous emails, since I haven't heard from you about when you will be returning to your job here at Perry and Company. Please could you be in touch at your earliest convenience, otherwise I will consider your contract of employment here to be terminated as of the end of this week.
> Yours
> Bruce Perry

The second one said,

> Darling!? Where are you?!! I haven't spoken to you in days, what have you been up to? How is London? I saw a picture of Hyde Park with the daffodils out in force in the *Times* yesterday, it made me think of when you were little and we used to walk through Kensington Gardens after your flute lesson, do you remember? I took you to Barkers for lunch in the cafe after your Grade 4 exam, wasn't it? It made me miss London terribly, isn't it funny! Oh darling, I miss you!! Please call, let me know you're OK. Oscar sends lots of love, he is standing behind me as I write this. Darling one more thing, you will be back in time for his 60th won't you? (He's not standing behind me now.) He would be so upset if you weren't there. Must go darling xxxxxxxxxxxxxxxxxxxxxxxxxxxxxx
> Mummy xxxxxxxxxxxxxxxxxxxx

And the third one had been sent at eight that morning. It was called 'Perfect' and it simply said,

Kate. You NAILED it. Loved the article. I knew you could do it. It's fresh, it's fun, it's really sweet! Readers are going to love it.

I want to talk to you about a contract. And your next column for us. Don't book any flights! Call me as soon as you get this.

Sue

Kate leant back in her chair and stretched her hands above her head, high into the air, till her sides ached. She drew her legs up under her chin, pulling the tattered old jumper over her knees. Her heart was hammering inside her chest. She'd known that email from Bruce was going to come; over the last week or so, she'd deliberately avoided calls from the agency, reasoning to herself that they were getting on fine without her, and the real reason Bruce was getting in touch was to fire her and replace her with the bodacious Lorraine. But now – she bit the tip of her finger, thoughtfully. Did she really have the nerve to email Bruce back and tell him to stick his job? Wasn't that just saying she wasn't going back to New York?

She knew it wasn't. No, if the last few weeks had taught her anything, it was that she should not be doing that job any more. She had to start being brave and get out there, not moulder away at Perry and Co. She had been quiet and diligent, but her heart wasn't in it, she didn't enjoy any of the books Bruce represented, she didn't believe in the world of Perry and Co, where one author – Anne Graves – held sway over everything, an author who'd long ago stopped trying to write good books and was merely content to deliver something half-baked, year after year, later and later, because millions of people across the United States had been convinced by her publishers that hers was a name they could trust. She didn't like Doris, and Doris hated her. She was

382

pretty sure Bruce didn't like her much either, it struck her suddenly with certainty. It wasn't a job she cared about, why had she let herself do it for so long, then? Kate shook her head.

She had told Mac last night that since she'd come back to London, she was finally working things out for herself. Well, time to put that into action. She pressed 'Reply' and typed Bruce a long, apologetic email taking full responsibility for her behaviour and thanking him for everything, and then a separate card, which she addressed and stamped, in a fit of organization. Right. Done. And it felt pretty easy. Liberating, in fact.

She was half-way through a reply to her mother, telling her to calm down in as nice a way as possible, when the phone rang. Kate checked her watch. It was ten-thirty. She wasn't due at her dad's till about three-ish. She clutched the now-cold mug of coffee and picked up the receiver.

'Well?' a brisk voice demanded on the other end of the phone. 'What on earth happened last night?'

'Francesca,' said Kate, with some relief. 'Hello.'

'I had a meeting at eight-thirty this morning, just got out of it, otherwise I'd have called sooner. So . . . ?'

'Why do we have this relationship when all of a sudden all you're interested in is me and Mac?' Kate complained. 'How are you, Francesca? What's happening with Pav, have you seen him lately since you slept with him by accident at the Christmas party? What are your hopes and dreams?'

'Shut up,' said Francesca. 'Pav's back with his girlfriend, the stupid twat. And as for you and Mac, that's practically the only thing I know about you in the last two years, since you disappeared off the face of the frigging earth. And I still don't even know what happened! Man!'

Kate took a sip of her coffee and pulled unenthusiastically

383

at the untouched toast which sat next to her, cold and slightly soggy. 'Look, Francesca . . .' she began, warily. She wasn't ready to be reminded of it all yet. She paused. 'It's pretty horrible, so . . .'

Francesca's voice softened. 'Oh, Kate. I'm sorry.' She sounded genuinely contrite. 'I wasn't calling to force you to tell me, honest. I just wanted to make sure you were OK. It was such a weird vibe last night after he arrived, between the two of you. I can't believe Zoe doesn't know something's going on, don't you two ever *talk*?'

She sounded like Mac. 'Well, we left together,' said Kate defensively. 'She probably imagines . . .' She didn't finish, curiosity suddenly, overwhelmingly getting the better of her. 'What time did he get back this morning?'

'Well, sometime after six o'clock,' said Francesca. 'I was in the shower when he came in. He was quiet as a mouse, too. But I didn't see him. I yelled out "Bye" when he was in the bathroom when I left and he yelled back.'

'Mmm,' said Kate. 'What – what did he yell back?'

'Well – "Bye", too.' Francesca sounded apologetic. 'Sorry.'

'Right,' said Kate. She knew he wouldn't have said 'By the way, I'm in love with Kate, and I left her this morning, but I'm just back here for a shower and change of clothes and then I'm going to buy her a big bunch of flowers and go back to her flat to shag her senseless again and then take her out for lunch somewhere nice, possibly by the river.' But a small part of her hoped he would. She stamped her foot. She was a stupid girl.

Francesca asked curiously, 'So he left you at – what? Five?'

'Five-thirty, yeah.'

'Blimey,' said Francesca. 'That's early.'

'Yes,' said Kate. 'Oh god, Francesca. He was so angry.'

'About what?'

'Well –' Kate sighed. 'Give me a couple of minutes to fill

you in, and if the yen starts to crumble you have my permission to cut me off. OK?'

So she told Francesca everything. About the night together all those years ago. The affair last year. Last night. The letters from Charly. How he'd left. When she'd finished, Francesca was silent, and then she said,

'Wow.'

'I know, sorry.'

'Yeah. Wow.' Francesca exhaled, loudly. 'You two are hopeless.'

'That's the problem,' said Kate. She added sadly, 'Do you know something? I promised myself I wasn't going to think about it for a little while, but I can't help just wondering if that's the last time I'll see him. And it's probably for the best.'

She didn't know what she wanted Francesca to say. She just wanted her to be honest. Francesca made a strange sound, and then she said,

'You know what?'

'What?'

'I think you may be right.'

'Oh.'

'Oh babe. It's hard, but really – how would it ever work? You're both too – messy from the past. He's got his own stuff, too. His job's really busy – he's looking for somewhere else to live, you know.'

'Yes. I know.' Kate bit her lip, grimacing. She thought for a second and said, 'I was so sure it'd work last year. I kept having these dreams, kept thinking I saw . . . I saw Sean and Charly. You know? They were everywhere, in the dreams, wherever I was.' She'd never said any of this before. 'It was like my punishment. Even though I knew they were dreams, they were so real, it was . . . awful.'

'Forget about her,' said Francesca.

'I can't,' said Kate. 'Now there's this letter thing.' She banged her fist gently against the wooden surface of her desk. 'God, I don't want to see her.'

Francesca made a huffing sound. 'Course you don't! She did you a favour though.'

'How so?'

'Getting you away from Sean, in my opinion,' she said. 'Imagine if you'd married him.'

'Yeah. Maybe,' Kate said, uncertainly.

'No maybe about it. You were such a little mouse in his presence,' Francesca said. 'You weren't yourself. You stopped saying interesting geeky facts, you stopped talking about your job – and you had this really important job too, while he was moving stupid program data around from one computer to another! You'd sit there and gaze up at him like he was fucking – Zeus or something!' Her voice was loud; she obviously realized it and said, after a moment, 'And as for that cow Charly, well. I just think it was bad luck, you know? We all make friends who we think are the greatest things since sliced bread. Especially at work. You just got really unlucky, that's all. She was a bitch, you always knew she was a bitch, but you never really knew she was *evil*, did you? Who could have known.'

'You're right, you know.' Kate nodded, blinking in amazement.

'I think they're probably miserable together,' Francesca went on. 'You know, Bobbie saw them last year, in some Vietnamese restaurant in Dalston. It was BYO and Sean hadn't bought the wine and Charly was having this massive go at him.'

'Gosh,' said Kate, fascinated. 'Is that true?'

'Yep, she looked awful, apparently,' Francesca said with relish. 'But she was always one of those people whose looks were going to go early on. Good riddance to bad rubbish, I say. And god, you know we all wish we could change what happened that day, but the one thing I don't think any of us would change is you splitting up with Sean. He wasn't right for you. He's weak. A weak, weak man.'

This was all news to Kate, and she was astounded. 'I had no idea,' she said, but as she said it she realized pretty much all of it made sense. 'Why didn't you say any of this to me?' she asked Francesca.

'When?' said Francesca, snorting loudly. 'Kate, when?'

'Yeah.' Kate nodded, startled at the easy honesty of this conversation. 'I know.'

'Let me ask you something,' Francesca said. 'You talked to Zoe about any of this?'

'No,' said Kate. 'No way. She's got enough on her plate.'

'I think that's your problem,' Francesca said, elliptically. 'You should have told her.'

'Maybe.' Kate squirmed in her seat. She still felt guilt about Zoe, in a variety of different ways. 'One thing at a time, eh? Hey. Let's have dinner tonight. My treat. To say thanks. You've been an amazing friend since I got back, don't know what I would have done without you.'

'Hm,' said Francesca darkly. 'Well, I don't know about that. Dinner'd be nice though. Where?'

'You pick.'

'Great.' She was silent. 'Yes. I've got an idea. I'll – I'll text you, when I've booked somewhere.' She changed tack, suddenly, and Kate forgot the strange tone in her voice. 'Oh god, I've got to do some work –'

By lunchtime, Kate felt much better. She'd accomplished more that morning than she'd ever expected to, and it filled her with an intoxicating sense of freedom. She spoke to Sue, who was so kind, and so positive, and she asked her to do another article for next week, and then to Lisa, checking on her dad and her plans to see them all that afternoon.

Francesca, in her bluntly affectionate way, had made her see things she'd never thought of before. And she was right about Mac, too, little though Kate wanted to hear it. Perhaps it was best to sweep all of this out, with this new sense of purpose she had. Consign it, once and for all, to the past. She didn't understand him, though she thought she had. But she understood his wanting to preserve his sanity, to not want to get dragged back into all of that again – even though it had been so good. Like investigating a sore tooth with one's tongue, Kate probed her feelings on the previous night – and wasn't surprised when, as ever, it hurt to the touch. Perhaps it always would.

She was having a shower when she heard the phone ring again, but they didn't leave a message. She got dressed, humming, and popped the 'thank you for everything' card she'd written to Bruce into her bag. The feeling of lightness that was washing over her did not vanish. She ran down the stairs, looking out of the windows onto the blue sky; another beautiful day, when would this gorgeous weather end? Because it had to end, sometime.

As she flung open the door, patting her bag to make sure she had her keys, Kate screamed with surprise. There, on the doorstep, grinning manically at her, just like she did in those dreams, in her nightmares, was Charly.

CHAPTER THIRTY-SEVEN

Kate stared at her. As if she were in a museum, staring at a curiosity piece.

'Hello, Kate,' said Charly.

Almost calmly Kate noted Charly's hair was thinner; perhaps that was the pregnancy, though, it sometimes made your hair fall out. She knew that, one of those random facts she'd picked up somewhere. It fell, lankly, about her shoulders, it was a bit too long.

'What are you doing here?' Kate said, steadying herself against the door. Everything felt as if it were in slow motion. She looked down, dreading seeing Charly's pregnancy in evidence, the child she was carrying, hers and Sean's baby. Charly had a neat, nice bump. She was wearing a stripey top, a pretty long gold chain, flat shoes, skinny jeans, a little jacket. The uniform of a thousand girls who cram into TopShop on Saturdays, only on someone heavily pregnant it looked different.

'Did you get my letters?' said Charly. She'd forgotten her voice, that curiously husky, yet high-pitched, slightly mockney voice. 'I wasn't sure.'

'Yes,' said Kate, nodding politely. 'Yes, I did get them. Lovely, they were.'

'I didn't mean the stuff I –' Charly began, but Kate interrupted her.

'Look, Charly, I'm late, and I have to –'

When she looked back on this encounter, she found it hilarious that she might have just walked away because otherwise she'd have been ten minutes late for Lisa. Though she should have done – who was Charly to keep Lisa waiting?

'I need to talk to you,' said Charly simply.

'OK,' said Kate, crossing her arms. 'Fire away.'

Charlie was waiting for her to expand on this; when she didn't, she said, visibly discomfited, 'Well – I want to say sorry.'

Kate watched her, breathing slowly. She just didn't know how to react: why wasn't she feeling more emotional? Why wasn't she trying to kick Charly, why didn't she spit on her, or run away, calling her vile names? Wasn't that what she deserved? She was vulnerable now, so much more vulnerable than she'd been when they'd been friends. And she just couldn't do it.

'How did you know I was back?' Kate said suddenly.

'That doesn't matter.' Charly waved her hand, impatiently, and Kate saw a flash of the old Charly – imperious, careless of others, concerned only with herself, not this watered-down, colourless version in front of her now. 'Can I – can I come up? I just want to talk to you for a moment.'

Kate stared at her, anger finally hitting her. 'Are you serious? You want to come up – up to the flat? This flat?'

'Yes,' said Charly. She looked obstinate. 'Only for a bit.'

'No way!' said Kate, almost laughing. 'This is a joke.' She walked down the steps, shaking her head. 'I'm going, Charly, bye.' She started walking down the road, as fast as possible.

'Sean's having an affair,' Charly said loudly, after her.

It was eerily quiet on the street, and the words echoed. Kate stopped, and turned around.

'What?' she said.

'He's having an affair.' Charly came down the steps, slowly; Kate noticed how she shuffled, her movements were painful. 'With someone at work; I don't know her, I know who she is, though.'

There were lines around Charly's mouth that hadn't been there before, sharp little lines that made her lips look like a rosette when she spoke. From smoking, Kate knew; from sucking on endless cigarettes, pursing her mouth; she looked again at Charly, and she couldn't even remember why they'd been so close, but she felt a pang of sympathy for her, for this girl in this situation. This girl. Because Charly was this girl, the one who'd taught her how to do tequila slammers, taught her how to chat someone up in a bar, made her grow her hair and ditch the glasses, sat through countless shopping expeditions, patiently saying Yes or No to everything Kate tried on. Who'd argued with their landlord when they needed a new sofa, insisted on sending back a bottle that was corked, who'd stayed in on Friday nights with her, watching 'Friends' and 'Frasier'. She had made her laugh, made her confident, made her feel like a person in her own right in the world. She had shaped her life, been a shot in the arm, been the spark on a fuse.

Kate had forgotten all of that.

She'd had to.

And now –

She faced her. 'What do you want me to do about it? Sympathize? I know how you feel.'

'Yes, you must,' said Charly, quietly. 'Look –' she grabbed Kate by the arm. 'Let's just go there and talk, can we?' She gestured to the pub down the road. 'That's why I've been writing to you. When I knew you were coming back –

look –' she licked her lips; her eyes were misty with unshed tears. Kate was transfixed. 'I have to make my peace with you, before this baby comes. I sort of think it'll make everything alright.' She swayed a little on her feet.

'You OK?'

'I need to sit down,' she said, impatiently, with a flash of the old Charly. 'Fuck it. Just one coffee or something. Sean's picking me up in an hour.' Kate's eyes flew wide open. 'It's OK, he's just going to wait around the corner, you can be gone by then. God I hate being pregnant.' Kate was silent. 'I do. I wish I was . . .'

Don't say it, Kate thought, please don't say it.

'I wish this had never happened. I wish I'd never met him.'

Kate wanted to walk away; she was repulsed by her, by what she was saying, by the fact that Steve was dead because of her and Sean. But she couldn't just leave her there. Walk away and not finish this.

'OK,' said Kate. 'I'll need to call my stepmother. Just one coffee, then.'

The pub was twenty yards away; anonymous, brown, neutral, serving burgers and tapas and coffee for young professionals, not old men. It was slightly soulless; Kate had never been in there before, and she was glad of that, suddenly. She turned to Charly.

'I've only got fifteen minutes. OK?'

'Fine,' said Charly.

They walked into the pub, silently, and sat down.

'It was the attraction mixed with the dislike, you know,' said Charly, sipping her coffee, rubbing her stomach, her feet up on the other side of the banquette. 'I was so used to getting anyone, I know it sounds crap, but I was. He was different, you know. He really hated me.'

392

Kate nodded. She had made up her mind to say as little as possible. She was just going to ride out the numbness, the absence before the pain starts, when the plaster is pulled off.

'He hated me and then, one day when you were out of the flat – you'd gone to a meeting about your new job – he came over; you were late. I said he was being rude, he just ignored me and sat there waiting for you.' She curled a section of hair around her finger; god, thought Kate, she doesn't even know I'm here. 'Then we had a big argument and suddenly – well . . .' She trailed off. 'We were doing it. In the sitting room.' She looked away at the memory.

'God, I hated him,' she said. 'Really despised him, for making out he was such a wannabe family man, all lovey-dovey with you, crawling up to your dad and all your friends, and then fucking me when you were out, or Jem was out, or . . . wherever we could.'

Kate didn't feel angry. She wondered, almost curiously, why, how she could hear Charly talking like this and not feel anger. She just felt sad for her younger self, for how stupid she must have looked.

'The day of your dad's wedding, you know? He was vile to me all day, and then he was furious because he couldn't have me. And what did he do? He proposed to you instead.' She shook her head, marvelling at herself, at him. 'His face the next day, when you came out of your room and told me . . .' Kate swallowed. 'Like it was a game, you know? Part of it all. We were so into each other, the things we would do to each other, it was like a drug. It scared me. I think we both wanted to get caught, by the end. I certainly did.' She stirred her coffee, and looked directly up at Kate. 'I was glad when you walked in on us.' Her eyes opened. 'Fuck me. Isn't that awful. Really glad. I thought, OK, well at least it's out in the open now. I was glad.'

393

Kate spoke then, her voice craggy with misuse. 'But – Charly, what happened after – how can you look at it like that?'

'Well, of course that was awful,' said Charly. 'Of course it was.' She looked uncomfortable. 'Absolutely devastating.'

This is unreal, Kate thought. She's a robot. She's not a real person at all. She said, tentatively,

'Did you feel like maybe . . . with Steve's death and everything . . . that you had to stay together, after all of that? Prove it was real to everyone?'

'Of course not,' said Charly, sharply. 'We were always going to end up together, me and Sean. We just wouldn't have wanted that to happen. That's all.'

Kate didn't know what to say. Because she just didn't believe her.

They made polite conversation after that. Where was she having the baby? The Whittington? How nice. What was she going to do, would she go back to work? Three days a week at *Woman's World*, she'd see how it went. They were living near Bethnal Green, how was the flat? Good, great, but Sean had to do some more work to the nursery, he was being crap about it, and he still hadn't finished the plastering in the hall, it was really annoying . . . It was funny, how hilariously perfectionist Sean had been about getting their flat right. He'd obviously tired of DIY. Kate told her about seeing Sue Jordan, but she was unwilling to discuss much more, there was something about Charly that deeply unsettled her now. Something desperate, as if a part of her had died and the rest of her knew it but couldn't work out quite what was wrong. She seemed to have shrunk, too – Kate realized that her heels were always so high it gave the impression of natural height. And when they were living together – well, she'd just been a different girl, brash, totally sure of herself. Kate had been pretty much the opposite.

Strange, then, that she had everything Kate had wanted, and Kate didn't want it any more. She wanted to be on her own, to walk to the tube station and go and see her dad, her sister and her stepmother. She was so, so glad she didn't have to get in a car and go home with Sean. Strange, she barely thought of him. She hadn't allowed herself to, so angry she had been with him, but so strange that he should have slipped out of her life so easily. When leaving Zoe, Francesca, her father, Dani and Lisa, not to mention Mac – leaving all those people behind in London caused her pain, constant, low-level pain.

I thought I was dead inside, she told herself, as Charly described in some detail the new girl at *Woman's World*. I thought I'd shut all of that out . . . and that's the reason it made me so unhappy. Because I love them, I love them all. And shutting out Charly and Sean – it was easy, because they're . . . not the people I thought they were.

The realization hurt her, but it comforted her too, because that's what real life is all about. It hurts to love people, because you expose yourself to them, and they can hurt you, so much. Here, in front of her, was the girl in whom Kate had had complete, idolizing faith, and she had broken her heart. She, and Sean.

Charly's phone vibrated on the table, jangling loudly into Kate's thoughts. She started.

'Oh . . .' said Charly, picking it up. 'He's waiting round the corner.'

'In case I go mad at the sight of him and throw something at him?' Kate said, trying not to sound like that was exactly what she wanted to do. Charly smiled vaguely, like she wasn't really taking it in.

'Yeah . . .' she put the phone in her bag, without replying. 'Listen. We have to talk about it. Did you know?'

Kate didn't understand what she meant. She shook her head, curiously.

'Did you know . . . when he was cheating on you?'

'Oh.' Kate felt awkward. Just because it made her feel stupid. 'Er . . . you know what? I don't see why I should tell you.' She smoothed her fingers across the wooden varnish of the table, leaving a fingerprint smear.

Charly's head drooped a little; she stroked her bump, for the first time. 'OK. OK, yes. Of course. I can see why.'

Glad you can see why, you fucking *mentalist*, Kate wanted to shout, but she didn't; she couldn't. Instead, unbending a little, she said, 'Look. If you want to know . . . No. I had no idea. I trusted him, which was my mistake.' She paused. 'You'll never trust him, will you?'

'What do you mean?' said Charly, blinking violently, as if someone was shining a bright light in her face.

'I mean, you can't trust him, because when you met him he was my boyfriend, my fiance, and you were sleeping with him behind my back for – what, two years? When I was your best friend, you were everything to me, he was everything to me.' She smiled, to hide her grimacing, as tears filled her eyes. She blinked them back, as if she were surprised at their appearance. 'And you wonder why you can't trust him after that? How could he betray me like that? How could you? So the two of you are locked together in this kind of weird old web of . . .' she was running out of words, now, 'web of *something*, I don't know, and you deserve each other, you *deserve each other, Charly*, and I can't feel sorry for you. Because he did it before and it ruined my life and it did, actually, kill someone. Or had you forgotten that bit?'

Charly flicked her hand, languidly, even though she was still blinking, strangely. 'Of course I hadn't. But this is different, this time. It's some girl at his company, I know who she is –'

'Shut up,' said Kate, standing up. 'Look, just shut up, I'm going.' She grabbed her purse and keys, and turned around, and there he was, Sean was in the doorway, twice as large and American-football-player-handsome as she remembered, and she just stared at him. Her hands flung out involuntarily and her purse slid to the floor. She bent down to pick it up, and he said,

'Kate. Hi. So . . .'

His eyes raked over her; Kate raised her hand to her pony-tail, swinging behind her head, and clenched her hair in her hand. She gritted her teeth.

'Hi,' she said, and she raised herself up as tall as she could, thanking the Lord and all His seraphim for her height, the gangliness at school that she used to hate and now loved, and the fact that she had put her high-heeled boots on that morning. 'I was just going actually. Bye, Sean.'

And with that, she turned on her heel, something she had always wanted to do, and strode out, feet clacking loudly on the wooden floor, and for the first time in her life she felt like Charly must have felt, walking away from all those situations, totally in control, and it meant nothing to her, nothing at all. She carried on walking, oblivious to the sound of Charly calling her name.

CHAPTER THIRTY-EIGHT

Kate caught the tube to Holborn that evening. She was meeting Francesca in Exmouth Market, and she was early. She walked through Bloomsbury, hands sunk deep into the pockets of her jacket, and she looked around her as she went. The streets were busy, as always in Bloomsbury. Students, tourists, old couples, people sitting outside the Brunswick Centre under heated lamps. She walked around the edge of Coram's Fields, through the sedate, quiet Mecklenburgh Square, and crossed Gray's Inn Road. She loved the fact that, in this part of town, it seemed as if every other house had a blue plaque on it, marking the presence of some worthy who had lived there. Often they were incredibly famous and you stopped and said, 'Huh! Thomas Hardy lived here? Wow!', surprised that one of the greatest novelists in the English language had chosen to live in an OK but not that nice Pooterish villa overlooking the train tracks leading into Paddington. Just as often, however, they were people of whom Kate had never heard, but she liked that too, liked knowing that at 21 Mecklenburgh Square lived both Sir Sayeed Ahmed Khan, a nineteenth-century Muslim reformer and scholar, *and* R.H. Tawney, British historian and writer (but not at the same time). Kate's own favourite, as a late convert to karaoke, was David Edward Hughes (1831–1900), who had lived at 4 Great Portland Street. He had invented the microphone, and she would always be grateful to him for that.

It had been a long day, and a longer night, but now she knew her time in London was coming to an end, she owed it to herself to keep on going. Things kept falling into place, these last couple of days. Not necessarily the way she would have liked, but perhaps the way she might have predicted. Mac had said she kept her heart locked away. Well, if that's what it took to get her through that strange afternoon with Charly, then fine. She thought about Charly, about how she couldn't see past her nose, how she hadn't altered at all, apart from the baby growing inside her. Kate saw now, the way she never had before, that they were totally different in that respect. Charly had seen it, she hadn't. For Kate had changed outwardly, because she dressed better and had nicer hair and bought flowers for her flat and could talk to people at parties, more than when she was twenty-two. But that didn't mean she was different. She was the same, just more grown-up. Same Kate. That, after all, was what was happening to them all, like it or not.

But she knew the next stage, where she felt all of this more deeply, would hurt her when it happened. She hated leaving London with her relationship with Zoe still so formal. She didn't know how to cross the final divide that separated them. Perhaps that had been what forced her to drive Mac away. And she couldn't think about that, yet.

So she didn't, she walked instead, and she watched people go by, and when she got to Exmouth Market she was early, so she walked a little further, up to Sadler's Wells, where *Rigoletto* was on that night. The audience was just starting to mill into the theatre. She stood for a while watching them all, the excitement of the pre-theatre crowd, the pretty fairy-lights that hung in the trees outside. From her position on the opposite side of the road she could see people's expressions, could tell if they were tired or excited or apprehensive, or if they'd had a bad day; the deliciousness of observing others unconscious of it. She felt totally alone, a unit of one, and it felt good to be on the other side of the road, watching from the sidelines.

When she reached the Ambassador on Exmouth Market, a few doors down from Moro, she decided to go in, even though she was still a little early. It was a sparse, frugal place, with white walls, floorboards, and a collection of junk-shop furniture, but the menu was all fresh, local produce, and the wine list was great, and Francesca loved it there. But as Kate opened the door, someone else behind her held it open for her.

She turned around.

'Zoe?' Kate said in surprise. 'What are you doing here?' She kissed her, in the doorway, and they got tangled up in each other's arms, until Zoe pushed her friend firmly over the threshold.

'I'm here to meet you,' said Zoe. 'Francesca's not coming.'

'What? Why?' Kate said.

Zoe's expression was set. 'She rang me. We had a talk. And I'm here instead.'

'Right,' said Kate, and she felt guilty.

'Francesca told me about Mac,' said Zoe, propelling Kate firmly to a rickety table and chair. She pushed her down on the shoulder, and sat down opposite her.

'Oh,' said Kate, waving to signal for a waiter. 'What – what did she tell you?'

'That you slept with him, and he ran out this morning.'

Kate felt nervous, Zoe looked furious. 'It wasn't like that. Look, Zoe, I didn't tell you because –'

The waiter appeared. 'Goodeveningladies.' He rubbed his hands together, impishly. 'Well, well. Can I –'

'Can you give us a moment,' said Zoe firmly. 'Just a little while. OK?' She nodded at him. 'Oh. Tell you what. Bring us a bottle of white wine in about five minutes.' She turned back to Kate. 'Where was I. You, Mac . . . um you . . . Yes.' She crossed her arms. 'You didn't tell me. And you didn't tell me that you came back last summer, and you didn't see any of us.'

'Well – I did, you see I –' Kate faltered.

'Oh, I know about that too,' Zoe said. 'You and Mac. Oh, Kate.'

'Zoe –'

Zoe looked around the room, which was pretty empty, and she said in a clear voice, 'She told me about Charly and Sean, too. You saw them today. And about the letters.'

Kate's heart was racing. Zoe was being scary. She hadn't seen her like this since   since when.

'For god's sake Kate, why didn't you tell me any of this?' said Zoe. She looked down, and smoothed the gnarled varnish of the table with her fingers.

'About what,' said Kate, helplessly.

'Exactly,' said Zoe, shaking her black hair. 'Exactly. About everything, Katy, why don't you tell me anything any more?'

'You've got enough on your plate,' Kate said, taking her hand. 'I can't bother you with all of that, I don't want to after everything that's happened –'

'That's *exactly* it.' Zoe banged her fist on the table. 'You're my best friend!' she said. 'We tell each other stuff, OK?' She looked down. 'Well. We *should* tell each other stuff, anyway,' she said, quietly.

'I can't ring you up and tell you about Charly and Sean, not after what I did to you,' Kate exclaimed. Her throat felt thick. 'I can't say, Oh by the way, I saw my ex-fiancé today,

401

and his pregnant girlfriend, who's been writing me weird letters, and neither of them seems to care, and it's all my fault . . .'

Her voice grew louder. The waiter watched them, openly curious, and Kate dropped her voice instead.

'I said to Mac this morning . . .' she said. 'I told him too . . . I don't think you understand what happened that day.'

'I do,' said Zoe. 'Kate –'

Kate held out her hand. 'He saved my life. He pushed me out of the way. I was the one running away. I always run away. And Steve was the one who saved me.' She swallowed. *And it should have been the other way round.*'

'No,' said Zoe.

'It's true.' Kate balled her fingers into her eye sockets. 'It was my fault. I should have died. It was my fault.'

'It wasn't your fault,' Zoe cried, interrupting her. 'Kate, it wasn't your fault! There's something I've never told you.'

There was silence.

The two friends looked at each other.

'It's not your fault,' Zoe said, covering Kate's hands with hers. She spoke softly, leaning in. 'Look at me.'

Kate kept her hands pressed to her eyes. She found it impossible to look at her friend.

'Oh god.' Zoe said something under her breath. 'I should have done this a long time ago. Kate, oh Kate.' She pulled her fingers away from her face, staring at Kate, her eyes ablaze. 'It's not your fault! Look, you are *not* to blame for this, and I can tell you that till I'm blue in the face but you have to believe it yourself.'

'You told me to go,' Kate said softly.

'Of course I did!' Zoe cried. 'It was the funeral, I'd lost my husband six days before and I was five months' pregnant! Of course I told you to go, I was crazy! Because you kept coming round and trying to help, and no one could help me, *no one*, and you just didn't get it, and I – I –' she shook her head. 'I'm *not* going to cry. I wanted you out of my hair for a bit. You know? And you were so busy hating yourself I think you thought you were unclean, or something, and better out of it and so you left without even saying goodbye! And I hated you for leaving!' She banged her fist on the table again. 'You were my best friend, I just lost my husband, and you ran out on me when I was about to have another baby!' Her voice cracked. 'I needed you, Kate, more than anyone else then I needed you. And you left.'

'You never said,' Kate tried to justify herself, but even to her ears it was weak.

'Neither did you,' said Zoe. 'Neither did you. And it's all so ridiculous, Katy. Because if it's anyone's fault it's mine, you know. I'm the one who should hate myself.'

'What?' said Kate, almost laughing. 'You? Are you joking?'

'No, no,' said Zoe, and she leant in again. Her eyes bored into Kate's, a clear, unflinching gaze. 'This is what I mean.' She swallowed. 'It was never your fault. It was mine, if anything. You know. You see . . . I knew about Charly and Sean.'

It was quiet in the restaurant; Kate stared at Zoe, unblinking, till she could feel her eyeballs dry. She didn't know what to say. 'You knew – you knew they were having an affair? You –' She trailed off.

'Yes.' Zoe nodded, her eyes never leaving Kate's. 'I knew. Steve told me. We had huge rows about it. I wanted to tell you. But I didn't know what to do. I thought perhaps it would burn itself out. I couldn't destroy your world. You were so happy, you'd been such a shy, unconfident thing, and now there you were –' she smiled at the memory. 'You were suddenly all grown-up, all happy and glossy and successful, and you had this wonderful life, and you *adored* him. You just adored him.' Kate opened her mouth to speak, but Zoe held up her hand, to stop her. 'I couldn't destroy all that for you. So I kept trying to get Steve to work on her, get her to see what she was doing.' She grimaced, biting her lip, and her voice was unsteady. 'Or to talk to Sean, make him understand how stupid he was being. I thought it might work out . . . you'd never need to know. So I never told you.

'We knew what Sean was doing. We knew it was going on. Steve's the one who took the decision to drive round there that day. I had lunch with you to distract you. And you know, I can't help thinking – if Steve or I had told you, months earlier, none of this would have happened. You see? You're the last person who should be blaming yourself. He . . .'

And then Zoe's face crumpled, and she slid her tiny hands over her face, fingers pressed furiously to her skin, and she cried.

'I was so wrong,' she sobbed. 'It was all my fault. I was so wrong, and I'll live with that for the rest of my life. Without Steve, for the rest of my life. Oh god. I'm so sorry, Kate.'

Kate pushed her chair out and stood up, she crouched on the ground next to her sobbing friend, and threw her arms around her, and they stayed like that, not speaking, just holding each other, for a long time. Out on the street people carried on walking by, and Kate watched them, unseeing, as she hugged Zoe tightly, the view blurred with tears. She couldn't speak.

'She said we needed to talk,' Zoe sobbed, dashing tears away from her cheeks.

Kate cleared her throat. 'Who said that?'

'Francesca. She said we were both being stupid . . . We have been, haven't we?'

Kate nodded. She brushed a tear away from Zoe's cheek

with her thumb, and sat back down in her chair. 'We have,' she said. 'Not any more, but we have.'

This was their reckoning, the build-up of everything that had needed to be said for two years and more, and strangely there was little else to say. Zoe sat back and breathed out heavily.

'Pff!' she said, smiling rather soggily. She blew her nose loudly on the paper napkin. The waiter looked up at the noise; these crazy girls who burst in to a nice quiet gastropub, started yelling at each other and then sobbing hysterically, were they going to order something, at last, finally, at last? He clutched his notebook hopefully.

Kate wiped her cheeks with her fingers. They were both silent, staring at each other, as the waiter approached carrying a bottle of white wine and some glasses.

'Are you ready for the wine?' he said, a little nervously.

'Ooh, yes,' said Zoe. 'Yes please.' As he retreated, she said, 'Well. Well well.' But they both ignored the wine.

Despite herself, Kate opened her mouth, to ask Zoe something, and then she shut it again, and smiled at her friend. It was all retread, and it would always be there for discussion. She was just relieved that it was all out in the open; what a day, what a day, she thought.

'Well,' she said, 'gosh.'

'Indeed,' said Zoe.

Kate grabbed her best friend's wrist. 'Look. We're OK now, aren't we?'

'Of course we are,' Zoe said, crossly. 'We were before, if you hadn't been such an ostrich about it. We've always been OK, I love you Katy, it'll take a lot more than Charly Willis and Sean Lambert to shake us. Urgh,' she said, her mouth a wavy line of distaste. 'I can't believe it. I bet he cheats on her, too. You mark my words.'

Something stopped Kate from telling Zoe this was true. She didn't know why, she just knew she didn't want to be involved with them any more, didn't want to poison Zoe's life with anything about them either. Best to walk as far away as possible from it all, that was it. As the waiter set some bread down on the table, she said instead,

'Who's got the children?'

'Mac,' Zoe replied briefly.

'Oh right.' Kate poured the wine. 'That's nice.'

'Very nice of him to come over twice in two days, but that's Mac for you,' said Zoe. She exhaled deeply again. 'Phew, I feel about ten years younger.'

Kate raised her glass. 'You look it.'

'Well, while I'm on the subject,' Zoe said untruthfully. 'You and Mac. Look, I know you two have some weird kind of sex thing going on –'

'It's not a weird sex thing,' Kate said hastily. 'And it's not –'

'Let me finish.' Zoe waved her arms at her, peremptorily. 'Whatever it is, it's weird, anyway, and don't think I didn't know something was going on by the way, he used to freeze whenever anyone mentioned your name –'

'Nice,' said Kate.

'I just wish you two could sort it out.' Zoe flapped her hands at Kate. 'I know it's silly, but it's true – I *know* he likes you, you know, and you quite clearly have a thing for him.'

Kate pulled at a piece of bread. 'We've been there,' she said firmly. 'Look, Mac and I have always had – we always have – well, we'll always be close, OK? But it's a timing thing. I just think it wasn't meant to be.'

'Why do you think that?' Zoe put her elbows on the table.

'It's timing,' Kate repeated eventually. 'We had a chance at it. I think there's too much water under the bridge for us to go back and start again.'

'I don't buy it,' said Zoe.

'It's true,' said Kate. Francesca thought it was true, too. And she was right, she knew. She was starting to see everything much more clearly. 'Look at my mum and dad. I actually think they're partly still in love with each other, or at least they think they are. But the timing's wrong now. They couldn't get back together, even if they were free to. They've got different lives now, they live thousands of miles apart . . .' She thought of her father's rage, his loathing of Venetia mixed with his open lust and admiration for her, which had peppered her teenage years. Her mother had left him, like Kate had left Mac – perhaps for the same reasons, or perhaps for others, Kate still didn't know.

'No, Kate,' said Zoe. 'It's the opposite. I've known you since you were five. You're not about to repeat the mistakes your parents made. OK? You're nothing like them.'

'Well, that's not true,' said Kate. 'They're my parents.'

'Yes, but genetics aren't everything. I think a lot of stuff skips a generation. Especially now I've got children. I see what they've got that neither of us had. And I'm telling you, you and Mac are not your mum and dad. Seriously.'

'He's always trying to fix things,' said Kate. 'I'm not ready. I want to sort it out for myself.'

'Fair enough,' said Zoe. 'But you can't blame him for trying, can you? Not if he's in love with you? And I've seen him with you. He is. In love with you.'

Kate looked away. 'Oh darling. He's not. He just wants to make everything alright. Sort everything out, wipe the slate clean. Honestly, after last night – well, this morning . . . it's over. Really.' She shook her head. 'I'm going back to New York, and that's that.'

Zoe looked disappointed. 'You really are?'

'Yes,' Kate said firmly. 'But properly this time. I'm getting a place of my own, moving out of Mum's. And I'll be back lots, if this column for *Venus* comes off. You're going to come out and visit, too. Hey!' She waggled her finger. 'You could come with Diggory! Leave the children with your mum for a few days!'

'Steady on there,' said Zoe, laughing. 'We've had two dates, Kate. We're not about to start hopping over to New York on mini-breaks. But I'll come! Yay!'

'Great,' said Kate. 'Even Dad's coming in a few months, when he's better, and he's bringing Lisa and Dani.' She thought of her mother, briefly. 'I'll tell Mum if you're in town. She'd love to see you. But I wouldn't dare tell her dad was staying with me.'

'You need to ask your mum what happened between those two,' said Zoe, reading her thoughts. 'I've never understood it, myself. Don't you want to know?'

'Sort of not,' said Kate, holding her wine glass to her cheek; she was hot.

'Why not?'

Kate tried to explain. 'I don't know. If the last couple of years has taught me anything, it's that . . . there are some things you're just not meant to understand.'

'I'll drink to that,' said Zoe. 'Cheers.'

They clinked glasses and smiled. The waiter reappeared with the menus.

'Will you ladies be staying for food?'

'You bet,' said Zoe. 'And – can you bring us two glasses of champagne, please?' Kate started forward. 'We should raise a glass, not to everything that's happened, but to us,' Zoe said as the waiter retreated. 'Seriously. Never forget I love you, Kate. We all love you, me and Flora and Harry.'

In under a minute, two glasses of champagne appeared on the table, and Zoe raised hers. 'To Steve, to you, and to me,' she said, sticking her chin out. 'Steve, we'll always drink to you, darling.' She held her glass high in the air, and looked up to the ceiling, then back at Kate. 'To us, all of us.'

'To all of us,' Kate agreed, and they drank.

CHAPTER THIRTY-NINE

'So, what time's your flight tomorrow?' Her father pushed his hair back out of his face.

'It's at nine-thirty.' Kate held up her hand, to shield her eyes from the sun. She shook her feet out, stretching on the wide steps. 'I've got loads to do and I haven't done it, still. Got to see Mr Allan now he's back again, got to pack of course, and I've got to make sure everything's tidied away properly, you know.'

'Of course,' said her father, who was utterly uninterested in domestic matters, unless they specifically pertained to him. 'Yep. You know, Kate —'

Kate leaned forward. 'Dani, perhaps don't go any further. OK? It's a busy road.' She turned back to her father. 'I meant to say, that reminds me. I've got to drop the spare keys off at the estate agent's too. They're showing people round next week.'

Her dad hadn't mentioned finding a new tenant for her flat since she'd first seen him and she wondered if he'd just forgotten or was being tactful. She wasn't sure. He turned to her now, smiling.

'I'm glad,' he said. 'Good, so you are going to rent it out again?'

'Yes,' Kate said. She put her hands out behind her, and looked up at the clear blue sky. 'I can't have it empty, I need the money, you need the money. You've been so kind, Dad, thanks a lot. I don't think I ever thanked you properly, for bailing me out of the flat after Sean went off.'

Her father looked embarrassed, and a little flustered. 'Don't be ridiculous,' he said. 'Not at all, who wouldn't?'

'I know you want a tenant in there again,' said Kate. 'They say it'll be a couple of weeks, honestly –'

Daniel Miller put his hand over his eldest daughter's, as Dani sat at their feet, a few steps below. 'Kate,' he said, softly, 'you misunderstand. I wanted you out of that flat because I couldn't see how you could ever be happy there . . . after what happened. Not because I wanted the rent. Please.' He sat back, shaking his head. Just as Kate felt herself breaking into a grin, he rather spoilt the effect somewhat by adding, '*Please*. That my daughter should go without a home? Never!'

'*Never*,' Dani bellowed loudly at their feet. 'Oh *never*!'

Kate laughed, but her father scooped his youngest daughter up into his arms. 'You monkey,' he said, tickling her.

'*Monkey*,' said Dani, dramatically. 'Oh, monkey, monkey, monkey.'

'You used to do that, too,' said Daniel, tickling Dani, who was wriggling and screaming.

'Do what?' Kate said.

Dani screamed loudly with pleasure and Daniel released her, a flash of irritation on his face. 'Shh Dani,' he said. 'You used to impersonate me when you were a little girl.'

'Like that?' Kate was amazed.

Her father scratched his chin. 'Oh yes. You'd appear in the kitchen after we'd put you to bed, and repeat these dreadfully pompous things I'd said during the day but

411

obviously forgotten.' He chuckled. 'It used to make me so crazy, but your mother said you'd grow out of it.'

'That's so funny, I don't remember that at all.'

'Well, she was right,' Daniel said. 'You grew out of it.'

High up in the sky, a tiny plane, almost invisible, cut a white trail through the blue expanse above her. Kate shook her head.

'Thanks, Dad,' she said.

They were silent for a moment, as Dani watched them.

Daniel sighed. 'Isn't this lovely.'

They were sitting on the steps at the front of the Albert Hall, which was eerily quiet for a Thursday afternoon; Kate had met Daniel and Dani for coffee, and they'd gone to Patisserie Valerie on the Brompton Road, and Dani had demanded a huge strawberry-filled pastry, of which she only managed three bites. Lisa was picking up Daniel's prescription and running some errands in her vast SUV; Daniel therefore was in charge of his daughters, for a couple of hours. Afterwards, they'd walked to the Albert Hall, nostalgia for the old days overcoming Daniel and Kate, and there they sat, looking down towards the Royal College of Music, Daniel's alma mater, quietly chatting and waiting for Lisa to pick them up, as Dani ran around the balustraded terrace, singing softly to herself. She had told Kate she was a princess, or Maria in *The Sound of Music*, she hadn't decided yet.

'So what will you do back in New York?' her father asked.

'I'm not sure,' said Kate. 'Sue's going to give me some freelance work, and I'll start getting some contacts out . . .' she paused. 'My column's in next week's edition of *Venus*, so let's see.'

'How can Girl about Town write a column about New York?' her father asked, wryly.

'Maybe it'd be good,' Kate said. 'Girl about New York

Town instead.' Daniel said nothing. 'Maybe interviews, I could be a stringer for them, do their stuff out of New York, contact other people who I knew from *Venus*, see what's available . . . We'll just have to see.'

In truth, it had been so long since she was in the magazine world she wasn't sure if anyone would remember her. Kate Miller, one of the youngest features editors in town at twenty-seven, the girl who disappeared off the face of the earth: writing the column for Sue had been enormous luck, she knew it, and she was still almost speechless with gratitude to her although, as Sue put it, 'You deserve a bit of good luck, Kate. So get over it.'

Now she was older, wiser, calmer, saner, and she didn't know what the future held for her in New York – she just knew she was going back there, even though –

'And you don't want to stay here?' her father said, sitting up straight and fiddling with his cuffs, interrupting Kate's thoughts as Dani, who had overheard this, danced over to them.

'Hey, Kate!' she said. 'Will you stay?'

'No,' said Kate, scooping her little sister into her arms. 'But I'll come back lots to see you, and I'll take you to the zoo next time to see the giraffes.' Dani was going through a big obsession with giraffes. Kate blew raspberries onto her sister's neck, and she screamed. Daniel looked weary suddenly, and a little bored.

'I'm going to get a place of my own there, too,' Kate said. 'Dad, you should come over when you're better.'

'Well, I'll have to, with the Manilow album,' her father said, with bravado. He looked around, at the Albert Hall, glowing red behind him. 'And they want me to do another series of *Maestro!* for Christmas, if I'm up to it.'

'I'm not sure about that,' said Kate, frowning, but Daniel ignored her.

'. . . So yes, it'll be pretty hectic . . . Anyway,' he said casually. 'You're moving out of your mother's then?'

'Well, it's about time,' Kate said, releasing Dani, who clambered onto the step below, in between her legs. 'Poor Mum and Oscar, I should think they're longing to have some time to themselves, now they've had a chance to get used to me not being there.'

And then her father said, impulsively,

'Give her a message, will you?'

The tone of his voice reminded Kate of utter desperation, of the way she had to struggle not to mention Mac's name to people, to ask how he was, just trying to glean some minute, significant detail about him. She stared at Daniel, in surprise.

'Mum? Yes – of course, Dad, what is it –?'

Her father pursed his lips and gazed ahead, into the distance, his aquiline profile set. He looked like a Roman bust in the V&A, Kate thought. He was silent for so long she thought he wasn't going to say anything, and she was about to chip in instead, to tell him about how Mr Allan had seen him play here all those years ago, when suddenly he said,

'Tell her I still think about Sheffield.'

Kate was disappointed. She'd been expecting something more romantic. *You are the key to my violin case and my heart.* Well, something like that. 'You still think about Sheffield?' She repeated it, uncertainly.

'Yes.'

'Well – but Dad. Will she know what that means?'

Daniel clutched his hand to his heart, briefly. 'Yes,' he said simply, and then was silent.

Dani wrapped her hands round Kate's ankles, as Kate sat next to her father, thinking how strange it was that he was now so human to her, suddenly. And wondering, wondering what it meant.

414

'Yes, it's much better now,' Lisa said, biting her lip as she turned the monster car around a corner. 'He sleeps through the night, and he's in such a good mood now, thank *god*.'

'I hear you,' said Kate. 'He seemed to be today, that's for sure.'

'Is it this way?' Lisa asked suddenly.

'Yes,' said Kate. 'Thanks, Lisa, it's really kind of you to drop me off.'

'Not at all, not at all.' Lisa sounded cross. Kate turned to watch her, but her expression was unreadable behind her huge mirrored wraparound shades. Kate cleared her throat.

'Lisa,' she began. 'I just wanted to say – thanks, you know.'

'You've said thanks,' said Lisa.

'No, I mean – for this past month or whatever. It's been –' Kate searched for words, and realized she had them already. 'It's been lovely. Just wonderful. I had no idea how –' *well this would work out*, she was going to say, then realized you couldn't really say that about a father's near-death experience. 'I've loved seeing Dad, and getting closer to Dani and – and you, Lisa.' She sounded about ten years old; she stopped. 'Thanks, anyway,' she finished. 'I don't think it can have been easy, sometimes.'

'You're right,' said Lisa, neutrally.

'Oh . . .' said Kate, slightly taken aback.

'You were a right bitch to me at first, Kate, you know that don't you?'

'No I wasn't!' said Kate, defensively. 'I wasn't!' She knew she didn't sound convincing.

'You were,' said Lisa. 'It's a fact, let's not dwell. It wasn't so much you, anyway. That boyfriend of yours – yuck. He treated me like I was a Thai prostitute, practically, your dad's young mistress.'

'Really?' said Kate, fascinated. 'God, I'm sorry. I was different then, things were different then – I – he –'

'You weren't that different,' said Lisa, as they turned onto the Edgware Road. 'You were the same, Kate. Same cross, gangly, geeky little girl who was the apple of her daddy's eye. You still are –' she held out a hand, as Kate opened her mouth '– but then you were living the life you thought you ought to be living. Now – well, I'm sure you wouldn't ask for any of what's happened. But it's been good for you.'

'Er . . .' said Kate. 'Thanks?'

'You should thank me,' said Lisa, bluntly. 'Your father's a nightmare to live with, you know he is.' She grinned. 'Imagine if you had to cope with all of that on your own. I can quite see what your mother had to put up with. You should love me, you know.'

'I do love you,' Kate said, realizing it was true.

'Right, fine,' said Lisa, sticking out her bottom lip. Sun bounced off her sunglasses. 'Right,' she said again, as they climbed up Maida Vale, towards the flat.

Kate looked out of the window, at the streets she knew so well; this time tomorrow she'd be back in New York, sitting in the dining room with her mother and Oscar. How strange to think it, and yet –

'He still talks about her, you know,' said Lisa. Her voice was deathly quiet, almost under her breath.

'Who?'

'Your father. Still talks about your mother. In his sleep, a lot of the time. Just says her name, I don't know why.'

'Really?' said Kate, and she could believe it.

'Yeah,' said Lisa, turning into Elgin Avenue. 'Yeah. She's quite a ghost, your mother. He'll always love her, you know.' She pulled over.

'I don't think so,' said Kate.

'I know so,' Lisa said, turning off the engine. She patted Kate's hand. 'You look so like her, these days. It's really strange.'

Then she leant over, and kissed her on the cheek.

'Don't run away again, like she did,' she said. 'Come back soon. Not just for your dad. For Dani and me, too. OK?'

'OK,' said Kate, trying to see Lisa's eyes through the glasses. She hugged her. 'Thank you – for everything.'

'Whatever,' said Lisa, waving her hand dismissively. 'Safe flight, you. Call us, OK? And don't fucking leave it so long this time.'

It was six o'clock; her last night in the flat, in London, for who knows how long. Kate let herself in, wearily, and looked down in surprise. There on the floor, slid under the door, was a handwritten note; her blood ran cold, fear spiralling in her chest. She looked again. It was attached to a magazine.

This is the kind of post I like getting; hope you do too. Your first piece for Venus, enclosed. Congratulations, Kate. I always knew you were a star.
*   Sue Jordan*

CHAPTER FORTY

It was Saturday, and the day dawned, cloudy and rainy, the sort of weather you only get in the UK, where one can't imagine there was ever such a thing as a blue sky, or a sun shining on those sad daffodils, flattened by the wind of the previous night. It suited Kate's mood. She drank tea in the kitchen, looking around her home in the damp grey light. Her bags were packed, she was ready to go, there was nothing more to be done – other than see Mr Allan, who was going on the Heathrow Express with her.

There was a sad, back-to-school feeling to the day, like the previous few weeks of spring and sunshine had never really existed, but Kate knew they had. She knew she was different, that her time back in her home town had changed her, for the better. She was stronger, she was back to her old self – no, not her old self, perhaps, but on the way to being her own person, for the first time since she was a young girl, probably.

As she was putting her own copy of *Venus* back in her dresser, and wondering when she should go up to Mr Allan, the doorbell rang.

'It's Geraldine Garley,' a voice came over loudly on the

418

intercom. 'Hi there. From Prince's, the estate agents? I just want to measure the flat, my colleague didn't do it yesterday. Can I come up?'

'Of course,' said Kate, pressing the buzzer.

Geraldine was short, stocky and very determined to impress. She was also clearly furious that she was having to do this.

'It's a busy time of year for us, Kate,' she said, pointing the electronic measuring gun at the opposite wall and zapping it viciously. 'And I don't see why I should have to pick up Nigel's pieces, just because Nigel is a total and utter w- Oh!' she said, coming to and remembering where she was. 'Seventeen, six. Great. Nice place,' she said, looking round.

'Thanks,' said Kate. She perched on the edge of the sofa, watching her. 'Do you want a cup of tea or anything?'

'Tea? No thanks, Kate. I'll just – fifteen. OK, and nine inches. Well you know what they say about nine inches, eh!' She bellowed, loudly.

'I do indeed,' said Kate, trying not to wink, like someone out of a seaside postcard.

'So why you moving?' Geraldine asked. She got out a clipboard. 'Jesus! He hasn't even filled out the – men. That's men for you! Bloody useless! Fucking Nigel! Well, now I've gone and done it Kate, I've sworn in front of you and we're absolutely not supposed to. Please accept my apologies.'

'Don't worry about it,' Kate called from the bedroom. 'It's fine, honestly.'

'So where you off to?' Geraldine said, following her in.

'I'm going back to New York,' said Kate. 'I live there. I was just over here for a bit, so I'm renting the flat out again after I've gone.'

Geraldine was only half-listening. 'That's great, Kate. That's great. You like New York, do you?'

Kate loved the way people asked questions like this in

London. It was basically a polite way of saying, 'Are you stupid? Why do you live there?'

'Love it, yeah,' she said. 'It's great, you ever been?'

'Couple of times.' Geraldine finished scribbling down something and looked up. 'Tell you what, though. If you're talking about cities, I prefer Paris.'

'Really?' Kate said. She was surprised, she didn't know why. She had Geraldine pegged as more of a Las Vegas kind of chick. 'Do you?'

'Yeah. Paris is lovely. Really beautiful. Dog shit and stuff, and it stinks of fags, but it's great. You can walk anywhere. It's small too. I liked that. Me and my boyfriend went there just before Christmas last year.' Her face lit up. 'Walking along the river. All those pretty little streets and stuff. Lovely. You want to think about going there. It's so romantic.'

'That's nice,' said Kate.

'Yep, it is,' Geraldine said, hugging herself. She snapped out of her reverie. 'Well, it will be again, if I make my bloody bonus. I'm the one who paid for it.'

'Well, fingers crossed,' Kate said. She added, jokingly, 'If you get shot of this flat first, perhaps you can go to Paris again.'

'That's what I'm thinking, and if Nigel thinks he's getting his useless little hands on it – oh my god, I'll kill him, Kate!' Geraldine chuckled. 'I'll fucking kill him. Oh, now. Now look. I've done it again. My god. My apologies.'

'It's really OK,' said Kate, seeing she looked quite alarmed.

Geraldine hit herself gently on the head with her clipboard. 'Best be off before I get myself into more trouble,' she said. She looked over at Kate's bags. 'Nice to meet you, anyway. You going soon?'

A voice behind her in the open door made her jump, suddenly.

'She's going in five minutes, and I've come to collect her.'

'Mr Allan!' Kate said, turning round to greet her neighbour. She kissed him on the cheek. 'Oh, you're really here. I really have to go. Oh dear. Thanks again, Geraldine.'

'Thank you, for choosing Prince's,' said Geraldine, almost bowing, and she shut the door behind her.

'Who on earth was that young lady?' said Mr Allan, coming into the sitting room and looking around him in bemusement.

'Estate agent,' said Kate, putting the remote controls on top of the TV. 'OK.'

'I could hear her voice from the flat upstairs. Well,' he continued, 'this is a sad day, isn't it?'

'Oh,' said Kate. 'Don't, Mr Allan. I'll cry, honestly.' She held her hand out to him. 'I don't want to go. I'm feeling homesick already.'

'Cry? Rubbish,' said Mr Allan. 'You are a strange girl, Kate. Here you are, back off to New York, which you were constantly telling me was the best city you'd ever laid eyes on, and all of a sudden you don't want to be there any more? Honestly.' He picked up a case. 'Make up your mind.'

'I'll take that one, it's –' Kate was going to say heavy. She corrected herself. 'It's lighter.'

'Rubbish,' Mr Allan said again. 'Now, before we go, here we are. Let me give you something.' He rummaged around in the capacious pockets of his overcoat. 'I have a present for you. Where did I put it. Here.'

He produced a paper bag with something wrapped inside it, and a plastic case. Kate unwrapped the bag.

'It's chorizo!' she said. 'Er. Thanks?'

'Fresh from the lush plains of Mallorca.' Mr Allan smacked his lips. 'Now,' he said. 'You can't take that into the States with you. There'll be six foot seven immigration officials all over you if you try to enter the country with that on your person. So, I thought I'd look after it for you.'

'You're going to look after a Spanish sausage for me,' Kate said.

'There's another present,' Mr Allan said, ignoring this. 'Now, where – ah, in the case. There we go.'

'"*Chappell Quartet: Songs for Lovers*"' Kate read out. 'This is you?' she asked.

'Me and the band, yes,' said Mr Allan. 'We cut that disc in 1960, you know. On my tenth wedding anniversary. To the day.' He nodded. 'Yes. Thought it was the last word, and then three years later that kind of music was absolutely dead. We became what we are,' he said, lovingly holding the CD and gazing at the playlist. 'A band of old fogies. Even back then, when we were relatively young. Haha.'

Kate's eyes flicked over the songs. '"That's All",' she read out. 'Well, of course that one. "There's a Small Hotel", "I Get Along Without You Very Well". "I Remember You" – that's Oscar's favourite. Oh, Mr Allan. What a beautiful album cover too. I love it.' She paused. 'Thank you. Thank you so much.' Her finger rested on the last song. '"It Never Entered My Mind" – I don't know that one.'

'Rodgers and Hart,' Mr Allan said, filling the gap. 'Saddest song in the world. So beautiful. Listen to it.' He sang a few lines, quietly. His voice was croaky, a little shaky, but true.

She took the CD and put it in her bag, so he wouldn't see her eyes filling with tears for him. There was silence.

'What will you do?' she asked him, breaking the tension. She wanted to know.

'Me? Oh, you know. I'm not sure.'

'Will you stay here?' said Kate.

'Well, again, I'm not sure.' Mr Allan blinked, looking around the room as if searching for something, and she realized with fear that he was older than she liked to admit. 'Sheila wants me to live with her, and you know, that's fine, I get on with her, but I'm pretty happy here, you know? I

422

lived with Eileen here for over forty years. Of course it'll be strange that she's not there any more. Getting into my hair.' He smiled. 'But I have my friends, I'm going to do some gigs, I think, for old times' sake. I've got to clear out the flat a little bit, not too much though. And you know – I've got my memories, and as the song goes, I'll have my love to keep me warm.'

'But what about if you –' Kate began, and then stopped.

'I'm old enough to be able to look after myself,' he said, firmly. 'I don't need anyone.'

Kate wanted him to understand. 'Yes but take it from me, Mr Allan. No man is an island. You need to rely on people, people who care about you.'

'Well, I can, I can,' he said rather snappishly. 'All except you, of course.'

Kate stepped back, as if he'd slapped her.

'I'm sorry, my dear,' he said gently. 'I don't mean it like that, of course. I just mean that, you know what?' He took off his glasses and fixed her with a steely, but kind, stare.

'What?' said Kate, returning his gaze.

'I'll miss you. That's all. I will bloody miss you, Kate. You coming back into my life just when I needed you most – a bit like an angel, the vicar said. You are an angel.'

'Me?' Kate was astonished. 'Are you sure he meant me?'

'I mean you,' Mr Allan said, seriously. 'You arrived as they were taking Eileen's body away. If that's not someone looking out for me in my darkest hour, I don't know what is. I thank God for it.'

'I really don't think –' Kate began, and then she stopped.

Mr Allan walked into the centre of the room. 'You can say I'm a silly old fool, who doesn't know what he's talking about, his wife's died and he's got a God complex, but there are things we don't understand, and there are things that are awful which happen for a reason, far beyond our ken.

423

And I believe someone sent you to me to look out for me in the days after Eileen – went.' He picked up the heavier suitcase. 'You gave me strength. Strength to carry on. Now, you think about that, dear Kate, next time you're telling yourself everything's your fault and no one loves you.'

Mr Allan wheeled the suitcase to the front door.

'We're going now,' he said. 'We'll be late otherwise. I don't want you walking round this flat saying goodbye to everything. I want you to walk out of here, with your head held high, and we'll go to the airport in style. God bless you, Kate.'

Terminal Three at Heathrow was like Armageddon. Plastic sheeting everywhere, walls open to the elements, the low sound of drilling, bags lying around on trolleys, in a worryingly relaxed way – whose bags were they, and why were they just casually being abandoned? – and queues and queues of people, some of whom didn't even seem to be sure for what purpose they were queuing. When Mr Allan stopped one old lady and asked her if this was the queue for the check-in to JFK, she said, faintly,

'I don't know. I've been here for nearly an hour and nothing's moved. I've lost the will to live.'

The screen on the board said the flight was scheduled to depart on time, at two p.m. but, at nearly one p.m., Kate still hadn't checked in. As she and Mr Allan waited, shivering in the breeze from the open wall nearby, Kate said,

'Shall I tell them I'm –'

'I have already, if you're going to New York,' said a man in front of her firmly, as if he took pleasure in grimly disabusing her of the notion that her case was special – again, a very British trait, she thought. He added irritably, 'I told them my flight was at two about an hour ago, and they said it'd be moving in a minute.'

'Ooh, the liars,' said Kate, trying to sound lighthearted, but feeling increasingly stressed. She wanted to leave, she'd made up her mind to leave, she had to leave. Please, she said in her head, don't let there be some hitch. I'm not mentally equipped for a hitch. I'm mentally equipped to go to New York, don't fuck with me, Lord.

'Honestly,' she said, turning back to Mr Allan, for the third time, after they'd been waiting for half an hour. 'You should go. I'll be fine, just go.'

'No, no, no!' said Mr Allan, rocking on his heels, his eyes shining. He liked a bit of drama. 'I'll wait to see you through security. Come now, my dear. What else will I have waiting for me at home?'

'I just –' Kate stamped her feet to keep warm, impatiently. 'This isn't a very good goodbye, that's all. Dribs and drabs. And I don't want you to get cold.'

'That's very kind of you,' he said 'But I'm not a child. I'm fine.'

Fifteen minutes later, just as Kate was starting to accept that, very possibly, she might miss the flight – for what if she and the man in front were the only ones not to have checked in yet and they simply didn't hold the plane? – salvation arrived, a woman with a clipboard and an understanding manner, and Kate and her companions were ushered into the until now empty Upper Class section, to be checked in. Mr Allan looked around him, anxiously.

'You OK?' Kate said. 'Nearly there.'

'Yes, yes,' said Mr Allan. 'About time.'

'Wow,' said Kate, hauling her bags onto the conveyor belt. 'At last,' she said, trying not to sound chippy to the woman checking her in. 'Is it a full flight?'

'Yes,' said the lady behind the desk, her mouth pursed in disapproval. 'It's a full flight, madam, and I'm afraid you're very late to be checking in.'

'But the –!' Kate began, trying not to yell something unforgiveable.

'Stay calm,' Mr Allan whispered in her ear. 'Close your eyes and count to ten. God bless you, Kate.'

Since there were only two possible responses, going mad and shouting at her, or remaining totally silent and counting to ten, and since she wanted to get on the flight and didn't want to risk violence, Kate bit her lip, closed her eyes, and counted to ten.

And when she opened her eyes, the woman was staring at her, strangely, and when Kate turned around, Mr Allan had gone.

'Where did he go?' she said.

'Who?'

Kate waved vaguely at her side. 'The man who was with me. The old – the elderly gentleman. Where did he go?'

The woman shrugged. 'I don't know. Sorry. Didn't see him.'

'Yes, but he can't have just disappeared,' Kate said, trying to stay calm. 'He didn't just vanish into thin air. Didn't you see him at all?'

'It's very busy here this afternoon, in case you hadn't noticed,' the woman said, with a real edge to her voice. 'Was he checking in for the same flight as you? Because if so, he's very late as well and needs to come to the desk. Otherwise, madam, I think you'd better go through.'

Kate looked wildly around her. 'But – he was just with me! I can't just leave him.'

'Excuse me,' came a voice behind her, and she wheeled round.

'If you're not going to move out of the way,' said a hard-faced lady, with a bag clamped under her arm, and an embarrassed-looking husband next to her, 'then we'll miss our flight and I will actually be entitled to sue you for compensation.'

426

'Oh my god,' Kate said. 'Are you serious?' She said this with such force the woman stepped back, clearly wondering if she was dealing with a psychopath. 'My friend – Mr Allan – he's gone missing, he was here a second ago and now he's gone off, and this lady won't help me at all, and just because that holds you up for *ten seconds*, you want to sue me?'

'Look, just please excuse me,' said the woman, her face a rictus of unpleasant smugness. 'Some of us have to catch that flight.'

'Stupid cow,' Kate muttered. God, she hated this country, and she would be glad to leave. She picked up her passport, casting a disgruntled look at the check-in lady, and slunk away, her heart racing.

Where was he? Mr Allan wouldn't have just left without telling her – would he? She didn't know what to do – she couldn't leave without saying goodbye to him, but she didn't want to miss her flight: what would he say if she did? Or perhaps he wanted her to stay so much he'd done this on purpose?

Kate shook her head; he wasn't that bad. Or was he?

She hung around outside the Gents for a few minutes, anxiously checking her watch and feeling a bit weird, but there was no sign of him, and five minutes later found her hurrying through departures, worry seeping through her, draining her. She was late, she was worryingly late, and she didn't know what to do. The hall was thronged with knots of people, occasionally bunching up to make way for a stewardess clacking her way through the crowd, pulling a trolley behind her, or airport staff in dazzling fluorescents. She was right about airports, she thought. They were stressful and – in this case, totally, horrifically chaotic – and they were the least romantic places in the world.

It was one-twenty-five. She'd have to go through, she couldn't wait. She hoiked her bag over her shoulder, took a deep breath, and got into the queue for security.

She was fishing through her things, making sure she wasn't carrying her little bottle of perfume, when a voice said,

'Thank god. There you are.'

She looked up, in confusion 'Mr −' But the words died on her lips.

Mac was standing in front of her, behind the security ropes, breathing raggedly, sweating slightly, shaking. Kate jumped, and her hand flew to her mouth.

'You −' she said, but the words died on her lips. She stared at him, both hands on her cheeks.

'Where the hell have you been?' he said, almost angrily. 'I've been looking for you for twenty minutes!'

'What on earth − you −' Kate began again. 'Where's Mr Allan?' she said, incoherently. 'Did you see him?'

'Yes, of course I did,' said Mac. 'I saw you in the queue. I was waving at him to come away, and when he did, I explained everything, and got him to step aside, so I could surprise you −' he grimaced, ruefully. 'He said to give you his love, and he told me to get on with it, but by the time we'd finished talking, you'd disappeared. It's so bloody crowded in here,' he said wrathfully. 'I couldn't see you, and I nearly missed you, and Kate −' he took her hands away from her cheeks, and clasped them in his own. 'I wanted to see you.'

'Step aside please miss,' said someone behind her. Kate looked at her watch, and stepped aside. People started filing past her, towards the security checks.

'I know you've only got about a minute,' he said, reading her thoughts. 'I know − this is all wrong, it's too rushed, it shouldn't have been like this, I've been waiting for you for god knows how long, but I found out from Zoe when your flight was going and I knew I had to come down because

Kate – I love you. I'm sorry about the other night.'

'It doesn't matter,' Kate said. 'I'm sorry – you were entitled to it. After the way I treated you, it's the least I could
do –' She moved forward a little, and someone pushed past
her, knocking her even closer to him.

'Kate,' he said. 'It's not a game with me, never has been.
I didn't just want a one-night stand with you. I'm glad I left
last week. I don't want to freak you out again.'

'You were right, though,' Kate said. She was breathless.
'I shut you out. I had to, Mac. *That's why I don't* deserve
you.'

Mac's face was without expression; but his eyes held hers.
'It was stupid of me. Pathetic. I suppose a part of me wanted
to hurt you, you know.'

'I hurt you,' Kate said. 'You –'

'It doesn't matter now,' he said.

'It does,' Kate said, quickly, too quickly, she wanted to
talk to him as much as possible in the time they had left.
'It does. You and me – we've never been you and me, have
we? We've never really been on a date – unless you count
two weeks together non-stop as a date.' She smiled, and he
smiled. 'That's what I worry about, I suppose,' she said.

'I know what you mean,' Mac said. 'That it'll never get
any better than this for us, that we're not destined to be a
couple, just ships who pass in the night?'

'Yes,' she said, relieved he understood.

'But I don't think that's true,' he said. He cleared his
throat. 'All along, I've been trying to make things right, and
I was wrong. *You* were right. I just wanted to tell you that.
I came here to tell you . . .' He smiled carefully at her. 'We've
done everything the wrong way round. I was wondering if
you wanted to go on a date sometime.'

'A date?' she said, shaking her head at him. The crowd
behind her swelled, pushed her forwards.

'Yes,' he said, his fingers holding hers. 'How about we go for a coffee one day. Or perhaps a pizza. There's a lovely place I keep hearing about in Battersea. Or go to the cinema, see a play.'

The noise around them seemed to get louder; someone appeared behind them, trundling a case full of bottled water for the newsagents behind.

'Hey,' a voice said next to her. 'Hey – you were in front of me, weren't you? Aren't you coming?' The man who'd been behind her in the queue appeared at her side. 'You know they're about to close the gate?'

He moved on, brusquely, shaking his head, leaving Kate gazing at Mac. She gripped his hands tighter.

'This is – impossible,' she said.

'I know. I know, darling. I'm going to say this quickly. OK?'

'OK,' Kate said, smiling. He leaned forward and kissed her.

'I've got an idea,' he said. 'You see, you know and I know what's been wrong with you and me. We've done it the wrong way round. We fell in love with each other the first night, and then we went backwards and backwards, till we were like passing strangers to each other. Don't you agree?'

She couldn't say anything; she just nodded. He slid his arms around her waist. 'I don't know, but perhaps we should start from the beginning again. I'm staying in London, I'm looking for a flat. Stay here too. Come on a first date with me. Let's do it the right way round.'

'This is the final boarding call for flight BS080 to New York. Would all passengers for flight BS080 please go to Gate 27. Gate 27 for flight BS080 to New York.'

'How can you be that sure?' she cried. 'What if fate's trying to tell us something, that we'll never be together? That we've tried, you know we've tried, and it'll never work?'

He paused, and swallowed. 'I don't believe you,' he said, fiercely. He clutched her wrists.

'You do,' she said. '*That's* why you left. You do. And I think I do too. I think it's too late.'

'Kate,' Mac's face was white, his nostrils flared. 'Don't do this.'

'I love you,' she said, tears streaming down her face. 'I don't want to go.'

'But you are going, aren't you,' he said, and he stepped back from the tape barrier that separated them, and turned around to leave. 'And you know what? I don't think I should have come here today. Perhaps you're right, it's too late.'

She watched him, as did her fellow passengers, who were gaping at them curiously. Her hands dropped to her sides; but he turned back and caught one, her left hand, and pressing her palm to his face, kissed the ball of her thumb, gently.

'Perhaps you're right.'

And then he was gone.

Kate swallowed, and turned back to the queue. One-thirty. She looked at one of the guards, showed him her ticket. His eyes opened wide.

'You'd better go through now,' he said, and pushed her along, down towards the fast-track queue, and she disappeared through the archway, towards departures, away from Mac, one step further away from London.

CHAPTER FORTY-ONE

There was a sign on the way into Manhattan from JFK airport; Kate had noticed it before, it had been there for a while. It said: WELCOME HOME!! from your friends at American Airlines

Kate had slept the sleep of the emotionally exhausted all the way to New York, and had woken up with panda-smudged mascara eyes and what she told herself was a clear head. Before passport control she ducked into a Ladies, washed her face, put on some tinted moisturizer and lipgloss, put her lenses back in. She wasn't going to walk into JFK looking like she'd just come back from a night out with Pete Doherty.

She was fine, she told herself. She was back. She wanted to talk to someone, she wanted to say 'Hello, I'm Kate, and do you know what's happened to me? Do you know where I've been?' Because suddenly, she wanted to talk. She wanted to explain how she felt, she wanted to clap her taxi driver on the back (gently, so as not to throw off his suspect steering even more) and say,

'How do you find your job? Because I've just left my job, and I'm really pleased about it. Except I have to find another one PDQ – pretty damn quick, that is!' She wanted to give him an interesting fact as the beautiful, gun metal skyline of Manhattan loomed up in front of them, she wanted to say,

'Have you tried the whispering wall in Grand Central Station? You can hear what someone's saying from thirty yards away? It's amazing.'

or

'When they built the Brooklyn Bridge, that's the first instance of the bends, because the men who were doing it were diving so deep and coming up so quickly, isn't that interesting?'

or

'My best friend Zoe had a third date with this bloke called Diggory yesterday, and I've had to come back here and I don't know how it went! It's her first date since her husband died, three years ago, isn't that incredible of her?'

or

'I'm going to see my mum again and I feel like it's for the first time in years, which is weird because I only saw her a month ago, it is weird. But I feel like I understand her a bit more, Mr Taxi Driver, are you listening, do you care?'

and, finally

'Can you take me back to the airport please? I think I've made a terrible mistake.'

But she didn't say any of that, of course she didn't.

And then she rode into Manhattan, and the sky was blue and the cabs were yellow and the trees were green, and it was its old, glorious self, and they rode through the park, cutting across town to the Upper West Side, and Kate hung out of the window, not wanting to talk now, like a dog on a family trip, her eyes eagerly scanning everything in the city she loved so much. The supermommies, jogging with their pushchairs, the businesswomen in pencil skirts and thick, massive trainers, striding fiercely back from the office, the families heading home after school, the harried businessmen crouched on the edge, the lines of traffic honking and yelling, the noise, the cheerful, aggressive, straightforward noise and bustle. She had missed it so much, longed to be here so much, it was the balm to her soul that she always needed and never more so than today.

Strange, then, that it felt so odd to be back. When she'd moved here, she had been wildly, ecstatically in love with the place, with everything about New York, with the Upper West Side, with the fact she could walk to the world's best deli in five minutes, the fact that she could shop at Anthropologie, her favourite clothes store, the fact that she could eat burritos from Chipotle whenever she wanted, that the pavements were wide, and clean, and people were friendly and polite, that things worked, and when someone came to mend something they actually mended it, instead of scratching their arse and saying, 'I could do it . . . but it'll cost you, I'm afraid . . . Best to just buy a new one.' But as the cab climbed through the streets up towards Riverside Drive, Kate looked out of the window and smiled, it felt different, she didn't know why. She had just loved it here, loved everything about it, but it wasn't where she belonged. The thought shot through her, disloyally, before she could dismiss it.

They were crossing Amsterdam Avenue. Was it the same for Venetia, she wondered? Did her mother truly belong here, or would she always long to be back in London? Kate honestly didn't know the answer. They were drawing up outside the apartment now, and the driver popped the back of the cab, and hopped out to fetch her suitcases. She paid him and he immediately zoomed off, leaving Kate standing

434

on the curb, staring up at the apartment building, wondering for the second time in a few weeks, though in a different location, why she was here.

The first time Kate had come to visit her mother in New York was the first time she'd ever been to the city, and she remembered it still with a clarity undimmed by her subsequent residency there. She was fifteen. It was summer, the school holidays, and everyone kept saying it was far too hot, humid, unbearable, even. But Kate had loved it. Maurice the doorman had just started to work at the building, a month after Venetia and Oscar had moved in there, and he called Kate 'newbie', and said she should call him the same. Her mother took her to Bloomingdales, and bought her clothes – primary coloured, Benetton-esque sweatshirts that didn't suit her at all, but which she adored and kept in her drawers for years afterwards. They had ice-cream floats, and they rented boats in the park. The city was curiously empty, everyone else was away, New York was theirs; Oscar taught her all the lyrics to 'Manhattan' on that very same subject. They saw *A Chorus Line*, which Kate and Oscar adored, but Venetia thought was awful. And she was with her mother, most importantly, for three whole weeks. Time to tell her lots of things, about her bedroom at home, about school, about Zoe, about how they were putting on *Macbeth* the following term, about how she had kissed Gavin Roberts *twice* now, once at the party Jude had in her parents' garden while they were away, then the following week outside the cinema on the Finchley Road where they'd gone to see *Dave*. Did this mean Gavin was her boyfriend? And perhaps they would talk about Dad, about how sad he was without her, about how shocked all their friends were that she'd gone, left Kate behind and gone.

They didn't talk about that, of course. They talked about

everything else but that, and nothing else, because Venetia didn't say and something about her mother meant that Kate knew not to ask her. They shopped, and chatted, and walked, and lazed on the sofa in the stifling apartment, and sang as Oscar played the piano, and after three weeks Kate went home again, hugely grown-up on the airplane by herself, and when she got back the next morning to the rickety old house in Kentish Town, she found her father asleep on the sofa, sunlight strobing through the gap in the rug that served as a makeshift curtain in the sitting room. Daniel wanted to know all about her mother, but Kate didn't tell lots. She wanted to keep the memory safe, holy almost. And thus was her post-divorce relationship with her mother formed, and it had continued to be the same ever since.

She realized, now, as she stood at the bottom of the steps up to the apartment building, that they were neither of them perfect parents, though they both suffered from her idolizing them. They'd tried, they hadn't deliberately wanted to hurt her, they were just a bit hopeless, no better and no worse than any parent, and that didn't mean she loved them any the less. But a lot of water had gone under the bridge since she was last here, though it wasn't that long ago. Where had she heard that phrase? She shivered, and climbed the stairs.

As she banged through the front doors, Maurice leapt up from behind his desk and said, with a huge smile on his face,

'Kate! Why didn't your mother let me know today was the day you were coming back? Well, well. Give me those bags, young lady. I'll call the elevator for you. It's great to see you! You have a good trip? How's your father?'

'He's much better, thanks,' said Kate, squeezing Maurice's arm. 'How are you?'

'I'm good, I'm good,' said Maurice, putting her bags by

the lift. 'It's been pretty crazy round here, you know, though. Mrs O'Reilly's been sick, but she's getting better. Your mother got a new coat for summer, Kate, it's beautiful. You know the board's finally talking about getting quotes in to have the floors redone? Yes, I know.' He nodded solemnly at the importance of this as Kate stared at him. 'Plus,' he finished, 'don't get me started on the new coffee machine they put in at Rick's!'

The lift doors clanged open. 'Thanks for the info,' said Kate.

'No problem,' said Maurice. 'It's great to have a young face around the building again!'

'Thanks, Maurice. I'll see you later,' said Kate, getting inside. 'It's great to be back.'

'OH MY GOODNESS!' a voice cried loudly as she emerged from the lift. 'MY BABY GIRL IS BACK!!'

A pastel rush of cashmere and strawberry blonde hair pulled her out of the lift and wrapped itself around her; Venetia had been prowling the corridors, alerted by Maurice to her daughter's arrival. She stepped back, holding her daughter's face between her hands, and her large, blue eyes sparkled with pleasure.

'Hi Mum,' said Kate, submitting gratefully to her mother's embrace, as Venetia hugged her again. 'How are you? Oh, it's good to see you.' She sank into her mother's embrace, remembering how she smelt – a mixture of Chanel perfume, shampoo and some kind of hand cream. Venetia's cashmere sleeve was soft, her cheek was soft, her hair was soft – her cheekbones were sharp, though, and she crushed Kate's face against her own angular bones, hugging her tightly as she did.

Are you a goody, or a baddy. Are you a goody, or a baddy.

'I have missed you SO MUCH!' Venetia cried, stroking

Kate's hair so heavily that it hurt. 'I have missed you! Haven't I, Oscar, haven't I?'

'Yes,' said Oscar, who had appeared at the doorway and was watching his wife and stepdaughter in fond amusement. 'Hello Kate, darling.' He kissed her warmly on the cheek, and stepped back, wiping his hands surreptitiously on the teatowel that was over his shirtsleeved shoulder.

'Look at you,' Venetia said then, staring at her curiously. 'You look different. Did you get a haircut?'

'No,' said Kate, clutching a strand of her hair. 'I didn't.'

'You look – did you lose weight?'

'I wish.'

'You look a little angular around the face,' Venetia said, looking her over with an appraising stare. 'I think you did lose some weight, darling. Which is strange, seeing as how no one in England eats vegetables.'

'Yes, that's totally true,' said Kate, taking off her jacket. 'I haven't eaten a single vegetable all the time I was there. They don't grow them there, you know.'

Venetia ignored this. 'Oscar made lunch,' she said, smiling her great big smile. She slung Kate's bag over her shoulder. 'He made burritos.'

Kate was ravenous. 'Lovely,' she said.

'Let's eat,' said Oscar. 'We'll eat and then we can talk. We want to know how you are. How was it, being back? Not too horrible I hope? We were worried about you.'

'Bless you,' said Kate, as they came into the apartment. It looked so small, somehow, like a dolls' house. She stared round, as if she hadn't been there for years and years.

'We need to talk about tomorrow,' said Venetia. She held her daughter's hand.

'Tomorrow?' Kate said blankly.

'The party!' said Venetia. 'Come on Kate, you haven't

forgotten! A MONTH back there and you've forgotten every-thing, haven't you?'

Why do you think I came back, Kate wanted to say crossly. For this stupid party. Why else do you think I'm here? She looked at her mother curiously, trying to imagine her back in England, trying to think of her as an actual mother, or sitting in a room with her father. She couldn't see it. Venetia pushed her hair out of her eyes with her arm, and smiled at her daughter, her beautiful, clear skin almost luminous in the sunlit hallway.

'It's OK,' she said then, in her low, luscious voice, and Kate remembered then, how she could do that, how she sort of always understood. They stared at each other for a moment.

She's the same height as me, Kate thought. She even looks a bit like me, I'd never noticed before.

'Come on,' said Oscar fondly, watching them both. 'If the flatbread wilts now I'm blaming both of you.'

'Hah,' said Venetia, going into the dining-room, clutching Kate's hand. 'So, tell me everything. Did you see Zoe? And is Francesca still as hard as nails? How's your father? Is that child still a nightmare?'

'Zoe had a date last week, Francesca's really well actually, and Dani is surprisingly adorable,' said Kate, sitting down. 'Sorry Mum, but she is.'

'Why should you be sorry?' Venetia sounded disingen-uous. She took a sip of water and hummed.

'No idea,' said Kate, pouring her mother some wine. 'Dad's much better, too. He's back in the studio next month, doing an album for Christmas.'

'Oh, really?' said Oscar. 'Already? What is it?'

'It's – it's an album of Barry Manilow covers,' said Kate. 'Come on. You know, he's a really good songwriter, actu-ally,' she added defensively, as Oscar and Venetia howled derisively with laughter. 'Oscar, you like him!'

439

Oscar held up both hands in defence. 'I'm sure he is "a good songwriter",' said Venetia, smiling at her daughter, her face alight with some strange emotion Kate could not place. 'It's just – come on, darling. When we were married he was with Deustche Gramophon, doing Paganini's most obscure Concerti. It's – er – it's just different, that's all.'

Kate suddenly remembered her father's message. *I still think about Sheffield*. She watched her mother, searching for some clue. Parents, she thought, smiling back at her. They are strange, and she thought of Lisa yesterday, and Oscar, and how they were practically parents to her – better, in lots of ways. Mum and Dad are mad, she realized, though she knew it of course, and she merely nodded at Venetia and carried on, deliberately changing the subject,

'But yeah, they're all really well.'

'Good,' called out Oscar, placatingly, as Venetia sipped some water thoughtfully. 'So, what else is new?'

'Oh. Well, I saw Charly and Sean,' Kate said casually.

'You *what*?' said her mother, holding her water-glass in mid-air, as if she'd been frozen. 'You – what? How come? What?'

'I saw Charly. And Sean.' Kate was smiling.

'*What?* Oh, my . . . grrr,' said Venetia, tossing her hair and making a strange, animal sound in her throat. 'My goodness, if I saw that little – that little *madam*, what wouldn't I do to her . . . What happened?'

Kate sketched in, very briefly, the story of the letters and the meeting itself. When she'd finished, Kate looked at her mother curiously. She was almost red with anger.

'My god, the nerve,' Venetia muttered. 'So what happened?'

Kate swallowed the rest of her drink. She was silent for a while. 'You know what? I got over it, that's what happened.

It was the most satisfying cup of coffee I've had in a long time.'

Her mother looked unconvinced but Oscar, who missed nothing, emerged from the kitchen at that moment carrying the burritos and the little bowls of guacamole, sour cream, cheese and chilli, and he said, simply, 'So, sounds like it worked out for the best.'

Now was not the time to say, 'I'm moving out, by the way.' Now was not the time to tell them about Sue's offer. She was home again, back in New York, she had decided to come back and she was going to make it work now, strange though it felt. 'Yeah,' said Kate, quelling the feeling she had inside 'I think it did.' Her fingers dug into her palm, as she remembered Mac's face, his lips on her palm, what he had said – she felt pain, sharp, shooting pain. She had made her decision, for better, for worse, and she was back.

CHAPTER FORTY-TWO

And gosh it was lovely being back, waking up in New York in the spring, almost the beginning of summer. The weather wasn't too hot, she didn't have to go back to Perry and Co, and so Kate realized the next morning that she was free to simply get on with her lovely life now in New York, starting with Oscar's much-anticipated birthday party that evening. She got up early, she rang Betty and left a message, wanting to fill her in on everything, unsure of how best to explain it all to her. The last time she'd seen Betty had been her last night in New York. She had nearly kissed that guy Andrew; how weird it was, how far away it seemed, like another life.

During the day Kate helped her mother; they went to the grocery store, they dropped by the caterers, to deliver the decoration for the top of cake that Venetia had chosen: a little plastic man playing the piano, naturally, with 'Happy Birthday' sticking out on top. In New York, even the cake decorations were better.

She picked up Oscar's present, the complete Beethoven piano sonatas which she'd had bound, with Oscar's initials stamped in gold on the front, from a store off Columbus Avenue, and she and Venetia had their hair blow-dried,

Venetia reading the *Times* and laughing gaily with the hairdresser; Kate flicking avidly through *People*, glad of a fix of US celebrity gossip that she'd missed since she'd been in London.

The salon was a few blocks away from the apartment building. Kate and her mother walked back together, arm in arm, towards Amsterdam Avenue. The streets were unusually quiet, but the blossom was out everywhere, frothing, frivolous. When she'd left, the leaves had barely been out; now the best of the spring was here, and she always thought this was when she loved New York most; Kate felt as if she were in a film. They walked under the white and green trees, like characters in a Madeleine story, in a Fred Astaire movie.

'I missed you, darling,' said Venetia. She looked from left to right, as they crossed the road. 'It's funny I always still do that, isn't it!' she said, patting the printed silk scarf she'd wrapped over her hair, to protect it from the Manhattan winds.

'What?' said Kate, watching her.

'Look left and right, as if I were in London, and all that.' Venetia took Kate's hand and pulled her across the wide road, almost running. 'I *did* miss you darling,' she said again, as they reached the other side.

'Oh mum, I'm sorry,' said Kate. 'I missed you too – I've been so lucky, having you let me stay here –' she clutched her mother's arm. 'Honestly – what would I have done if I couldn't have come to you, three years ago?'

'Don't be silly,' Venetia said. 'Gosh, though,' she said, in her artless, dramatic way. 'I sometimes think you would have been better off.'

'What do you mean?' Kate asked, bewildered.

Venetia released her arm from her daughter's clutches.

'Well,' she said, considering carefully. 'Are you your mother's daughter?'

'Well obviously I am,' Kate said.

'I mean, perhaps running away isn't the answer. It was for me, I don't think it was for you.'

Kate saw what she meant. They were on a street corner; she could hear someone playing the piano; she stopped, listening out for the music, straining to hear notes.

'What is it?' she asked.

'Don't know,' said Venetia briefly. 'I can't hear it.'

But Kate could hear it. It was 'Rhapsody in Blue'; how delicious, how clichéd, someone in their apartment on 77th and Broadway playing Gershwin, framed by the cherry blossom. It was almost too New York; that had been what she loved about the city; it was a cliché, a wonderland, all for her. She remembered something, then, as she watched her mother, who was fixing her scarf in place.

'Mum,' she said, and added, carefully. 'Dad asked me to tell you something.'

Venetia stopped.

'What?' she said. 'He – did he have a message for me?'

'Yes,' said Kate, wondering how she knew. Venetia's hand fluttered on her cheek, then her breastbone.

'Let's walk,' she said, softly. 'Tell me.'

She set off at a long, fast pace, which Kate matched; they were physically very similar, she realized, so she could have got her height from her mother, or, like Dani, from their father, or both. The music faded, the languorous, slicing phrases disappearing as they walked. She fell into stride with her mother, and they were silent for a few seconds, and Kate said,

'Well, he said to tell you he still thinks of Sheffield.'

It sounded so prosaic when she said it. 'Sheffield'. Like 'Terminal 3'.

'Sheffield,' said her mother. She was looking at the ground. 'Wow.'

'Yep,' said Kate, hating this, wishing they were back at the apartment. This was it, though.

'Are you sure?' said Venetia. 'Nothing else?'

'No,' said Kate, feeling guilty. 'Sorry.'

'Sheffield . . .' said Venetia. She glanced at her daughter, her expression unreadable. 'Thank you, Katy. Thanks.'

'But Mum – what does it mean?' Kate said, unable to quell her curiosity.

Venetia walked on a little further, past another apartment block, past a slew of pink blossom. Her mother sighed, and threw her head back a little.

'Kate – Kate,' she said. 'Can I ask you something?'

'Yes,' said Kate, nodding furiously.

'Do you know why I left your father?'

'Erm,' said Kate, not wanting to sound too eager. 'No, actually, Mum, I don't know why.'

'Well, I should have left it another year,' her mother said, almost conversationally. 'I should have waited till you were fifteen or so. You were too young and it was wrong of me. I will have to live with that for the rest of my life. You know?'

'Mum, I don't –'

Venetia was babbling, her voice quite without its usual girlish inflections. 'I pay for it every day, in one way or another; when I think about how I let you down it breaks my heart every day, but I just couldn't take it any more.' She took a deep breath. 'And god. I must say, your father saying that just goes to prove it.'

'What?' Kate said. 'About Sheffield? What, Mum? What does it mean?'

Venetia turned to face her, and Kate saw her mother as a woman, the woman she must have been.

445

'It's the reason I left your father,' she said, with a tiny laugh. 'And it was selfish of him to ask you to give me the message, wicked and selfish.'

'It wasn't like that –' Kate felt uncomfortable. 'We were talking about you and I always wondered . . .'

'There's no big secret,' Venetia said. 'You think there's some big secret, there isn't.' She wrinkled her freckled nose and exhaled loudly. 'God, Kate, I left him because he was a nightmare to live with. He made me miserable. I used to find any excuse to go to the shops, pop out for milk, and I'd cry all the way there, all the way back.' She began counting off on her fingers. 'He criticized me constantly, I never knew where he was. And if I asked him – pfff! Oh, he'd go mad. He belittled me in front of everyone. He slept with countless other women, he had these terrible rages, he never did the shopping –' listening to this, as it filtered through her head, Kate loved the fact that sleeping with countless other women was almost on a par with not doing the shopping '– and it got to the point where I couldn't take it any more.'

Her eyes were sparkling with tears, and Kate stroked her arm. 'Oh mum. I had no idea,' she said, trying to work out what to say. She knew her father had been a nightmare to live with, he still was, but she had been protected from it – by her mother, by him, because until she grew up and had a mind of her own, she was still his little girl.

'He's a monster, Kate,' Venetia was laughing, almost hysterically. 'And I can say that because I still love him, I'll always love him. I just can't live with him. We weren't good for each other. We made each other miserable. That's why I ran away.'

'That's all?' Kate said, and hurriedly corrected herself. 'I don't mean that's all – it's a lot, Mum, it's just I always thought there was some terrible secret . . .'

'On our thirteenth wedding anniversary he was playing with the Hallé in Sheffield. The Mendelssohn. I surprised him in the dressing room beforehand. He was with the first trombonist,' said Venetia. 'She was sitting on his lap.' She shook her head. 'God, it sounds like a French farce. So ridiculous.' Drawing herself up a little, she said with touching dignity, 'And I am not ridiculous. But she was just one of many, and god, she was so young! About twenty! I couldn't take it any more.'

'That was "I still think about Sheffield"?' Kate asked with incredulity. 'I thought it'd be some wonderful romantic story.'

'In Sheffield? In a dressing room with peeling wallpaper and a cheap little brass player with big tits?' said Venetia, bitterly. 'God no.' She put her arm around Kate. 'Is he cheating on Lisa?'

'I have no idea,' Kate said, feeling a stab of loyalty to Lisa, understanding even more so now that her life must sometimes be difficult. 'But you know, I don't think so,' she said. Venetia looked at her.

'You and me – we were both in the same boat, that's why when you turned up here, so strange, you wouldn't talk about Sean and Charly, or Steve, or Zoe, or anything – that's why I just let you stay, didn't put any pressure on you. I wanted you to feel you had a home here, that you didn't have to worry about anything.'

It was sunny on the wide street, but Kate felt a cold wind to her heart, suddenly, as she saw how prescient her mother had been. Venetia took her arm and they carried on walking.

'And when you came back last year after those mysterious two weeks away – I know you were away that long darling, Maurice told me, really, I'm not stupid – well, I didn't say anything, because I knew you just had to work it out for yourself.'

'Yes,' said Kate, nodding violently. 'I did. I think I have

now, Mum – but I think I've screwed it all up even more.'

'How so?' said her mother.

'Every how so,' said Kate. 'There was this man. I should have been with him from the start,' she turned her head towards the sun, blinking. 'He's the one I was with in London. Zoe's brother-in-law. Mac.'

Venetia nodded. 'I know Mac. I remember Mac. That good-looking doctor who spent all night of your engagement party pretending not to look at you. Nice man.'

Of course she knew, Kate thought. Venetia missed nothing. 'I left him, I wasn't ready . . . And now I think it's too late.'

'Why do you think he's the one for you?' Venetia asked almost conversationally. She waved an elegant hand at someone walking along the pavement, the other side. 'Hello, Karina!'

'Um –' Kate tried to sound articulate. 'You know Sean?'

'Yes.'

'Well he was wrong for me and I couldn't see it. Because everything was disguised with him. He looked good, but he was bad inside. He was tall and comforting, but actually he let me down.' Kate carried on talking, though her throat was tight, sore. 'I thought I needed someone to look after me, and actually, I was better off on my own.'

Venetia was nodding violently. 'Go on,' she said. She patted her daughter's arm, comfortingly. Kate could hear the birds singing, loudly now, in the trees.

'Mac – he's right for me, and he wanted to look after me too, but I didn't want that. I couldn't see it. It's exactly the opposite. Sounds mad I know.'

'It's not mad.' Her mother looked sad. 'I wish it had been the same with your father.'

They were opposite the apartment building now. She kissed Kate on the cheek.

'Let's go inside. My darling baby'll be wondering where we've got to.'

448

Venetia tripped up the stairs, almost skipping. 'Hello, hello,' she cried, as Maurice came out from behind the desk.

'I'll see you girls later,' he said. 'Mr Fienstein must be very excited.'

'He certainly is,' said Venetia.

Maurice said, 'He really is a very lucky man, Mrs Fienstein.'

'Oh, he knows it,' Venetia sang, looking up at Maurice from underneath her lashes as the lift doors sprung open. 'Baby, he knows it.'

Kate sighed. 'Come on, Mum,' she said, trying not to laugh. 'It's nearly party time.'

Back at the apartment, the Robertsons had rung to say they were definitely coming, but Joel Robertson was worried about what to wear, and Mrs Cohen was now coming solo, because Mr Cohen wasn't well, and Mrs Da Costa had popped by to offer to help. Oscar had a) drawn up a list of songs that he might, if asked, possibly consent to play at the (hopefully enthusiastic) gathering b) crossed it out and started again, several times.

'I don't know what to do for an encore,' he said, fretfully, as Venetia and Kate arrived back. 'What if they want something – you know, really jazzy.'

'Darling, give 'em the old razzle dazzle,' said Venetia, depositing the bags on the sofa and taking off her wrap. 'You'll be wonderful. Won't he, Kate?'

'Of course he will,' said Kate, loyally, extracting the coffee beans they'd bought from the bags and putting them in the little galley kitchen, as Venetia flung her arms around Oscar and kissed him.

'Oh Oscar darling,' she said, repeatedly kissing his cheek. 'Birthday boy tomorrow, party tonight, ooh la la! Look!'

Oscar grabbed her hands, and brought them in front of

him. Kate watched them, torn between slight embarrassment and real affection, and feeling something inside her, a
voice that wouldn't go away now.

'I have a present for you, Venetia darling,' he said,
solemnly. 'Kate, you too. Wait there.'

And he vanished down the long parquet-floored corridor
towards their bedroom. Kate stood next to her mother, rather
excited – what was it?

He reappeared a minute later, carrying two little bags.

'Tiffany?' said Venetia. 'Oh, Oscar, no . . .'

Kate looked at the pale-blue confection being held out to
her. 'Oscar. Wow,' she said, taking it and opening it up to
find a little box, wrapped in white ribbon. She opened it,
feeling almost nervous.

Nestling in the white silk padding was a chain and a
pendant. A platinum chain, with a heart-shaped pendant,
covered in diamonds, a tiny thing that bulged and glittered
in the light from the lamp.

'Oscar!' Kate cried. 'Oh my god. You shouldn't have!' She
looked up, to find her stepfather watching her, a curious
expression of sadness mixed with – what was it? Love? Kindness? Emotion? All those things were written on his face.
She hugged him.

'I love you Kate,' he said, his voice choking with emotion.
'Dear girl, thank you for coming back for the party.'

'Of course I would –'

He gripped her arm. 'I know what it cost you,' he said.
He shook his head, forbidding her from further speech. 'You
were right to come back, but I know what it cost you. I love
you –' he added, as Venetia, who had been having consid-
erable trouble with her box, managed to get it open to reveal
a diamond tennis bracelet, dotted with hearts, and the
screams of joy that greeted the unveiling of this present
could, as Mrs Cohen said to Mr Cohen, on the floor below,

be heard all the way in Hackensack, and what could they ever do about it? Sweet girl, Venetia, but boy, was she loud.

So from mid-afternoon onwards a stream of caterers, waiters and servers flowed in and out of the apartment, setting up the buffet, building ice-sculptures, arranging flowers and moving furniture, so that the vast living room was split into two, with the piano and room for a little dancing at one end, and chairs at the other end for people to sit and eat.

Kate's mother, though she loved to pretend to be a drama queen, was in fact intensely practical in many ways; it amused Kate, the co-dependency she and Oscar imposed on each other, each behaving to type around the other but actually more than capable of finding the salad cream and booking a doctor's appointment (Oscar) and booking a car and filing tax returns (Venetia).

So, actually, at seven o'clock Venetia and Oscar were ready for their guests, who were due to arrive from seven-thirty, the caterers had left but the waiters had remained, the sun was starting to set over the park, fiercely red, flooding the last light of the day into the big airy room, and only Kate was missing.

Because Kate was in her room, staring at her phone. One side of her hair was pinned back, the other side hung like a curtain across her face. She was in her dress, but her feet were bare, and her room was littered with makeup, shoes, clothes, half unpacked, half still in bags and boxes. She pressed '121' again, and listened to the message, barely able to understand what she was hearing.

'Hello, Kate. It's Geraldine Garley, from Prince's? The estate agents? We met on Friday? I just wanted to let you know we showed the flat today, to a gentleman, and I think we may have a tenant, Kate. He can move in on Monday!'

Kate had listened to the message four times already. She liked this next part.

'I must say, I've never dealt with such a speedy let, in all my years here. Well . . .' (There was some hilarity in the background of the message; the sound of her colleagues laughing.) *'I've only been here eighteen months you know. But . . . still, it's incredibly fast.'*

Then there was some rustling of paper; Kate held her breath again, even though she knew the ending.

'A doctor, actually, he says he knows you. Kate, isn't it a small world? Doctor Mac Hamilton, his name is. Anyway, he said he'd already seen it the previous week? I didn't know you were showing it before then, Ms Miller. He wants it from Monday, and that's why I had to let you know . . . Um . . .' (she cleared her throat, a degree of perplexity in her voice) *'And . . . he specifically asked that I ring you and tell you something – he said he knew you? OK. He said he had to see it again to realize he didn't want to let it slip through his fingers. He said it doesn't need fixing, that it's perfect as it is. Well, so I should hope so. There's one more thing, what else did he say? Hold on . . .'* (more rustling of paper) *'Hold on a second. I wrote it down. Right, he said . . . "Tell her I'd be happy to take her out for dinner to discuss it."'* There was a pause. *'Oh. I don't get that part! I hope he still wants the flat. Nigel, where have you put the –'*

The doorbell buzzed, as Kate jumped, and the phone fell out of her hand. The first guests had arrived.

'Kate, dear?' Oscar called. 'Are you coming? What are you doing in there?'

And Kate stared around the room. 'I don't know,' she said, in blind panic. 'I'm an idiot. I don't know.'

CHAPTER FORTY-THREE

Five months later

Autumn came, after a terrible, wet summer, and surprised everyone by arriving with a beautiful, gentle September. Kate was always annoyed by people who claimed, with the air of one who is a little bit original, to 'love' autumn, who said it was their favourite season. What rubbish, she always thought. It wasn't just that it started getting darker at night – what's good about that? It was that it rained. It was slippery. Leaves fell everywhere, and made everything more slippery. It was impossible to dress, because one spent the whole time longing to don one's new autumnal clothing, usually involving brown or grey knitwear of some description, and when one did, one stepped outside for the day to discover that it was, actually, twenty-three degrees.

Kate wrote as much, in her column that last week of September, and as she gazed out of the window, towards the just-setting-sun, she chewed her pen (which she hated herself for, it was a disgusting habit, and she'd once got a splinter of biro caught in her throat and nearly choked) and pressed Save. The weather was changing today, definitely, she thought. Summer was definitely, finally over. It was nearly October.

She didn't want to be late. She looked at her watch: six o'clock. Pushing herself up and away from her desk, she stood up, and stretched, yawning loudly. She went into her bathroom, which still had the smell of fresh wallpaper. At Zoe's insistence, she'd had the bathroom wallpapered, in this gorgeous black and white, Swedish cartoony design she'd seen in a hotel in New York. It was waterproof, and she loved it. She'd had Hollywood star lights put up around the mirror, and she switched them on, slapping her face and looking critically in the illuminated mirror. She looked back at herself, and smiled, though part of her still thought that growing out her fringe was a mistake. At least it was getting to the stage where she could get away with an insouciant, jewelled clip effect.

With surprising speed Kate put on some powder, some mascara and some lipgloss, and then pulled on her little black cropped linen jacket, which was her summer/autumn jacket/coat dilemma salvation (she'd written about that the week before in her column, and was still going through the emails from readers about where they could buy it and what to do when it got colder). She wound her scarf around her neck and, shutting the door lightly, paused at the top of the stairs.

'Night, Mr Allan!' she called up.

The door opened, after a few seconds.

'Have a lovely evening, Kate,' came a faint, warm voice. 'I heard the yawn, thought you must be about to go out. Do enjoy it. Let me know, won't you?'

'Of course,' she said. 'I'll be up tomorrow morning for coffee. OK?'

'OK,' he said.

'What are you listening to?'

454

'Miles Davis. Miles Davis, you ignorant girl. Goodbye.'

'Bye!'

The door closed, and she ran down the stairs.

The air was rich with rain and wet leaves as Kate came outside. She smelt woodsmoke, drifting on the evening air from the gardens down the road. People were hurrying out of Maida Vale Tube station as she crossed the road and ran inside, glad of the warmth of the usually-stuffy Underground. Well, she thought to herself, autumn really is here if I'm glad that the Tube's warm. It's the sign.

She sat down on the train and pulled open her book. Her mother had just sent her *The Talented Mr Ripley*, which she'd never read before, and she was enjoying it with the sort of addictiveness you usually get with chocolates or, in Kate's case, Marmite. The train was quiet, going the wrong way back into town. When they got to Marylebone, someone skidded on a free evening newspaper lying on the ground; he paused, in mid-air, waving his arms, and then reached out to grab the pole next to Kate; she reared back in alarm, holding out a hand to stop him falling. He steadied himself, and smiled at her, embarrassed, and she smiled back at him, embarrassed that they had almost had contact, that he had almost looked foolish. But other than that it was quiet, almost soporific, and Kate's eyes closed just a little.

She was tired. She had babysat Harry and Flora the night before, while Zoe and Diggory went out to dinner for his birthday. She was still recovering. Last week she'd babysat while they went to the final Prince concert at the O_2 centre. The children had been exhausted from a big afternoon at the park and they'd fallen asleep right away. Last night, however, had been a nightmare of getting up, going back to bed, bad dreams, arguments, bargaining, and recriminations (on Kate's part, in her head). She thought, resentfully, that the sooner Diggory moved in with Zoe and they stopped having to go out on dates the better. Francesca always got out of babysitting, because of her long hours. Mac seemed to want to, the crazy man, but then he was their uncle, and his working hours meant often he couldn't. Kate got stuck with it more than she wanted and she moaned vociferously about it to Zoe. But really, she couldn't have loved it more.

She was remembering the rhyme Flora had been chanting the night before, the pattacake pattacake one, and it chimed exactly with the rhythm of the quiet carriage, and she might easily have missed her stop had her book not fallen into her lap and roused her with a start. She hopped off the train, her heart beating fast.

Tickets to *Much Ado about Nothing* had been sold out ever since they'd announced who'd be in it: a famous Hollywood star, who'd never acted in the West End before, but the reviews were amazing, and people genuinely said she was pulling off the part of Beatrice, that the chemistry between her and the grizzled, experienced RSC actor doing Benedick was so amazing it had to be seen to be believed. Kate couldn't wait. It was her favourite play. She got off the Tube a stop early at Oxford Circus, and walked through town, past Liberty's, through Soho Square, stopping to look in the windows of shops, smiling at the hardy drinkers still out on the pavements. She walked fast, weaving in and out of the throngs, avoiding eye contact, hugging herself against the now-chilly evening, enjoying being out, being bumped by people, living here, walking towards the theatre, towards him . . .

Down the side alley, before Great Windmill Street, was the theatre, and there, waiting for her, like she knew he would be, was Mac. He was holding two programmes.

'Hello,' she said, her heart beating even faster. She kissed him, as he slid a hand around her back, pulling her towards him.

'I got two programmes, you see,' he said stepping back. 'After the programme debacle of the Open Air Theatre date, I thought I'd better not risk it.'

'You're learning all the time,' she said. 'I missed you.'

He wrapped both his arms around her. 'I missed you too,' he said, and kissed her again. 'How was your day? Did you get the column done?'

'Nearly,' she said. She took his hand. 'I've got tomorrow as well. How was yours. Did you do that craneotomy?'

'Tracheotomy. Stop watching Grey's Anatomy,' Mac said, grinning. He scratched the side of his face, and touched his knuckles lightly against her cheek. 'Where are we going afterwards?'

'Back to mine?' she said.

'I meant for food, but back to yours is fine,' he said, fishing in his pocket. 'Although Francesca says to tell you, she's away all weekend. Oh, and my room needs serious vacuuming.'

'Why does she think I'd want to know about that?' Kate said, sternly. 'Isn't the vacuuming your problem?'

'Two separate points,' said Mac, hurriedly. 'Very separate. She's away all weekend. First point. Second point, I need to hoover.'

'Great,' said Kate. 'So you're coming home with me tonight. And I'll come over on Friday evening, and you'll have hoovered.'

'I can guarantee it.' He smiled at her; she smiled at him, they looked at each other for a long, long time.

'Let's go in,' he said eventually. 'Are you ready?'

'Oh yes,' Kate said. 'I'm ready.'

ACKNOWLEDGEMENTS

First of all, thanks to my wonderful Mum and Dad. Huge thanks to Pippa and Rebecca as ever for everything, and Brendan and Caroline O'Reilly, Thomas Wilson, Jo Roberts-Miller, Sophie Hopkin, Nikki Barrow and Clare Betteridge. Thanks to the following people for the conversations we've had about why we live where we live: Vicky Watkins, Pamela Casey, Nicole Vanderbilt, James Coleman, Lance Fitzgerald, PJ Mark and Simon, Megan and Jasper Mulligan. (Special thanks to Bea, Felix and Harriet for the flowers.)

I would never have finished this book without the support and encouragement of Clare Foss, my favourite Headliner in an extremely crowded field. Thank you so much, Clare and thanks too, as always, to Jane Morpeth. And Marion for telescope advice!

Thanks as always to Mark Lucas, and everyone at LAW, Kim Witherspoon and David Forrer (and to Mr Forrer for the Chrysler Building fact). And to Louise Burke and Maggie Crawford at Pocket Books, who make me love NYC that little bit more.

Finally huge thanks to everyone at HarperCollins, especially Victoria Hughes-Williams, Helen Johnstone, Sarah

Radford, Lucy Upton, Leisa Nugent, Lee Motley, Clive Kintoff, Wendy Neale and Amanda Ridout. I am eternally grateful to the super-talented Claire Bord for every little thing, thanks so much CB. Finally, to Lynne Drew, who is amazing. Thanks for understanding that the brand diamond is in my sitting room.

If you enjoyed

the love of her life

you'll love Harriet Evans'
bestselling novel,

a hopeless romantic

Read an extract now…

CHAPTER ONE

Laura Foster was a hopeless romantic. Her best friend Jo said it was her greatest flaw, and at the same time her most endearing trait, because it was the thing that most frequently got her into trouble, and yet falling in love was like a drug to her. Having a crush, daydreaming about someone, feeling her heart race faster when she saw a certain man walk towards her – she thrived on all of it, and was disastrously, helplessly, hopelessly incapable of seeing when it was wrong. Everyone has a blind spot. With Laura, it was as if she had a blind heart.

Anyone with a less romantic upbringing would be hard to find. She wasn't a runaway nun, or the daughter of an Italian count, or a mysterious orphan. She was the daughter of George and Angela Foster, of Harrow, in the suburbs of London. She had one younger brother, Simon, who was perfectly normal, not a secret duke, nor a spy, nor a soldier. George was a computer engineer, and Angela was a part-time translator. As Jo once said to her, about a year after they met at university, 'Laura, why do you go around pretending to be Julie Andrews, when you're actually Hyacinth Bucket?'

But Laura never stopped reality getting in the way of fantasy. By the time she was eighteen she had fallen for: a runny-nosed, milk-bottle-glasses-wearing primary-school outcast called Kevin (in her mind Indiana Jones, with specs); her oboe teacher Mr Wallace, a thin, spotty youth, over whom she developed a raging obsession and calluses on her oboe-playing fingers, so ferociously did she practise (she would stand outside his flat in Camden in the hope she might see him; she wore a locket which contained a bus ticket he'd dropped around her neck); and about fifteen different boys at the boys' school around the corner from hers in Harrow.

When she went to university, the scope was even greater, the potential for romance limitless. She wasn't interested in a random pull at a club. No, Laura wanted someone to stand underneath her window and recite poetry to her. She was almost always disappointed. There was Gideon, the budding theatre director who hadn't quite come out of the closet. Juan, the Colombian student who spoke no English. Or the rowing captain who was much more obsessed with the tracking machine at the gym than her. Her dentist, who charged her far too much and then made her pay for dinner. And the lecturer in her humanities seminar who she never spoke to, and who didn't know her name, who she wasted two terms staring at in a heartfelt manner.

For all of these Laura followed the same pattern. She went off her food; she mooned around; she was acutely conscious of where they were in any room, thought she saw them around every corner – was that the back of his curly head going into the newsagent's? She became a big, dumb idiot whenever any of them spoke to her, so fairly often they walked away, bemused that this nice girl with dark blonde hair, a sweet smile and a dirty laugh who seemed to like them was suddenly behaving like a nun in a shopping centre, eyes downcast, mute. Or they'd ask her out – and then Laura, for her part, usually came tumbling down to earth with a bang when she realised they weren't perfect, weren't this demigod she'd turned them into in her mind. It wasn't that she was particularly picky – she was just a really *bad* picker.

She believed in The One. And every man she met, for the first five minutes, two weeks, four months, had the potential in her eyes to be The One – until she reluctantly realized they were gay (Gideon from the Drama Society), psychopathic (Adam, her boyfriend for several months, who eventually jacked in his MA on the Romantic Poets and joined the SAS to become a killing machine), against the law (Juan, the illegal immigrant from Colombia), or Josh (her most recent boyfriend, whom she'd met at a volunteer reading programme seminar at work, decided was The One after five minutes, dated for over a year, before realizing, really, all they had in common was a love of local council literacy initiatives).

It's fine for girls to grow up believing in something like The One, but the generally received wisdom by the time Laura was out of university, as she moved into her mid-twenties, as her friends started to settle down, was that he didn't really exist – well, he did, but with variations. Not for Laura. She was going to wait till she found him. To her other best friend Paddy's complaints that he was sick of sharing their flat with a lovesick teenager all the time, as well as a succession of totally disparate, odd men, Laura said firmly that he was being mean and judgemental. James Patrick – Paddy to his friends – was a dating disaster, what would he know? To Jo's pragmatic suggestions that she should join a dating agency, or simply ask out that bloke over there, Laura said no. It would happen the way she wanted it to happen, she would say. You couldn't force it. And that would be it, until five minutes later when a waiter in a restaurant would smile at her, and Laura would gaze happily up at him, imagining herself and him moving back to Italy, opening a small café in a market square, having lots of beautiful babies called Francesca and Giacomo. Jo could only shake her head at this, as Laura laughed with her, aware of how hopeless she was compared to her level-headed, realistic best friend.

Until one evening, about eighteen months ago, Jo came round to supper at Paddy and Laura's flat. She was very quiet; Laura often worried Jo worked too hard. As Laura was attempting to digest a mouthful of chickpeas that Paddy had marvellously undercooked, and as she was trying not to choke on them, Jo wiped her mouth with a piece of paper towel and looked up.

'Um . . . Hey.'

Laura looked at her suspiciously. Jo's eyes were sparkling, her heart-shaped little face was flushed, and she leant across the table and said,

'I've met someone.'

'Where?' Paddy had asked stupidly. But Laura understood what that statement meant, of course she did, and she said,

'Who is he?'

'He's called Chris,' Jo replied, and she smiled, rather girlishly, which was even more unusual for her. 'I met him at work.' Jo was a conveyancing solicitor. 'He was buying a house. He yelled at me.'

And then – and this was when Laura realized it was serious – Jo twisted a tendril of her hair and put it in her mouth. Since this was a breach of social behaviour in Jo's eyes tantamount to not sending a thank-you card after a dinner party, Laura put her hand out across the table and said,

'Wow! How exciting.'

'I know,' said Jo, unable to stop herself smiling. 'I know!'

Laura knew, as she looked at Jo, she just knew, she didn't

know why. Here was someone in love, who had found The One, and that was all there was to it.

Chris and Jo moved into the house she'd helped him buy after six months; four months after that, he proposed. They started planning a December wedding, a couple of weeks before Christmas, in a London hotel. Jo eschewed grown-up bridesmaids, saying they were deeply, humiliatingly naff, much to Laura's disappointment – she was rather looking forward to donning a nice dress and sharing with her best friend on this, the happiest day of her life. Instead, she was going to be best woman, and Paddy was an usher.

It seemed as if Jo and Chris had been together forever, and Laura could barely remember when he hadn't been on the scene. He slotted right in, with his North London pub ways, his personality so laidback and friendly, compared to Jo's sometimes controlled outlook on life. He had friends who lived nearby – some lovely friends. They were all a gang now, him and Jo, his friends, Paddy and Laura, some-times Laura's brother Simon, when he wasn't off somewhere being worthy and making girls swoon (where Laura was always falling in love, Simon was usually falling into bed with a complete stranger, usually by dint of lulling them into a false sense of security by telling them he worked for a charity). And there was Hilary too, also from university and christened Scary Hilary – because she was – and her brother Hamish, their other friends from work or university, and so on. And so Laura's easy, uncomplicated life went on its way. She had a brief, intense affair with a playwright she thought was very possibly the new John Osborne, until Paddy pointed out he was, in fact, just a prat who liked shouting a lot. Paddy grew a moustache for the autumn. Laura got a pay rise at work. They bought a Playstation to celebrate – games for him, karaoke for her. Yes, everything was well within its usual frame, except Laura began to feel, more and more, as she looked at Jo and Chris so in love, and as she looked at the landscape of her own dull life, that she was taking the path of least resistance, that her world was small and pathetic compared to Jo's. That she was missing out on what she most wanted.

Under these circumstances, it's hardly surprising that the next time Laura fell, she fell badly. Because one day, quite without meaning to, she woke up, got dressed and went to work, and everything was normal, and by the next day she had fallen in love again. But this time she knew it was for real. And that's when everything started to go wrong.

CHAPTER TWO

Chris the groom coughed and stood up, looking rather nervous. Laura smiled at him, pretending to listen. She should have been paying attention but she was daydreaming, in a reverie of her own. She was thinking about her grandmother, Mary Fielding. Laura's grandmother was the person Laura loved most in the world (apart from whoever it was she was in love with at that moment), even more so perhaps than her parents, than her brother.

Mary was a widow. She had lost her husband, Guy, eight years before, and she lived on her own in a small but perfectly formed flat in Marylebone. There were various reasons why Laura idolized Mary, wanted to be just like her, found her much more seductive than her own parents. Mary was stylish – even at eighty-four she was always the best-dressed person in a room. Mary was funny – her face lit up when she was telling a joke, and she could make anyone roar with laughter, young or old. But the main reason Laura adored her grandmother was that Mary had found true love. Her husband, Guy, was the love of her life, to an extent Laura had never seen with anyone else. They had met when each was widowed, in Cairo after the Second World War. Mary already had a daughter, Angela, Laura's mother. Guy also had a daughter, Annabel, whom Laura and Simon called aunt, even though she wasn't really related to them.

Because of her mother's natural reserve, it was Mary whom Laura told about her love life, her latest disasters, the person she was currently in love with. Because she lived in central London, and so not that far from Laura's work, it was Mary whom Laura called in to see, to talk to, to listen to. And it was Mary that Laura learnt from, when it came to true love, in large part. She did not learn it from her own unemotional parents. No, she learnt that true love was epic stuff.

One of Laura's favourite stories was how Mary and Guy had realized they were in love on a trip out to the pyramids to see the sun rise. It had been pitch black as they rode out, crammed in a Jeep with the other members of their club in Cairo. And as the sun rose, Guy had turned to Mary, and said, 'You know I can't live without you, don't you?' And Mary had replied, 'I know.'

And that was that. They were married six months later.

George and Angela, by contrast, had met at a choral society function off the Tottenham Court Road, when they were both at university. Somehow, Laura felt this wasn't quite the same.

'You are the love of my life,' she heard a voice say. 'The woman I want to grow old with. I love you.'

He was staring at her intensely, his eyes boring into hers. Laura raised her hand to his chest, and said, breathlessly, 'I love you too.'

Beyond them the sun was rising, flooding the vast desert landscape with pink and orange colour. Sand whipped in her face, the silk of her headscarf caught in the breeze. She could feel the cold smoothness of the material of his dinner

472

jacket against her skin, as he caught her and pulled her towards him.

'Tell me again,' Laura whispered in his ear. 'Tell me again that you love me.'

And then, suddenly, a microphone crackled loudly, jerking Laura back to reality, as someone cleared their throat and said,

'To my beautiful wife, Jo!'

'Aah,' the wedding guests murmured in approval, as Laura came back down to earth with a bump. There was some sniffing, especially from Jo's mother up on the top table, as Chris raised a glass to his new bride, kissed her, and then sat down to a welter of applause and chair-shuffling.

'Aah,' Laura whispered to herself, leaving her daydream behind with a sigh. She looked at Jo, her best friend, so beautiful and happy-looking, and found tears were brimming in her eyes. She turned to her flatmate Paddy, sitting next to her, and sniffed loudly.

'Look at her,' she said. 'Can you believe it?'

'No,' said Paddy, raising an eye at Chris's cousin Mia. Paddy had recently begun to teach himself how to raise one eyebrow, in a 'come to me, pretty laydee' way. This involved several hours of grimacing into Laura's hand-mirror in the sitting room of their flat, whilst Laura was trying to watch TV. She got very irritated with her flatmate when he did this, and was frequently telling him that being able to raise one eyebrow was not the key to scoring big with the ladies. Wearing matching socks was. As was having a tidy room. And not acting like a crazy stalker when some girl said no after you asked her out. These were the things that Laura frequently told Paddy he should be concentrating on, and yet, much to her deep chagrin, he ignored her every time. For Paddy's retort would always be that what Laura knew about dating was worthless.

What a perfect, happy day, Laura thought, as she gazed around the room, clapping now the speeches were over. She was gripping her glass, searching for someone. Suddenly her eye fell on Jo and she watched her for a moment, truly radiant, happy and serene in an antique lace silk dress, her hand resting lightly on her new husband's as they sat at the top table. Laura couldn't help but feel a tiny pang of something sad. It wasn't just any bride sitting there in the white dress, with the flowers and the black suits around her. It was Jo – Jo whom she had danced with all night in various Greek nightclubs, with whom she had spent hours in Topshop changing rooms, whom she had stayed up all night with whilst she sobbed her heart out after her last boyfriend Vic dumped her. It was her best friend, and it was weird.

She blinked and caught Jo's eye, suddenly overcome with emotion. Jo smiled at her, winked, and mouthed something. Laura couldn't tell what it was, but by the jerking of her head towards the best man, Chris's newly single brother Jason, Laura thought she could guess what Jo was on about. Laura followed her gaze, shaking herself out of her mood. Jason was nice, yes. Definitely. But he wasn't . . . dammit, where *was* he?

'Who are you looking for?' said Paddy suspiciously, as Laura cast her eyes around the room.

'Me?'

'Yes, you. Who is it? You keep looking round like you're expecting to see someone.'

'No one,' said Laura, rather huffily. 'Just looking, that's all.'

'There's Dan,' said Paddy.

'Who?' asked Laura.

'Dan. Dan Floyd. He's raising his glass. He's talking to Chris.'

'Right,' said Laura calmly. 'Ah, there's Hilary. And her mum. I should go and say –'

'Laura!' said Jo, coming up behind her, dragging someone by the hand. 'Don't go! Here's Jason! Jason, you remember Laura?'

'Hey. Of course,' said Jason, who was an elongated, blonder version of Chris. 'Hi, Laura.'

'Er,' said Laura. 'Hi, Jason, how are you?'

There is nothing more likely to induce embarrassment in a single girl than the obvious set-up at the wedding in front of friends. Laura smiled at Jason, and once more cast a fleeting glance around the room. Where was he?

'Good, thanks, good,' said Jason, as Jo nudged Paddy and grinned, much to Laura's annoyance.

'See the match on Wednesday?' Paddy asked Jason, in an attempt at blokeish comradeship.

'What match?' said Jason.

'Oh . . .' Paddy said vaguely. 'You know. The match. The big game.'

'What, mate?' Jason repeated, scratching his head.

'Anyway, great to see you, mate,' said Paddy, changing tack and banging Jason hard on the shoulder, so that he nearly doubled up. 'So, Laura was just saying – Laura? Help me out here.'

Jason gazed at Paddy, perplexed. Laura looked wildly around her, searching for an escape, and then someone over Jason's shoulder caught her eye.

'Jason split up from Cath two months ago,' Jo hissed in her ear, in a totally unconvincing stage whisper, as Laura gazed into the distance. It was him, of course it was him, she would know him anywhere. 'You know, he's living in Highbury now? Laura, you should –'

But Laura was no longer standing next to her, she had turned around to say hello to their friend Dan, who had appeared by her side. Vaguely she heard Jo's tutting, vaguely she was aware that she should be making an effort.

For Jo hadn't seen the look on Laura's face after she was tapped on the shoulder by Dan. In fact, Jo and Paddy hadn't been seeing quite a lot of things lately, and if they had, they would have been worried. Especially knowing Laura like they did.

'You had a good evening, then?' Dan was saying to Laura, smiling wickedly at her.

'Yes, thanks,' she replied, looking up at him, into his eyes. 'Good speeches.'

'Great,' he said, shifting his weight so that he was fully facing her. It was a tiny movement, almost imperceptible to Jo, Paddy, or any of the other hundred and fifty people in that room, but it enclosed the two of them in together as tightly as if they were in a phone box.

Dan smiled at her again, as Laura pulled her shawl over her shoulder and she smiled back helplessly, feeling her stomach turn over at his sheer perfectness. His dark blond hair, the boyish curling crop which curled over his collar. His tanned, strong face, wide cheekbones, blue eyes, lazy smile. He reminded her of a cowboy, a farmhand from the Wild West. He was so relaxed, so easy to be with, so easy to be happy with, and Laura glowed as she gazed up at him, simply exhilarated at the prospect of a whole evening in his company – a whole evening, where anything could happen. Suddenly she could barely remember whose wedding it was.

He was here. She was here with Dan, and he was hers for the rest of the evening, and for those hours only she could indulge herself with the secret fantasy that they were a couple who'd been going out for years. Perhaps they were married already. Perhaps Jo and Chris had been the only witnesses at their beach wedding in Barbados

476

two years ago. Dan in a sarong – he would suit a sarong, unlike most men. Her in a silk sundress, raspberry pink, her dark blonde hair falling loose behind her back. Some spontaneous locals and other couples gathered at the seashore, crying with joy at how perfect, how in love they obviously were, totally pole-axed by the strength of emotion, the purity of their love. Laura and Dan, Dan and Laura. Perhaps . . .

'Laura!' a voice said sharply. 'Listen!'

Laura realised she was being prodded in the ribs. The lovely bubble of daydream in her head burst, and she tore herself away from Dan, and looked around to see Paddy glaring at her.

'I was talking to you!' he said, affronted. 'I asked you a question four times!'

'I'll see you later,' Dan murmured, shifting away from her. 'Come and find me, yeah?' and he very lightly ran his hand over her bare arm, a tiny gesture, but Laura shuddered, looked up at him fleetingly, even more sure than ever, then turned back to Paddy. As Dan moved off, he raised his glass to her, and smiled a regretful smile. Laura screamed inwardly, and turned away from him towards Paddy.

'Sorry,' she said. 'What was it?'

'Is this fob watch too much?' said Paddy, fingering the watch hanging from his waistcoat. 'I think it is. I'm not sure, but perhaps it overloads the outfit. What do you think?'

'Ladies 'n' gennlemen,' came a bored-sounding voice from the back of the room. 'Please make your way back into the Ballroom. Mr and Mrs Johnson are about to perform their first dance. Ah-thann yew, verrimuch.'

Laura looked wildly around her, as if trying to prioritise the many tasks on her mind. She glared at Paddy, who was still obviously waiting for an answer.

'Yes, it is,' said Laura wildly. 'Far too much. I totally agree. In fact, it's hideous,' she said crossly. 'You'd better take it off and throw it away. I'm going to the loo – see you in a minute,' she finished, and hurried away.

Dan, Dan, Dan. Dan Floyd. Even saying his name made her feel funny. She muttered it on her way to the loo, feeling sick with nerves, but totally exhilarated. Laura had got it bad. She knew it was bad, and she knew if any of her friends found out they'd tell her it was futile, she should get over it, but she couldn't help it. It was meant to be. She was powerless in the face of it, much as she'd tried not to be. Dan Floyd, looking like a ranger or an extra from Oklahoma!, calm, funny, and so sexy she couldn't imagine ever finding any other man remotely attractive. Laura wanted him, plain and simple.

She had constructed a whole imaginary life for them, based around (because of the Oklahoma! theme) a small house in the Wild West with a porch, a rocking chair – for Laura's granny Mary – corn growing as high as an elephant's eye in the fields, and a golden-pink sunset every night. Mary would drink gins on the porch and dispense wise advice, and would sit there looking elegant. Dan would farm, obviously, but he would also do the sports PR job thing that he did. Perhaps by computer. Laura would – well, she hadn't thought that far. How could she do her job in the prairie? Perhaps there were some dyslexic farmhands who'd never learnt to read properly. Yes.

Her friend Hilary was in the loos when she got there, washing her hands. 'Oi,' she said. 'Hi.'

Laura jumped. 'Oh. Hi!' she said brightly. 'Hey. Great speech, wasn't it?'

'Not bad,' said Hilary, who didn't much like public displays of affection, verbal or physical. She ran her hands through her hair. 'That idiot Jason's there, did you see?'

'Yeah,' said Laura. 'He's quite nice, isn't he?'

'Well,' said Hilary, in a flat tone. 'He's OK. If you like that kind of thing.'

'He's split up from Cath,' Laura said encouragingly.

'Yeah, I know,' Hilary replied coolly. 'Hm. I might go and find him.'

'OK. See you later,' said Laura, and shut the door of the cubicle. She rested her pounding head against the cool of the white tiles. She was stressing out, and she couldn't help it. It was the first time she'd seen Dan since they'd kissed, so fair enough. But she didn't know what to do. Dan had got to her. The worst bit of all was, she didn't just fancy him something rotten. She really liked him, too.

She liked the way he was always first to buy a round, that the corners of his blue eyes crinkled when he laughed, the rangy, almost bowlegged way he walked, his strong hands. She liked the way he rolled his eyes with gentle amusement when Paddy said something particularly Paddy-ish. She liked him. She couldn't help it, she did. And she knew he liked her, that was the funny thing. She just knew, in the way you know. She had also come to know, in the last couple of months, that there was something going on between her and Dan. She just didn't know what it was. But somehow, she knew tonight was the night.

Dan was a friend of Chris's from university. He'd moved about five minutes away from Laura about six months ago, round the corner from Jo and Chris towards Highbury – and she'd known of him vaguely since Jo and Chris had got together. In July, Dan had started a new job, and more often than not Laura found herself on the tube platform with him in the morning. The first couple of times it was mere coin-cidence. Now, at the end of summer, it was almost a routine. They would buy a coffee from the stall on the platform and sit together in the second-to-last carriage, deserted in the dusty dog days of August, and go down the Northern line together until they got to Bank. And they would read Metro together and chat, and it was all perfectly innocent.

'Dan? Oh yeah, we're tube buddies,' Laura would say nonchalantly, her heart thumping in her chest.

'They're transport pals,' Chris and Jo would joke at lunch on Sundays. 'Like an old married couple on the seafront at Clacton.'

'Ha, ha, ha,' Laura would mutter, and then she would blush furiously, biting her lip and shaking her hair forward over her face, burying herself in a newspaper. Not that they ever noticed – it's extraordinary what people don't notice right under their noses.

But to Laura it was obvious, straightforward. From the first time she'd recognised him on the tube platform, that sunny July day, and he had smiled at her, his face genuinely lighting up with pleasure – 'Laura!' he'd said, warmth in his voice. 'What a nice surprise. Come and sit next to me.' Through the sun and rain of August, September and October she would run down the steps to the tube platform, hoping he'd be there, not knowing what was going on between them. They had built up a whole lexicon of information. Just little things that you tell the people you see each day. She knew when his watch was being mended, what big meeting he had that day; and he knew when Rachel, her boss, was being annoying, and asked how her grandmother had been the previous day. Out of these little things, woven over each other, grew a web of knowledge, of intimacy, and one day Laura had woken up and known, known with a clarity that was shocking, that this was not just another one of her crushes, or another failed relationship that she couldn't understand. She and Dan had something. And she was in love with him.

Oh, the level of denial about the whole thing was extraordinary, because you could explain it away in a heartbeat if you had to. 'We go to work together, because we live round the corner from each other. It's great – nice start to the day, you know.' Whereas the truth was a little more complicated. The truth was both of them had started getting to the station earlier and earlier, so they could sit on the bench together with their coffees and chat for ten minutes before they got on the tube. And that was weird. Laura knew that. Yes, she was in denial about the whole thing. She knew that, too. It had got to the stage where something had to give – and she couldn't wait.

Laura collected herself, breathed deeply, smoothed the material of her dress down, and came out of the loo to put on more lip gloss. She realised as she looked in the mirror that she was already wearing enough lip gloss to cause an oil slick – it was a nervous reflex of hers, to apply more and more when in doubt. She blotted some on the back of her hand, and strolled out of the door nonchalantly, looking for Paddy or Hilary, someone to chat to. It was strange, wasn't it, she mused, that at her best friend's wedding, knowing virtually everyone in the room, she could feel so exposed, so alone. That on such a happy day she could feel so sad. She shook her head, feeling silly. Look over there, she told herself, as Jo and Chris walked through the tables of the big ballroom, hand in hand, smiling at each other, at their friends and family. It was lovely. It was a privilege to see. Out of the corner of her eye she saw Hilary pinning Jason against a wall, yelling at him about something, her long, elegant hands waving in the air. Jason looked scared, but transfixed. Another man scared into snogging Hil, she thought. Well done, girl.

Someone handed her a glass of champagne. She accepted it gratefully and turned to see who it was.

'Sorry,' whispered Dan casually, though he didn't bend towards her. He said it softly, intimately, and clinked his glass with hers. 'I thought I'd better leave you to deal with Paddy's sartorial crisis by yourself. Where did you go?'

'Loo,' said Laura, trying to stay calm, but it came out, much to her and Dan's surprise, as a low, oddly pitched growl. He smiled. Laura smiled back, and ran her hand through her hair in a casual, groomed manner, but forgot the lipstick mark of gloss still adhering to the back of her hand. Her hair stuck to the gloss, and her hand became caught up in her hair as she flailed wildly around with her hand in the air, covered in hair.

'Arrgh,' said Laura, despair washing over her as she stood in front of Dan. Her hand was stuck. Dan took the champagne out of her other hand, put it on a table, held her wrist and slid her fingers slowly out of her hair. He smoothed it down, swiftly dropped a kiss on the crown of her head in a sweet, intimate gesture, and put his palm on the small of her back as he guided her through the room onto the terrace.

'Thanks,' whispered Laura, trying to walk upright and not cower with embarrassment. 'I should go back out, to see the first dance, look . . .'

'No problem,' said Dan calmly. 'In a minute. I just want to do this.' And he slid his hand round her waist, drew him towards her, and kissed her. No one else was watching, they were all turned towards the dance floor where Mr and Mrs Johnson were dancing. They were alone on the terrace, just the two of them.

Dan pulled her towards him, his hands pressing on her spine, his lips gentle but firm on hers. He made a strange, sad sound in his throat, somewhere between a cry of something and a moan. Laura slid one arm around his neck and drew him further towards her. The other arm was by her side, she was still holding the champagne glass. It tilted, the champagne spilt, and neither of them noticed.

After a short while, they broke apart slowly, and said nothing. There was nothing to say, really. Laura drained the meagre contents of her glass and leant into Dan. They stood there together as the music died away and applause rippled out towards them, aware of nothing else but themselves, alone in their bubble.

'Well,' Dan said eventually. 'I didn't know that was going to happen tonight,' and he put his arm around her.

Laura twisted round, looked up at him. 'Oh yes you did,' she said, smiling into his eyes. 'Of course you did.'

That was Laura's second glass of champagne, and she found Paddy and Hilary on another terrace having a cigarette so she joined them. After her third glass, thirty minutes later, she was a bit tired. After her fourth, she felt better again and she'd eaten from the buffet as well. After her fifth and sixth, she danced for an hour with Jo and Chris and their other friends. And after her seventh glass, she didn't know how it happened, but she found herself in one of the free taxis going home with Dan Floyd, and they were kissing so hard that her lips were bruised the next day. And that's when it really started, and Laura went from knowing lots of things about Dan and how she felt about him and her place in the world in general to knowing nothing. At all.

At one point during the night, she propped herself up on her elbow and leant over him, and kissed him again, and he kissed her back and they rolled over together, and Laura pulled back and said, 'So . . . what does this mean, then?' It just came out.

And Dan's face clouded over and he said, 'Oh gorgeous, let's not do this now, not when I want you so much,' and he carried on kissing her. Something should have made

Laura pull away and say, No, actually, what does this mean? Are you going to tell your girlfriend? When will you leave your girlfriend? Do you like me? Are we together? But of course she didn't . . .

CHAPTER THREE

Yes, Dan had a girlfriend, Amy. Just a tiny detail, nothing much. They were as good as living together, too – although she still had her own place. Another detail Laura tried to forget about. She had almost managed to convince herself that if she didn't tell anyone about her – well, what was it? A 'thing'? A 'fling'? A fully formed relationship just waiting to move into the sunlight of acceptance? – her liaison with Dan, then perhaps the outside world didn't matter so much. And it didn't, when she was with him. Because he was The One, she was sure of it. So it became surprisingly easy for Laura, who was basically a good girl, who never ever thought she could do something like this, to turn into a person who was sleeping with someone else's boyfriend.

She had tried, after Jo and Chris's wedding. She told herself – and Dan – that it wasn't going to happen again. She bit her nails to the quick about it because, much as Laura might be clueless about some things, she was clear about other things, and one of those was: don't sleep with someone who has a girlfriend. She'd already tried going cold turkey from him, as autumn gave way to winter, and as she realised she was falling for him, badly. She tried avoiding him at the tube

485

station – but she couldn't. She tried to forget him – but she couldn't. When she thought about him, it was as if he was talking to her, pleading with her, communicating with her directly. Laura, it's you I want, not Amy. Laura, please let me see you, his eyes and his voice would say in her head, until the noise got so loud it was all she could hear. Every time was the last time. Every time was the first time.

Laura knew it was wrong to be thinking like this. But she assuaged that secret guilt in her head with the knowledge that Dan and Amy weren't getting on well. Dan himself had told her it wasn't working out. Well, he had in so many words, with a sigh and a shake of the head, in the early days of their coffee mornings together on the tube platform. And she knew from Jo that Dan was going out with Chris and his other mates more, playing more football, watching more football, in the pub more, working harder. Added to which, no one in their group ever really saw Amy. They were together, but they were never actually together. She was completely offstage, like a mystery character in a soap opera whom people refer to but who never appears. You know when a couple are happy together – mainly because you don't see either of them as much, and when you do they're either together, or they talk about each other. Or they're just happy. You know. Laura knew – as did everyone else – Dan wasn't happy with Amy. Dan wanted out, he just didn't know how to get out.

And, actually, Amy wasn't really her friend. They occasionally all went out for drinks, Jo and Chris, Dan and Amy, Hilary, Paddy and Laura and so on, especially now Chris and Dan had moved nearby. But Amy rarely came along, and in any case, Laura had long ago realised she couldn't stand her. Never had been able to, in fact. Because not only was Amy a quasi-friend of hers, they had also been at school together, many moons ago, and there is no more mutually suspicious relationship than that of two ex-schoolmates who are thrown together several years later. Added to which, Amy had been one of the mean girls who had teased Laura relentlessly about her love for Mr Wallace the oboe teacher, and had spread the subsequent rumours surrounding Laura giving up the oboe. She'd even told Laura's mother Angela about it, at a school concert, all wide-eyed concern. Angela Foster had got the wrong end of the stick, and assumed Laura was being pestered by Mr Wallace. She'd complained. He'd nearly been fired. The whole thing was deeply embarrassing. So Laura's dislike of Amy was genuinely historical, rather than based upon the fact that Amy was with the man Laura felt quite sure she loved. This made her feel better, in some obscure way.

Amy ate nothing, exercised obsessively, talked about shoes and handbags the entire time (like, the entire time) and she played with her beautiful red hair. Non-stop. It was her thing. She always had, even when she and Laura had been eight-year-olds in plaits and virgin socks at school. Twenty years later, the same white hand would smooth down the crown of its owner's hair as Amy softened her voice to tell a sad story – about a friend's mother's death, or something bad in the news. Or said something deeply meaningful at the pub, which made Laura want to gag childishly on her drink.

The thing was, Laura knew Amy was the kind of girl men fell for, even though she led them a merry dance. Laura wasn't. She was nice, she was funny, but she knew she was ordinary, nothing special. Why would anyone, especially Dan, choose her when they could be with Amy? Why was it he got her so well, laughed at her jokes? What amazing thing had led him to think of her as this perfect person for him, just as she knew that he was her Mr Right? It perplexed her, as much as it exhilarated her. It was extraordinary, it was magical, and so even though it was underhand and stressful, she carried on doing it.

going home

Some families warm your heart.
Lizzy's makes her head spin.

Home. For most it's a place of calm and safety. For Lizzy Walter, things are a bit more complicated. Keeper House – the family home deep in the countryside – has always been where Lizzy can escape from her London life and ease her heart and mind. But trouble is on the horizon.

For a start, her entire family are hiding something. Then the love of her life makes an unexpected reappearance – just when she thought she was starting to get over him. And now Keeper House itself is in peril. By the time the Walters gather for a summer wedding, the stakes have never been higher – for Lizzy, for her family and for love...

978-0-00-719844-3 • £7.99

a hopeless romantic

Have you ever fallen for the wrong man? Over and over again? But do you still believe in fairytale endings?

Then you must be a hopeless romantic, just like me.

ve just had my heart broken (again …) and so have taken some time out on a family holiday to Norfolk – possibly not the greatest idea in the world. nyway, I had made the decision to remove my 'rose-tinted' glasses and swear off ALL men and EVERYTHING romantic (including my beloved Doris Day boxed set and Georgette Heyer novels) for good.

Then I met sexy and mysterious Nick, the manager of stately home Chartley Hall and suddenly found myself falling for him, even though he's got a murky secret or two in his closet.

But do I want to open my heart for it to only be broken again? Or could Nick really be The One?

You'll have to read on to find out …

Love

Laura x

978-0-00-719846-7 • £6.99

Save 10%

when you buy direct from
HarperCollins – call 08707 871724.

Free postage and packing
in the UK only.

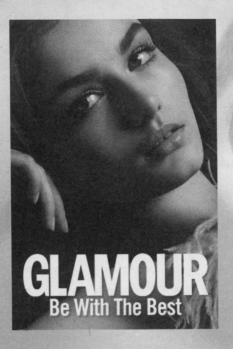

GLAMOUR
Be With The Best

WIN

A day behind the scenes at GLAMOUR, the Number One glossy fashion, beauty and lifestyle magazine for 21st century women.

If like Kate, lead character of *The Love of Her Life*, you've always had a desire to immerse yourself in the world of magazines, don't miss out on your chance to spend a day with the team at Glamour and find out what really goes into putting the magazine together each month.

Simply log onto
www.harpercollins.co.uk/loveofherlife
to enter